THE SHADOW OF DEATH

The Hunt for a Serial Killer
by Philip E. Ginsburg

"Ginsburg is riveting as he gets down to the brass tacks of [psychologist John] Philpin's method." —*Kirkus Reviews*

"Ginsburg makes excellent work of the ongoing investigation . . . [and] time and again goes beyond the facts of the case to evoke the shifting fears of the affected communities."
—New York *Daily News*

. . . *And praise for Philip E. Ginsburg's*
true crime bestseller
POISONED BLOOD:

"Illuminating . . . An astonishing and complex case, and one which the author ably unravels . . . [Ginsburg] keeps us on the edge of our seats." —*The Washington Post Book World*

"One of the most riveting true crime stories in memory."
—*Publishers Weekly*

Also by Philip E. Ginsburg

POISONED BLOOD

The Shadow of Death

Philip E. Ginsburg

JOVE BOOKS, NEW YORK

This Jove Book contains the complete text of the original hardcover edition. It has been completely reset in a typeface designed for easy reading and was printed from new film.

THE SHADOW OF DEATH

A Jove Book / published by arrangement with Charles Scribner's Sons

PRINTING HISTORY
Charles Scribner's Sons edition published 1993
Jove edition / February 1995

ISBN: 0-515-11547-9

A JOVE BOOK®
Jove Books are published by The Berkley Publishing Group,
200 Madison Avenue, New York, New York 10016.
JOVE and the "J" design are trademarks belonging
to Jove Publications, Inc.

PRINTED IN THE UNITED STATES OF AMERICA

10 9 8 7 6 5 4 3 2 1

To CA,
who waited until I was ready,
and SEG,
who waited until I was almost ready.

acknowledgments

For someone who spends so much time working by himself, the writer of a book like this depends rather heavily on the help of others.

I could not have told this story in so complete and detailed a way without the help of all those people who took the time to answer my questions. Among them were Captain James Candon, Noreen Crocker, Corporal Tim Crotts, Chief Joseph Estey, Kathy Falzarano, Robert Grover, Captain Glenn E. Hall, John Halpin, Pauline LeClair, Bob Merchant of the Vermont Department of Transportation, Deborah Mozden, Jane Grey North, Janet O'Brien, Mike Quinn, Pamela Rowe, Carolyn Sprague, Wayne Weiner, Lieutenant Bill Wilmot, and Sergeant Clay Young. Several people gave an extra measure of their time and attention. They included Jane Boroski, Sergeant Mike LeClair, Corporal Mike Leclaire, Stephen Moore, Sergeant Kevin O'Brien, and Chief Michael Prozzo; I extend to them a special word of thanks. And there were a number of others who were willing to help but preferred to do so anonymously; I honor their wish and assure them that my thanks are no less heartfelt because of their discretion.

Among these people, named and unnamed, were some for whom helping me brought the anguish of recounting and reliving painful events. I want them to know that I understand the special generosity involved in their assistance, and I offer them a special word of thanks. I hope they will find the evidence of their sacrifice in the pages of this book, and that they will think it was worth it.

Bob Condon of the *Claremont Eagle-Times* was kind enough to offer assistance with the gathering of photographs, in a period when other demands on his time were especially heavy. I had professional help from Don Blades with photographs from the *Rutland Herald,* and other photographic help from Paul Montgomery of the *Keene Sentinel,* who also wrote the best of the many newspaper stories trying to make sense of the series of killings in the Connecticut Valley. I want all three of these gentlemen to know I appreciate their professional courtesy.

Two people were especially generous with their time and advice. I came to admire many of the police officers I met in New Hampshire and Vermont, and the memory of Ted LeClair will always represent for me the best qualities of such men and women. He was dedicated, compassionate, good-natured, and courageous under pressure. And he was kind without expectation of return. I will always be grateful.

John Philpin became not only a source of information but my instructor in forensic psychology and criminal profiling, far exceeding the effort any reasonably self-protective person would invest in a neophyte. In addition to expressing my everlasting gratitude, I want to make clear that any errors of fact or interpretation in the areas of my mentor's expertise are solely the responsibility of the pupil, not the master.

I had two readers, RG and CA, indispensable critics who sent signals from the real world. Both were critical enough to make their compliments seem genuine, and complimentary enough to make their criticism bearable; the combination requires great wit and equal kindness. Without them it would have been considerably harder to keep on.

I know from experience with others that I was lucky to have the help of Nancy Ray with transcriptions. Once again I have also been fortunate in the publishing professionals who have offered me a hand. I continue to appreciate the help Susanne Kirk gave me in getting started, and she set a high standard as an editor. Bill Goldstein has proved a worthy successor, wise in his guidance and extraordinary in his patience, which I tested excessively without finding its limits; and in the end he gave me back a better book than I gave him. Hamilton Cain has been quick and smart with the logistical help I've asked for. And Elizabeth Knappman, my agent, has been lavish with her enthusiasm and reliably astute in her advice. All these are blessings one can not take for granted, and I do not.

author's note

The story told here is true, the actors real people, the events actual happenings, all as close to an exact recounting of the facts as I have been able to come through hundreds of hours of interviewing and many hundreds more of research.

The reader should be aware, however, that of necessity certain elements of the story have been altered. Names have been changed, along with some elements of personal description, to protect the privacy of certain individuals, and to protect the legal rights of persons who have not been formally accused of crimes. Other details of cases are either absent from this account or altered because the police withhold them as an aid to the solution of the crimes; no criminal will find here details that will help him escape detection, and no damaged soul will find authoritative particulars for a false confession.

One other form of deviation from empirical fact should be mentioned. Where the thoughts of characters are reconstructed, it is done on the basis of those characters' own recollections. Where the speech of characters is quoted, it is in some cases based on contemporary accounts, like newspaper stories, diaries, and meeting notes. In other cases it may be based on the memories of the speakers and of those who heard them speak. Since recording error, fallible memory, and the mysteries of the human spirit preclude exactitude, the author begs the reader's indulgence for this exercise of artistic license.

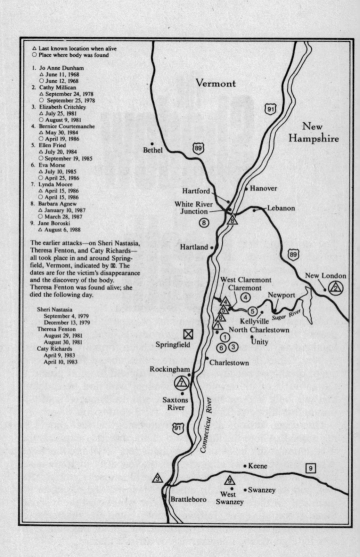

△ Last known location when alive
○ Place where body was found

1. Jo Anne Dunham
   △ June 11, 1968
   ○ June 12, 1968
2. Cathy Millican
   △ September 24, 1978
   ○ September 25, 1978
3. Elizabeth Critchley
   △ July 25, 1981
   ○ August 9, 1981
4. Bernice Courtemanche
   △ May 30, 1984
   ○ April 19, 1986
5. Ellen Fried
   △ July 20, 1984
   ○ September 19, 1985
6. Eva Morse
   △ July 10, 1985
   ○ April 25, 1986
7. Lynda Moore
   △ April 15, 1986
   ○ April 15, 1986
8. Barbara Agnew
   △ January 10, 1987
   ○ March 28, 1987
9. Jane Boroski
   △ August 6, 1988

The earlier attacks—on Sheri Nastasia,
Theresa Fenton, and Caty Richards—
all took place in and around Springfield, Vermont, indicated by ⊠. The
dates are for the victim's disappearance
and the discovery of the body.
Theresa Fenton was found alive; she
died the following day.

Sheri Nastasia
   September 4, 1979
   December 13, 1979
Theresa Fenton
   August 29, 1981
   August 30, 1981
Caty Richards
   April 9, 1983
   April 10, 1983

Vermont

New
Hampshire

• Bethel

Hartford • Hanover

White River
Junction

Lebanon

Hartland •

New London

West Claremont
Claremont

Newport

Kellyville
North Charlestown

Springfield

Unity

Charlestown

Rockingham

Saxtons
River

Connecticut River

Sugar River

• Keene

West
Swanzey

• Swanzey

Brattleboro

The Shadow of Death

prologue

This is the story of death in a small, quiet place, of how it touched a community and the people who live there, of how they endured, and how they fought back.

We live in a time when the ways of death have multiplied, emerging in new weapons, new diseases, new impulses to horror in the human mind. The newspapers and television inform us daily that in communities all over our country, there is a new kind of murderer, one who chooses his victims without motive, strikes again and again, and often eludes capture for long periods. We learn from the media that the new way of death he brings has become a commonplace.

But that is not true everywhere. This is the story of a place where once, not so long ago, the idea of a serial killer was remote, even foreign, to the everyday lives of people. We may read and hear about these things, but that is not the same as waking up one morning to learn that they have come to our neighborhoods, our streets, our homes. That is what happened, beginning in the middle of the 1980s, to the people living in a small section of the valley of the Connecticut River in New Hampshire and Vermont.

Just a few years earlier there had been a forerunner of what was to come, a first appearance of this new thing. A killer had roamed the Valley, preying upon young girls. But like the first high winds of a great storm, his arrival could not foretell the still more terrible destruction that would follow. This first experience seemed an aberration in the quiet life of the Valley. There was no way for the people living there to anticipate that this first killer would be followed by another, one who would place them among those remote and dangerous places they had only read and heard about in the news. It is the specter of this second killer that inhabits the Valley still. The crimes he committed against individuals became crimes against all who live in the Valley.

Among the people of the Valley today, there are those who think they know who did these crimes. They live with that belief, and the fear and anger it creates, every day.

And then there are those—including some of the investigators who have worked on these cases—who are *sure* they know who did these crimes. And for them, it is even more difficult to live with the knowledge that their certainty cannot—not yet—be substantiated nor validated in court.

And finally there is the great majority of the people who live in the Valley. Among them are a few whose daughters, mothers, or wives have been taken from them in the cruelest way, without time to understand or prepare. But most are ordinary people who crossed paths with someone who was later murdered, people who were the friend or fellow worker or neighbor or the kind of acquaintance who said hello on the street, or who were merely the relative or friend of someone who bore one of these connections, to a woman who became a victim of the Valley killer. This network of associations spread in the end to touch almost every person in the Valley.

These people know only that someone has committed these terrible acts against individuals and against the peace and order of the whole community. And each in some degree has felt the loss, and each at some time has felt the fear that such loss might somehow, sometime, touch them in a still more personal way.

These are the survivors, for whom the unsolved homicides in the Valley remain truly unsolved, those who know only that somewhere an impalpable menace still stalks their lives, still travels the roads of their towns and villages. These are the people who live life every day in the shadow of death.

BOOK I

Isolated Incidents

one

It had been raining steadily in the Valley for two days.

All of May had been wet, and by now it was getting hard to remember a day when it hadn't rained. Total rainfall for the month was approaching record levels.

Even in ordinary times it was impossible to go anywhere in the Valley without being aware of the presence of running water, friendly, cheerful, comforting. It flowed under a bridge beneath the road, it splashed and gurgled near a familiar path through the woods, it trickled across a meadow to fill a cow pond, it moved with slow majesty in the Connecticut River, which both separated and connected New Hampshire and Vermont. The big river formed the spine of the Valley, flowing always just below the consciousness of everyone who lived within a dozen miles of its banks on either side.

But now the water was out of control. All up and down the Valley roads were closed and students were sent home early. Town and village schools stayed closed on Tuesday in Cavendish and Chester and Londonderry on the Vermont side of the river, and roads were washed out in Weathersfield and Ludlow. In the little city of Springfield, twenty feet of sidewalk collapsed at the corner of Mount Vernon Street and Gulf Road.

On the New Hampshire side, the Sugar River, a favored

trout stream that fed the Connecticut, was overflowing its banks throughout Newport. Downstream from Newport, the business district of Claremont was safe up on its hill, but on the flats below, where the Sugar River flowed through the Beauregard Village section just before joining the Connecticut, the fire department was keeping watch. Volunteers were helping to scoop out debris and clear culverts, to keep the water from backing up and washing over the roads.

Beauregard Village was the last place anybody saw Bernice Courtemanche.

Bernice's boyfriend, Teddy Berry, called her at work at the Sullivan County Nursing Home on Wednesday. They arranged that Bernice would come to meet him at his sister's place in Newport after she got off work at three o'clock.

Bernice decided to go home to get some things before heading over to Newport, so she asked Bonnie Spicer, who was getting off work at the same time, for a ride into Claremont. From the nursing home, in the little town of Unity, it was less than ten minutes' drive north to the house in Beauregard Village, where they had been living with Teddy's parents. She'd get a snack and change, then hitchhike the ten miles east to Newport. She hitched rides a lot these days and it was a good way to get around, but she was due to get her driver's license soon and she was looking forward to it. She wouldn't have to depend on strangers so much.

Bonnie dropped her off at the corner of Main Street, where it came down the hill from the center of Claremont, and Citizen Street, which led off to the left across the Sugar River into Beauregard Village. It was still overcast, but the rain had let up, at least for a while.

Teddy's parents, Janet and Arthur Berry, lived in a small yellow house a few blocks into the village. They arrived home around three-thirty. Janet stayed outside in the truck with the motor running while Arthur ran inside to get something. Bernice was sitting at the kitchen table eating a peanut butter sandwich. She told Arthur she was planning to go to Newport to meet Teddy at his sister's. He offered her a ride. She said, no, she'd get a ride easily enough.

Teddy wasn't worried at first. They hadn't been definite about what time she'd get to Newport, and he knew Bernice might have had trouble getting a ride. It wasn't until darkness fell that he started wondering what was holding her up. He called home first but she wasn't there.

Maybe she had gone to her parents' house. When he phoned he learned that her parents had rushed off to Boston with Bernice's younger brother. He had gotten a fish hook caught near his eye and they wanted him to get specialized attention at the Boston Eye and Ear Infirmary. That was close to two hours' drive, so they would be late getting back. Could Bernice have gone with them? No, she hadn't been around.

Around six-thirty Teddy and his sister's husband, Robert, went out to see if they could find her. They drove the ten miles from Newport to Claremont, searching the roadside and anywhere she might have gotten sidetracked. In Claremont they checked all the likely places. No luck. Finally they decided to sleep on it. Bernice was an independent type. They told themselves it was just possible to imagine her staying away overnight, and maybe something had kept her from calling so far. It wasn't like Bernice to just take off and not come back the next day; she'd turn up, they said to each other. But their hopeful imaginings didn't carry much conviction.

In the morning there was still no sign of her, and no word. At twelve-fifteen Teddy called the Claremont police. Bernice Courtemanche went into the official records as a missing person.

The rain and cloudy skies had intruded on the activities of the long Memorial Day weekend, but it wasn't as if Mike Prozzo ever got very far away from his work, no matter what he was doing. He hadn't expected it to turn out that way. He had hated the idea of being transferred to the detective division when the chief first told him about it. It had felt like a punishment. That had been two and half years ago, and at the time he couldn't imagine anything that suited him more than being a uniformed cop, walking the streets, keeping an eye on things.

Prozzo had grown up in Claremont and it felt as if he knew everybody in town. As a child he had just assumed he would go into the family business. His father had come back from World War II and started a dry-cleaning store, naming it Veterans Cleaners in honor of his recent experience and his fellow soldiers.

It was a real family business. Michael's grandfather, uncle, and mother had all worked there with his father at one time or another, and his older brother and sister had helped out while they were in school. But by the time Michael was finishing high school at St. Mary's Catholic in Claremont, it was clear that his older sister and brother had other career plans; she was on her way to becoming a hairdresser, he was going to business college, majoring in accounting. Michael, who was helping out in the store himself now, was his father's last hope to take over the business.

The problem was, they couldn't work together. The old man knew how he wanted things to be done, and that was that. And as Michael got older, he started to feel he knew how things ought to be done, too, and it wasn't always the same way his father wanted.

"We're both thick-headed Guineas," Prozzo said years later, his smile taking the sting out of the coarse ethnic slur he had heard more than once as a young man. Being Italian really had nothing to do with it; the story of a father and son clashing at close quarters was as old as time, and there was no room for compromise.

At the same time, Prozzo had harbored good feelings about cops and their work ever since he was a child. There were always beat cops around his father's store, and when he was eight years old a veteran Claremont officer named Arnie Foosse had given him a police whistle. Michael and a friend sat on a stoop on Washington Street and blew the whistle at cars that looked like they were going too fast.

In high school he discovered that other people accepted him as a leader. He was chosen cocaptain of the soccer team and elected an officer of the student council. And when he went into the National Guard soon after graduating from high school, he was singled out for promotion to PFC, then to corporal, and later to sergeant.

Prozzo wasn't given to self-analysis, but in later years it occurred to him that these experiences contributed to his feeling that he could never get along in the dry-cleaning business. When he finished Guard training in South Carolina he went back to the store, but it didn't feel right any longer.

"At that point," he recalled, "in my father's business he was the leader and I was the follower, and I would rather have been the leader. I always liked leading people, and I don't like following.''

It was easier to make the decision than it was to tell his father about it. For all the conflict, they were still close, and Michael didn't want to disappoint his father. He was still living at home, and he eased into the police department at first, with part-time work as a ''special.'' He helped out on traffic duty or worked special events when he wasn't needed in the dry-cleaning store. Then a full-time position opened up in the department. Prozzo applied and was accepted. The critical moment had arrived.

''I can remember like it was yesterday,'' Prozzo said, ''going home and telling my father that I wasn't going to work for him any longer.'' His laugh betrayed the tension of the moment even when it was close to two decades in the past. The elder Prozzo had been taking his midday break from the store, sitting in his armchair in the corner of the living room at home. The television was on but it was hard to tell if he was watching or dozing.

''I need to talk with you for a minute,'' Michael said to his father, and then he told him he was going to work full-time in the police department and wouldn't be helping out in the store anymore. The reaction was curiously muted, and Michael was relieved, but he could tell from his father's manner how disappointed he was.

Now it was more than two decades later, the elder Prozzos had just sold the dry-cleaning store and moved to Florida, and their son had risen steadily in the Claremont Police Department. In 1981, when he was a lieutenant in charge of the uniformed division, he had applied to become chief, but the job went to someone else. When the new chief transferred him to head the detectives a few months later, Prozzo was convinced that insecurity was responsible for the move, that his visibility in the community as head of the uniformed officers on the street posed a threat to his boss, a newcomer to Claremont.

That wasn't the only reason for his disappointment with the shift. Prozzo had no interest whatever in being a detective. The duties of an officer on patrol fit him like his sharply tailored uniform shirt. Ducking in and out of stores and restaurants and bars, anywhere people gathered, stopping to chat on the street, keeping up with what was going on in town, anticipating problems and preventing them from developing, resolving disputes, collaring troublemakers, none of that seemed like work.

Prozzo *knew* these people. He was a glutton for professional self-improvement—he had once figured out that in less than eighteen years on the force he had spent a total of almost two years in courses of various kinds—and he was especially proud of having been selected in 1978 to go to the FBI Academy, where cops from all over the country learn about the latest law-enforcement issues and techniques. But he also knew that police work in a small place like Claremont depended on knowing the community and its people much more than on technology and methods. That was the part of the job that he loved. For a gregarious person like Prozzo, a man who moved among the people of Claremont like a fish in a pond, being a street cop was as easy and natural as breathing.

Even so, within a year or so after he had been taken away from the uniformed division Prozzo could hardly remember why he had objected to the idea so strenuously, and his disappointment had turned into gratitude to the chief who had made the move. Perhaps the chief had understood something that wasn't visible to Prozzo himself. Prozzo loved the work.

In the two and a half years since the transfer he had instituted a series of changes to make the detective division function more efficiently, but the part Prozzo enjoyed most was the change he felt in himself. He had learned how to see the broad picture, how to manage a case, how to talk with suspects, how to work within the legal restrictions to gather evidence for a prosecution.

Most of all, it was the interview, the confrontation with the suspect, that he loved. It was a psychological game, and it required a feel for people, a gut-level understanding of character and personality. The transfer to detective work offered a whole new set of challenges, and Mike Prozzo found that his ability to meet them was a rich new source of professional achievement and satisfaction.

But now, as Prozzo returned to work after a long Memorial Day weekend, his enthusiasm was about to run head-on into a case that would gradually expand to touch every corner of the community in which he was so deeply immersed, and his professional confidence was soon to be tested in a way that went far beyond anything he had ever experienced.

Leafing through the preliminary reports turned in by detectives and officers in his absence, Prozzo saw little at first in the case of Bernice Courtemanche to produce the chill of concern that usually signalled something special. A seventeen-year-old girl with no apparent reason to take off was missing. Officers had checked with her boyfriend, Teddy Berry, his parents and sister, Bernice's parents, a couple of her teachers, a supervisor at the nursing home. There wasn't anything in these preliminary interviews to distinguish Bernice Courtemanche from a lot of other runaways.

"She's not the first juvenile that we've had missing," Prozzo thought to himself. Even in a quiet place like Claremont, that happened all the time.

The truth was, it had been happening more and more in the last few years. In the previous twelve months, 237 adults and 95 children had been reported missing in Claremont. In a single year, the number of people who disappeared for long enough to provoke a report to the police department equalled one of every forty-four people in Claremont.

Among almost a hundred children reported missing in the twelve months before Bernice Courtemanche disappeared, a three-year-old had wandered less than a block to her grandmother's house, then found her way home twenty minutes later. A sixteen-year-old girl turned up at the home of friends after a day and a half; it was the fourth time she had run away. A retarded eight-year-old wandered away when his brother, who was assigned to watch him, got distracted; he was found after ten minutes in the bushes near his house. A two-year-old was snatched by his mother from a department store; the parents were fighting for custody of the child. And little clusters of youngsters, ten to fifteen years old, were constantly disappearing for a few hours from Orion House, a local home for troubled children. These cases, where the children were located within a short time, usually hours, at most a couple of days, were typical.

But there were exceptions, tragic exceptions. The year before, just a dozen miles away, across the river in Vermont, an eleven-year-old girl had been kidnapped on an April Saturday. Her body was found the following day; she had been murdered. Long after the case had been solved her parents were left with the thought that somehow the horror might have been prevented. They initiated a lawsuit against the local police department, claiming it had not reacted quickly or comprehensively enough to the report of the kidnapping.

And it was the possibility of this kind of exception, the thought that a child might have come to harm, that sharpened the attention of anyone who heard a report that a young person was missing.

In March of 1984 the mayor of Claremont, partly in response to the Vermont case, had appointed a committee to upgrade the city's procedures for handling missing-persons cases. The committee was to focus especially on cases involving children. One member was the chief of police, Adam Bauer. Chief Bauer named a young detective, Bill Wilmot, to serve with him on the committee. Two months after that, Wilmot was working with Mike Prozzo on the disappearance of Bernice Courtemanche.

At first look it wasn't clear to Prozzo how the case should be treated. At seventeen, Bernice Courtemanche seemed to be on the borderline between adult and child. She was working at the nursing home, no longer dependent on her parents, living with a boyfriend away from home; but she was still living as a dependent with adults, Teddy's parents, she was still going to school, and she still had a few months left as a minor.

The information alone was equivocal: was Bernice Courtemanche an adult who could be expected to come and go on her own, or a child whose disappearance should be treated as an emergency from the first minute? It was time that provided the answer. The passage of a few days after Bernice Courtemanche's disappearance combined with what was known about her so far to work a subtle change in Prozzo's thinking: the business before him was shading from a missing-person case into a potential criminal matter. Bernice Courtemanche was looking more and more like a victim.

That afternoon, Prozzo went to see Teddy's parents. Mrs. Berry did most of the talking, while her husband sat quietly, satisfied with being in the background. She said that Bernice and Teddy seemed very much in love. They had been talking about getting married. Mrs. Berry had enjoyed having Bernice living there, had come to think of her as being like a daughter.

She thought Bernice liked it, too, appreciated the freedom from the tension in her parents' home.

It soon emerged that Mrs. Berry was unhappy with the effort the police were making to find Bernice. It didn't seem like they were doing anything. Why weren't they out looking for Bernice?

This kind of criticism wasn't anything new for Prozzo and he tried not to take it too personally. The family of a victim always focused on their own fears and found it hard to imagine that there was other business the police had to handle at the same time. And so much of what the police were doing was invisible to anyone outside the department.

Prozzo considered it part of a commander's job to deal with this kind of impatience. In a small place like Claremont that meant offering himself in person as a whipping boy and trying to make the people feel better. He waited patiently while Mrs. Berry vented her frustration. Then he outlined for the Berrys what the department had done already and what they were planning to do in the next several days.

"I want you to know we're concerned about Bernice and we're doing everything we can to find her," he said. "We do care."

Mr. Berry seemed to accept Prozzo's explanation, but his wife still wasn't satisfied. Prozzo resolved to stay in touch with her, keeping them informed about all the activity aimed at finding Bernice that the public wouldn't be able to see.

Among the early reports, Prozzo had found one from somebody who worked in a sheet-metal shop on North Street, a mile or so from Beauregard Village, where Bernice had last been seen. The caller had seen her get into a white pickup in front of Frank's Neighborhood Store, across the street from the sheet-metal shop. There were two or three guys in the truck, he said. North Street would have been a natural route to take toward Newport.

No one had found any further trace of her on North Street, though, and a few days later Arthur Berry, Teddy's father, appeared at the front window of the police station. He wanted to talk to somebody. He had heard a rumor that Bernice had been seen getting into a white pickup. He owned a white pickup, he told the officer, and he was concerned that the police might think he had something to do with Bernice's disappearance.

Though Arthur Berry's worry was a tribute to the speed and scope of the gossip network in Claremont, Prozzo wasn't taking him seriously as a suspect in the disappearance of his son's girlfriend. Berry had been the last person to see her, he was with his wife at the time, and they were together afterward, during the time that Bernice would have been leaving for Newport.

Teddy Berry was another matter. A boyfriend, lover, husband was always an obvious prospect when you were looking for someone who might harm a woman. Prozzo spent most of Tuesday tracking reports about Bernice and working on other cases. He was on the day shift, supposed to finish at five o'clock, but the case of the missing girl was taking on a feeling of urgency. Workdays were going to be longer for a while. It was almost eight o'clock before he could catch up with Teddy Berry for an interview.

Teddy was barely older than Bernice and seemed very young to Prozzo. Things were going great between them, he said. They were planning to get married and get an apartment of their own. They had talked about buying a car together and driving to Florida for a vacation later in the summer.

He admitted that they had argued a couple of weeks before, but it was about something minor. "I wouldn't do anything to hurt her," he said.

He confirmed that Bernice did hitchhike at times, but she was careful. If the driver were a woman, she wouldn't hesitate, but if it were a man she'd check him out before taking a ride, and Teddy was sure she wouldn't get in if there were more than one man in the car.

"She wouldn't go this long without contacting me," Teddy said. "I think something bad has happened." He couldn't picture what it was, but she wouldn't just disappear unless she was dead or kidnapped, or. . . . The thought trailed off into realms of vague but shocking speculation.

The detective now felt comfortable in dropping Bernice's boyfriend as a suspect in her disappearance. He had a good alibi, and beyond that, the boy's concern was too genuine, and his actions had been consistent with the role of a young man shocked and upset at the disappearance of someone he cared for.

Bernice Courtemanche was the descendant of a historic migration. Thousands of French-speaking Canadians had come down from rural Canada in the decades on both sides of the turn of the century to take jobs in the textile mills and shoe factories of New England. Like Beaulieu and Therriault and a thousand others, Bernice's family name had lost its rounded French dignity to the stiff Yankee tongue of New England. In Bernice's generation everybody, even people of French descent, pronounced it ''Cootermarsh.''

At Stephens High they said Bernice missed class more often than her teachers would have liked, but she did all right. At seventeen she was getting ready to move on, and most of her attention was clearly elsewhere, with her boyfriend, her work, her future. A teacher who saw her almost every day said there hadn't been any obvious change in her mood.

''She wasn't part of the 'in crowd,' '' one teacher said, ''but she was no loner. And she certainly didn't seem as if she'd want to do any harm to herself.''

Bernice had enjoyed her work as an aide at the nursing home. She had gone out there because her mother worked there, and she did willingly whatever needed to be done, helping to care for the patients and clean up. She got along fine with the other staff people and the patients.

The Courtemanches lived in a trailer in Unity, not far from the nursing home. Bernice's father worked at the Dartmouth Woolen Mill, one of the few working remnants of the days when the mills had dominated the economy of the Valley. Life had been tense for Bernice at home with her own family, but now that she was living with Teddy at his parents' house, things were a lot better. Though the move was a short one in distance—there were only about fifteen thousand people in Claremont, New Hampshire's ninth-largest city, and everything seemed close together—it brought a big improvement in her life. The Berrys seemed to like her and enjoy having her around.

Prozzo found two telling details in the reports that made it look as if Bernice Courtemanche had more than routine reasons to stay around, at least in the short run: Two days after Teddy reported her missing, she was due to receive a paycheck for $113 at the nursing home. And the same day, she had an appointment to take the test for her driver's license; she had been talking about getting her license for weeks, looking forward to it eagerly.

As Prozzo's portrait of the missing girl continued to grow more detailed, the case took on an ever more ominous look.

Even in the week of Bernice Courtemanche's disappearance, the biggest crime stories in the Claremont area were about a barn fire that was the latest in a series of suspicious early-morning fires over the last six months—there was little damage because the barn was so saturated by the rain—and a Plainfield woman who was angry because roving dogs that had been killing her laying hens for months had finally gotten the last three of a flock that had once numbered twenty-five.

Not so long ago in Claremont, even the worst crimes had a kind of domestic feel to them, seemed to grow out of everyday affairs. Once they had been ground up fine by local coffee-shop discussion and street-corner theorizing, such happenings seemed understandable, manageable. Someone knew, and soon everyone knew, that two men who got into a fatal argument had hated each other since they fought over a girl in high school, or that the boy who killed his father had been taking revenge for years of abuse. There was a history, a reason for what happened. Things could be explained.

But somewhere along the line, everything had changed. Families flew apart and nobody seemed to know why, except to say, "It happens all the time." The more serious forms of violence, even killings, seemed to come more frequently, and often someone died and nobody knew who they were, or where they had come from, much less who might have wanted to kill them. Claremont was changing, and with it the business of the police was changing, too.

On Friday uniformed officers under Captain Pete Hickey fanned out along the banks of the Sugar River, searching for any sign that Bernice had somehow gotten sidetracked and passed that way. Other officers retraced the route along the roads between the bridge near the Berrys' house and Newport, ten miles away, where she was supposed to have met Teddy. Detectives from the Newport Police Department drove all the possible routes on their side of the town line. There was no trace anywhere.

Late Saturday afternoon, a man who worked at the small airport in Lebanon, New Hampshire, eighteen miles north of Claremont, reported having seen Bernice Courtemanche the day before. She was getting out of a white Ford Falcon at the first exit from the interstate, just across the river in Vermont. He recognized her from the picture in the paper earlier in the week. Claremont asked the Vermont State Police to check the story out, but they were unable to learn anything more.

By now, all the happier outcomes were starting to seem unlikely. The department released information about the missing girl to the *Claremont Eagle-Times*. A small story appeared on the front page of the Sunday paper. Under a picture of Bernice smiling broadly, the story announced that the Claremont police were "seeking information as to the whereabouts of Bernice L. Coutermanche." The misspelling looked like something inspired by a phonetic reading of her name. The story described her as having hazel eyes and long dark brown hair, and said she was five feet ten inches tall and weighed 140 pounds. Some people who knew her were a little surprised to see how tall she was. Somehow she hadn't seemed that big. Maybe it was because she was still so girlish. Perhaps it was her diffident manner.

The same day the story appeared, Teddy Berry brought Bernice's purse to the police department. She had left it at his parents' house. There were medications, some earrings, a datebook, the usual essential clutter of daily life's small baggage.

"She wouldn't have left without taking this stuff along," Bill Wilmot thought. The purse just reinforced the growing pessimism about what had happened to Bernice Courtemanche.

Later that day Officer Angela Mains phoned the Sullivan County Nursing Home to find out what had happened with Bernice's paycheck. She was told that Teddy Berry had picked it up on Friday, using an authorization slip signed by Bernice. Officer Mains checked with Teddy, who said Bernice had authorized him to pick up the check because she was planning to take the test for her driver's license on Friday and wouldn't be going in to work.

The idea with a missing-person case was to jump on it hard from the start. Usually the investigation was interrupted by the person's return, if not within hours, at least within a day or two.

And if the person didn't turn up voluntarily, the best chance the police had of finding them came in the first two or three days, no more than a week, when the trail was still warm. The background check, the interviews, the search of the most likely places, all the routine of police, family, and friends, normally turned up the missing person or persuaded everybody that the person had taken off voluntarily. Either way, that put an end to the police role. There was no law against running away from home.

Even so, if the person didn't return, there were still a few things left for the police to do. In the next week, the Claremont police sent a flier describing Bernice Courtemanche to other local departments in New Hampshire and Vermont, state police throughout New England, and a national search service for missing children. Beyond following up leads as they came in, there wasn't much more they could do.

On Monday the *Eagle-Times* ran a tiny story on an inside page reporting that Bernice was still missing, inviting anyone with information to phone the Claremont Police Department. It added the information that she had been wearing a blue denim jacket, denim pants, and brown suede shoes when she was last seen. She had been missing for six days.

That was the last mention of the missing girl in the newspaper. Over the next few weeks there were occasional reports from people claiming they had seen Bernice Courtemanche after she was reported missing; in time they all proved to be mistaken.

In the offices and stores of Claremont, over coffee in the diner on the square, in the bars, when people talked of Bernice Courtemanche, there was usually someone present with a relative or friend who knew the missing girl or her family. After all, they were saying, she wasn't the most faithful person about going to school, and everyone knew that kids around her age were taking off all the time. Maybe it was wishful thinking rather than conviction, a defense against the anticipation of tragedy, but the consensus was that Bernice had taken off on her own. She'd show up.

Among those who knew her better, by now the early optimism had subsided along with the flood waters. Teddy Berry's mother was having vivid nightmares in which she saw Bernice tied to a tree. "Please, help me," Bernice pleaded in the dream, "somebody come and help me." For weeks Janet Berry had searched the woods, hoping that the nightmare was somehow offering a sign, a lead to what had happened to her son's girlfriend.

For the family of the missing girl, for Teddy and his parents and Bernice's friends and the people who worked with her, now there was only uncertainty, but it was an ambiguous, double-edged uncertainty. There was the desperate need for some resolution, the urgent wish to know what had happened to Bernice, but as days became weeks and the likelihood of a happy ending diminished, the possibility of knowing became increasingly fraught with dread.

And for Mike Prozzo there was a sense that this was not an ordinary case of a missing person. Bernice Courtemanche had too many reasons to like her life, there were too many signs that she was not someone who would run away, and there was too little cause to think she was the victim of an accident. It was still not something that Prozzo wanted to put in words; in fact the idea existed almost entirely beneath the level of conscious thought, but Prozzo couldn't shake the feeling that something was seriously wrong.

So far, though, the circle of those who glimpsed the specter of tragedy lurking behind events was limited, confined to a few investigators and the small number of people who had known and loved Bernice Courtemanche.

That would soon change.

two

March 1982

Ellen Fried loved the outdoors whatever the season, needed the freedom and the solitude, but spring was special. Something about the green, the newness, everything opening up after the long winter. It was an especially beautiful time here, where she had grown up, a small town in New York State, nestling into the southern reaches of the Catskill Mountains.

And this year there was something else: the coming of spring brought the anticipation of change, an unfamiliar mixture of melancholy for what would soon be the past and excitement at what might come next, the end of one part of her life and the beginning of another.

Maybe that was what brought on the breakup with Tommy. Ellen had known him a long time, and it seemed as if she'd loved him forever. They shared a passion for country life, the woods, riding bikes, and swimming, but there had always been a dark side to his joy, and lately it had come to bother her more and more.

There had always been an ease and flow to their time together, getting high and listening to loud music, laughing, and making love. She loved his gentleness and sense of fun, and she also loved the wildness in him and what it brought out in her, the excitement of riding fast on his motorcycle, the rock-

and-roll side of their life together.

But Tommy went beyond that, drinking heavily at times, using it as something beyond recreation, needing it in a way that scared her. It seemed too important to him. Those were the times when she pictured the wildness as a demon that fastened on to something inside and sucked the responsibility and drive and ambition out of him.

She had passed through her own time of searching and indecision, several years of college interspersed with times of work and uncertainty. Finally she had made her decision, gone back home to live, and entered nursing school.

Now she was twenty-four years old and it was starting to feel as though this time in her life would soon look like the distant past. In just a few months she'd be finishing nursing school and she knew she couldn't let everything familiar, the people and things she loved—home and her parents and the place where she had grown up—swallow up her own ambition, her yearning for freedom and independence. And part of leaving, she knew, of starting the next phase of her life, would be getting free of Tommy.

It wasn't easy. She'd break away and then a day or a week later she'd regret it and try to get in touch with him again. Or he would call and she would be tempted to give in.

"I love Tommy maybe more than anyone ever," she said, "and I walk out on him. I hurt him so bad. It hurt me a lot. But when I surrender my life to him, I'm depressed."

Then she'd be driving down the highway, Aretha Franklin on the stereo laying down every woman's claim to independence and respect, and suddenly Ellen would feel better again, confident that she was doing the right thing.

There were times when she imagined herself alone, away from all this—family, place, lover—and she seemed to lose her sense of who she was. Then, over the months, as she began learning to imagine her new life in a new setting, daydreaming about how it would be, she gradually started to rebuild her idea of herself.

"Off and on," she said one day, recalling an evening when she had begun to recognize her confidence coming back, "it stayed with me. My long lost friend. My self."

By March she was starting to feel certain about her decision: she would leave all this behind, go somewhere else to find a job, start fresh on a new life. She read a biography of Jack London, the roving author of *The Call of the Wild.* She was impressed by his all-out approach to life, the way he gripped his years and used them to the fullest, and she was a little unsettled by the way he burned up and died at forty.

Tommy was still holding on and a part of her wanted to give in, yield to the powerful magnetism of the familiar. Then in April she met Jeffrey. He played the fiddle, and the sound took a grip on her heart.

"Anyone would love him," she said, "and several do."

She saw herself as new and unformed, full of great possibility but still without the power she would one day acquire. And yet, she was surprised and delighted to find that he seemed to return her feelings. It was a happy distraction from the pain of breaking with Tommy, and from her guilt about the pain she knew she was causing him.

Immersed in the pleasure she was taking from this new affection, needing the reassurance it brought her, she had no wish to give much attention to what might happen later. The possibility that leaving this place, this period of her life, might soon force her again to go through the process of separation, this time from Jeffrey, seemed remote and weightless.

She began looking for nursing jobs, going off for interviews in the fading Toyota she thought of as "old Rusty." She drove up north through New York State, along the upper reaches of the Hudson River Valley, then crossed into Vermont to check out a hospital in Burlington, 275 miles from her home. From Burlington, just forty-five miles short of the Canadian border, it was south and east to the Connecticut River, crossing all of Vermont in less than an hour and a half.

Just across the river in New Hampshire she visited the Mary Hitchcock Memorial Hospital in the little college town of Hanover. She found the place preppie and snobbish, smugly self-assured.

"If I got a job here I'd definitely need to live outside the town," she said.

She considered Portland, Maine, too. Apart from her feeling about the rarefied air of Hanover, she liked these places with their small-town feel and countryside all around, the outdoor life just on the other side of the window at every moment. No big city would do for her.

She graduated in June, celebrated with family and friends, and stayed around to enjoy the summer, her last at home before moving away to begin life on her own. During the summer she marked time, picking fruit to make money.

One evening after work she drove out to the swimming hole where she had gone so often with friends in the past. When she came out of the water she walked upstream to the clearing where kids always gathered. There, sitting around a campfire, she found a group of boys she knew.

They were drinking beer, cooking venison over the fire, planning to sleep outdoors. They welcomed her enthusiastically, making her feel at home.

"Just like old times," she thought to herself, "me with wet hair and bare feet, standing by the fire to dry off and warm up," and soon Tommy was in her mind. They had been there together so many times, just like this.

"He'll hear that I was here," she thought, "the guys will tell him."

And then he was there, walking along the footpath, coming out of the woods like a figure in a dream, and the old joy rushed back, both of them forgetting for a while that things were not the way they had been, that everything had changed.

The next day she was miserable again, wishing that she could hold on to the simplicity and easy joy of the past, knowing at the same time that she could never go back, that she had to move on.

All summer she swung back and forth between regret and excitement. At times she told herself wistfully that she didn't have to leave, that she still had a choice. But beneath all the wavering and uncertainty, she knew she had made her decision and wasn't going to change it. She began the process of separating herself from Jeffrey.

In August she took the occasion of her twenty-fifth birthday to reflect a little about her life. Now that she had made her decision it was typical that she thought as much about the pain she was causing Tommy, and now Jeffrey, as about her plans for the future.

She postponed the moment, continuing to pick fruit through the fall to make money, but finally she accepted a job at the Valley Regional Hospital in Claremont, New Hampshire. Claremont was a small city just twenty-five miles south of

Hanover and it enjoyed the same riverside setting, but it was a whole world away in atmosphere and style. It was a small working-class city without pretension. The hospital served the whole Connecticut River Valley on both sides of the river. It suited Ellen just fine.

She took a temporary room in Claremont and before the end of the year she found a much nicer place away from the center of town. She spent New Year's Day of 1983 moving into the new place, several rooms in a rambling frame building on Chestnut Street. The back of the house overlooked Monadnock Park, and just beyond the park flowed the Sugar River. Off in the distance the thin white mantle of an early-season snow was broken only by Route 11 climbing the first hill on its way east to Newport.

During the previous summer, struggling with the pain of separation from everything familiar, facing the break with the place where she had come to adulthood, Ellen had wondered how it would all come out. Finally she had arrived at a simple statement of what she wanted: "I need a house, a job, a chance to live and see."

Now she had achieved all of that.

July 1984

It wasn't as if you ever forgot about a case like that, not as long as there was a young woman still missing and nobody knew where she was. It wasn't like the ordinary run of police business. That kind of disappearance, sudden, unexplained, people waiting for someone like Bernice Courtemanche in Newport on an ordinary day and then she doesn't show up, a thing like that left a hole in the community that just wasn't supposed to be there.

A cop who took his responsibility seriously would feel that kind of damage in a personal way, would never feel completely comfortable until it was repaired. And anybody who knew anything at all about Mike Prozzo would know without giving it a second thought that he was that kind of cop. It was like having it on your list of Things to Do Today, find Bernice Courtemanche, and then when you didn't get it done one day it carried over to the next, and the next, and the next. And even if you couldn't get it done, it was always there, always on the list, hovering in that part of your mind that would always be uncomfortable with unfinished business, responsibilities unmet.

The police weren't the only ones, either. Other people had it on their minds, too. On the street it seemed that every other person had something to say about it to Prozzo, some casual comment or question about the progress of the investigation. And every day or so at least one person came in or phoned with some kind of tip, and some days there were several. A Claremont man came in to say he thought he had seen her in town the day after the disappearance; it turned out he didn't know what she looked like. A woman claimed she had spotted Bernice, and it turned out she was right, but she was confused about dates; the day she had seen Bernice was before the Wednesday of her disappearance. And so it went, with none of these tips producing anything solid to indicate what had really happened.

Still, there were a lot of other things for the police to think about, plenty of robberies and auto accidents, vandalism and abandoned cars, bar fights and speeding violations, the daily business of police departments everywhere. And as the weeks slipped by, the amount of useful work Prozzo could do on the case of Bernice Courtemanche shrank steadily.

So while he never forgot about it, and in fact hardly a day went by when Claremont's chief detective didn't think about Bernice Courtemanche and her family and the fat file of information about her that the department had gathered in a cabinet not far from his desk, by midsummer Prozzo was once again immersed in the routine events of ordinary days in Claremont.

Among those events, the report of a car parked by the side of a country road on a slow Friday in the third week of July attracted no particular attention at first.

Jarvis Lane was a dirt road in a wooded area a little more than two miles from the center of Claremont. The narrow lane saw little traffic besides snowmobilers in the winter, blueberry pickers in the summer, and an occasional car passing from Plains Road over the hill to Route 12, which ran parallel to the Connecticut River, another mile west of town. An officer on patrol reported seeing the car parked with its righthand wheels resting in the grass and matted leaves just off the edge of the road.

The vehicle, an elderly Chevelle, was parked about three-quarters of a mile up the lane from Plains Road. The officer found that the doors were locked and nothing seemed to be amiss inside the car. It looked as if the owner had left it there and gone for a walk.

A routine check of the license plates with the Registry of Motor Vehicles showed that the car was registered to an Ellen Fried at an address on Broad Street in Claremont. The next day the car was still there. Jarvis Lane was not the kind of place where someone would be likely to leave a car and go camping overnight. An officer was dispatched to check with the owner.

It took most of the day to find someone at the Broad Street address who knew that Ellen Fried had moved out a few months before. She was still in Claremont, but nobody knew her new address. Maybe after dark, when people came home, someone at Broad Street would provide the information.

The following day, two nurses from the Valley Regional Hospital reported that a colleague had failed to show up for work on Friday and Saturday. She had been scheduled to work from three in the afternoon to eleven at night. It wasn't like her, they said, she was a responsible person, more than responsible, highly dependable and always considerate of the people she worked with. She wouldn't even be fifteen minutes late for her shift without calling. Her name was Ellen Fried.

By now several officers had looked around in the woods near the car without finding anything. A more systematic search was organized for late Sunday; a hastily assembled group of officers and auxiliary police found nothing unusual.

Monday morning a detective went up with a local pilot in a small plane to see if any trace of the missing woman could be spotted from the air. When that turned up nothing, officers were dispatched to borrow all-terrain vehicles, one from the Suzuki dealer and another from the Gulf station on Washington Street. At midmorning a state trooper arrived with a bloodhound. Mike Prozzo joined him and they began tracking back and forth across the area around the car; first they searched on both sides of the road, then slogged up and down the banks of the river. All these efforts were fruitless.

"A possibility of foul play exists at this time," Chief Adam Bauer said, in the stiff language of foreboding the police use with reporters everywhere. Detectives spent the rest of the day organizing a large-scale search effort for the following day.

By the middle of the morning Tuesday, more than thirty fish-and-game officers, firefighters, and police officers had gathered on Jarvis Lane. An officer of the Fish and Game Department described the search area, a rough triangle of woods bounded by the dirt road, railroad tracks to the west, and the Sugar River on the north, less than a square mile all together.

"Even a child couldn't get lost in there," the officer told the searchers standing solemnly in loose ranks along the side of the road. Certainly an adult could find her way out, unless something had happened to her. They should assume that if Ellen Fried were in there she would be on the ground, injured, unconscious, or dead.

A small group was sent to walk the railroad tracks, moving as far north as the high trestle bridge over the Sugar River; with the trains running through on their way to Montreal and back, anything could have happened if someone got onto the tracks. The rest of the volunteers spread out in a line about twenty-five yards apart. The leader signalled and the line disappeared slowly into the woods, like water soaking into a garden, each searcher scanning the ground to the left and right while trying to stay even with the men on each side and keep an equal distance from both. By nightfall they began filtering out again, less orderly now. They had covered most of the ground, without success.

Wednesday morning most of the group reassembled to finish the search, but by now a sense of futility was setting in. No one was surprised when the line of searchers reached the final boundary of the target area without turning up any sign of the missing woman.

As the search expanded, Mike Prozzo's detectives and other officers were gathering information about Ellen Fried. There were several reports from people who thought they had seen her shortly before or after the Thursday when she disappeared. One man said he had seen her in a market buying cold cuts Friday afternoon; the detectives had learned by then that she was a vegetarian, and in any case the identification seemed shaky. They discounted the story.

Most of the other reports of sightings also fell apart under scrutiny, but there was one story the police were not able to dismiss. Someone had seen Fried's car driving through Claremont with a canoe lashed to the top. Fried had not been in the car. The driver was described as a man with brown hair and a dark complexion.

The personal details began to form into a portrait of the missing woman. She was about five feet seven inches tall, slim at 125 pounds, with dark blond hair and distinctive green eyes. Her ears were pierced in three places. She was last seen at the end of her shift at eleven o'clock Thursday night, but no one seemed to know what she had been wearing when she left the hospital. It might have been her nurse's whites, she might have changed into street clothes, nobody was sure.

As far as the investigators could find out, she lived a quiet life and valued her privacy; she preferred to live without a telephone. Nevertheless, people in the house found her friendly and accommodating. One tenant had heard the sound of a banjo drifting out of her apartment from time to time.

Ellen liked the idea that her life was simple, uncomplicated by a lot of possessions or worries about security. It was important to her that she lived in a community where she felt comfortable walking out of the house without locking the doors behind her; she often left her car parked with the keys in the ignition.

Among those who knew Ellen Fried there were some who thought Claremont was really not as safe as she seemed to assume, but she continued to arrange her life her own way, and she wasn't alone. Most people thought of the Valley as a quiet, rural place, maybe a bit behind the times, a little out of the mainstream, a place where an older, friendlier way of life was still preserved, and that was just the way she liked it. Maybe her view of the place was based more on wishful thinking, on what she wanted it to be, than on what it was becoming, but in that she was like the vast majority of people, those who lived in the Valley and those who viewed it from the outside. And her way of seeing her surroundings, her trust and sense of security, had never been violated, never been contradicted by events.

The missing woman hadn't talked much to the people at the hospital about what she did when she wasn't working, but no one thought she was the kind of person who could have gotten into trouble in a bar or club; that wasn't the kind of place she liked to go for recreation. There was a young man she saw quite regularly, often spending the weekend with him in outdoor activities like camping and fishing, cross-country skiing in the winter. His first name was Erim, his family was from the Middle East somewhere, but no one seemed to know much more about him. He lived somewhere in the countryside, only occasionally had a car that was running, and like Ellen he lived without a telephone. More than one person used the word *hippie* in talking about him.

Ellen had clearly valued her single existence, the freedom, the sense that her life was her own to manage as she wished. That had remained a kind of barrier between her and the men she had been close to, including Erim. At the same time she confided to one source that her greatest wish was to find the one man, the one relationship, that would overcome her reservations. She was friends with a couple who had two young children and she often daydreamed about having a family of her own. She was delighted when the friends brought their children to visit at her apartment and the daydream came true, the children playing marbles and dominos on the living-room floor.

She had been working at the Valley Regional Hospital since late 1982, a little over a year and a half. It was a small institution catering to Claremont as well as Windsor and Springfield in Vermont, and the surrounding small towns on both sides of the river. It was overshadowed in some people's minds by the Mary Hitchcock Memorial Hospital in Hanover, a half hour up the Valley. The Hitchcock was affiliated with the Dartmouth Medical School, which gave it access to the most advanced technology and expert physicians. Valley Regional couldn't compete in those areas, but the staff there liked to think they provided a kind of personal care that patients couldn't find in Hanover, and everybody thought Ellen Fried fit in perfectly.

"She was an excellent nurse," someone said, "empathetic and caring." In fact, she brought a kind of fresh energy and commitment to the work that some of the more experienced nurses looked at with wonder. Beyond the point where others would begin to grow tired or lose patience, she always seemed able to smile at a difficult patient or take on a disagreeable task. She talked about a nurse's responsibility to the patient and the profession with an idealism that would have bordered on being annoying if she hadn't been so devoted to her work.

At the hospital the regular weekly staff meeting was scheduled for Friday, exactly a week after Ellen Fried had disappeared. If she turned up, one of the nurses said, they would cancel the meeting and hold a joyous welcome-home party instead.

"You read about things in the paper," one of her co-workers said, "and even when you don't know the people involved, you feel bad about it. But when it's right in your own backyard, it really hurts."

The woman might have been speaking for many people in Claremont and the surrounding area. The feeling was starting to take hold that the disappearance of Ellen Fried was something more than an isolated incident.

It was less than two months since Bernice Courtemanche had disappeared. There was still no explanation of what had happened to her, but as long as her disappearance had been the only event of its type, it was possible to keep a certain psychological distance. Seeing an update in the newspaper, catching her name in a bit of street-corner gossip, a person could think of her disappearance as somehow a singular event, a private matter, particular to Bernice. But now there was another woman missing, and the first hint of a question began to force itself into the consciousness of Claremont: Could the two cases be related? Was there some event, some person, some danger, that tied the two events together? Was this now in some sense a wider matter, something that affected the whole community, that could reach beyond the individuals involved? As the sense of loss began to sink in, any man or woman might begin to wonder: Could this affect me or someone close to me?

Friday came and the nurses at Valley Regional held their weekly staff meeting as scheduled. It was increasingly difficult to sustain any form of optimism about what had happened to Ellen Fried.

During the following week the posters began to appear

around town. The picture of Ellen Fried was taken from a snapshot. It showed her looking slightly down and to the side, with a small smile on her face. It conveyed the impression of a woman who was both self-confident and self-contained. Some of the posters had been put up by the police, but others were the work of a women's group that thought it might be catching the first slight odor of something that could be a danger to all women. Handwritten notices began to appear on bulletin boards around town asking anyone with information to come forward.

One central puzzle remained: Where had Ellen Fried gone when she left work? No one had seen her after 11:00 P.M. Thursday night. Reports that she had been sighted continued to come in, but none of them proved out. Then a lead turned up from a surprising source. Through the missing woman's family, the detectives learned that she had talked on the phone with her sister, Heidi, in California, soon after leaving work Thursday night.

Without a phone in her apartment, Ellen was forced to depend on public booths. She had located several around town that were convenient for one reason or another. Working from phone company records, the detectives traced the call back from Heidi to a phone at Leo's Market, a convenience store on Main Street in Claremont, less than half a mile down the hill from the central square. The phone was placed in an open two-sided enclosure hanging on the front of the building. Ellen could park her car nose in and make her calls without moving more than ten feet from the driver's seat.

The two sisters had been close for several years, making the effort to stay in touch, and the conversation went on for the better part of an hour. Heidi reported that the discussion had ranged back and forth over family and personal matters. For the most part it had seemed like many other phone conversations the sisters had shared, but there was one exception. It hadn't seemed like anything special at the time, but in retrospect it seemed to become significant, even frightening.

They had been talking for some time, Heidi recalled, when Ellen paused for a moment.

"That's strange," she said.

"What?"

"A car. Just drove through."

There was a pause. Then Ellen spoke again. "Hold on a minute."

There was the sound of the phone being put down. Moments later, Heidi heard the distant sound of an engine turning over. Ellen returned to the phone. She had wanted to make sure the car would start before hanging up the phone. They talked for a few minutes more, then hung up.

That was the last contact the detectives could find that anyone had with Ellen Fried before she disappeared. The passing car was interesting, particularly with Heidi's impression that something about it—Had it passed through more than once? Did Ellen have the feeling that the driver was examining her? Was there something familiar about the driver?—had made Ellen wary. But there was no clue in the conversation about what might have happened to Ellen after she hung up the phone.

Facing a dead end in the investigation, the police arranged to search the missing woman's apartment. It was neat, everything in order, and there was no sign of anything out of the ordinary. Perhaps it was because there seemed to be nothing that could provide any immediate help with the search for the missing woman, but no one took fingerprints from the apartment. That would turn out later to be a significant omission.

Friends and fellow workers refused to accept Ellen's disappearance as final. In the middle of the third week without news, some friends decided to try to find her boyfriend. On August 7 a man presented himself at the reception window of the Claremont Police Department.

"I'm here about Ellen Fried," he said. "I'm her friend."

His name was Erim Nasoglu, he told an officer who sat down with him, and he had been seeing Ellen Fried for some time. Her friends had located someone who knew where he lived and tracked him down, driving out to his house in Simonsville, Vermont, about thirty miles from Claremont. They had been hoping that Ellen, against everything they knew about her personality, might have decided for some reason to drop out of her life and hole up with him in the country. Or at least that he would know something about where she was. Their hopes had been frustrated. It was the first Nasoglu had heard about her disappearance.

The friends had told him that someone had been sighted

driving Ellen's car with a canoe lashed on top. He and Ellen had been planning a fishing trip a few weeks before, he told the officer, and he had been driving around, making preparations. If the person sighted with the car was someone else, he said, that would be a good lead, because she would never let anyone but him take the car and she didn't own a canoe herself.

The timing and the description of the driver in the sighting reported earlier matched Erim Nasoglu's story exactly. The person the witness had seen driving Ellen's car was her boyfriend, preparing for the fishing trip. The report was not going to provide any evidence of what might have happened to her. The last significant lead had evaporated.

Across the river in the tiny town of Felchville, Vermont, a psychologist named John Philpin had been following newspaper accounts of Ellen Fried's disappearance with particular interest.

It was strange that the news stories about Fried never mentioned Bernice Courtemanche, who had disappeared less than two months before. Maybe it was a result of the general innocence of outlook in the Valley, a lack of experience with the kinds of terrible things that happened in big cities. Or maybe the papers were just going along with the police, who didn't want to alarm people, didn't see any good reason to upset the community with speculation about some connection between the two disappearances when there was no evidence that they had anything in common. People were disappearing all the time and there was no reason to think there was anything more here than sad coincidence.

John Philpin didn't share the general outlook in these matters. Any innocence he had ever enjoyed in matters of violence was long gone, first shaken by the events of childhood, later banished by professional experience.

In a few weeks it would be exactly three years since a series of chance events had changed Philpin's professional life irrevocably, in the process bringing him face-to-face with the kind of unfathomable violence that still seemed remote and exotic to so many of his neighbors. During that time, he had trained himself to bring his knowledge of psychology to bear on the analysis of crimes. In the process he had built a wide acquaintance among police officers on both sides of the Connecticut River, men who had first contributed to his education in criminal investigation and had then become his friends, and he had developed a deepening familiarity with the details of their work.

Almost from the start Philpin had seen something in the disappearance of Ellen Fried that could not be separated from the stories about Bernice Courtemanche just weeks earlier. Even from the sparse details that had appeared in the newspapers, Philpin got the feeling that neither of these women looked like a typical runaway, neither had any obvious reason to disappear, and both seemed to have strong connections to the continuity of routine, to everyday life.

In May, Philpin had cut out newspaper stories about the disappearance of Bernice Courtemanche. Now he took out a fresh file folder and wrote the name Ellen Fried on the tab. He gathered up the earlier clippings, combined them with the new ones about Ellen Fried, and put them into the folder.

Philpin had met Mike LeClair, a detective with the Vermont State Police, when he had first worked with investigators on a case three years before. Since then they had stayed in contact, and lately Philpin had worked with LeClair on the murder of a young girl in Vermont. Philpin voiced his concern about the New Hampshire cases to LeClair one day.

"You know," he said, "I think they've got a serial killer over there in Claremont."

Book II

Innocence at Risk

three

It hadn't been that long ago, the warm autumn evening when a thirteen-year-old girl named Sheri Nastasia disappeared in Springfield, Vermont.

That was only five years before the summer when the names of Bernice Courtemanche and Ellen Fried were thrust into the consciousness of the Connecticut Valley. But the Valley had seemed like a very different place then.

To be sure, the changes had started, were well under way in fact, and already they had gone a long distance toward altering the character of this narrow fifty-mile strip of land running north and south along both sides of the Connecticut River. But there is always a period between the time when things change and the time when people recognize the new reality and begin adjusting to it. In that sense, most people in the Connecticut Valley were still living in the past.

The two states that faced each other across the river here in its upper reaches ordinarily lived more intimately with history than most American places. New Hampshire and Vermont were states whose past was tightly intertwined with the nation's origins. Their present, because they were situated at a slight remove from the most dynamic centers of American change, had not so overwhelmed memory as in many places to the south. Tiny graveyards dotting the landscape, winding country roads that traced their origins to early cart roads and footpaths, austere old houses with narrow windows, the kind of small farms that were disappearing from much of the rest of the country, all these things were daily reminders that this northern edge of New England bore much of the past in its living heart.

From the start these two small states had rested physically and politically at the edge of the new nation, New Hampshire defining itself in relation, and opposition, to Massachusetts at its southern border, Vermont moving in the wake of New York to the west. And in between, the rows of towns facing the Connecticut River from opposite banks often felt more social and economic affinity to each other than to the states at their backs. The first towns in what later became Vermont were originally established in the middle of the eighteenth century by the government of New Hampshire, and in 1781 a clutch of towns on the east bank of the river came close to pulling out of New Hampshire and joining up with Vermont. There was even some sentiment for carving out a new state in the Valley, within the natural boundaries of Vermont's Green Mountains to the west and the Sunapee and Monadnock ranges in New Hampshire on the east.

In the end things remained as they had been, the border between the two states running down the west bank of the river, but the sense that the Valley was a place apart remained palpable two centuries later. Identity flowed easily back and forth across the river, over the privately owned wooden bridge with the twenty-five-cent toll between Charlestown and Springfield, and across the big steel-arch bridge on the interstate highway up north from Lebanon to White River Junction, conveying more sense of movement than of change. The Valley had a newspaper that assumed its name and called itself the *Valley News,* refusing to choose sides; a museum that took a piece from the name of each state and called itself Montshire; and a school district, reputedly the only one in the nation, that served students in two states.

Well beyond the middle of the twentieth century the Valley remained a place of small farms and modest factories. The sheep that once supplied the nation's wool had given way to dairy cows, and the textile mills and shoe factories that took their power from the abundant flowing water had largely been replaced by small machine shops and manufacturing plants, but the character of the place still owed more to the early decades of the century than it did to the years of rapid change since World War II.

All that began to change for good with the coming of the interstate highways. Beginning in the late 1950s the four-lane divided highways began pushing up from Boston into New Hampshire, northward first to Concord, the capital, then westward over I-89 across half the state to the Connecticut River and into Vermont. From western Massachusetts I-91 flowed due north along the Vermont bank of the Connecticut River, forming a strong new spine for the Valley, crossing I-89 at White River Junction. By 1970 the last links were in place, measurably shortening the passage between north and south, opening the way for a historic migration.

Even before the last segments of the new roads were complete, people from other places—flatlanders, the old hill Yankees liked to call them—were following them northward, coming to ski or to look at the autumn leaves or just to escape for a while the growing pressures of their cities and suburbs. And, slowly at first, then with gathering momentum, they came to stay.

Through the 1960s and 1970s they came, fleeing Massachusetts and New York, fleeing cities and high taxes, fleeing crowding and crime and schools that were becoming like prisons, fleeing the sense that everything, that life itself, was disintegrating. In Vermont and New Hampshire they found a green and gentle land, small communities with enduring connections among their people, a kind of safety and simplicity that had seemed lost forever to the larger places from which they had come. And the highways gave them continuing access to the things—relatives, work, the urban amenities—they had left behind.

The population of New Hampshire grew by more than half between 1960 and 1980, Vermont's by almost a third. In the Connecticut River Valley, still remote even with the greater ease of travel, the effects of the influx were muted. Even so, the population of the two dozen towns and two small cities between Hanover, New Hampshire, and Brattleboro, Vermont, grew by more than 20 percent in the two decades.

But there was irony in this great flow of migrants. Their numbers, their ways, their very newness began relentlessly to subvert much of what they had come to find. Their housing developments and condominiums became blemishes on the bucolic rural scene, their demand for services drove up tax rates, their separateness undermined community, and their numbers overwhelmed intimacy.

As the invasion of population and capital took hold it changed the very shape of the Valley. It was as if the vitality was draining slowly from the centers of the towns and small cities onto the roads radiating away from them, roads that connected them with the highways, then the interstates, and with other places. There was a new restlessness here, a need for something more than the settled, familiar life of the town, an urge to be moving, going somewhere else. Increasingly the people of the Valley, like much of the rest of America, were taking to the road, for work, for social life, for recreation. The center could not hold them.

Sheri Nastasia was one of those who had seemed to spin away from the old settled orbits of life in the small valley towns. Her parents were divorced, and at first Sheri and her eleven-year-old brother had lived with their mother in Florida. In July of 1979 they moved up to Springfield, Vermont, just a dozen miles south of Claremont, to live with their father. John Nastasia was a truck driver for an oil company. Most days he was on the road. He tried to arrange for baby-sitters or asked a neighbor to keep an eye on the children, but most of the time they seemed to run free. Police officers soon became accustomed to seeing Sheri on the streets long past dark, often with her little brother in tow. At first the children's idea of fun was ice cream and soda and the freedom of the streets at a time when most kids their age were being tucked in bed. The month they moved to Vermont, Sheri turned thirteen.

With a population of just over ten thousand, Springfield was one of the larger places in the Valley. A little concentration of machine-tool plants had given it one of the steadiest economies in the Valley, too, but by 1979 foreign competition was undermining its strength. Over the next ten years it would be one of the few places in the Valley to lose population.

Though it was a town, governed by a board of selectmen,

Springfield was distinct from the smaller places in the Valley, where life and activity were more private, less visible. Springfield looked like a small city. Its business was visible on the street, condensed into the space of a few blocks. The town center held a motley mixture of plain three-story office buildings, their street-level fronts opened up to make display windows for stores, an occasional wood-frame structure with professional offices, and a few brick buildings that looked as if they could once have been the homes of wealthy families. Now they had been converted to accommodate businesses.

In the center of town, crowded into the midst of the commercial life along Main Street, stood the First Congregational Church, an impressive building with six two-story fluted columns in front and a steeple rising to a high gold mast. Many days, at the edge of the sidewalk in front of the building, a blackboard issued an invitation: "Senior Citizens—Today's Menu: Liver and Onions, Tomatoes Stewed, Boiled Potatoes." Lunch was three dollars, but for those over sixty, a donation was optional.

That was the surface of daily life in Springfield, but just beneath it there was an undercurrent of something darker, flowing from the center of town out to the little shopping plaza, a distance of less than a mile, then back to the center, restless, searching.

Daylight rendered them less visible, but after dark there was a constant traffic here of people with nothing much to do, nowhere else to go, no one to go home to. Among them there were those known to the police as drifters and minor drug dealers, drinkers and brawlers and loiterers, a kind of small-city street furniture. And there were those who were drawn to them, lured by the sense of movement and action: teenagers driving too fast and making too much noise, young men looking for drugs, the occasional women looking for diversion or maybe a little cash, older men looking for the women.

And among them, before long, was Sheri Nastasia, often wearing brief shorts and a halter top, with her long, dark blond hair hanging down her back, a thirteen-year-old girl who looked older, old enough to drift along with this human current, certainly too old to be thrilled by ice cream and soda and the chance to stay up late.

On a warm Tuesday night in late August, an ordinary late-summer night, Sheri Nastasia went out as usual. And as usual, she had no particular destination. She never came home.

She was reported missing the next day and the local police began an investigation. Lots of Springfield police officers were familiar with Sheri Nastasia. There were places that cops walking the street or riding in a patrol car kept an eye on without thinking about it, certain houses where there had been trouble, shadowed areas behind buildings, an alley outside a bar where knots of people formed and dissolved through the night. Sheri Nastasia had been turning up in those places all summer. Beat cops and detectives talked to the people who hung around there, the men and women who moved routinely along the strip between the center of town and the shopping plaza. They all knew Sheri Nastasia, and they all had noticed her around in the last day or two, especially the men. But no one had an idea where she could have gone. Or at least no one had an idea they were willing to talk about. Even at the best of times there was something furtive about these people, something guarded. Now, when there was some mystery, a question of what might have happened, a possibility of trouble on the street, they seemed to draw back into themselves, pulling shades, drawing curtains, closing doors as they went.

A detective soon found a man with a room in the same house as the Nastasias who said he had seen Sheri walking along River Street about midnight on Tuesday. A dark car, maybe green, he thought it looked like a Pontiac Firebird, slowed to match her pace, then followed alongside as she continued walking. After a few moments the car stopped and Sheri got in.

That was the only solid lead that turned up. The investigators did what they could with it, checking out a number of people with criminal records, some that involved sex crimes and young girls. They turned up at least one case where a possible suspect owned a Firebird. None of these efforts produced anything useful. There were reports that Sheri had run away from home before, mad at her father, mad at limits, mad at life, returning several days later. In the absence of any evidence to the contrary, it seemed likely that she had just decided to take off on her own again. Most people thought that she'd probably turn up soon, the way these teenagers did, seeming a little surprised that anybody had noticed she was gone.

They were wrong. Three and a half months later, a truck driver taking a break at a rest area on Route 103, ten miles south of Springfield, found a body. Time and exposure had reduced the remains to little more than bones.

It was snowing when the driver made his discovery. The local police soon arrived, sealed off the site and the surrounding ground, and put in a call for the mobile crime lab from the state authorities. By the time the technicians arrived and prepared to go to work the area was covered with snow. It was a laborious process, trying to clear away the snow and examine everything minutely for any tiny trace of evidence. They didn't come up with much beside the skeleton.

The bones and teeth provided enough evidence to allow a positive identification. It was Sheri Nastasia.

Apart from the identification, the investigators didn't have much to work with. The condition of the body made it impossible even to be sure about what had killed Sheri Nastasia. The investigators were proceeding on the assumption that she had been abducted and killed, but strictly speaking there was insufficient evidence for an official ruling that the cause of death was homicide. She had suffered broken ribs and a broken leg. If she had been murdered, the medical examiner concluded, it had probably been done by strangulation, but that was the most that could be said. The hyoid bone, the one in the neck that would probably show if she had been strangled, was missing.

As for finding the person responsible, the problem was the opposite of the one the police usually faced, where they could subject a limited number of potential suspects to close scrutiny. Here there were too many suspects. All the rough inhabitants of the dim downtown corners, all the careless thrill-seekers who were drawn to them, any of them could have done this. One after another, the police checked them out.

One detective was amazed at how many of the suspects failed polygraph examinations, the so-called lie detector test, men who later proved to have solid alibis.

The detective came to the conclusion that the people of the streets had an abundance of things to feel guilty about, things that could produce the fugitive perspiration, the skittering pulse, that gave them away to the polygraph operator. Maybe they had played at sex with this underage girl, or had tried to, or just wanted to, or knew somebody who had, or maybe they had provided this child and her brother with beer or drugs. There were certainly crimes here, but none of them involved the disappearance of Sheri Nastasia. Even the sighting of Sheri getting into the car had led to a dead end. Other than that, no one had seen a thing, no one had an idea.

From an investigator's point of view, the case was a disaster.

"Everything that could have gone wrong went wrong, right from the beginning of that case," one of the detectives recalled later. From the snow that interfered with the gathering of evidence to the lack of leads and solid suspects, nothing seemed to favor the investigators. Over the next several months, in spite of intense activity, it turned into the kind of investigation where the police never felt they were close to the truth about what had happened and who was responsible. And then, as more months passed and the first anniversary of Sheri Nastasia's disappearance approached, it began to seem that the case would never be solved without some kind of surprising break.

It was two years before the death of Sheri Nastasia returned to force its way again into public consciousness.

four

August 1981

It was an image that would stick in Joe Estey's mind for a long time afterward. It wasn't like most memories, fading gradually over the years. If anything, this one seemed to get more vivid, more disturbing, especially after he had children of his own.

Estey had turned thirty that spring but he was a latecomer to police work. A lot of people who ended up as cops had decided in high school, or even earlier, that that was what they wanted to be, and many of them started their careers soon after high school or military service. Estey hadn't become a cop until he was twenty-six, and by then he had tried a lot of other things. He had grown up and graduated from high school in Brattleboro, a small city near the Vermont bank of the Connecticut River, and headed off to Boston University, thinking about majoring in physical education. Once there he found he had no idea why he was doing it and left after a year. He had worked at a ski area, managed a clothing store, sold furniture. One day he saw an ad in the newspaper for a part-time deputy sheriff. For some reason, maybe it was just boredom, he went to take the exam.

"It was really just a lark," Estey recalled, but he did well on the test and got the job. After a one-week course in the basics he started working a few hours a week, guarding county prisoners being transported from one place to another, working security details at school dances and basketball games, still working full-time at the furniture store. There was a kind of romance to wearing the uniform, and the variety of the work was always stimulating, so when there was an opening for a full-time juvenile officer Estey put in his application. He got the job.

It wasn't long before Estey knew he had found a career. Coming late to police work had given him time to see cops from the other side of the badge. He knew they could often seem stiff and intimidating to the ordinary citizen. His own approach was low-key, unassuming, and people seemed to respond well to him. Soon he moved on to the Springfield Police Department, thirty miles north of Brattleboro, and by the summer of 1981 he was the department's chief investigator.

Estey was at home enjoying the soft early evening of a summer Saturday when the phone rang.

"Joe, you'd better come on in," the voice said. "We've got a girl missing."

Theresa Fenton had begged for permission to go on a bike ride. She had been up late the night before at a slumber party with girlfriends, and she had gone into town earlier in the day to a backyard fair a girlfriend was giving to raise money for a muscular dystrophy charity. It seemed like enough for one day, and it was getting close to dinnertime, but when she persisted her parents gave in. At twelve she was a lively and confident child, pushing steadily at the limits of her independence. She wanted to ride a circular route, but her parents asked her instead to take a shorter trip, heading south on the Old Connecticut River Road and then retracing her route back home, a total of four miles or so. Theresa agreed and set out a little after six o'clock.

As six-thirty passed and the time crept toward seven and beyond, at the Fentons' house attention became concern and concern became worry. Could Theresa have broken the agreement with her parents, seeking to challenge herself, and pedaled farther along the River Road to make the loop back on Route 5? It wasn't like her to defy authority in that way, but what else could have delayed her?

Family members set out to look for her, and the word

quickly spread to neighbors along Putnam Road. Several volunteered to help in the search. A number of passes along her planned route turned up no trace. At eight o'clock it was growing dark; Theresa's grandmother called the Springfield Police Department.

There was a poignancy to the description of Theresa in the police broadcast that undercut the idea of the strong, independent person who had set out on her own for a bike ride: a girl well under five feet, weighing about ninety pounds, wearing blue jeans and sneakers. It was a child that was missing.

As Joe Estey and other officers were assembling at the Springfield Police Department, a neighbor of the Fentons, twenty-nine-year-old Richard Craig, was heading out to join the family's search. He drove south with a companion along Route 5 and took the fork onto the River Road. As dark fell, Craig perched on the hood of the car with a flashlight, scanning the areas at the edge of the road and beyond that were not touched by the sweep of the headlights. Past the thin margin of woods next to the pavement, a bank dropped off to the river flowing peacefully through the night below.

They had been searching about forty-five minutes when the car reached a place where the bank dropped off steeply to the river. Something just beyond the rim of the roadside border returned a small sliver of the flashlight's beam. Craig peered over the edge, then scrambled down the bank. A bicycle lay in the brush several feet below the top of the bank. The flashlight's rays had reflected off a piece of the bike's chrome. It was a girl's bike and it looked like Theresa Fenton's. They rushed back to report their find.

The bike was quickly identified as Theresa's. The place where it had been found was about two miles from her house, next to the route she had promised to take. She had kept to the agreement with her parents.

By eight-thirty the police search was organized and volunteers all over town were dropping their normal Saturday evening activities to join in. Besides the police officers dispatched by the Springfield department, off-duty policemen, city firemen, and volunteer firefighters joined the neighbors and friends who had begun the search. As word spread among the searchers that the bicycle had been found, the focus narrowed to the area along the River Road and Route 5 north and south of the discovery site. Volunteers continued to arrive throughout the evening, until there were dozens of people combing the woods and fields. When the last of them quit at two-thirty in the morning, no further sign of the missing girl had turned up.

The location of the bicycle near the top of the steep bank suggested that Theresa might have fallen down the slope and into the river. By six in the morning the searchers had assembled again. Joe Estey and Vermont state trooper Mike LeClair organized the police and civilian volunteers, dispatching groups in every direction from the focal point where the bicycle had been found.

Half a dozen men with masks and wetsuits had also showed up; in addition to a diving team from the Springfield Police Department and another from the Vermont State Police, two local men, amateurs, had volunteered to help out. They slipped into the water below the spot where the bicycle had been found and began combing the river bed and the banks downstream. An official from New Hampshire, which owns the Connecticut River to the low-water mark on the Vermont side, showed up to oversee the water search.

Meanwhile, searchers fanned out along the logging roads and trails to the north and south of the place where the bicycle had been found, searching the woods and gravel banks. To the west, away from the river, lines of volunteers pushed through the fields where corn stood higher than a man's head. Police officers checked the few houses to ask if anyone had seen a strange car or anything unusual. Overhead, another local man who had volunteered his services tracked back and forth in his helicopter, searching roads and clearings.

Bloodhounds were brought to the place where the bicycle had lain. They seemed to pick up a scent briefly, then became confused.

By one o'clock the divers had searched a large swath of river without turning up a clue. The water was clear and moving calmly. They were convinced that if she had fallen in they would have found some sign. That, and the bloodhounds' failure to find a trail leading away from the site, suggested that Theresa might have left the scene in a car.

A little after two o'clock a Springfield man named Torrey Walters and his two children left their car just off Mile Hill

Road, about ten miles from the center of the search for Theresa Fenton, and walked down a gravel road into the woods. They were going for a few hours of fishing, but in general this was an area where people went not so much to find nature as to avoid the scrutiny of others; beer cans and plastic bags, the remains of drinking parties, cluttered the side of the road and the occasional clearing. There were signs here and there that the woods had been used for target practice or the illegal dumping of trash.

A few hundred yards down the road they turned off into the undergrowth, heading toward the stream. As his children scrambled in their cheerful orbits around him, Walters slowly became aware of a sound that separated itself from the gentle hum of nature on a sunny summer afternoon. He turned his head until he located its source in a tangle of brush. It was difficult to identify at first, a sound that seemed so out of place in this mild and happy time, but after a moment it resolved itself into something distinctly human: it was a low moaning sound.

Walters moved toward the sound to investigate. As he waded into the brushy tangle, a movement caught his eye. A foreign shape raised itself from a clump of dirt and leaves. It was an arm, a thin, pale arm, waving weakly in the air.

Ten miles away, the call on the car radio came to Joe Estey like a punch in the stomach.

"They've found her, Joe. She's hurt, hurt bad. Over by Mile Hill Road."

"Ah, shit," he said, in a long sighing whisper.

It was surprising how much hope had survived the eighteen hours of fruitless searching since Estey had received the first phone call at home. All along, without thinking about it, he had been hoping that Theresa Fenton would come walking out of the woods, safe, whole, happy. It was only now that he fully realized the extent of this hope, at the moment when he felt it leaving him in a rush that was almost physical, as if all the air had been sucked out of his body.

Estey and Mike LeClair, the state police detective, turned onto the narrow gravel lane off Mile Hill Road as the ambulance crew was preparing to leave. Theresa Fenton was still alive.

Estey set about his work, the routine of investigation, talking to Torrey Walters, examining the place where Theresa Fenton had been found. The bottles and scattered bits of litter gave the place a shabby look. Dirt and leaves mixed with hemlock needles had been scraped into a low pile, partly covering the girl's body. Blood had seeped into the ground and congealed on the spot where she had lain.

The fisherman described what he had heard, the moaning sound that had drawn his attention, and what he had seen, the frail arm of a child, a watch on the wrist, waving haltingly in the air. It had been as if she were trying to summon help.

And that was the image that Joe Estey would never be able to escape. It was a scene he had never viewed himself, and yet it burned itself into his mind as if it had come to him in a nightmare. He thought of the child, torn in a moment from the reassuring certainties of her life, knowing somewhere in her consciousness that she must be gravely injured, lying overnight in the unknown, in the dark and cold. A child, alone.

And from that terrible isolation, a small arm reached out bravely against the dark, begging for help that could not come in time.

five

The ambulance carried Theresa Fenton to Springfield Hospital, ten minutes away. A quick examination showed that she had suffered severe head and internal injuries. Numerous cuts and bruises suggested the possibility that she had been beaten. The doctors decided that the sophisticated emergency care she would receive at Dartmouth's Mary Hitchcock Hospital was worth the additional delay in getting her there. Around four o'clock Sunday afternoon the ambulance set out for Hanover, thirty miles up the Valley.

The discovery of Theresa off Mile Hill Road added a second area of focus to the investigation. The volunteers, who had numbered close to a hundred by the time the news spread that the missing girl had been found, were no longer of any use. Now the burden shifted to the professionals. Joe Estey and Mike LeClair, the state police detective, turned their attention to the new location, dispatching investigators to look for anyone who might have seen some part of what had happened to Theresa Fenton. By nightfall on Sunday officers had talked to more than three dozen people living near both locations. No one was able to provide any help.

Stories about Theresa Fenton made the front pages of Valley newspapers on Monday. The last of thirty-five paragraphs in the *Rutland Herald* made a connection that probably had not occurred immediately to many of its readers:

> It was slightly more than two years ago that another Springfield girl, 13-year-old Sheri Nastasia, was declared missing. Her badly decomposed body was found Dec. 13, 1979, near a rest area on Route 103 in Bartonsville.

Sheri Nastasia's disappearance had worried some and frightened others, but there was too much uncertainty about the circumstances, and her links to the community were too weak to inspire powerful and universal sentiment when they were broken. The discovery of her body months later failed to clarify what had happened—even an official finding of homicide had been impossible—and thus failed to focus the community's emotion on her case.

The case of Theresa Fenton was a different matter entirely. From the moment many of the firefighters and off-duty police officers called in for the search showed up with neighbors who wanted to help out, the fate of Theresa Fenton became a matter of intense common concern for the people of Springfield and surrounding communities.

The newspapers reported that Theresa was "an exceptional student, very good in all her classes," and active in the chorus, band, and cheerleading. She had been named Student of the Month several times during the previous year in sixth grade. She was to begin junior high school on Wednesday.

Monday evening, almost exactly forty-eight hours after she had failed to come back from her bike ride, Theresa Fenton died. She had never regained consciousness.

The news spread fast, and with it came a buzzing cloud of gossip, rumor, and speculation. There were those who had heard the police were preparing to arrest a suspect, others who thought they knew who it was, still others who thought the killer would strike again soon and set out to protect themselves and their families.

The Board of Selectmen called an emergency meeting to consider the town's response to the tragedy. They voted quickly to appropriate $1,000 toward a reward for information leading to a solution of the crime.

"We shall spare no time, no manpower, no willpower, nothing, in our efforts,'' the chairwoman announced. Each of the five selectmen rose to support her statement and praise the efforts of the police.

A dozen residents gathered at the office of a Springfield lawyer to set up a committee to raise money for a private reward fund. Collections were taken up at factories in the Springfield area, and before the day was over collection jars were appearing in many of the local businesses. The Chamber of Commerce, the Merchants Council, a union local representing workers in machine-tool factories, and many individuals came forward to pledge their support.

The chief of police, Peter Herdt, called a press conference the next morning. Herdt had rushed back to town Monday from North Carolina, where he had just begun his first vacation in two years, after getting word of Theresa's disappearance. It was necessary ''to clear up confusion'' about what had happened, the chief said, and about the progress of the investigation.

''At this point there are no leads,'' Herdt announced to the press. The department had a dozen men working on the case ''around the clock,'' he said, and state police had assigned ten troopers to work with them. The investigators had received a flood of calls from citizens offering tips and assistance. There had been ''tremendous cooperation'' from the public, the chief said, and he looked forward to seeing it continue.

''I hope the public doesn't overreact,'' Herdt told the reporters. ''This is an atypical event.'' There were no grounds for hysteria, he said, with local people barring their doors in fear.

All this was meant to reassure the public, to avert panic, to stimulate the flow of information that might help the investigators, to inspire confidence in the commitment and the capabilities of the police and officials pursuing a solution to the crime. Behind the scenes, however, things looked much less reassuring.

Experienced investigators knew that most of the time either you had a good suspect in the first day or two or you settled down for a long, and sometimes fruitless, investigation. It was just an instinct that detectives developed, and it was by no means infallible, but it gave them an early feeling about how things might turn out. In the case of Theresa Fenton, the intense investigation that had begun as soon as she was reported missing had produced no sighting, no clear evidence, not even a strong suspicion.

One of the investigators gave voice to the general pessimism.

"This thing may never be solved," he said.

The police and the searchers, their families, friends, and neighbors, heard about Theresa Fenton on Saturday night and Sunday morning, but it wasn't until later on Sunday, after she had been found, that the news spread widely throughout Springfield and the surrounding areas. That was when John Philpin heard about it.

Monday it was the lead story in all the papers. When Philpin arrived at the office he shared with two other psychologists, people were talking about it, and when he went out to lunch it was the universal topic of conversation. When he arrived at the office Tuesday, he hadn't seen the papers yet. The news came with the secretary's first words of the day.

"Theresa Fenton died last night," she said.

Philpin paused to absorb the sadness of the news, and then spoke.

"When they catch him, it'll open some eyes in this town," he said. "It'll be a name that everybody will recognize."

Philpin could see that the flat statement required some amplification. "I mean, it'll turn out to be some local guy who did it," he said.

Philpin's response to the news of Theresa Fenton's death was not the impulsive offhand remark it seemed to be. He had been engaging in a kind of bleak competition with himself for several years, studying and analyzing this kind of violent, public crime.

Even before that, Philpin had taken more than a passing interest in violence. Later in life, with the combination of an adult's perspective and a psychologist's insight, Philpin was able to look back on his childhood and find there some clues to the origin of this preoccupation. Philpin's father, an immigrant from Scotland, had often responded to a harsh working-class existence in the tough Roxbury section of Boston with an anger that was inflamed by alcohol. Two of John's older brothers had followed their father's path, eventually slipping into lives dominated by alcohol and drugs. The second brother had served time in Walpole State Prison for attempted murder.

There had been a pervasive sense in the Philpin household of being outside of things. Both parents spoke with the rich brogue of their native Scotland. Philpin's mother recalled for the family memories of coming to the United States early in the century amidst the squalor of a ship's steerage. She worked as a waitress and was eager eventually to become a citizen; her husband steadfastly resisted the idea, and John recalled a home filled with a pall of anxiety about the world outside, compounded of his mother's fear that she might be deported and his father's resentment at the conditions of his life.

The elder Philpin, a highly intelligent man who had no more than a sixth-grade education, a voracious reader of serious books, never found work that interested him and never held for long the jobs that he did find. Mrs. Philpin worked when she could, but the income was meager and the family was often on welfare. Her husband was constantly ill with what the family referred to as "stomach problems" and "heart trouble." It wasn't until he was older that John realized these illnesses must have had their origins in alcohol.

Several years later, soon after he had graduated from college, Philpin visited the Charles Street Jail in Boston, a place he believed he had never before entered. Once inside he was suffused with an overwhelming sense that he had been there before. At first he put it down to déjà vu, the elusive sense that one has viewed a scene before, when logic and memory say that it could not have happened. But what Philpin remembered was too solid, too detailed for that—the oppressive brick walls, the dingy corridors, everything painted in dull institutional colors—and gradually it came back to him. Eventually he recovered a memory, long since faded, of going with his mother to visit his father, "in the hospital," she had said. Philpin now became convinced that she had taken him to see his father at the Charles Street Jail, that his father had been locked up in the drunk tank.

"There was craziness in that house," Philpin recalled of his home, a trace of the childhood anxiety still evident in his voice decades later. "It was real off-the-wall craziness. You never knew when somebody was going to erupt." One night, John's father, drunk, set himself on fire. Another time one of the brothers, in an alcoholic fury, broke the door down. Philpin remembered climbing out a window onto the fire escape in his pajamas, trying to flee the danger and the rage.

The last of six children, John set out along the same path as his father and brothers. At eight, on a visit to his grandmother in Nantasket Beach, he was caught by the police after breaking into a beach house with another boy by throwing a rock through the window. He continued getting in trouble periodically through the eighth grade. That was the year when a combination of repeated mischief and bad grades kept him in trouble most of the time. But it was also the year his life started to change.

It was a number of factors that brought him up short, as Philpin recalled it. During the school year he took an IQ test, and though he never found out the score, word trickled back from teachers that the test indicated he had unusual intelligence. The family moved to Hull, a town not far from Boston but slightly more hospitable to aspiration than the old neighborhood. And John was placed in some classes that were more demanding; he came to understand that other people, teachers and school officials, thought he could do better than he thought himself. But most of all, what brought the change was the realization that if he didn't do something quickly he was likely to end with the same kind of chaotic, self-destructive life his older brothers had already fallen into. It was a point his parents must have made many times before that, Philpin remembered later, but without much effect. At last, rather suddenly as he recalled it, he decided he wanted to change his life. And then he did it.

During that summer Philpin determined to be "the best student that ever there was." Four years later he finished high school first in his class, the valedictorian, chosen most likely to succeed, a better-than-average baseball player. He was accepted at Harvard—only the second student from Hull ever admitted there, he was told at the time—and awarded a large scholarship.

Philpin majored in English and, with the help of work-study jobs and large loans, graduated in 1965. He took a job at the Massachusetts Mental Health Center, expecting to stay for a year before accepting a fellowship in English at the University of Washington. He had been active in protesting the Vietnam

War, and the fellowship would offer a draft deferment. But student deferments were cancelled, and the mental health center offered an occupational deferment; the hospital desperately needed male workers. Philpin went to work as an aide on a unit of fifteen seriously disturbed teenagers. With other aides he was responsible for helping the young people through the day, serving as an anchor to the ordinary. Because of his education, Philpin was also asked to do some tutoring. He ended up staying in the job for four years. He found he like the youngsters. He became curious about their illnesses, wondering what could have happened to disrupt their mental lives so dramatically. He began reading books on mental illness. Something in their need, in the tragedy of young lives so terribly damaged, touched him. Perhaps he felt a special empathy with young people whose lives were going out of control, and found in his own experience some hope that they could be rescued.

Over the next decade Philpin got married, moved in stages northward to Vermont, and passed through a series of jobs working with troubled children, deciding finally to study for a master's degree in counselling. At the time of Theresa Fenton's death he had worked as a private therapist under supervision in a group practice for four years; in a few months he would receive his license and set up his own practice. Now that he had reached his late thirties, even with all the changes, it was not hard to find in the way he approached his profession vivid traces of his early experience.

In the group practice Philpin had seen clients of all kinds, people who were unhappy with themselves and their relations to those around them, but a significant part of his counselling work was with criminals. They were men referred to him by the courts for treatment, usually in conjunction with a jail sentence. In addition, other therapists passed on to him patients who were violent or seemed capable of rage.

"Nobody else wanted them," Philpin remembered later. "Who wanted to spend a day or more at work in a jail? Who wants to try to give a psychological test that requires digital dexterity from a guy in chains?"

Philpin didn't particularly enjoy treating these patients, who were sometimes threatening or offensive, often resistant to treatment. But their manner and circumstance were not so completely alien to Philpin as they were to many of the other therapists, particularly the women. Aware from youth of all the rationalizations and manipulations that come so easily to alcoholics and drug users, Philpin was a tough man to con. Experienced with the role of will, of conscious decision and intention, in shaping his own life, he looked with skeptical eyes on his patients' attempts to blame their crimes on their upbringing or other forces outside themselves. Exposed early in his life to anger and violence, Philpin kept those destructive forces at a distance by knowing them intimately, turning them over and over in his mind, understanding their lure and their danger.

It was probably this combination of intimacy and disgust with the violence that some humans do to others that gave rise to the exercise John Philpin had engaged in periodically for the several years before he heard of the death of Theresa Fenton. Reading in the newspaper of some unsolved violent crime, usually a murder, Philpin had found himself intrigued by the puzzle: who did it, of course—you always wanted to assign responsibility—but beyond that, what *kind* of person did it, and why did he do it, and how did he do it, and what was the relationship between the person and the reasons and the methods?

He began by talking about his thoughts to people at work, other psychologists, cops. Then he took to making notes, speculations really, about the details of the crime, things the police either hadn't found out yet or hadn't released to the newspapers, and setting them aside. Eventually he was writing down a page or more of analysis, reasoning from the outlines of the crime to a prediction about the kind of person responsible, three or four characteristics maybe, a little essay about each. Then he would seal the notes in an envelope and toss it in a desk drawer to wait for the arrest and trial. It was a challenge, like a school exam, the chief difference being that no one could know when it would be graded, if ever.

Usually, though, the cases were solved, and Philpin would gather what information he could, from the newspapers, from cops and prison staff he'd met in his counselling work with the cons. He'd search for holes in his reasoning, analyzing why he missed what he did, slowly building a mental catalog of cases.

At the same time, Philpin was reading—popular books

about crimes and killers, the developing professional literature in psychology about sociopathic killers, histories and sociological studies that were adding a wider perspective. The literature of murder, and particularly multiple killings, seemed to expand geometrically as the nation became more and more aware that something new and frightening was happening. Finally, sometime in the middle of the 1980s, this new phenomenon took on a name in the American popular consciousness: serial killer.

By then, John Philpin was already deeply immersed in the hunt for a real serial killer in his own backyard.

The investigation of Theresa Fenton's death was not going well.

Deep into the second week, Springfield and state police detectives worked long hours in what Chief Herdt referred to as "saturation tactics." Herdt had come to Vermont from Oakland, California, where big-city methods had evolved to counteract big-city crime. He found himself wholly in tune with the idea, recently adopted by the Vermont State Police, of pouring every available officer, state and local, into the investigation within hours of a major crime. The technique had been used in Vermont for the first time less than a year earlier and had led to the quick solution of a double murder.

But the saturation technique wasn't working in Springfield. Investigators had made an intensive search of the woods in the area where Theresa Fenton had been abducted and the area where she had been found. They had canvassed houses in both areas, and a week later they had returned to search the woods again. They had followed up dozens of leads phoned in or passed to officers on the street, interviewed over two hundred people, including close to thirty potential suspects, and administered more than a dozen polygraph tests. Nothing had brought them any closer to solving the crime, and slowly the fourteen-hour days were taking their toll.

More than half the twenty-member Springfield police force had been working full-time on the case since the beginning. On the second weekend many of the officers stayed up all night Friday and most of the night Saturday, pursuing a lead that proved fruitless in the end.

"Everybody's eyes look like burn holes in a mattress," Chief Herdt's secretary said.

In the following days it was clear that fatigue was setting in; officers were catching up on their sleep and there was a noticeable lull in activity at the Springfield police station.

At the same time, fear born of the sense that a new and special kind of danger had been loosed on the town was continuing to grow.

Mixed in with the dozens of calls to the police offering help were several each day complaining about the pace of the investigation, demanding angrily that the police find the killer of Theresa Fenton. They were just "letting off steam," a police officer allowed charitably, people who were frightened and insisting that the police do something to take away their fear. They were like children frightened by shadows on the bedroom wall, crying for the protection of a parent.

The crime had almost immediately given rise to a variety of fearful rumors and by now they were "running rampant," one resident reported. Word was circulating that other children were missing, that the Fenton case was only one incident in a terrible rash of similar crimes. Chief Herdt was forced to announce that all missing children in town had been accounted for and that no child had disappeared.

School officials were swamped with phone calls from parents concerned about the vulnerability of their children as they walked to the bus stop and waited for the school bus. Many parents began escorting their children to the bus stops, others were driving them to and from school. One parent who lived near Mile Hill Road, where Theresa Fenton had been found, drove from his home into town and reported that there was not a single bus stop along the route of several miles without one or more parents standing among the children or sitting nearby in a car. Many families introduced curfews, even for older children, and imposed new limits on where they could go in town.

In spite of the fears, attendance was close to normal in the opening weeks of school; there was no sign that children were being kept home. And the community continued to express its sympathy for the Fentons and its determination to contribute to a solution of the crime. More than five hundred people turned out for Theresa's funeral at St. Mary's Roman Catholic church, including a hundred seventh-graders, children who would have been her classmates, who signed up to ride over from the junior high school on a yellow school bus.

The reward fund had collected cash and pledges approaching $10,000. In the first two days alone a glass fishbowl on the counter at Morse's Market on Park Street had filled with five- and ten-dollar bills, close to $300 in all.

"It's amazing," a clerk at the market said. "Kids come in and put their candy money into it."

In all these ways, Springfield was trying to come to terms with what had happened, and the *Valley News,* based in Lebanon, New Hampshire, twenty-five miles north of Springfield, summarized the impact of the murder on the town:

> The slaying of 12-year-old Theresa Fenton has rocked Springfield like no other crime in recent memory, leaving residents of this town where it couldn't happen shaking their heads at the fact that it did.

Several weeks after Theresa's death, the town's Board of Selectmen revised a report, approved weeks earlier, in order to insert a request that the state legislature consider reinstituting the death penalty. The members agreed that stricter penalties were needed to prevent acts like the brutal murder of Theresa Fenton.

But beyond all this there was another reason for the crime's dramatic impact: people who had lived in Vermont all their lives had almost no experience of this kind of crime—sudden, apparently without ordinary motive, taking an innocent child as its victim.

And it wasn't only the natives who were shocked and surprised by what had happened. Newcomers, the people who had been responsible for the dramatic increase in the Valley's population over the previous dozen years or so, were shaken by the sudden eruption into their lives of something they thought they had left behind.

Even the chief of police expressed similar sentiments. During his almost ten years on the Oakland police force, Peter Herdt had served as a detective on the robbery squad and a member of the SWAT team, immersed in a relentless tide of violent crime. It was the time of the anti-Vietnam War riots on the Berkeley campus and the kidnapping of Patty Hearst by the Symbionese Liberation Army, which later took credit for killing Oakland's superintendent of schools. At the age of thirty-four, after seeing fellow cops shot down on the job, several of them killed, Herdt had decided to move with his wife and four children to a rural area. Three years later, he found himself immersed in the case of Theresa Fenton.

"We moved here to get away from all this," Herdt said, alluding to the violence of the Fenton murder.

Herdt was giving voice to an idea that the murder of Theresa Fenton was forcing upon the people of the Springfield area, one that would spread through the Connecticut River Valley like the shadow under a fast-moving cloud: We had reached a time in American history when no place was remote enough, no place small or innocent or *friendly* enough, to escape the reach of this vicious fury that was loose in the land.

six

A lot of these psychologists were as strange as their patients, Joe Estey was thinking.

When Estey had left Boston University during his freshman year it was because so much of the work seemed far removed from real life. That was how he thought of psychologists. So many of them seemed to be highly educated but lacking in basic common sense.

Lloyd Merwin was a perfect example, twitchy and ill at ease, probably the kind of guy who had stood by his locker in high school watching what everybody else was doing, too nervous and remote to join in.

Chief Herdt, however, had developed the feeling that they needed some kind of new perspective on the investigation, and Merwin seemed like a place to start. The chief had a brisk manner that sometimes seemed out of phase with the more relaxed ways of small-town New England, but it came with a disciplined professionalism that had made a positive impression on the Springfield department. He had earned a master's degree in criminology from Berkeley and made an attempt to stay on top of the latest developments in police work.

Chief Herdt had raised the idea of getting someone to help develop information about the killer of Theresa Fenton. Herdt had seen reports from the FBI unit at Quantico, Virginia, which had been working on a set of new techniques for the last several years and was just beginning to publish the results. They had been trying to devise methods for analyzing the scene of a murder, the condition of the victim, anything that could be learned about the abduction and treatment of the victim, all with the aim of working backward to draw a portrait of the unknown killer. A profile, they called it, and there had been a few cases where the information had been helpful in focusing an investigation and drawing up a pool of potential suspects.

Estey and Herdt had been in the chief's office talking about profiling when the chief brought the conversation to a point: "Let's look into it," he concluded. "Who might be able to help us?"

The only possibility Estey could think of was Lloyd Merwin, who was a probation officer with a background in psychology. The chief investigator knew of him because psychological counselling was sometimes required as part of a criminal's sentence or offered to a victim of sexual assault, and Merwin's office would be involved in providing it.

"Why don't we see if he has any ideas?" the chief said, and a few days later when Merwin appeared at the station the chief asked if he could give them a few minutes. Once Herdt had explained what they were after, the probation officer said he didn't know anything about profiling himself, but he was acquainted with another psychologist who had taken an interest in it. Chief Herdt asked Merwin to see if the psychologist thought he might have anything to contribute to the Fenton investigation, and whether he'd be interested in talking with the police about giving them a hand.

John Philpin's reaction was immediate and enthusiastic.

"Sure I'd be willing," Philpin told Merwin. Hell, it was exactly like what he'd been doing on his own for several years. This would add the excitement of a real hunt, the chance to help catch a killer.

But there was something more, another reason. "The impact on this town was incredible," Philpin recalled, still touched by the memory years later. "I thought that anybody who could do anything to help should do it."

A few days later Estey gathered up the case file and drove

over to Philpin's office. The investigator's first impression of Philpin did little to contradict his notion of psychologists. Philpin was a little over six feet tall and slim, with a full head of black hair that crept over his collar in the back and an abundant beard that was just beginning to show the odd fleck of some lighter color. His manner was reserved, almost placid, but he harbored an intensity that occasionally glowed in his eyes. At those times, with the dark cloud of hair and the sense he gave of being wholly self-contained, the overall impression was of a mountain hermit who had descended among the plain folk. The corduroy jeans and tan lace-up lumberjack boots that Philpin favored served to strengthen the impression. The only indication he gave of concern for conventional professional dress was a shirt with a button-down collar, but he wore it without a tie and left it unbuttoned at the neck.

Still, people were much more relaxed about that kind of thing in the Valley than they might be in Boston, or even in nearby cities like Rutland, Vermont, or Manchester, New Hampshire, and Estey's reservations quickly disappeared as they began talking. Philpin was a heavy smoker, but he politely asked permission from his guest before lighting up, and unlike a lot of smokers he seemed genuinely prepared to refrain if asked. He had an easy, unpretentious manner, and his interest in the Fenton case seemed professional and sincere. They were soon deeply immersed in the file.

Two hours later they had gone through the thick pile of reports, with Estey providing commentary and Philpin responding with further questions. The broad outline of the case that emerged merely whetted Philpin's appetite. He didn't have a ready-made plan of how to proceed. Apart from his little predicting game, he had never done this before. But as he listed for Estey the additional information he wanted to see, a pattern began to show itself in his curiosity. He needed to look at Theresa's diary, wanted to interview her parents and the children who had been with her the night before she disappeared, the friends she had seen during the day before she left on her bike ride. Philpin was pushing for everything that could contribute to a portrait of Theresa Fenton, the victim of this crime. Instinctively, he wanted to understand her as completely as possible, to learn to think like her. What did she like and what did she dislike, what interested her and what frightened her, what did she think of herself and how did she get along with her friends, what were her aspirations?

The goal, of course, was to draw a portrait of the man who had killed Theresa Fenton. But the killer had left behind no more than a fleeting scent of himself, and no living person was known to have seen him. The only person who had seen him, who had confronted the man face-to-face, was Theresa Fenton. If the investigators were ever to look into his face, it could only be through her eyes. Now, to reconstruct Theresa's vision of the killer, to see what she had seen, Philpin must first come to know Theresa. It was as if the soul of Theresa Fenton might briefly be recovered from the arms of death.

"I want to thoroughly *be* a twelve-year-old girl if I can," Philpin thought. "I want to be *this particular* twelve-year-old girl."

It was a strange idea on the face of it, a man closing in on forty trying to bring his mind in line with that of a girl just entering pubescence, and over the next few years Philpin would gradually broaden his approach to drawing the profile of a killer. But the process of identifying with the victim would remain a key element in his method, and one that would eventually lead him into treacherous psychological waters.

Now, though, a combination of instinct and all that he had read told Philpin that the way to the killer was through the victim. With no experience in crime reconstruction except his amateur exercises, no method except what he had found in his readings, he would simply have to trust his common sense and his curiosity.

At first, Philpin wondered what kind of reception his curiosity might receive. Estey wasn't the only one who had started with reservations about the working relationship between the police and the psychologist. Philpin had wondered how easily the police would share information about the case with an outsider, even one they had invited into their circle. In the following weeks he was pleasantly surprised at the openness of the officers he came in contact with. Joe Estey, in particular, seemed to be giving the benefit of the doubt to this unconventional form of cooperation. He brought Philpin every document he requested, arranged interviews with investigators and members of the public, accompanied the psychologist to the key locations, and served as a sounding board for all Philpin's questions and speculation.

Philpin's first thoughts about the case, tossed off so easily in the office that first day, had not been as casual as they seemed. "It'll turn out to be some local guy who did it," he had said.

And he had anticipated the reaction of all those, the majority it seemed, who shared the belief that it couldn't happen in a place like this, that such evil could not be born amidst the small-town tranquillity of Springfield, Vermont: "When they catch him," Philpin had predicted, "it'll open some eyes in this town."

After his meeting with Joe Estey, Philpin threw himself into the investigation with all the energy he could summon. Estey came to Philpin's office at least twice a week, bringing reports and materials Philpin had asked for, sitting down to answer questions and talk about the case for an hour or two.

"If anybody notices how much time I'm spending here," Estey joked one day in the psychologist's office, "they're gonna think I've got one hell of a problem."

Estey was impressed with Philpin's grasp of details. The psychologist was interested in things the police didn't ordinarily look at closely, matters of personality and nuance behind the hard facts of the case. Estey found the give-and-take with Philpin stimulating; it counteracted the natural tendency of any investigator to get in a rut, to look at new things in old ways. The psychologist's approach added a new dimension to police routine.

It was amazing, when you started looking at all the possibilities suggested by the theories, how much work there was to do. Joe Estey and Mike LeClair, the state police detective, compiled lists of suspects—adults Theresa might have known and trusted, men who had been arrested for sexual offenses or assaults involving women and young girls, people who had aroused the suspicion of a neighbor or acquaintance.

The number of suspects grew steadily as the investigators combed arrest records, interviewed potential witnesses, chatted with their own neighbors or people who stopped them on the street. Hundreds of names were recorded, sifted, considered; some could be eliminated with a quick check of the records or a phone call; they had been away, or in prison, or at work, or dead. Already in the early stages of investigation, more than 100—someone counted 114 before giving up—were put down for further inquiry. Dozens more were added as time went by. Many of them, even most, seemed unlikely prospects, but thoroughness required that every one be checked out. Each one was interviewed, details of their alibis were verified with witnesses, and some were asked to undergo a polygraph examination.

Two of the reports were very intriguing. Sandy Freeman, a police dispatcher in Springfield, knew right away that what her husband, Willard, had seen could be significant. Willard Freeman was a steady, reliable man, a truck driver for the phone company. He said he had been driving on Route 5 Sunday afternoon when a car came out of the River Road onto Route 5. The River Road formed a loop between Route 5 to the west and the bank of the Connecticut River next to the road on the east. The car had appeared at the southern end of the loop.

"He came screaming out of there," Willard Freeman said. It was a red car, he recalled, some sporty model, he couldn't say what type. The time was shortly after 6:40 P.M.

The other report was from a woman who had been taking her dog to the kennel on River Road, just north of where Theresa's bike had been found. She had been travelling south when a car passed her, going in the opposite direction, moving fast enough that she noticed its speed. It had been red, she recalled, low and speedy-looking. As close as she could pin it down, the time must have been several minutes after six-thirty.

Neither Willard Freeman nor the woman with the dog had seen the driver, and neither could recall enough detail about the car so it could be used to produce suspects, but their observations did contribute to a tentative picture of what had happened to Theresa.

And there was a third report that dovetailed with these two. Bobby Johnson, a nineteen-year-old from Springfield, had been driving south on the River Road with a bunch of friends in the car when they saw Theresa on her bike heading in the opposite direction. They had identified her later from a picture in the paper.

That sighting indicated, Estey concluded, that Theresa must have reached the end of the road, where it rejoined Route 5, and turned around to head toward home. She had held to the agreement with her parents. Bobby Johnson had a reputation for wildness and didn't seem like the most reliable witness, but careful questioning of his passengers confirmed the information and they were able to narrow down the time they had spotted Theresa to about six-forty. In fact, Bobby Johnson could have offered more about Theresa's disappearance, information that might have changed the course of events, but he was not about to offer it to the police now. By the time he changed his mind, it would be too late.

What Johnson and his friends did say was reinforced by an experiment that Estey and LeClair had performed. The two detectives had set out to reconstruct the timing of Theresa's bike ride. They located a girl close to Theresa's age and size, a neighbor, and asked her to ride out from the Fentons' house, then south on Route 5, taking the fork onto the Old Connecticut River Road, on past the point where the bicycle had been found, to the junction where the River Road rejoined Route 5, then back up the River Road and home. Added to the time Theresa left home, a little after six o'clock, the time the girl took to get to the spot where the bicycle had been found came to about 6:40 P.M. That corresponded neatly to the estimate from Bobby Johnson and his friends.

It was curious, the way these facts fit together, shaping themselves into a picture of a man, possibly two or more men, in a low, sporty red car, cruising close to the area where Theresa had been kidnapped, around 6:40 P.M. that Sunday. A little more information—the make and year of the car, the license numbers, someone recognizing the driver—might have provided the identity of the killer. But none of that information was emerging. In this case, the facts had their limits; they were not going to lead to the killer by themselves.

John Philpin had always depended on his ability to manage facts, to think logically. It was this capability, after all, the power of his mind, that had rescued him from the rough life and the bleak prospects of his father and brothers. But he had never fully trusted logic alone, and he had always made room alongside it for the creative flow of imagination. He had begun college majoring in philosophy, but after taking a writing course had switched to English. Even after getting his Ph.D. in psychology he fantasized about going back for a master's degree in creative writing, maybe becoming a writer. He still wrote poems and fragments of stories from time to time, and a more personal kind of writing he did in a journal had become one of his most satisfying diversions. Now, trying to construct the profile of a killer, he was finding that the Fenton case called on both types of thinking, logic to compile and arrange facts, imagination to discern the flow of human action that lay behind them. Into the rushing stream of fact the detectives were creating, Philpin now fed the product of his imagination, the emerging portrait of Theresa Fenton.

Philpin had painstakingly assembled the impressions from his own interviews with Theresa's parents and grandparents, her friends, teachers, and others who had known her. He read her diary, and he pored over the novel she had been reading before she died, *Flowers in the Attic,* a horror story by V. C. Andrews. He was coming to feel he knew her, knew her as well as it was possible to know someone you had never met, and what he was learning supported those first anguished comments by her teachers to the newspaper reporters. There had been little exaggeration in the public picture of Theresa Fenton as an accomplished, responsible, and likeable child. She was one of those children in whom the adult-to-be has already become visible without erasing the lively innocence of the child.

It all added up to a portrait of a girl who knew her own mind. She was beginning adolescence, starting to find areas—boyfriends, school dances, bedtimes—where her wishes were pressing against her parents' limits, and she was capable of occasional resistance. A central character of *Flowers in the Attic* was a thirteen-year-old girl locked in an attic with her siblings; Philpin came to feel that Theresa had identified with the girl, with her confinement, which operated as a metaphor for the restrictions imposed on a young girl by family, society, and school. But compared to many forms of adolescent rebellion, Theresa's response was mild; a lot of the energy others her age might have channelled into anger she used up in physical activity and competition. Her final bike ride had come after an all-night slumber party with little more than an hour of sleep, followed by a full day of activity, yet she was described as ''full of piss and vinegar'' when she left the house, lively and energetic, off for an adventure.

Philpin was convinced that she would find—''would have

found," he had to correct himself, since she was a living presence in the picture he was painting of her—she would have found a way to grow up gracefully without the need for dramatic defiance of her parents' wishes. She was not willful, Philpin concluded, simply confident. She liked to know what she was doing, to be in control of her circumstances. And she was capable occasionally of indignation, even anger, when she felt her autonomy being threatened.

All this suggested to Philpin that she would not be easily intimidated by psychological means or by authority alone. On the other hand, there had been two incidents in which she had been exposed to weapons—a knife in one case, a gun in another. Even though there had not been any direct threat, Theresa had displayed an exaggerated anxiety.

With an emerging sense of Theresa Fenton's character and experience, Philpin and the detectives moved on to questions about the events of the evening she disappeared. Why had she been so eager to ride her bike along that particular route at that particular time, Philpin wondered, after she had been up late the night before and busy all day? Could she have arranged secretly to meet a boyfriend her age, perhaps someone she had a crush on? Could she have been enticed to join an older boy, or a group, someone with a car, to do something her parents might not have approved of? The more the psychologist learned of Theresa, the less likely it seemed. She had accepted limits on the time allowed for her ride. She wouldn't have gone back on the commitment.

Could she have been watched, perhaps by someone along Mile Hill Road, stalked until she was vulnerable? There had been no pattern to her bike rides; no one could have known where she would be at a given time.

What about a chance meeting with an older teenager, or a group, kids fooling around, racing up and down the River Road? Could she have been lured into trouble that started out looking like fun? It wasn't Theresa's kind of fun, and beyond that she wouldn't have gotten into something so loose, unstructured, uncontrollable. She wouldn't voluntarily put herself in a situation she wasn't sure she could get out of at any time she wanted, not for the promise of peer approval or adventure or wild fun or anything else that Philpin could imagine.

Philpin tried to picture the scene, Theresa's confrontation

with her attacker, attempting to see it the way she would have. There were at least three things about getting into someone else's car, stranger or not, that Theresa would have found unacceptable: spurning the authority and wishes of her parents, submitting to potential risk, and yielding control of her circumstances. Philpin sensed in her a resolve, a degree of commitment, that even the threat of force alone would not shake. That left two possibilities: either it was somebody she knew, perhaps an adult she had reason to trust, or it would take actual force, coercion, to make her go along. And there was the bicycle: it had been found leaning against a tree, as if carefully placed there. Philpin learned that Theresa had been proud of her bicycle and taken meticulous care of it. It seemed unlikely that she would have abandoned it voluntarily.

That began to suggest an interpretation of the autopsy results. The child had been beaten, the medical examiner said. It had been a "deliberate" beating, not the result of an uncontrolled frenzy. She had been struck at least four times in the head with some kind of object. It was these blows that had killed her. They had crushed her skull and left at least one indentation with a distinctive shape, but these were not the only marks. There were bruises on her right cheek and lower lip and a broken upper right incisor, suggesting one or more blows to the face. There was another mark, more like a scrape, on her face. There was a bruise on the right side of her neck and an abrasion on the left side that could have been caused by choking. There were bruises on one arm. And there was an odd, shallow, puncturelike wound in the middle of the abdomen that the medical examiner described as "healing."

Theresa had been fully dressed when she was found. The autopsy showed swelling around the vagina and a small tear in the skin of the rectum. When detectives asked for an interpretation of these facts, the impression circulated that they had not been caused by sexual attack. Theresa had fallen on the arm of a chair a few days before her death; the fall was understood to be the probable cause of the damage. The investigation proceeded on the assumption that there had not been any sexual assault. This would turn out to be one of those failures of communication that plague enterprises where a number of individuals bring many kinds of expertise to bear on a single question.

There was one odd piece of information from the autopsy. Some leafy matter had been found inside the waistband of Theresa's pants. Could it have been placed there intentionally, or gotten caught there somehow? It would have made more sense if there had been evidence of sexual assault. Under the circumstances, no one was sure what to make of it.

In the woods off Mile Hill Road, Philpin gazed around him at the debris of countless parties, and beyond that, deeper in the underbrush, the hidden place where Theresa Fenton had been found near death. Philpin tried to relax the logical part of his mind and let the place tell him what it would. The site was remote but heavily used, widely known. And the killer had moved back into the dense, entangling brush with his victim, dragging her across a brook, away from the familiarity and safety of the gravel road, away from Mile Hill Road, away from his car, from his means of escape. What Philpin saw, and what he felt, reinforced his first impression, that the killer was a man comfortable, possibly familiar, with his surroundings.

There was more. The killer had taken his time. It appeared that he had begun to bury Theresa, digging out a shallow depression, then stopped before completing the task. He had not quit entirely, though. He had continued trying to cover her, scratching leaves and twigs and dirt from the surrounding ground to place on her body. It all reinforced the idea of a man who felt at ease, who knew where he was. And there was another element here: the few bits of material would not have been enough to hide her from sight; it was more like an attempt at adornment, as if she had been anointed.

Philpin let his mind rove among these impressions. They brought forth images of burial and funerals, of cemeteries. There were dozens of tiny cemeteries dotted all over Springfield, three in the immediate area of the River Road, one near the Fentons' house. These were the family burial places of early settlers, long unused, the headstones now fallen and settling back into the earth, hidden by a century of leafy growth. Philpin imagined the people who had used the small burial grounds, their awe at the mystery of life and death. The shallow depression, the arrangement of the body in it, the little piles of debris, it struck him that there was an element of ceremony, of ritual, in what had taken place. There was something of religion in all this, Philpin sensed.

And somewhere behind this welter of clues and impressions and bits of information there lurked a man, the predator who had attacked a young girl, who in killing Theresa Fenton had struck a devastating blow against her family, her friends, and an entire community. It was time to begin assembling a portrait of the killer.

seven

November 1981–June 1982

Through summer's end and on into the fall, Theresa Fenton's bicycle ride filled the imaginations of the men investigating her death. At last they began to build slowly, to extend the sequence from what they knew of her movements to what they could only deduce, her course along the River Road to her confrontation with the killer, and on to her end. And John Philpin, now a member of the team of investigators, pushed on from there, seeking to enter the mind of the man who had killed her.

Philpin read the case reports, then read them again, interviewed subjects, discussed his conclusions with the detectives, incorporated their ideas into his thinking, reread the reports yet again. Through the fall and winter he found himself constantly coming back to the case at odd moments, while driving to and from work in his pickup, sitting in the office with a free hour between therapy clients, staring off into the distance in the middle of a conversation.

The case of Theresa Fenton, the work of creating a portrait of her killer, was tapping John Philpin's deepest passions, the legacy of his rough childhood and the resolutions of his adult life. It brought together the creative impulse to draw a portrait of people and events, the psychologist's need to understand a personality, the child's wish to help a helpless child and see adult cruelty punished, the adult's need to see justice done for the child and the community. The case was approaching the level of obsession with Philpin.

Joe Estey, Mike LeClair, and the other detectives and officers who had combed the areas between Theresa's home, the Old Connecticut River Road, and the place where she was found had made it possible to retrace her movements almost minute by minute.

But the question remained: How did the bicycle come to be placed so carefully against the tree, down the hill leading to the river? Perhaps the killer, having established control with a weapon or other threat, forced Theresa to hide the bike so she would be more difficult to trace, and even while struggling with her fear she had retained her meticulous concern for her bicycle.

Once he had her in the car, excited by what he had done, preoccupied with driving, her captor would have been less able to control her directly. Perhaps now he was making it clear to Theresa what he planned to do with her. Typically this would involve some form of dominance and control, often expressed through sexual mastery. At this point, now that he had made explicit his ugly intentions, now that Theresa could no longer be in any doubt about what he had in mind, it would have been consistent with her personality to challenge him.

Philpin imagined Theresa reacting indignantly, in spite of her fear: "You're sick, you're crazy. I'm going to tell, I'm going to get you in trouble."

Expecting docility and submission, the man is shocked, then frightened, even humiliated; his sense of himself, his spurious notion of competence and mastery, is shattered. He strikes out in fury, backhanding the right side of her mouth as she faces him, bruising her cheek and breaking a tooth. He grips her neck to bring her under control again.

More than the threat or mild force that first made her cooperate, this violence has made plain to Theresa the danger that she faces. She is intimidated into submission, robbed of any impulse to direct confrontation.

By now they have stopped, either at Mile Hill Road or some intermediate site. The attacker pulls her from the car, or she tries to flee. As she leaves the car she falls to the pavement or against a rock, scraping her face.

At this point, while Theresa is at last frightened into compliance, the killer is bathed in fury. He may not have admitted to himself what he had in mind when he set out, may have told himself that he was seeking only company or friendship; now those things are no longer possible, and it is her fault, this girl who would not trust him, refused to cooperate with him. He understands that she will not be dominated. She is independent, powerful, her freedom is threatening to him. The girl herself, her very existence, is a danger.

There is a practical side to this danger: she could report him to the authorities. But that is not all. Now in his mind she has taken on some other form, represents something else, someone else, something frightening in his past and in his soul. He walks her into the woods, perhaps prodding her before him, needing her to face away from him so he can act, so he can do what must be done, what she has brought upon herself. He begins to batter her with some hard, blunt object.

He strikes her repeatedly, seeing before him a menace that will not be conquered. She is felled by the first blow, but still she is in control and he must strike again, and again, until at last she is subdued, still and beyond stillness, and the threat is vanquished.

When he has finished he moves quickly to find a safe hiding place, carrying her body to the final site. He is not aware that she has survived the battering. He moves easily in the woods, knowing where he is heading, disturbing little as he goes. He finds an isolated spot in the bushes, then scratches out some cover in an attempt to bury the body. Now he is tense, uncomfortable with the fact of what he has done, afraid of being observed. The burial only partly finished, he hurries to his car and leaves.

There was one major problem with this version of events, Philpin concluded. It was unusual, even rare, that violent dominance of a man over a woman did not take the form of sexual assault. It was becoming a commonplace to psychologists in the early 1980s, if not yet to the public at large, that rape was not so much a sexual act as one of violent domination. Yet it was understood at this point that there was no evidence of rape or other sexual violence in the attack on Theresa Fenton. That inconsistency would trouble Philpin and the investigators for several months more.

Philpin surrounded his profile with reservations. Once you came down to it, he told the police, this was merely an exercise in informed speculation: a profile is based on probabilities; where it provides details, that is an attempt to help the investigators, not an indication of certainty. Investigators should not exclude any suspect simply because he didn't fit the profile, and no suspect, not even the killer if he were eventually caught, should be expected to have all the characteristics of the person in the profile. That said, Philpin laid out his portrait.

The killer was a resident of Springfield, Philpin said, refining his original instinctive reaction to the local residents who said, "It can't happen here." Knowledge of the sites where Theresa Fenton was picked up and abandoned would be confined to local people. And no roaming killer from afar would venture even those few miles from the interstate highway, so deeply into the maze of narrow back roads. And it follows that he owns or has regular access to a car or pickup.

Through the winter and into the spring of 1982, Philpin hunted down every available piece of research on serial killers and psychopaths in general, desperate to match his knowledge to the task. It wasn't easy. It would be almost ten years before serial killers would become the subject of best-selling books and hit movies. Even among experts, the first rumblings of interest were just being heard. Published knowledge was still sparse.

At first Philpin had pegged the killer's age between the late teens and early twenties. But as he read the psychiatric literature and thought further, he sensed that the personality emerging from the profile was that of someone a little older, perhaps into his twenties, even beyond.

The published research was beginning to establish a distinction between organized and disorganized killers: the former were prepared, systematic, precise, as if adhering to a detailed plan for the attack. In the most extreme cases they played out grotesque scenarios, making real the fantasies they had labored over in imagination, working through and refining the selection of the victim, the attack and abduction, the ritualized preparation for death, the killing, manipulation, and disposal of the victim. Such systematic killers tended to be older, more experienced. The man who had killed Theresa Fenton seemed to fit that mold. She had been captured in daylight, subdued quickly, moved efficiently, assaulted, perhaps moved again, killed in a deliberate way. The sequence suggested someone prepared, perhaps practiced in the skills of this brutal enterprise.

Philpin imagined a deeply immature personality. He probably lives with his family, Philpin wrote to Joe Estey, and they will fall within the broad middle class. If he is in the upper part of the age range he may have left the area to go to college or join the military; in that case he would have carried out the killing on a vacation, leave, or unauthorized visit home.

He is indulged by his mother, but his father either neglected him entirely as a child or oppressed him through rough criticism and rejection, perhaps even some form of physical or sexual abuse. The combination would create a personality that was fearful and extremely sensitive to any hint of attack that bears the potential for humiliation. It is of the utmost importance to him to impress other people, to be seen as masterful, confident.

The killer gets along reasonably well with adults, older people, Philpin wrote, but he is awkward with peers. He is particularly uncomfortable in social situations with women. He finds it easier to be with younger girls, whom he can impress with his car, money, or other material things. He spends a great deal of time watching television or immersed in his own fantasies.

Philpin could not escape the feeling that had come upon him in the woods where Theresa Fenton had been found near death, her body placed with care, partly buried, as if she had been anointed: the killer was a man moved by religion, touched by ritual, a churchgoer.

Afterward, Philpin speculated, the high tension of the attack and killing, along with subsequent feelings of guilt or anxiety over possible capture, caused changes in the killer's behavior. He would have increased his use of alcohol or drugs, thrown himself into school or work, intensified his participation in church. These changes would have been visible to those closest to him. The killer's mother, ever indulgent and uncritical of her son, may suspect that he was involved in the killing of Theresa; or, it is possible that other family members know of his involvement, especially if he is living with his family, either because he is at the lower end of the age range and still in school, or older and living at home for some other reason.

But there was one important element to be added to the profile: Research had shown that certain serial rapists were highly selective in their choice of victims. They spent long periods cruising the roads, looking for prey who fitted their fantasy picture of the act they were about to perform. Philpin thought of the many rapists he had interviewed as a consultant for police departments. Serial rapists, the researcher pointed out, were psychologically akin to serial killers; some killers, too, could be expected to spend long hours searching for a victim to match some standard. Philpin thought everything about the abduction and killing of Theresa Fenton suggested a man on the road, a careful selection of the victim. This must be a man who cruised the roads, searching for just the right victim.

In the fall the investigators had copied a great pile of case documents and sent them off to the FBI's Behavioral Science Unit in Quantico, Virginia. The unit had become the driving force behind the emerging discipline of criminal profiling. The first efforts at profiling had focused on serial killers and mass murderers. In addition to working on federal cases where the FBI was directly involved, Quantico agents helped local and state police in selected cases by analyzing the data and providing theories about the crime and the criminal.

John Philpin helped compile the materials with high expectations. Surely the masters of this new field would provide incisive, helpful analysis. For several months there was no response except requests for more material. In December additional documents were sent off to Virginia. When there was no answer after several weeks, Philpin was authorized to find out what was happening. He phoned Quantico and was told the analysts needed still more material.

In March, Philpin tried again, finally reaching an agent who was familiar with the case. The FBI wasn't going to produce a profile, he told Philpin. Over the phone he offered some thoughts about what had happened to Theresa Fenton. It was an almost total disappointment.

The agent offered alternate theories. In one hypothetical scenario Theresa was sideswiped by a car and knocked from her bicycle; the damage to her brain was caused by the fall, and the odd indentation in her abdomen was caused by a sharp fall forward against the center post of the handlebars. To Philpin, it sounded as if the Quantico analysts had been reading about some other case. A second possible sequence was a casual encounter with a young man that degenerated when he went further than Theresa would accept. The agent described a man seventeen to nineteen years old, inadequate, slow in school, probably casually acquainted with Theresa, taken suddenly with rage, just as suddenly pulling back from the results of his assault, overtaken by regret.

The agent's third interpretation found the facts to be consistent with an assault intended from the start to be sexual. It was here that the most useful element of the FBI's analysis emerged. The agents had pored over the autopsy photographs. The bruising and the tear could not have been caused by a fall. These were unmistakable signs of sexual assault. The attacker had penetrated his victim, probably with either his fingers or some object.

Most of the FBI analysis seemed either nonsensical or redundant, but the confirmation that the attack had been sexual eliminated inconsistencies in Philpin's version of events and his profile of the killer. That explained a finding that had appeared to be incompatible with everything else: the leaves found under Theresa's waistband. Now it appeared that her pants had been removed, then neatly replaced after the sexual assault, catching up a fragment of leaf as they were slid on. In addition to validating the sexual character of the assault, these findings made the attack seem more programmed, more deliberate, sharpening the impression of a controlled, experienced killer. The facts reinforced Philpin's instinct. He revised his estimate of the attacker's age upward, to the late twenties or older.

The Quantico analysis leaned toward the idea of a younger killer. Though it was difficult to pin down the FBI's view without a written version of their analysis, it was clear that there were other points at which the novice and the masters saw the case differently. The Quantico experts believed Theresa and the killer had probably known each other, that she had gone along voluntarily at first. Philpin's instinct pointed with growing conviction to a different view: this was a confrontation of strangers.

Soon after Philpin began working on the Fenton case, Chief Herdt and Joe Estey had brought up the possibility of using the profile information to goad the killer into the open. If the investigators knew what kind of person he might be, they could release information calculated to play on his weaknesses. Suspects could be watched for signs of anxiety or paranoia; the killer might be provoked to reveal himself to someone who would then come forward with information, or the killer might even be prompted to relieve the anxiety by coming to the police himself.

In the fall of 1981, a few months after the murder of Theresa Fenton, Philpin proposed a plan to smoke out the killer. With the passing of time since the killing, he reasoned, the killer's initial anxiety and fear of capture would have subsided. The strategy should be to restore the tension by announcing that the police possessed evidence suggesting the identity of the killer or connecting him to the murder site. The public statement would admit that it might take a great deal of work to follow these leads to the man who abducted Theresa Fenton, but it would be only a matter of time until the police were knocking on the killer's door.

The message could be validated by releasing bits of information only the killer would know, facts that had not yet been revealed to the press. The message to the killer would be clear: the police are absolutely convinced that they will catch you; it may not be tomorrow, it may not be next week, but you will be caught.

Philpin was told to go ahead and prepare materials for use in a press conference. For several weeks he worked to compile a list of points common to his profile and the ideas the Quantico agent had offered over the phone. Under pressure to eliminate inconsistencies between his own views and the FBI's, in the end Philpin went along with the agent's notion of a younger man, contrary to his own emerging theory. The result, once the truth eventually emerged, reinforced Philpin's willingness to trust his own instincts in future cases. For now, though, he accepted his status as a neophyte and yielded to the need for a single, unified view.

On a Wednesday morning in the middle of June, Chief Herdt, Joe Estey, and John Philpin sat before a blackboard in a meeting room at the Springfield police station. With Philpin doing most of the talking, they painted a portrait of a man deeply troubled by what he had done. Their words were carefully crafted to both provoke the killer into revealing himself and persuade him that he would be received with professional sympathy and understanding if he came forward.

Chief Herdt opened the meeting, introduced Philpin, and informed the reporters that the psychologist was making a contribution of his time to the police department and the town. "This profile is the product of countless hours of volunteer work," the chief said.

The FBI had also produced a profile, Herdt said, and the two had been combined. "There were numerous areas of overlap," he told the reporters.

In his description of the profile for the assembled reporters, Philpin acquiesced in the FBI's view that the killer was probably in his late teens or early twenties and was at least casually acquainted with Theresa Fenton, in spite of his doubts on both issues. That was why, as the *Rutland Daily Herald* reported, Theresa was not initially frightened or intimidated by the man who approached her on the River Road.

Consistent with the FBI's estimate of the killer's youth, Philpin also speculated that the attack on Theresa Fenton was his first violent criminal act, even though there had been widespread discussion of a connection to the death of Sheri Nastasia. There was no point making the killer think that surrender would subject him to charges in other cases. That could wait for later.

"The incident began innocently enough," Philpin told the press. "When he approached her he probably wasn't intending to kill her. Then something in him snapped. The violence was spontaneous."

Passing on the FBI's elaboration of its portrayal of a younger man, Philpin described him as being of average intelligence but not a good student, probably in the bottom quarter of his class. He was strong but not athletic.

"He can appear to be congenial and unassuming," Philpin said. "He can act confident, even cocky, and he wants to impress people, but in actuality he's probably failed in most areas of adjustment.'' He probably didn't date much or get along well with women of his age. His relationship with his mother was the most significant in his life.

Finally, Philpin attempted to summarize the killer's state of mind. Like the rest of the description, it was meant to offer clues by which family and acquaintances of the killer might validate any suspicions they had been reluctant to act on. It was also intended to show the killer that the police understood him, that they could see how events could have gotten out of control, carrying him from an ''innocent'' beginning to a terrible end. There was even an implication that the authorities empathized with him, recognized the fear and anxiety that must be troubling him. The words carried an offer of relief, the chance of resolving the tension by coming forward.

''He probably wishes it never happened,'' Philpin said. ''Chances are he has no overwhelming reaction of guilt, but he has a strong fear of being apprehended. He probably hasn't told anyone about it, for fear of getting caught.''

Chief Herdt ended the press conference by pledging never to close the investigation. It had been almost ten months since the crime, and the department had worked on the investigation virtually every day since it happened.

''I'm never giving up hope,'' he said. ''I'm not a quitter.''

The press conference had been a long shot, an attempt to stir things up as the investigators approached a year without a break in the case. There was a flurry of phone calls with new leads to follow up, new suspects to investigate, even a few new paranoid fantasies that disturbed people wanted to share with the police. None of the new information produced anything useful.

And then, a few weeks later, an odd stroke of luck provided another important piece of evidence about the killer of Theresa Fenton and helped to solidify John Philpin's views of the case. Bobby Johnson's sighting had helped to confirm that she was heading for home before she was abducted, and his estimate of the timing had contributed to the precision of the investigators' timetable of her movements.

Now, nine months later, he was arrested on charges of possessing and intending to sell drugs. Seeking leniency from the police on the drug charges, Johnson suddenly became more cooperative about remembering what he had seen in the Fenton case.

He had seen Theresa first as they passed going in opposite directions. That was what he had reported in the days after her disappearance. But that was not all he had seen.

"I saw her in the rear-view mirror," he told the police. After passing her, he had looked in the mirror to see a car behind him heading in the same direction, facing the girl on her bicycle. The car and the bicycle passed each other, heading in opposite directions.

"Then the car slowed down and stopped," Johnson recalled. "And then she stopped, and he started backing up."

As Theresa straddled her bicycle, the car backed up until it had come even with where she stood. At that point Bobby Johnson and his friends pulled out of viewing range and Theresa Fenton was left to her fate.

"Why didn't you tell us this back when we first interviewed you?" a detective asked Johnson.

"Well, shit," he responded, "When you asked me that the first time, I forgot. I couldn't remember it."

And there was one other detail of Johnson's story that appeared tantalizing at first, even more so later. The car had been a Pontiac Sunbird and it appeared to be a dull gray. And the license plates looked like they were from New Hampshire.

No one was convinced that Johnson had suffered from memory failure during the first interview, but there was no apparent motive for his failure to cooperate. It must have been antagonism toward the police. A polygraph examination seemed to indicate that now he was telling the truth.

If that was the case, there was a problem with his description of the car. The two other witnesses who had seen a car on the River Road around the time of Theresa Fenton's disappearance had described it as "speedy" and "sporty," terms that certainly fit a Pontiac Sunbird. But both had also described the car as red. There was no way red could be confused with gray, the investigators thought. It was another puzzling discrepancy.

For John Philpin, though, the new information from Bobby Johnson helped refine his picture of what had happened on the River Road that afternoon.

"From Theresa's perception," he thought, "it must look

like the old 'I've got to ask for directions' kind of number. He backs the car up, acts a little confused, and goes from there.'' The method also reinforced Philpin's sense that this was a selective killer, probably one who cruised the roads hour after hour, searching for the perfect victim.

"When I heard that," he recalled later, "I knew it was a stranger." And the deliberate quality of the act suggested someone older, probably experienced in this kind of abduction, working out a fantasy scheme constructed well in advance. The man who attacked Theresa Fenton was looking less and less like the impetuous youth of the FBI profile.

And that led to another thought: This man they were hunting had probably attacked a woman before, may well have killed before. And there was a strong chance that he would try to do it again.

"It was a matter of waiting for the other shoe to drop," Philpin recalled later.

"The more I thought about it, the more I was convinced that the guy was going to kill again," he said. "It was just a question of when. I was totally convinced of that."

By now there were times when Philpin almost felt he would recognize the killer if he saw him on the street, but in fact he and Estey and LeClair knew they were as far from catching him as they had been the day Theresa Fenton was found in the brush off Mile Hill Road. With all the investigation, the questioning of suspects, and the assembling of facts and deduction about Theresa and what had happened to her, they knew a lot more than they had, but in a way, that made it worse.

Now, it appeared, there was another life at stake.

eight

November 12, 1982

There was nothing unusual about it, hitchhiking to Rutland, certainly nothing scary.

At the time, Dana Thurston didn't even give it a second thought. She was no stranger to thumbing a ride, and right now it was the only way she had of getting to see her boyfriend, Jerry Twitchell, who was in prison up there. It was no big deal, just some trouble he got in, but it made things difficult. The trip was about fifty miles from Brattleboro, at the southern end of the Connecticut Valley, where she was living with Jerry's brother, north and west to Rutland, the second-biggest city in Vermont. She could make it in a couple of hours or less, see Jerry, and get back by dark. It was midmorning on Friday by the time she set out.

The small, black-haired girl got picked up quickly by a man in a green van and they drove north up Route 5 to Putney, where the road eased back into contact with I-91, along the Connecticut River. She walked over to the interstate and it wasn't more than five minutes before a man in a blue Nova stopped for her. He took her another twenty miles north along the river and dropped her at the interchange in Rockingham where Route 103 led off westward toward Rutland. Rockingham was the next town south of Springfield.

It took a little longer to get a ride this time, maybe fifteen minutes or so, but eventually a man in a red car with Vermont plates pulled up and she got in. He was a smallish man, about five-foot-seven or five-eight, wearing a checkered flannel shirt, jeans, and cowboy boots. He had short, brown hair, parted on the side, and wore steel-rimmed glasses. He appeared to be in his early forties.

As they headed northward toward Rutland, slowing for the small towns that now and then interrupted the smooth flow of the two-lane road through hilly farm country, he asked her questions about herself. She had been in trouble, hard to control, they said. She'd had problems getting along with her parents, especially her father. They had gotten divorced and she had become a ward of the state. It hadn't been easy, but now she was seventeen and all that was behind her. She didn't go into detail, and the man didn't seem to mind. He was happy to talk about himself.

He told her he was divorced, with three daughters. The oldest was sixteen, married, and pregnant. He had been in the Navy, a nurse, stationed in New Orleans, and he'd been shot in the shoulder, ankle, and left hand. He didn't say how. His name, he said, was Stan. He went on about his work and his time in the Navy.

They had been driving less than an hour when they passed a sign that said Rutland, 13 Miles. With the intervals of walking and waiting for rides, Dana's trip had stretched into the early afternoon by now. A little farther along Stan pulled off the road into a small rest area.

"I've gotta take a leak," he told her.

He nosed the car to a stop, put on the brake, and opened the door to get out. If they didn't stop for too long she could be with Jerry in Rutland in another half hour, maybe sooner. Stan slid out of the car, then turned to lean back in, reaching down behind the front seat. Suddenly, as Dana idly watched him straighten up again in the door of the car, the world changed.

He was holding a gun, a shotgun, and the two barrels were pointing straight at her.

"Don't try to run away or scream," he said in a flat voice, "or I'll kill you."

She stared wordlessly at the gun. He slipped back behind the steering wheel.

He pulled at something on the top of the barrel and the gun opened. He pushed it toward her to show her the green shells inside.

"You can see it's loaded," he said. "You know I'm not fooling around." He settled himself and looked directly at her.

"It only takes one trigger and you'll be dead," he said, "so do what I say or I'll kill you." There was a coldness to his voice that gave it force; she was absolutely convinced that he meant it.

He backed the car up and swung out onto the road, now heading back in the direction from which they had come. He was holding the gun on his lap, wedged somehow between his legs, so that it pointed in her direction. It seemed to be aimed at her head. Now she noticed more shells on the seat, like the ones she had seen inside the barrel of the gun. These were red.

He drove easily, glancing over at her from time to time.

"You a virgin?" he asked.

"No," she replied. The fear had taken control of her whole body. It never occurred to her to lie.

He reached down and pulled out a bottle of Colt 45 malt liquor. He handed her the bottle and ordered her to drink it.

"We'll get drunk and then we'll have some fun," he told her.

Soon he began to talk about sex. His tone was insinuating, as if he expected her to get excited, and he kept looking over at her to see how she was reacting. He ordered her to remove her underwear, then put her shirt and jeans back on. With the shotgun pointing at her, she complied. He threw her jean jacket, red-and-blue vest, and underwear into the back seat.

"Please don't hurt me," she pleaded.

"As long as you do what I say," he responded, "there won't be any problem."

He began talking to her, mostly about sexual things, about masturbation, oral sex, intercourse, using the vulgar terms for everything. It wasn't as if she had never heard those words, but the way he said them, with the two big gun barrels pointing at her like open mouths, made it all sound disgusting. He kept urging her to drink more of the malt liquor. He was going to get her drunk before he had sex with her.

With his free hand, he reached over and touched her breasts, then reached down between her legs. She was immobilized with fear, but when he tried to force his hand inside her pants and press his finger into her, she resisted, pushing his hand away. He began talking about war, what happens when fighting men have women at their mercy, raping them at will.

"I like raping girls," he said. He wouldn't have any problem doing it to her, or killing her, if she didn't cooperate. He had picked up other girls like this, he told her, and he had been forced to kill two of them. He would do it again if he had to.

By now they were nearing the north-south corridor of the interstate and the Connecticut River, twenty miles north of where he had picked her up. In the Mount Ascutney area, just north of Springfield, he once again pulled over to the side of the road. She experienced a brief surge of hope that he was about to let her go, but he ordered her to take his place behind the wheel.

With him sitting on her right, she could clearly see the scar on his left hand. The skin on his hands was rough and chapped-looking, and there was grease under his fingernails. Now he was no longer occupied with driving. As they headed northward along the river, he took advantage of his freedom to touch her repeatedly, even leaning over to put his mouth on her body.

"You're really nice," he said. "You're the nicest I've ever picked up."

He had been drinking the malt liquor along with her, and by now they were running low. At the White River Junction exit he ordered her to turn off the highway. Moments later he directed her into the parking lot of a liquor store near the bus stop.

Keeping her close by his side, he walked into the store. As he occupied himself with picking out beer from a cooler, his attention was diverted momentarily.

She turned to the woman clerk, who stood behind the counter.

"Please help me," she mouthed, trying to keep her body still so that Stan wouldn't see her.

She shifted her body to shield her hand from his sight and

gestured frantically in his direction. The clerk didn't seem to understand. Dana tried to say more, shaping the words silently and pointing, but it was obvious she wasn't getting through. In a few moments Stan was back at her side. He placed two six-packs of Budweiser on the counter, asked for a soft pack of Marlboros, and paid up. Before she could figure out what else to do, they were back in the car. Now he was behind the wheel. Her chance was gone.

She was struck with a chilling certainty: He was going to rape her, and then he was going to kill her, same as he had killed those other girls he had talked about. There was nothing she could do about it. She could feel the fear churning inside of her.

"I don't feel so good," she said. "My stomach. I think I'm gonna be sick."

He didn't want her throwing up.

"We'll stop and get you something," he said.

In a few minutes they were in the business district of White River Junction. He pulled over to the curb in front of a small store, just down from the district court building.

"Go in and get yourself some Rolaids," he said. "I'll be right here watching. Remember, I've got the gun." He must be counting on her terror to make her obey, or had he convinced himself by now that she was enjoying herself, that she was going along with him voluntarily?

He sat behind the wheel, watching as she got out of the car and walked toward the store. As she entered the store she counted four customers, three men and a very heavy woman. There was a woman behind the counter.

"Help me," she cried. "He's going to kill me." There was a muffled quality to her scream that made it seem even more desperate. She was trying not to be heard, or seen. By somebody. But who? Who did she mean?

One of the men was paying for his purchase. He had seen everything she did, heard everything she said, but he didn't seem to understand. She watched him walk out of the store, her hope going with him. But once outside, he turned and waved to her through the glass doors. He was motioning for her to come out. Maybe he thought it was one of the other men in the store who was threatening her. He beckoned again for her to come out, out to where her captor waited at the curb in his car, waited to capture her again, to take her away with him, to kill her.

In an instant, she had made her choice. The man motioning to her was the only one who seemed to understand, the only one who had responded. She ran to the door, flung it open, and grabbed the man, spinning him around.

"Please, help me," she screamed. "It's him." She pointed to Stan, sitting in his car, just a few feet away. The stranger glared down at Stan.

"What the fuck are you doing to her?" he yelled.

Stan stared up through the windshield at the two of them, a blank look on his face. Would he use the shotgun, grab her, and drive off, kill them both?

"I don't even know her," he said in his flat voice.

She hardly heard what he was saying. She turned and raced back into the store.

"He's got a gun," she screamed at the woman behind the counter, "he's gonna shoot me. Call the police. Call the police."

It was eleven minutes past two when the call came over the police radio. Officer John Halpin was on patrol in Hartford.

A girl had become hysterical in the Progressive Market in White River, the dispatcher told Halpin. She claimed there was a man with a gun who was trying to kidnap her.

"It's a possible ten–ninety-six," the dispatcher said. The number code stood for mentally ill; the woman might be crazy, suffering from delusions. Halpin acknowledged the call and headed across the river. White River Junction, though better known from the old railroad days, was just a section of the town of Hartford. It took Halpin less than three minutes to get to the Progressive Market.

The young woman was sobbing, unable to catch her breath. She appeared to be hysterical. She was repeating the same words, over and over. After a moment, he understood.

"He was gonna kill me," were her words.

Halpin took a few minutes to help the woman calm down. She said her name was Dana Thurston.

"He had a gun, he was gonna kill me," she said again, but she was calmer now, beginning to feel safe, to believe that her ordeal was over.

Halpin asked where the man was now. She said she had seen him drive away. The clerk gave a brief account of what had happened, and the heavy woman said she also had seen the man in the red car drive away. It was becoming clear that this story was no fantasy produced by drugs or insanity. This young woman was terrified, not crazy.

The man who had challenged her captor was gone. Nobody in the store knew who he was. He was the only one besides the young woman herself who had gotten a close look at the car, who might have seen the license plate.

Back at the police station, Halpin sought out the department secretary to take notes and began interviewing the young woman. By the time everything was arranged and she seemed calm enough to give a statement, it was close to three-thirty. It had been about an hour and a quarter since Halpin had arrived in front of the Progressive Market. He began gently guiding Dana Thurston through a step-by-step account of what had happened.

Later, much later, when it was all over, when it had all degenerated into mere words, long, rambling conversations with the detective and the lawyer and the jailer and the psychologist, so many conversations you couldn't keep track of them all, then what he had remembered most about that day was the driving, the long hours of driving around, just thinking, trying to figure out what to do. That was what he had told them about, the driving and the drinking, and remorse, too, not for that day but for the other, for the little girl's death, and what the hell, maybe it was true. He told them that was what the gun was for, for the remorse, to use on himself, that he hadn't started out to find some girl and use it to control her. That had all happened out of drunkenness and coincidence, and once they were rolling, once they got into it, the beer and all, she was enjoying herself, she was going along for the ride. And they never knew for sure, for an absolute certainty, that it wasn't true, never could prove that wasn't really the way it happened.

But it was the driving, roads he knew from a thousand hours of cruising, just like this, cruising and thinking and looking, things flowing by, feeling drunk and loose, and then suddenly feeling it was too much, the malt liquor and the Budweiser, pulling off to the side of the road for a nap, then starting up again. By then he felt a little better, now that he was closer to home, still driving, still moving, off the main roads now, onto the little state road, heading west from the river, into a quiet rural area, and maybe he was going too fast, so when the curve came up he couldn't handle it. The car ran off the road and the wheels went up the bank and raised the whole side of the car until it tipped upward in a dizzying spin and rolled over with a thunderous crash of metal and spatter of spraying glass. The car lay upside down, wheels spinning in the air.

There was a long stillness when the car came to rest. The driver had not been wearing a seat belt and the crash had thrown him around, but he had stayed inside the car. He took a few moments to gather himself, then worked his way out of the car. It felt as though he had taken a blow to the head; otherwise, he couldn't feel any major damage. In a few minutes a woman came along. He flagged her down and asked her to call the police.

Once the woman had gone, he thought about the car. It was full of things that could mean big trouble when the cops got there. The gun alone could land him in jail by nightfall. And all the beer bottles. And the clothes, the shirt he had taken off, the girl's stuff.

He scrambled through the car, frantically gathering up everything that came to hand, making no effort to distinguish between things he could safely keep and things he had to get rid of. When he had assembled a pile he gathered it up and walked off into the woods. He was deep in the woods, close to two hundred yards from the wreck of his car, before he felt satisfied that he was well out of sight of the road. He scratched briefly at the ground, creating a shallow hole, flung the gun and other things down, and hurriedly scraped together dirt and leaves for a covering. Then he returned to the car.

In a few minutes, a green-and-yellow car of the Vermont State Police appeared. Troopers Dan Lavoie and Bobby Warner were getting near the end of their shift. Vermont troopers worked long hours, on duty and on call continuously, for five or six or seven days, then took three or four days off. This would be the last job for Lavoie and Warner before they went off duty.

As Lavoie took down information about the accident the two troopers looked over the man who had been driving the car. He gave his name as Gary L. Schaefer. He was thirty-one years old, though wire-rim glasses and a receding hairline made him look older. The car, a four-year-old Pontiac Sunbird, a sporty red two-door model with a white top, had been battered all along the sides and roof by the crash. Lavoie estimated the damage at $3,000, virtually all of the car's value. The vehicle was registered to Schaefer's mother, and he gave her Springfield address as his own.

Schaefer explained that he had encountered a deer racing in panic across the road, pursued by a snarling dog. He had swerved to avoid the two animals, he said, and the rising embankment at the side of the road had flipped him over. The troopers estimated the time of the accident at around 3:25 P.M. If the driver still seemed slightly disoriented, that was to be expected from someone who had just rolled his car, and Schaefer claimed he had been banged on the head in the crash. He had a headache, he said. Trooper Lavoie put it down as a "nonincapacitating" injury. Other than that there was nothing much to the accident, no property damage except to the car. It was a routine one-car accident.

By the time the troopers had arranged for the car to be towed and the driver delivered to the Springfield hospital for precautionary X rays, their duty was pressing against their free time. Lavoie and Warner returned to the state police office in Rockingham, just south of Springfield, to close out the shift. Lavoie finished filling out a routine accident report and threw it in a basket with all the other reports from the shift, their own and those from other troopers on duty. It was getting close to five-thirty, past time to start the weekend. Lavoie and Warner left the Rockingham office, headed for their homes.

Dana Thurston turned out to be an unusually observant witness. Some people find that fear narrows their attention to a few obsessive details of their surroundings. Dana Thurston was the opposite. She had been with Stan for close to two hours, first in apprehension, then in terror, and she had used the time well. From the start she had made a point of gathering details, hoping she would escape, hoping she could provide the facts that would help the police find this man and pay him back for what he was doing to her.

She described him minutely, down to moles on his forehead

and cheek. He was unshaven, maybe a day or two's worth of growth. His flannel shirt was checkered in red, black, white, and a little yellow. He wore designer jeans and his cowboy boots had square toes that were scuffed. She remembered his hands clearly, his menacing hands, chapped and rough, pale with reddish patches, the grime under his nails, the scar on his left hand.

The car was small, red or maroon with a white top, and there was a sunroof. It was fairly new, with Vermont plates. It could have been a Mustang, something like that. She knew cars fairly well; all the men she'd been around fooled with them. She hadn't had a chance to read the numbers on the license plate, but it had a pink inspection sticker dated July 24, 1982. The inside was red, too, and there was a sticker in the shape of the Playboy bunny stuck on one of the windows. There was a sheepskin cover on the driver's seat and a blanket covering the back seat.

It took close to two hours for Dana Thurston to tell her story. By the time they finished it was about five-twenty. Halpin summarized the key facts for the dispatcher and almost immediately a teletype message went out to all police departments and state police offices in Vermont, asking anyone who spotted him to stop and hold him.

Dana Thurston was much calmer by then. Someone had called her father and he had come to the station with his wife. It was five-thirty when they left for home.

As Dana Thurston was heading for home, police dispatchers throughout the state were rebroadcasting the bulletin to their patrol cars and officers on the street. In the next few days many of them made up printed notices for their bulletin boards. The Vermont State Police office in Bethel, thirty-five miles north of Springfield, put out its own bulletin. Bethel was the closest office to White River Junction, where Dana Thurston had escaped from the man who had abducted her. The short bulletin described the man and his red-and-white car, "possibly a Ford Mustang," briefly recounted what the man had done to an unnamed "female subject," and asked that troopers and local police keep watch for the man. At the top of the bulletin it said, in capital letters, *WANTED FOR QUESTIONING RE:* KIDNAPPING.

• • •

Dana Thurston returned to the Hartford Police Department a few days later to take a polygraph test, which validated her version of what had happened. She also worked with an officer to produce a composite sketch, assembling transparencies of facial features into a portrait of the man who had abducted her. The likeness was distributed to police throughout Vermont. By the time police departments throughout Vermont had caught up with the weekend's reports and bulletins early in the week, officers in many communities were watching for a red car like the one involved in the abduction of Dana Thurston. They knew they were looking for a lead in a case of kidnapping.

But there were some in the Valley who knew that in searching for that car they might be tracking bigger game. They were the few—officers in Springfield and the surrounding towns, state police detectives who had worked on the case of Theresa Fenton—who remembered that a small red car had been seen on the Old Connecticut River Road near the place where Theresa's bicycle had been found, a little more than a year earlier. Among them was Joe Estey, the chief investigator in Springfield, and Estey quickly learned that the man who abducted Dana Thurston had spoken to her of killing two girls.

Theresa Fenton and Sheri Nastasia. Sheri Nastasia had last been seen getting into a car in Springfield three years before. It had never been determined exactly what had killed Sheri Nastasia, but Estey, along with state police detective Mike LeClair and the other investigators, had always stood ready to make the link between her death and that of Theresa Fenton.

The inspection sticker looked like the best bet. How long could it take to go through the stickers for July 24? The next week John Halpin, the Hartford officer who had found Dana Thurston sobbing at the Progressive Market after her escape, drove up to Montpelier, the state capital, with Estey, LeClair, and another state police detective. It turned out that thousands of cars had been inspected on that date. The four detectives settled down to the tedious search.

After two full days of pawing through the records they had found barely a dozen that fit Dana Thurston's description of a sporty red car. Hundreds of man-hours later, each had been checked. Not one could have been involved in the kidnapping of Dana Thurston.

In the following days, officers throughout the Connecticut Valley looked closely at small red cars, checking them out in parking lots, looking into cars stopped along the streets, running license-plate checks, stopping dozens of them on some reasonable pretext to get a look at the driver and the inside of the car.

Meanwhile, a red 1978 Pontiac Sunbird with a white top and an inspection sticker dated July 29, 1982, sat for several weeks behind the Sunoco station near the junction of the interstate and Route 103, about ten miles south of the center of Springfield. The first night it was there, Gary Schaefer's brother Roger went down after dark and removed the cassette deck from the dashboard. It was Roger's equipment and he had installed it in his brother's car as a favor and for safekeeping, after removing it from a Chevy Vega he had junked. Soon after, Gary Schaefer went to the station and retrieved the sheepskin cover from the driver's seat.

In its own time, the insurance company concluded that the Sunbird was a complete loss. The bruised hulk of the car was taken on a truck to a junkyard, the Rosen and Berger Auto Parts Corporation in Rutland, and Gary Schaefer received a check. Schaefer soon bought himself another car. On the driver's seat he installed the sheepskin seat cover he had rescued from the old Sunbird.

There was nothing special about the accident report filled out by Trooper Dan Lavoie. The single sheet passed along the usual paper trail of the state police office at Rockingham and finally made its way into the filing system. The car involved was a 1978 Pontiac Sunbird. There was no space on the report to enter the color of the vehicle involved in an accident. There were only two people who knew the color of the car, who might have made a connection to the red-and-white car in which Dana Thurston had been a prisoner that morning: Dan Lavoie and Bobby Warner. And when the bulletin from the Hartford Police Department on the kidnapping of Dana Thurston arrived in Rockingham, Dan Lavoie and Bobby Warner had left for home; when they returned four days later, the bulletin had passed into that realm of less-urgent matters that recede into the backwaters of attention. In any case, Dana Thurston had guessed that the car in which she had been imprisoned was a Mustang, and someone in the Progressive Market had seemed to confirm her opinion. That identification had been incorporated into the broadcast bulletin; the newspapers reported Saturday that "police were on the lookout for an armed man driving a red Mustang car."

A number of people had connected the unknown man who abducted Dana Thurston to the faint trace of the man who had killed Theresa Fenton, and possibly Sheri Nastasia also. But no one was to make the connection between that man who attacked young girls and the small, slightly dumpy, nondescript man who wrecked his car on a country road and told the trooper a deer had run across his path.

Random circumstance, bad luck, fate, whatever it was that described or explained the tiny but unbridgeable gap between a young woman's terrifying ride and the rollover of a Pontiac Sunbird a little more than an hour and a mere thirty-five miles away—that failure of connection was to have tragic consequences just a few months later.

nine

August 1982–April 1983

Enough time had passed now since the killing of Theresa Fenton, a full year, that many people had found ways to forget. It is easier on the mind, necessary even, to treat such a terrible event as an isolated happening with no relation to others in the past or future. But that was not possible for those who were closest to the case.

Theresa's brother and sister, now six and nine, shrank from strangers; for the first time their parents kept the doors and windows locked. The Fentons found themselves wondering if Theresa's killer could have been someone with a grudge against their family. Was there a disturbed soul out there somewhere, nursing a bitter grievance over some imagined provocation, preparing for another act of revenge?

It was not only her family that was threatened, Barbara Fenton thought, but the entire community. At the end of the summer of 1982, Mrs. Fenton marked the anniversary of Theresa's death by writing an open letter to the killer and sending it to newspaper and television stations throughout the Connecticut Valley. The letter was signed by both the Fentons, but it spoke in a mother's voice.

"We still think about the details and often relive the anguish and pain that you caused," the Fentons told their daughter's attacker. They were plagued with questions: How had it happened? Why did the killer lose control? What made him so angry?

They asked the killer to consider the consequences of what he had done. "How many lives have been affected by your actions?" they asked rhetorically, and Mrs. Fenton's anguish showed itself in the answer: "Believe me, it was not just Theresa's tears and pain and life, but literally hundreds of others." As long as he was on the loose, the Fentons told their daughter's killer, he left the entire community in a state of anxiety.

The Fentons asked the killer to come forward and end the fear and tension, the community's and their own. But there was more, Mrs. Fenton told a reporter. A devout Roman Catholic, she had no interest in revenge for Theresa's death, but hoped that the killer might achieve reconciliation with God. And before that would be possible, Mrs. Fenton said, the killer must make his peace with his victim's parents. "I personally don't think that you can be truly and completely reconciled with God until you are also reconciled with us, her parents," Mrs. Fenton told her daughter's attacker.

From that terrible need and wish for reconciliation came the Fentons' extraordinary request: they wanted to meet the man who had taken their daughter's life.

Theresa's parents needed a chance, Mrs. Fenton said, to resolve their fears, get answers for their questions, and offer the killer their forgiveness. They would never be able to resume a normal life, return to ordinary activities in family or community, until they had seen their daughter's killer face-to-face.

In the meantime, the Fentons were unable to commit themselves to personal or community activities, for fear that the capture and prosecution of the killer would someday bring to the surface once again all the anguish of their daughter's ordeal and their own loss, throwing a shadow over ordinary life and pushing aside all routine commitment.

"When we make a commitment we stick to it," Mrs. Fenton told a reporter. "But involvement in the community is a way of healing. We feel that our lives are incomplete at this point, because the event is still not closed.

"Our life is suspended," Mrs. Fenton said. "We're in suspension."

• • •

The two girls walked along the edge of the highway, talking, keeping an eye on the traffic. It was late Saturday afternoon, a wet, cold day in the first week of April. Caty Richards and Rachel Zeitz had finished dress rehearsal for their ballet recital the next day and then headed down Route 106 toward Athens Pizza. They were both eleven years old, an age when girls can move easily from ballet to video games, but some kids were using the Pac-Man machine, so they bought a bag of potato chips and headed back toward Rachel's house.

They were near the entrance to the Pedden Acres development when a blue car passed. Moments later it passed again, heading in the other direction, going slowly as if the driver were lost. In a few minutes it appeared again, pulling to a stop alongside the two girls.

"Do you know where Joe Cerniglia's house is?" the driver asked. He had brown hair and wore glasses, Rachel noticed. Joe Cerniglia was a Springfield selectman, but the girls didn't know where he lived.

Caty, a friendly, outgoing child, was eager to help. She moved toward the car. The man got out and came around the car. One hand was jammed into the pocket on the front of his red sweatshirt. Rachel thought the sweatshirt looked familiar. When he spoke again, there was something new in his voice, a hard, cruel quality.

"What if I tell you, if you don't get into the car I'll kill you?" he said. He fixed Caty Richards with an unwavering stare.

Caty gasped and froze in place. The man never took his eyes off her. It was as if Rachel, only a few steps farther away, were not there. Rachel noticed a bulge in the man's belly pocket, bigger than a hand alone would make, as if he were holding a gun.

Caty moved toward the vehicle. Rachel backed away. Caty was sobbing now as she got into the car. Rachel turned to run as her friend disappeared from view and the car pulled away.

It didn't come right away. The girl was shaken by the experience. But gradually she started recounting what had happened and she turned out to be a surprisingly good witness. When Joe Estey had decided to become a cop full-time, his first job had been as a juvenile officer. He knew how unpredictable a child's memory could be; even a lot of adults missed things, failed to record in memory the details of what they saw, and children were even less reliable. But Rachel Zeitz was a different story entirely.

She had shown the presence of mind to run to the nearest house as the man drove off with Caty Richards. Now, minutes later, she was recalling the scene piece by piece, the man's slim build, his short, brown hair and metal-rim glasses. He seemed to be in his twenties, she thought, maybe six feet tall. The car was light blue, possibly a darker blue on top, and she thought the license plates looked like the ones everybody had, Vermont plates.

The man had been wearing blue pants. And the sweatshirt. She remembered the sweatshirt vividly. It was red, a bright red, with a hood, and the year, 1983, was printed on one sleeve in black lettering. There was more black lettering, in script, across the chest. She had seen one just like it, a classmate in the fifth grade at the Park Street School had the same sweatshirt.

A call went out to all Springfield cruisers to begin a search of every known parking and turnoff area in town, all the wooded places away from the main roads where people went seeking freedom from the scrutiny of others. They started with the area around Mile Hill Road where Theresa Fenton had been found. A bulletin was broadcast to departments throughout the state. It was less than an hour since Caty Richards had gotten into the light blue car.

It was a real contrast with the other abduction cases. In those cases they hadn't developed any leads until it was too late; this time, they had some facts to build a search on. Maybe this time they could find Caty Richards in time to keep her from harm. After Theresa Fenton's disappearance, the police and fire departments had worked with town officials to develop an emergency search plan to speed the town's response. The plan was put into effect. Within hours, scores of people were looking for Caty Richards. The mood around the police station was hopeful.

While Rachel Zeitz worked with an officer to create a composite picture of the kidnapper, Estey began tracking down the sweatshirt. Through Rachel Zeitz's classmate he learned that the shirts had been made up specially for a gathering of young people held at a local church. The lettering across the front said *Christadelphian,* the name of the church.

The Christadelphians were a fundamentalist group whose members asserted the literal truth of the Bible and believed that Christ would return and establish his kingdom on earth. The church was small, about eighteen families, fifty people in all, and close-knit; most of them lived in the part of Springfield near an intersection called Hardscrabble Four Corners and socialized mainly with other members. But there had been Christadelphians from other areas at the youth meeting where the sweatshirts were distributed.

Estey set to work to get a list of the people at the meeting and a roster of the church's membership. Then, late into the night, they ran the names one by one through the Department of Motor Vehicles computer, looking for church members who owned blue cars. They began making phone calls.

By morning, as the members of the Christadelphian Church gathered for Sunday worship services, word was spreading through the congregation that the police were searching out the people who had attended the youth conference.

It was a little after 9:00 A.M. when Ginny Collier, a teenager who had attended the conference, greeted one of the adult leaders of the youth group as he arrived at the little church for morning worship. He had been especially friendly to her, advising her about life in long, heartfelt conversations, writing her letters that referred to the Bible and popular songs for lessons about how to deal with personal problems. She had seen him about three o'clock the day before and he had confided in her that he was upset because he was unable to see his adopted daughter's baby, and also because the next day would be the first anniversary of his father's death.

The girl felt close enough to her confidant to tease him a little. "Hey," she asked him, "are the police after you, too?"

He looked startled. "What do you mean?" he asked.

"Oh, you know, they're asking people about the sweatshirts," she responded. She reminded him about the shirts made up for the gathering of Christadelphian young people.

He turned pale. "I'm not feeling well," he said. In a moment he had gone, headed for the bathroom. He returned a few minutes later. He had vomited. Quickly making his excuses, Gary Schaefer left for home.

There is no delicate way to spit tobacco juice into a foam cup, but Mike LeClair did his best to be unobtrusive about it, hiding the container in his big hand, dragging it tightly across his lower lip, then reaching over to put it back at the far edge of his desk, away from any visitor who might be offended.

Like a lot of the cops in the Valley, men who grew up in small towns, LeClair looked a little out of place sitting at a desk. He was over six feet tall and he was solid, too bulky to fit comfortably into half a small detectives' cubicle at the Rockingham barracks of the Vermont State Police. LeClair was comfortable outdoors, going on long hunting trips with his brother and friends, working on his house or in the yard. Folded up behind a metal desk he conveyed a sense of motion contained, the feeling you might get from seeing a hot-air balloon tethered in a strong wind. But that was where a detective spent a lot of his time, writing reports, checking files, making phone calls.

LeClair had been a detective with the Vermont State Police less than two years when Sheri Nastasia disappeared. Now here he was, three and a half years later, and finally it seemed as if the series of events set in motion that night might reach some kind of resolution.

LeClair had worked countless hours on the case of Theresa Fenton, and countless hours more on the case of Dana Thurston, the young woman who had been held captive by a man who claimed he had killed two girls before her. Through it all, LeClair had wondered always if any of these cases were related, waiting for the event or bit of information that would answer all the questions.

Now, at last, after all the false starts and fruitless searching, finally there was something to work with. Sunday morning LeClair took the composite portrait of the kidnapper that Rachel Zeitz had created and went to see James Millay, a lay minister of the Christadelphian Church. Millay would be able to help narrow down the possibilities, LeClair thought. He did more than that.

"Oh sure," Millay said, looking at the composite, "that looks just like Gary Schaefer." Schaefer was a first cousin of

Millay's, a fellow member of the church.

Millay went to get a picture of his cousin. Millay was right, LeClair thought: there was a striking similarity between the face in the photograph and Rachel Zeitz's composite.

Gary Schaefer had moved to Springfield from Pennsylvania with his family in the early sixties, when he was ten or eleven years old. After high school he had served in the Navy for ten years, stationed in Norfolk, Virginia, and Newport, Rhode Island. He had come back to Springfield two years earlier and rejoined the Christadelphian Church. He had recently been elected a custodian of the church.

Since his return Schaefer had been very active in the church, Millay said, faithfully attending Sunday services and Wednesday night prayer meetings, taking a special interest in the youth group. Three days a week he led groups of young people to visit with the elderly residents of nursing homes. Millay said his cousin had little or no social life outside the church. He was divorced and lived with his mother and younger brother in a white clapboard house about a half mile from the church. He was thirty-one years old.

"What's this about?" Millay wondered. LeClair described the abduction of Caty Richards the day before on Route 106.

"I saw Gary over there yesterday," Millay responded. He had passed his cousin on Route 106 near the entrance to the Pedden Acres development. Schaefer had been driving a light blue car, his mother's Pontiac.

Millay was able to narrow the time to between five and five-ten in the afternoon; he had been shopping at the hardware store just before it closed at five o'clock, then passed Schaefer minutes afterward. And there was more: He had seen two young girls walking along the highway at the same time. They fit the description of Rachel Zietz and Caty Richards.

Had he noticed what Gary was wearing? Oh yes, Millay said. He and Gary had waved to each other, he told LeClair, and he had noticed his cousin's red sweatshirt.

That was it, they had it, enough evidence to place Gary Schaefer at the place where Caty Richards had been kidnapped, at the time of the crime. And the identification was solid. It was time to go see Gary Schaefer.

Mike LeClair called Joe Estey at the station to make the

arrangements. It was late morning by now. If only there was still time to do any good for Caty Richards.

It wasn't that John Philpin thought about it every hour, or even every day. It wasn't even that every time Philpin and the others involved with the case of Theresa Fenton reconsidered the evidence or set out to investigate new leads, they consciously thought, "I know this guy is going to do it again." The consciousness was more like a small, unexploded charge in the awareness of each of the investigators.

Each had tried in his way to help solve the case, to catch the man who killed Theresa Fenton, and each knew he had somehow failed. And each felt the burden of that failure, a mixture of fear that the man would attack another young girl, and some share, however small, of responsibility for the consequences of that attack. No reasonable person could ever agree that they should share even the smallest part of that responsibility; in fact the opposite was true. Each of them had worked many hours of overtime, often without pay, sacrificing home life and other professional commitments, in the attempt to catch the killer, and Philpin had worked without any compensation at all. But those hours had made this search their search, had made this killer their enemy, and had made his continued freedom in some part their responsibility. This had gotten personal.

That was probably why John Philpin felt sick to his stomach when he heard the news about Caty Richards.

It was a Sunday, one of those nasty days that only early spring can create, with enough deep cold left in it to turn April showers into sleet, chilling the hope of winter's end. Philpin and his wife had been in Springfield shopping in the late morning. Heading back home after noon they were slowed almost to a stop by traffic backed up along the road a few miles north of town. Police cars filled the roadsides and a large area at the side of the road had been cordoned off. A little farther along, Philpin stopped at the store in Perkinsville, thinking to phone back to the Springfield Police Department to find out what was going on.

The phone call wasn't necessary. A crowd had gathered in the store and they were already talking about it. A body had been found. It was a girl, missing since the day before. Nobody knew the details.

"Could be anything," Philpin thought, holding the idea of Theresa Fenton and her killer at a distance. He decided not to make the phone call from the store. The phone was right behind the counter, in the open, where everybody could hear a conversation.

In a few minutes they were home and Philpin called the station. Joe Estey was out and the dispatcher didn't have much information. They had found the missing girl a little before one o'clock in the woods off Baltimore Road, about two and a half miles from where she had been kidnapped. She was dead. There were no details yet about how she had died, but they had a suspect.

It was around suppertime before Philpin reached Joe Estey. The question almost asked itself: "Is it like the Fenton case?"

"Yes."

"How was she killed?"

"She was beaten to death."

Caty Richards had been clubbed on the side of the head at least twice, possibly more, with some hard object. It appeared that the blows had been struck from behind. She had been found facedown in the mud, her jeans bunched around her knees, shirt pulled up over her face.

That was when it struck with sickening impact, the certainty that this was the crime they had tried to prevent.

Spring would be gone, then summer and fall, and it would be winter again, nine months later, before the formal process of law would finish with Gary Schaefer, and even then there would remain a sea of unanswered questions and unresolved concerns about what he had done and why he had done it. Yet, in this moment, John Philpin knew that what they all had feared was made real, and with the knowledge came the terrible sense that their best effort had failed.

ten

April 1983–January 1984

People in the Valley had known of Gary Schaefer only that he existed and that he had done evil, nothing more. Now there was a particular fascination in seeing the details of his portrait emerging slowly into public awareness, like an image appearing little by little on a sheet of photographic paper in a darkroom tray. And yet, there was a bland ordinariness to the man that defied the public yearning for some clear explanation of what had happened.

The arrest had been uneventful, except for a telling moment at the very beginning. The body of Caty Richards had been found at close to one o'clock on Sunday. At almost the same time, Mike LeClair and Doug Johnston, a Springfield detective, arrived at the Schaefer house, primed for action. At long last, a break in the string of abductions and killings was at hand. Other police cars waited out of sight nearby, officers at the ready to back them up if necessary. The tension was palpable.

Schaefer's mother let the two officers in and called to her son, who was upstairs in his room. The officers tensed as he came down the stairs.

"I've been sick," were his first words. And then he excused himself and walked to the bathroom. From behind the bathroom door, the two officers heard the retching and spitting sounds of a man vomiting. It was the second time that morning that the prospect of a reckoning had shaken Gary Schaefer to the point of nausea.

The officers had been braced for some dramatic act, an attempt at escape, perhaps, or resistance, or even self-destruction. LeClair and Johnston, experienced police officers, knew all those things were possible once a suspect was cornered. But Gary Schaefer had exhausted his capacity for drama. Once the discussion began, it proceeded almost like an ordinary conversation of acquaintances meeting on the street.

Schaefer worked as a mechanic for Thomas Soucy, a car dealer in North Springfield. He told the two detectives that he had spent Saturday afternoon in Rutland with his boss, picking up cars for the dealership. In fact, he said, the cars were late in arriving, so they hadn't gotten back until sometime after nine o'clock.

Schaefer's mother, who was standing by as the police officers talked with him, confirmed that he had left about two o'clock and returned around nine-fifteen. She said he had been wearing blue pants and a red sweatshirt he got at a church youth meeting. He had been driving her car, a light blue Pontiac J2000.

"We have a reliable witness who saw you in Springfield right around five o'clock," LeClair told Schaefer.

The sighting and the false alibi constituted sufficient cause to arrest him. LeClair placed Gary Schaefer under arrest. Thomas Soucy later told police he hadn't been anywhere near Rutland Saturday.

Afterward, LeClair and other officers returned to search the house. They worked until two in the morning, turning up the red sweatshirt and blue pants. On the pants they found a blond hair that looked the same color as Caty Richards's hair, a dusty blond. There were stains on the pants that might be blood, and on a pair of boots Schaefer had been wearing, as well. Other stains were found in the light blue Pontiac. And in Schaefer's car they found a sheepskin seat cover. All the confiscated items were sent to the lab for analysis.

As for Schaefer himself, people described him as mild-mannered, a reliable worker at Soucy Motors, a good neighbor, but it emerged that no one knew him very well. His family might have been an exception, but they weren't talking. He had two brothers and a sister. His father had worked at Bryant Grinder in town for twenty years. Since his father's death exactly a year earlier, Gary had taken care of his mother.

A grove of Norway spruces towered over the white clapboard farmhouse in south Springfield where Schaefer lived with his mother and his younger brother, Roger. The house sat atop a hill, surrounded by woods and fields. A small dog roamed the yard, barking at strangers, or nothing at all. Several of the houses closest to them were occupied by other members of the Christadelphian Church, which was half a mile away. Home, church, and work; as far as anyone knew, that was Gary Schaefer's life, nothing very dramatic.

Nobody seemed to have any vivid memories of Gary Schaefer's past either.

A longtime Cub Scout leader in Springfield thought he remembered Gary, but he wasn't sure. "I've had a lot of Schaefer boys in my packs," he said, "and I'm not certain he was one of them. But there was this very nice little fellow and I think it was him."

"I had him in some of my classes," said one man who remembered Schaefer from high school. "He was pretty intelligent. I don't remember him having any close friends."

Schaefer hadn't done much in team sports but he had run on the track and cross-country teams in his first two years of high school.

"He was a quiet youngster," the man who had coached the teams told a reporter for the *Rutland Herald*. He had once driven Schaefer home after school and the boy had been silent except when the coach spoke first. But he was earnest and hardworking.

"He was a learner," the coach recalled. "He did everything I asked him to do." The coach had considered that Schaefer had potential as a runner.

"That's why I got on him about his smoking," the coach said. "He would come in coughing his head off, and I told him to stop smoking." After two years the coach had left for a job in another town and Schaefer had dropped out of cross-country and track. He had continued smoking.

Like Schaefer's classmate, the coach remembered him as a loner. Past or present, no one could remember Gary as having a close friend, with the exception of James Millay, his cousin and fellow church member. Even a relative of Schaefer's who lived nearby and saw him often felt she had little to say about him, referring a reporter to Millay.

"They're close friends," the relative said.

However close they were, Millay's picture of Schaefer wasn't much different from anyone else's. Millay described his cousin as quiet, earnest, religious. His possible involvement in the case of Caty Richards, Millay said, was "a terrible thing."

"This is impossible for us to understand," Millay said.

The only public hint that Schaefer was anything but a quiet, pious man leading a dull and unremarkable existence was a notation someone had made on an affidavit submitted at his arraignment. Next to a brief reference to his ten years of military service, someone had written, "Had trouble in Navy." There were no details.

Even in the newspaper photographs of police leading Schaefer in handcuffs from jail to court and back again, his plain face, receding hairline, and slightly doughy body made the suspect look bland and indistinct, older than his thirty-one years.

Schaefer himself wasn't doing anything to sharpen the hazy public picture of him. When he stood before a judge on Monday wearing dirty white sneakers, brown pants, and a flannel shirt, his only words were the plea of "not guilty" he entered to the charge of kidnapping Caty Richards.

The kidnapping charge would be sufficient to hold Schaefer in jail while the investigators gathered evidence on other charges related to the death of Caty Richards and looked into other cases that might involve Gary Schaefer.

The police quickly made the connection between Schaefer and the attack on Dana Thurston five months before. On Tuesday they traced his wrecked car to the Rosen and Berger junkyard in Rutland, where it had sat untouched since Schaefer had rolled it over a little more than an hour after Dana Thurston escaped from her kidnapper. It was a red-and-white Pontiac Sunbird. The car was hauled back to the Springfield police station.

Early Wednesday morning Dana Thurston identified the car as the one in which she had been held captive. The car was dented, much of the glass was shattered, but there was no question. She recognized the colors, and the steering wheel she had held in her hands while the man had forced her to drive. The Playboy sticker was unmistakable. And her denim jacket and red-and-blue vest were still in the car.

Two days later, seven men stood with their backs to the wall of the selectmen's room in the White River Junction town hall. Each had a number from one through seven pinned to his chest. One by one they stepped forward and spoke: "Don't try to run away or scream, or I'll kill you."

Seated across from the men, Dana Thurston listened to them speaking the words her kidnapper had used. The voices only confirmed what she had known since the men walked into the room. She had begun shaking uncontrollably as soon as she saw them, saw the man who had picked her up on Route 103.

As the men filed out, she wrote the number five on the top sheet of a pad of paper. Number five was Gary Schaefer. Then she burst into tears.

A week later Gary Lee Schaefer was charged with kidnapping Dana Thurston and with reckless endangerment, threatening her with a gun. A rusted shotgun had turned up in the woods near other items Schaefer had thrown away.

And now Gary Schaefer largely disappeared from public view while the prosecutor and investigators hunted for evidence in the Richards and Thurston cases. Detectives were also checking to see if Schaefer had been on leave from the Navy when Sheri Nastasia was killed, and searching for any leads that might connect him to the case of Theresa Fenton.

Gary Schaefer was transferred after a few days from the local jail in Woodstock, not far from Springfield, to a newer prison up north in St. Johnsbury. He had been kept under close watch in Woodstock after a psychiatrist reported that he had suicidal tendencies, but the chief reason for the transfer was security. Schaefer had to be kept apart from other prisoners. Officials were concerned that he might be attacked.

"Within the prison world, child molestation is the lowest status of crime," the jail superintendent said. "People charged with those crimes take the most abuse from other prisoners."

As the summer passed, the prosecutor's office met with mixed results in its campaign to build cases against Gary Schaefer.

The strongest cases were those involving Caty Richards and Dana Thurston, but there were problems.

Tests showed that Caty Richards had been raped; charges of murder and sexual assault were added to the kidnapping count against Schaefer. It looked as if Rachel Zeitz would make a strong witness, but the physical evidence was shaky; the laboratory reported that the stains in Schaefer's car and on his pants and boots were not blood.

Prosecutors were confident Dana Thurston would make a good witness, too, but it appeared Schaefer would argue that she went along willingly. It might be hard to portray for a jury the terror that had kept her in Schaefer's control over such a long period and with several apparent chances to escape, especially since she had not been physically harmed.

As for Theresa Fenton and Sheri Nastasia, there were no witnesses and no physical evidence in either case. Bobby Johnson *had* seen a Pontiac Sunbird in his rear-view mirror, stopping and backing up to draw even with a girl on a bicycle on the Old River Road. But he had said the car was gray, a dull gray. It was clear that Johnson would have seen only the front of the car.

When detectives inspected Gary Schaefer's dark red Sunbird they found indications that someone had done body work on the front of the car. Gray primer would have been applied before the red was restored, and it was likely that the car had been on the road at times during the various stages of repair. Bobby Johnson could well have seen the gray, primer-painted front of Gary Schaefer's Sunbird, without realizing that the rest of the car was red with a white top. But none of this constituted proof, and neither Bobby Johnson nor either of the two witnesses who had noticed a sporty red car had seen its driver.

It was even more difficult to link the death of Sheri Nastasia to Gary Schaefer. There was the man who had seen her getting into a dark green Pontiac Firebird; Schaefer had owned a blue Firebird at the time. It was suggestive, but there was little more to work with; even the cause of death was speculative.

The solution to these problems came from the most unlikely source: Gary Schaefer himself.

At the end of September, after five months in jail, Schaefer wrote to the prosecutor, William Bos, accepting responsibility for the murders of Theresa Fenton and Caty Richards. In addition he admitted kidnapping Dana Thurston.

Schaefer's language was vague. He claimed to have only fragmentary memories of the time he had spent with his three victims. But what he did remember, along with the evidence presented to him by the police, caused him to believe that he had committed the crimes he was charged with, as well as the murder of Caty Richards. And Schaefer's religious beliefs, his attorney said, led him to feel that he was responsible for these acts in the eyes of God. These feelings, as well as a desire to avoid inflicting the pain of a trial on his family and fellow church members, prompted him to accept responsibility for the crimes.

"He is guilty in the eyes of God, as he sees it," Schaefer's attorney told reporters.

It was early December before all the other legal issues were disposed of and Schaefer appeared in court to formally accept responsibility. Two months of hearings and negotiation had produced an agreement in which Schaefer pleaded *nolo contendere*—no contest—to the sexual assault and murder of Caty Richards and the kidnapping of Dana Thurston. The plea meant that he admitted guilt and gave up his right to remain silent; in return the admissions could not be used against him if he were prosecuted on other charges.

In addition, Schaefer agreed to give a statement after sentencing admitting his "full involvement" in the death of Theresa Fenton. The state promised in return not to prosecute him in Theresa's death.

The agreement insured that Schaefer would be sentenced to thirty years to life on the murder charge and fifteen to twenty years on the sexual assault and kidnapping charges. The murder sentence would be the second-longest imposed in Vermont since the elimination of the death penalty several years earlier.

Even with good behavior, prosecutor William Bos said, Schaefer would not be eligible for parole in less than twenty-two years. And no parole board, knowing what Schaefer had done, would set him free even then, Bos predicted. Schaefer would stay in jail, Bos concluded with satisfaction, "for the rest of his natural-born life."

The plea bargain represented a good deal for the community, Bos told the press. The risk of an uncertain prosecution would be avoided, the community would be protected from Schaefer, and any fear that a killer might still be on the loose would be eliminated.

And Schaefer's agreement to talk about his "involvement" in the death of Theresa Fenton would put her family's mind at ease, as well as helping to resolve the community's apprehension. Bos had taken pains to keep the families of Caty Richards and Theresa Fenton informed about the negotiations with Schaefer; he was particularly aware of the Fentons' desire for more information about their daughter's fate. Schaefer's statement was in part a response to their need.

"I feel I owe it to them," Bos said.

The case of Gary Schaefer was closed, and yet it was hard to imagine that the brutal force of what Schaefer had done would ever fully dissipate.

The families of Schaefer's victims dealt in various ways with the horror and loss. Sheri Nastasia's family, already in disarray, had left Vermont shortly after the discovery of her body. Schaefer claimed to have no memory of any meeting with Sheri. In interviews with the authorities he speculated about what might have happened to Sheri and about the possibility that he might have been involved. He theorized that amnesia could have wiped out his recollection, but he never directly admitted to anything. Those who loved Sheri Nastasia were left not only with their loss but also with the imagined horrors that filled the vacuum of uncertainty about what had happened to her.

Even where there was certainty about Schaefer's deeds, imagination retained its capacity to torture those left behind. At the hearing before Schaefer's sentence was announced, Caty Richards's mother, Rosealyce Thayer, released a heart-rending statement imagining her child's terror and suffering in Schaefer's hands. She had been told that Schaefer was acting out of a hatred of women so deep that he tried to inflict the greatest possible pain and terror on his victims. She speculated that he chose young girls as his targets because they were female, but defenseless. She imagined the plight of Schaefer's victim:

"There is no blissful escape into the unconscious. He wants his victim to be fully aware of all of the horror he has carefully planned for her. Her only escape, her only release, is death. We have all been afraid at one time or another. At a time such as that, seconds appear to be endless. Caty was terrorized for three and three-quarter hours. Both mentally and physically, she suffered more in those endless hours than we ever shall in our long lives.''

Caty was the child of the Thayers' later years, her mother wrote. ''Children who are born to parents as old as we are very precious.

''Her hopes and dreams, her aspirations, became ours. A shining part of our future died with her, the best part of our lives is gone. At night, I wake to hear her voice, pleading, calling for help and protection which was denied to her. Her agony will always be with us.

''Our lives, our home, are now filled with a vast, bleak and aching silence,'' Mrs. Thayer wrote, and she quoted Caty's older brother: '' 'Now life is merely a series of events.' ''

Mrs. Thayer approved the sentence that had been negotiated with Schaefer and urged that he never again be allowed to walk freely on the street.

''We do not want other parents doomed to live the rest of their lives as we do,'' Mrs. Thayer concluded, ''hearing the clear voices of the children they can never see or hold again, calling for mercy and protection.''

In their search for some explanation of what had happened to their daughter, the Thayers criticized the Springfield police for what they said was a failure to react quickly enough to reports of the girl's kidnapping. An investigation exonerated the police, but the publicity highlighted the problem of distinguishing between runaways and victims and prodded a number of communities in the Valley to develop strategies for responding quickly to reports of missing children. Mrs. Thayer became active in organizations working for the safety of children and victims' assistance.

The parents of Theresa Fenton continued to seek a more private accommodation with their grief. They pursued their request for a meeting with their daughter's killer. A week after Schaefer's sentencing he gave the prosecutor's investigator the promised statement on Theresa's death. As in his earlier confession, Schaefer spoke vaguely about what had happened, professing failures of memory. Nevertheless, the prosecutor was satisfied that Schaefer had accepted responsibility for killing Theresa and satisfied the conditions of his sentencing.

A month later, Schaefer agreed to meet and talk with Barbara and Richard Fenton, Theresa's parents. In the two and a half years since Theresa's murder, Mrs. Fenton said, they had prayed for three things: that the killer would find the courage to confess, that he would turn to God, and that they could achieve "some type of reconciliation between that person and us."

Their meeting with Schaefer had been "the answer to those prayers," Mrs. Fenton said. She spoke gently of Theresa's killer, referring to him by his first name as if their mutual participation in the tragedy of Theresa's death had created a kind of familiarity.

She had found it difficult to accept that someone in Springfield could suffer from such severe psychological problems that he could brutally murder a child, Barbara Fenton said. How could such terrible sickness go unnoticed, she had wondered, how could such a person go unhelped, in a small, close-knit place like Springfield? After talking with Schaefer, she said, she knew.

Their conversation had led her to believe that Schaefer's fury was the product of a painful childhood, Mrs. Fenton said. Respect for his privacy prevented her going into detail, but she did not think of Schaefer as a monster, Mrs. Fenton assured a reporter.

"The best thing we got out of the conversation was an understanding of who he was as a person," she went on. "Gary is a very troubled person and he very definitely needs all our prayers."

Schaefer's confession and plea were acts of responsibility, Mrs. Fenton said, and she appreciated what she saw in him as a growing conscience. He had seemed interested in understanding how Theresa's death had affected other people. The Fentons' talk with him had seemed to heal some of their pain, she said.

"We were able to put a lot behind us," Mrs. Fenton said. "Not all of it. We'll never be able to put all of it behind us."

After it was all over, after Schaefer had admitted kidnapping Dana Thurston, Joe Estey went back through the boxes of case records trying to see if there had been any way they could have made the connection to Schaefer, caught him earlier, prevented the death of Caty Richards. Even in hindsight he could find nothing they could have done, nothing they should have done. Maybe there was a professional sense of relief in that. Otherwise, though, it did nothing at all to make anyone involved in the investigation feel much better about it. Nothing was going to help Caty Richards and the people who had loved her.

John Halpin never got over the failure to catch Schaefer after the kidnapping of Dana Thurston. Even nine years later, when he was asked about the case, he said he had just been reminiscing about it a few days earlier with Mike LeClair.

"That is one of the most frustrating things [in my career]," Halpin said. "I think about it almost every day."

Mike LeClair and John Philpin searched for their own kinds of understanding. LeClair had sat with Gary Schaefer in his mother's kitchen the day of the arrest and urged him to ease his conscience by confessing. LeClair had studied Schaefer all through the months of legal maneuvering, and after the sentencing he had written to Schaefer, describing what he thought had happened and once again encouraging him to offer a full confession.

In a series of jailhouse discussions with LeClair, Philpin, and various prison officials during the following months, Schaefer talked of the girls who had died, returning repeatedly to what he said were merely fragmented memories and conjecture about what had happened to them. LeClair became convinced that Schaefer had killed Sheri Nastasia: ultimately, in one of five long conversations with Philpin, Schaefer offered what seemed like a confession. He was charged with second-degree murder.

It all came to nothing. Schaefer's statements were eventually ruled inadmissible in court; a judge decided that LeClair and Philpin had manipulated Schaefer into confessing. The charges were dismissed.

The lack of a resolution in the death of Sheri Nastasia gnawed at Mike LeClair, a continuing professional and personal affront. More than a decade after the day he had rushed to Springfield to help the local police investigate the disappearance of a thirteen-year-old girl, LeClair's voice still rose slightly and took on a hard, passionate tone when he talked about the case.

"I'd still like to go back and do Schaefer again," he said. "And I might just do that some day." It almost sounded as if LeClair were challenging Gary Schaefer, letting him know that justice was not finished with him yet.

"I really would like to know," LeClair said, "for experience purposes, what motivates him and exactly how and why he committed the crimes he did. Because that would be very valuable in working homicide cases for detectives for a hundred years to come."

If they knew how long a killer like Schaefer kept his victim captive, how far he drove with her, what he did and where, they might know better how to react the next time a victim was taken, where to put the roadblocks, how long to leave them, how far away to check for a suspicious car.

But beyond that, it seemed, LeClair was driven by a simple need for knowledge. In part it was simply the facts that he craved, the satisfaction of knowing which theories, which deductions and guesses and speculations, had been right, and which had been wrong. But there was something else, as well, the need finally to look evil in the face and understand something of its source.

The case was closed, but it would never be finished. There would never be a full description of what had happened between Gary Schaefer and his victims.

eleven

The appetite in the Valley for information about Gary Schaefer and his crimes seemed insatiable, and yet for most people he remained an enigma. But not to John Philpin.

Philpin had read and reread the vast file, talked to family members and friends of Schaefer, interviewed Schaefer himself at length on five occasions, and pursued his research on serial killers and sexual psychopaths.

Schaefer had grown up within a strict family. His mother, in particular, was remembered as "extremely demanding," and there were stories of severe physical punishment by his father. The Schaefers attended worship services and other church functions at least three nights a week, in addition to Sundays. The children were discouraged from socializing, even talking, with children in the community who were not members of the church.

Forced back on their own company, a small group of family members and closely related Schaefer children had played together. When he was around school age, old enough to run with the group, Gary gradually became exceptionally close with one of these children, Anna, who was several years older. Over the next few years he became dependent on Anna, insisted on being with her in every spare moment. Especially through the long free days of summer, Gary followed Anna and her friends around like a faithful puppy. He seemed to prefer Anna's company to that of children his own age. Others recalled at least one summer when Gary and Anna took off their clothes and played for hours in a cemetery near where they lived, running naked among the tombstones. The connection with Anna became pivotal in Gary's life.

Some of Gary's relatives believed his relationship with Anna eventually became sexual, incestuous. Schaefer himself recalled an incident in the cemetery, before he was an adolescent, in which Anna and another girl stripped his clothes off and forced him to perform sexual acts with them. The combination of the child's mysterious sexual excitement and humiliating impotence became a defining memory for the man. It was not clear whether this incident had actually happened, but the memory, invented or not, had become for Schaefer a metaphor for sexual betrayal and a symbol of the need to avenge his humiliation.

The relationship with Anna took on a powerful intensity for Gary, so that as they later grew apart he felt that she was taking away something he could not bear to lose. As she moved on into adolescence and began dating, she quickly lost interest in the friends and activities of her youth, and especially in Gary. Before long she became pregnant. Hearing the news, proof of Anna's sexual intimacy with someone else, Gary became deeply upset; afterward his almost worshipful attachment to Anna was inverted into ceaseless hostility. His anger was transparent. Still emotionally and sexually immature, he felt abandoned, desperate at his loss.

Philpin, having assembled the story, recalled a psychologist's comment about rapists: "Some rapists harbor chronic excessive hostility toward the significant female figures in their early life development, particularly the mother, or in some instances an older sister or aunt." And certainly, Philpin thought, someone as close as Anna.

Schaefer's problems in the Navy, hinted at in the notation on the court documents, turned out to be charges of arson and illegal use of drugs, Valium and Demerol, stolen from the infirmary where he worked. He had been found guilty and sentenced to two years at hard labor.

There were other reports that associated these incidents with marital and sexual problems. In addition, three separate reports surfaced linking Schaefer to sexual molestation of female relatives, two of them children.

One attack took place within months of the abduction of Dana Thurston and bore a striking similarity to that incident. Schaefer drove the young woman around before parking in a rest area off the interstate highway, where he forced her to perform oral sex and other acts. When she attempted to resist, she said, Schaefer became furious and reached under the dash for something. The young woman thought it sounded like a heavy metal object. She was saved when another car drove into the rest area. Schaefer drove her home without saying another word.

Another report turned up: Schaefer had been arrested and identified in a lineup in 1974 as the man who attempted to abduct a thirteen-year-old girl in his car in Massachusetts; the charges were dropped when the girl's parents refused to subject her to the trauma of a trial.

This was the local man Philpin had imagined a year earlier, living with his family, his psychological life dominated by his mother, uncomfortable with his peers but at ease with young people because his age and experience gave him the means with which to impress them. The fixation on young girls, in particular, seemed tied to the intense, probably sexual and incestuous, relationship with Anna, and Gary's perception of betrayal in her withdrawal and marriage.

Here, too, connected to the idea of betrayal, was the fantasy of humiliation Philpin had foreseen, the terrible fear of subjection attached to a young girl through the degrading assault by Anna and her friend in the cemetery. And from that arose the fantasies of revenge, reprisal for betrayal and humiliation both real and imagined. There was one remarkable piece of evidence: investigators collected photographs of Schaefer's victims, his wife, and a married woman with whom he had had an affair. All of the women resembled Anna as an adolescent.

Schaefer's methods of stalking and killing corresponded neatly to Philpin's imagined picture of Theresa Fenton's killer. Schaefer had cruised the roads of Vermont hour after hour, searching for the perfect victim to play a role in his fantasy of revenge. His rituals of death and vengeance, enacted against young girls, incorporated the elements of pseudoreligious ceremony that Philpin had sensed in the woods. And Philpin had correctly anticipated that the killer's anxiety would expose him to the suspicion of those close to him: Schaefer's brother had accused him of killing Theresa Fenton. After the arrest, Joe Estey had compared Philpin's profile point by point with what was known about Gary Schaefer: thirty-one of thirty-nine points had matched Schaefer exactly.

In a sense Philpin had known Schaefer before he met him. That in itself gave the psychologist's work a slightly eerie feeling. But with it came an enduring sadness. Since the moment he heard on the phone of Caty Richards's fate, the deaths of Schaefer's victims had cast a pall over Philpin's analysis; no matter how good his profile, it had not been sufficient to save the life of a child.

The pursuit of Gary Schaefer had transformed Philpin's casual diversion into a profession. The publicity from his unpaid work on the profile in the Fenton case had brought him requests for help from police departments and private individuals throughout New England. He began work on a doctoral degree in forensic psychology.

"He's a psychological Sherlock Holmes," said a police detective Philpin had worked with on another case. "He's a wizard. When he's on somebody's tail, they better look out."

"Each time I get a new case, I'm completely immersed in it," Philpin told a reporter a year after the capture of Gary Schaefer. "I'm waiting for one that is the total challenge. I don't feel I've been challenged as I could be."

Philpin could not know that he would soon be drawn into a case that would test his skills to their limit and push him to the brink of a personal crisis beyond anything he could now imagine.

The death of Caty Richards, the capture of Gary Schaefer, and the link to Theresa Fenton and Sheri Nastasia symbolized the beginning of a change in the life of the Connecticut Valley that would soon come to seem inexorable and irreversible.

Caty Richards's mother spoke for parents who had children to worry about, but she might as well have been speaking for everyone in the southern part of the Connecticut Valley, where Gary Schaefer and his crimes had grown to dominate public consciousness over the last several years. They had learned something from the deaths of children and the capture of Gary

Schaefer that would never go away: "All parents will have to be cautious forever and forever," she said.

The idea of a person who could kill again and again, randomly, without motive, had once belonged to other places, other people's lives. Once the people of the Valley had lived with an innocent confidence that theirs was a place of rare peace in an ever harsher world. Gary Schaefer had shaken that confidence like a scream in the night. And now, a few miles away, events were taking shape that would destroy it forever.

Book III

Connections

twelve

People who were close to Eva Morse knew there had been times in the past when she had every reason to run away, just leave it all behind, give up, go somewhere else and hope it might be better. If she had done it then, no one would have been surprised. If the cops had treated her as a runaway back then, reacted slowly, figuring she'd come back when she was ready, or not at all, and that was her privilege, no one would have thought much of it. But now it was different.

Now that time was past. You would never say she had solved all her problems, or magically turned her life into the kind of smooth and easy middle-class dream she saw on television, not by a long shot, but things were definitely looking up. And of course, there was Jenny.

Eva Morse had a lot to overcome, although things had started out well enough. Her mother, Marie, came from a big, close-knit French-Canadian family in New Brunswick. The Ferlands had been going south to New Hampshire in search of work for decades and there was a good deal of visiting back and forth. There always seemed to be a lot of people around, especially in the summer, when relatives gathered and there was singing and dancing in the evenings.

In the summer of 1955, Marie needed a change of scene.

Her husband, Daniel, was an inveterate drinker and gambler, often disappearing for months at a time. Now they were separated and Marie was thirty-five years old, with children two, ten, and eleven years old. She decided to take the children south to visit with an uncle who lived in Charlestown, New Hampshire, along the banks of the Connecticut River. Soon after they arrived, someone arranged a blind date for Marie with a local man, Darwin Fuller.

Darwin was forty-four and had never been married. At first no one thought there was anything more than friendship between them, but after she went back to Canada he came to visit, and once he returned to New Hampshire he phoned Marie regularly. Eventually he persuaded her to come visit in New Hampshire again, and when they finally did get married, they were already expecting a child, Marie's fourth. It turned out to be a boy, and they named him Frank. A year later they had another one, a girl. They named her Eva.

Eva was a beautiful baby, with distinct features in a round face and lots of dark hair. "She looked like a little Eskimo," one member of the family recalled.

There was a sad irony in the fact that Eva should have been an unusually pretty baby, because once she was old enough to be aware of her looks they became a source of unhappiness that never left her in all her brief life. "I don't think she was ever as pretty in her whole life as when she was born," the family member said.

The Fullers lived in Charlestown, just across the river from Springfield, Vermont, where Darwin worked as a machinist at Bryant Grinder. Marie tried to keep up the traditions of her family from Canada, with a big family gathering for Thanksgiving dinner and a Christmas supper by candlelight.

Eva, the youngest, often seemed to stand apart from the gaiety. It was hard to remember a time when she wasn't overweight, the frequent brunt of children's teasing and the pitying glances of adults. Soon she was playing more with the boys than the girls in the neighborhood. In spite of her weight she was active and energetic, a strong swimmer and tireless hiker. She was tough and unafraid, removing her thick glasses to block and tackle with the boys in football games.

In elementary school Eva wore skirts and dresses like the

other girls, but as she became more self-conscious about her weight she came to prefer long pants to cover her legs and a sweatshirt or flannel shirt to conceal her bulk. She didn't seem to care if her clothes looked messy or there were holes in her jeans.

Much of Eva's development seemed to escape her mother. Marie had never seemed to recover completely after Eva's birth. She worked full-time at the Sylvania plant in Hillsborough, but she was anemic, often ill, and had little energy for close supervision of the children. The two youngest ones, Frank and Eva, were on their own a lot, and Eva's weight seemed a signal that something important was missing in her life.

When Eva was twelve, Marie died; she was fifty years old. In the next few years, everybody noticed a change in Eva. The three older children ranged from seventeen to twenty-six by then and had little to do with their half brother and half sister. With Darwin working, there was no one to watch over Eva and her brother, Frank.

Eva was getting old enough now to spend more time away from home, and soon she was spending it with people that nobody approved of, doing poorly in school, skipping classes, coming home late at night. After Darwin remarried, things seemed to get worse. His new wife, Lucille, wanted to start fresh. She seemed to have little interest in the children of Darwin's first marriage.

The first of Marie's five children, Noreen, had been fourteen when Eva was born, and from the start she had thought of Eva as more like her daughter than her sister. Noreen married Bob Campbell when she was sixteen and gave birth to her own first child within a year. After Marie died, Noreen and her husband moved to Connecticut, so she was no longer in a position to do much with Eva. Eva moved in with Joyce, the second of Marie's five children, who was thirteen years older than Eva. Joyce did what she could, but Eva seemed beyond her reach now, not a bad or dangerous adolescent, just adrift, living in a world no adult could enter.

In the late spring of 1975, around the time of her seventeenth birthday, Eva brought up the subject of babies with Joyce. It was an odd conversation, but nobody read any significance into it at the time.

"What would you do if I showed up with a baby?" she asked at last.

"I'd boot your butt right out of here, that's what I'd do," Joyce answered, not giving the subject much thought at all.

Noreen and Bob Campbell had moved back to Charlestown from Connecticut a few months earlier. The day after Father's Day, Frank, the brother who was just a year older than Eva, came by to tell Noreen that Eva was in the Claremont hospital. She had just given birth to a baby. He didn't have any more news than that, but he was on his way up to their father's house to find out what had happened.

As Noreen and her husband walked up the stairs to the second floor of the hospital, they heard screaming echoing down the stairwell. Noreen recognized her half sister's voice.

At the nurse's station Noreen identified herself and told the nurse they had come to see Eva Morse.

"Oh," the nurse said, "it's so sad. She's not prepared to give that baby away. Can't anybody in the family do something?" Eva's father had told the doctors that she would not be able to manage the baby by herself and that no one in the family was in a position to help her.

"Well," Noreen answered, "I'll see what I can do."

It had been more than twelve hours and Eva had not seen the baby yet. The hospital authorities had told her that because of her age she would have to give the baby up for adoption. She had been raging against the decision, insisting on seeing the baby.

"I want my baby," she cried when Noreen entered the room. As she calmed down and they began talking about what had happened, Eva turned her eyes away. She seemed ashamed.

"Please don't hate me," she pleaded with her half sister.

"I don't hate you," Noreen replied, "how could I hate you? But why did you go through this alone? Why didn't you come to me?"

Eva recounted the conversation with Joyce. She had taken Joyce's offhand comment as a blanket condemnation. "I thought if she wouldn't understand," Eva told Noreen, "you wouldn't either."

At seventeen, Eva was close to five feet seven inches tall and weighed over 180 pounds. Her weight had hidden her pregnancy from sight, and her fear and sense of isolation had kept her from sharing the secret even with those closest to her.

Noreen was devastated, imagining the gulf that they had allowed to grow between Eva and the rest of the family.

"I was totally crushed," Noreen recalled, many years later. "It was like somebody had hit me in the stomach with a sledgehammer. I just couldn't believe that she'd gone through that alone and never felt she could talk to me, never felt that I would understand."

The memory of her half sister's loneliness would return again and again over the years, made ever more poignant by later events.

Noreen talked with Eva about the responsibilities of raising a baby, how difficult it would be for a young girl on her own, but Eva was adamant: she wanted to keep the baby. Noreen arranged with a social worker for Eva to be declared an emancipated minor, which freed her from parental control. Eva and the baby, a girl she named Jenny, stayed temporarily with a friend. Soon after, when Noreen had gotten a place of her own, they moved in with her. Jenny's father, it turned out, was Bennie Willis, a boy Eva's age who lived in the neighborhood; his parents didn't want anything to do with Eva and the baby, and he wasn't in any position to do much for them himself, though after a while he started coming to see the baby from time to time.

Eva stayed on with Noreen and continued in high school, but her performance didn't improve and she showed little interest in studying. There didn't seem to be anything dramatic in her life, good or bad. Gradually, though, her family became aware of something unsettling. Eva was spending a lot of time with a girl named Sandy, and slowly it came to seem different from the usual friendship. Eva appeared obsessed with Sandy, spending every minute with her when she wasn't taking care of Jenny. Eventually Noreen spoke with Eva about it. Eva didn't quite know how to say it herself, but in the end it became clear: Eva was in love with Sandy.

The surprising thing about Eva's sexual orientation, those close to her came to feel, was how unsurprising it was after they thought about it. She had never been very feminine in any traditional way, and as one of Marie's aunts said, it was no wonder she had turned to women, after the way men had treated her. After all, Darwin had seemed to abandon her after he remarried, and even the father of her child had done the same.

Her brothers and sisters came to view Eva's lesbian life with varying degrees of acceptance. Noreen found that, as much as she wanted to support her youngest sister, she could never bring herself to approve. Still, she told Eva, she loved her no matter what she did.

Eventually Eva found a place of her own and moved out. She dated men, but her lovers were women. There was a small society of gay people in the Valley, with a few bars scattered around where they could gather and feel comfortable. Eva left school without graduating and took a low-paying job in a small factory.

Over the next several years, Eva changed jobs and lovers, but there was one constant in her life: she was devoted to Jenny. Though she lived in cheap apartments and never had much extra money, she provided for her daughter as well as she could and included her in whatever she was doing.

Eva never had enough money for a car, but she hitchhiked constantly. She always seemed able to catch a ride over the short distances between Charlestown and wherever she worked, and she developed a reputation for being punctual. She visited her brothers and sisters occasionally, bringing Jenny along to see her aunts and uncles and cousins, and she even wrote an occasional note or short letter to let Noreen know what was going on. But Eva's unconventional life and the crowd of outsiders who had become her closest friends raised a wall between her and the rest of the family. By the time she was in her mid-twenties, Eva seemed settled in her separate world. It was as if her sexual orientation, along with her obesity and mannish clothes, had formed a kind of armor, protecting her against the demands and expectations of a world she had never fit into very well.

That was why it was so surprising when she started showing signs of wanting to change her life. She had been living for some time with a woman named Carol Wilcox. Though Eva seemed dependent on Carol, the relationship had been turbulent, with periodic fights and occasional public scenes. Carol was impatient with Jenny; some thought she was jealous of Eva's devotion to her daughter.

And then it appeared that Eva was trying to separate herself from Carol. In the spring of 1985 she moved out of the apartment where they had been living together. Carol didn't want Jenny around, and for Eva, Jenny came first, before anything else in her life. They moved in with Rose Treat, a childhood friend who had remained loyal to Eva through all the times of disarray in her life. Noreen was living now in Keene, twenty-five miles away at the southern end of the Valley, and Eva wrote her half sister to say that she was trying to turn her life around.

When Eva finally came with Jenny to visit Noreen, she had some surprising news: she had begun dating a young man from Springfield. Eva looked different, too, her half sister noticed. She looked as if she had started paying attention to her appearance. She had a new hairdo and she was wearing a blouse that seemed more feminine than her usual shirts. She talked of a diet and she had already lost some weight. The visible changes in Eva were striking, Noreen thought, but even more significant were the pride and determination in her voice.

In June the family gathered to celebrate Jenny's tenth birthday. Eva had saved to buy her daughter a ten-speed bike. It was hard to tell which of them was happier: Eva's expression as she watched Jenny ride the bike glowed with her pride at being able to give her daughter such an expensive gift. Noreen took a lot of pictures at the party, and Eva talked about getting some time off from work soon. She wanted Noreen to meet her and Jenny one day for a picnic at a park in Surry.

Noreen was in Maine a little more than three weeks later, taking care of her mother-in-law for a few days, when her husband called from home. The Charlestown police had called to ask if they knew where Eva was. She had disappeared.

Noreen's first reaction came with a rush of fear: "It must be something bad, because she would never, ever, take off and leave Jenny without making sure she was taken care of."

The investigation of Eva Morse's disappearance was slow getting started. Though its population had almost doubled in twenty years, Charlestown was still a small place, with forty-five hundred people and a police department to match, three officers. It was manned only in daytime, and never with more than one man at a time. And the chief, the only experienced full-time officer, was on vacation when the first report came in from Rose Treat, the old friend Eva and Jenny had been staying with. The officer on duty when the call came was Bob Campbell, the former husband of Eva's half sister Noreen. Noreen herself had worked for a few years as a dispatcher in the department, and Bob was a part-time officer there.

Eva hadn't come home after work, Rose reported. She had left for work in the morning at her usual time, setting out to hitchhike the eight miles south to the J. H. Dunning box factory in North Walpole.

The investigation showed that Eva had arrived at work on time, at 7:00 A.M., but hadn't punched her time card. She made a phone call and then told a supervisor that she was sick and was going home, but someone who spoke with her had gotten the idea that she was going up to Claremont to see Carol Wilcox, her former lover.

The first stories that surfaced made Eva Morse look like someone who had good reason to take off and leave her life behind. Someone who worked with her said she had been depressed lately, and a friend said she had talked of going to Connecticut to learn how to run a bulldozer so she could get a better-paying job. There was a story that she had gone away once before without making arrangements for Jenny.

Charlestown was a small place and almost everybody had known Eva since she was a child. Some of their comments implied that Eva's friends were not the most responsible group and you could hardly expect anything different from Eva herself. There were hints that Eva had been upset about the breakup with Carol Wilcox. The consensus seemed to be that there was no great surprise in one of "those people" disappearing without warning.

Eva's half sister Noreen thought differently. It was several days before she could arrange to leave her mother-in-law's bedside in Maine to return home. Back in Keene she was disturbed to find that nothing about Eva's disappearance had appeared in the local newspapers. No one seemed to be taking the case seriously. Everyone, it seemed, police and friends and townspeople, was convinced that Eva was gone by choice.

Noreen was certain that they were wrong, and Rose Treat agreed. In conventional terms Eva's life was no model of success and happiness, but there was one thing that outweighed all the failure and discouragement, and that was her devotion to her daughter. Eva would not have left without providing for Jenny, no matter what anyone said about the past.

Noreen drove to Claremont the next day and put an ad in the *Eagle Times*. It included a description of Eva and the clothes she was wearing when she left home, a light blue windbreaker and jeans. The ad cost Noreen $14.80.

Alerted by the ad, the *Eagle-Times* sent a reporter to look into the story. On July 19 a front-page headline announced, "Whereabouts of missing Charlestown woman baffles police." It had been ten days since Eva Morse had disappeared.

The story reported that the police thought the disappearance of Eva Morse was different from the case of Ellen Fried, the young nurse who had been reported missing a year earlier after her car was found by the side of a dirt road in Claremont.

"There is nothing like a car left behind in this case to give you a place to start with," the investigating officer told the *Eagle-Times* reporter. They were searching the most likely spots along the Connecticut River, he said, but it didn't seem likely they would turn up anything.

"It's a lot of territory to cover," he said. "I could bring in the dogs, but where would we start?"

It was several days more before posters and fliers were put into circulation.

At seven-fifteen on a Wednesday morning in August, a little more than a month after Eva Morse had disappeared, police set up a roadblock outside the J. H. Dunning plant, hoping to find someone who might have been at the same place at the same time on the last day anyone had seen Eva Morse.

Among the drivers who were stopped and shown a picture of Eva Morse was a man who hardly glanced at it before he looked up at the officer.

"Oh, yeah, I saw her," he said. "On Washington Street. She was hitchhiking."

Not the day they were asking about, he said. Three weeks later.

There was no question that it was Eva Morse, the man said. He had grown up in Charlestown and gone to high school with Eva. She had been trying to get a ride eastward from Claremont toward Newport.

The report was puzzling, since it seemed unlikely that Eva

would have remained so near to home without contacting Jenny or being seen by someone else who knew her, but it raised the hope that she might still be in the area. It was the only grounds for hope that anybody could think of. Otherwise, the roadblock produced no leads.

But soon afterward a woman came forward in response to the publicity to report that she had picked up a hitchhiker who fit Eva's description outside the Dunning plant early in the morning on July 10. They headed north, toward Charlestown, where Eva Morse lived, but her passenger had made no move to get out.

The hitchhiker seemed to be going to Claremont, the woman thought, but she could only take her as far as the veterinary clinic where she worked, at Knight's Hill near the Charlestown-Claremont line. When the woman went inside the clinic her passenger was standing by the side of the road, thumbing a ride to continue her trip northward. Five minutes later the woman looked out the window of the clinic. The hitchhiker was gone.

Around that time Eva's half sister Noreen finished shooting the roll of film in her camera and dropped it off for processing. When she picked up the prints, they included the shots she had taken at Jenny's birthday party. She couldn't remember when she had last seen Eva looking so happy.

Now that it is possible to look back, to make chronologies and tie one event to another, it seems a conspicuous fact that at that point there were three young women who had disappeared from a very small geographical area within a short time. Now the three events bunch together, their similarities making them stand out like the three brightest stars in the night sky. In 1985, things were not so clear.

When Eva Morse disappeared, it had been a little more than a year since Bernice Courtemanche, the Claremont High School girl, set out to hitchhike to Newport to meet her boyfriend at his sister's house and never arrived. Less than two months after that, Ellen Fried, who worked as a nurse at the Valley Regional Hospital in Claremont, had put down the pay phone after a late-night conversation with her sister and vanished.

The police made only the most tentative connection between

Ellen Fried's disappearance and the earlier case of Bernice Courtemanche, and the newspapers followed suit. In the stories about Ellen Fried, there was no mention of Bernice Courtemanche.

The disappearance of Eva Morse, rather than focusing the speculation, seemed to scatter new possibilities into the mixture. It was almost exactly a year since Ellen Fried's car had been found abandoned, it doors locked, on Jarvis Lane. In that time the aggressive pursuit of a break in the two earlier cases had given way to a kind of detached watchfulness. There were obvious resemblances between certain aspects of Eva Morse's disappearance and the two earlier cases: the other two women had been seen last in Claremont, less than a mile apart, and Eva outside the veterinary clinic, only eight miles south. Like the others, Eva was a woman alone and on the road, and like Bernice Courtemanche she was hitchhiking.

But investigators noticed the differences first. Bernice Courtemanche and Ellen Fried had been leading apparently stable, conventional lives, with jobs, boyfriends, daily routines. Eva Morse had moved from job to job, changed her residence frequently, associated with a rough crowd. She had been on the fringe of trouble with the law: there had been a dispute and some people had broken into her apartment, roughed her up, and threatened to kidnap her daughter, Jenny.

And there was the issue of her sexual orientation. It was a sensitive matter, and no one could ever be sure how much it figured into the calculation, but the fact that Eva Morse was a lesbian made her seem more vulnerable, more likely to get in trouble, exposed to a whole different set of dangers from those that would affect the other two young women. For the police in the Valley, the facts of the three cases, rather than drawing them into a single pattern, seemed to separate them from each other.

That wasn't John Philpin's reaction. The psychologist had the grim authority of his experience with the Gary Schaefer killings to move his mind toward the vision of a pattern in the three disappearances. Schaefer had been in jail six months when Ellen Fried disappeared and Philpin took out a file folder, wrote her name on it, and combined the newspaper clippings he had saved about Bernice Courtemanche with the new ones about Ellen Fried.

The experience with Schaefer was still fresh in Philpin's mind after Ellen Fried vanished, when he suggested the existence of another serial killer to Mike LeClair. And a year later, when Eva Morse disappeared, it was just three months since the final charges against Schaefer had been dismissed. Reading the newspaper stories about Eva Morse, Philpin reacted without hesitating:

"That's number three," he thought.

There was a report that Eva had been on her way to see her former lover, Carol Wilcox, either seeking a reconciliation or trying to resolve an angry disagreement, nobody was sure which. Wilcox lived on the west side of Claremont, in the section called Beauregard Village. Leo's Market, where Ellen Fried had used the pay phone to call her sister in California just before she disappeared, was in West Claremont. The place where the Sugar River had rushed over its banks beneath Bernice Courtemanche's feet as she crossed the bridge from Beauregard Village to begin hitchhiking to Newport was about a mile north of Leo's Market, also in West Claremont.

John Philpin cut the stories about Eva Morse out of the newspaper and slipped them in with the clippings from the other two cases in the file labeled *Ellen Fried*.

What Philpin and the police involved with the three disappearances did have in common was a kind of heightened attention. It wasn't exactly like waiting for the other shoe to drop, not like the feeling the detectives had lived with in Springfield after Theresa Fenton's death, but for Philpin and some of the people who were closest to the cases there was at least a sense of anticipation, the beginnings of a curiosity about what might happen next.

thirteen

Most of the time the police radio was like white noise, intermittent bursts of routine business that barely touched the consciousness of the men and women in the police station.

Then, every once in a while, something changed, a little edge of urgency pushed its way into the normally laconic tone of the officers on the air, the pace picked up. At those times conversation in the station became tentative, concentration on other matters wavered, attention poised to fasten on the next word from the monitor. Something was happening.

This was one of those times. And there was nothing Mike Prozzo could do about it.

Ever since he had sat as a child on a Washington Street stoop and blown his police whistle at drivers who were speeding, Prozzo had felt a part of everything that went on in Claremont. Now he had been chief of detectives close to four years and his sense of involvement had taken the form of a professional commitment.

Three women had disappeared in fourteen months, two from Claremont, the other from just over the line in Charlestown. The last was Eva Morse, a little more than two months ago. They were three cases Prozzo had worked on from the start. He had followed up an endless procession of leads and theories, checked out every teletype from anywhere in the country about a body that might be one of the missing women, and all the work had produced nothing but questions.

Now Prozzo's instinct was telling him that the radio calls he was hearing on this otherwise routine Thursday afternoon were going to bring some answers. But as the calls followed one after the other through the afternoon, all he could do was listen. The calls were from Newport, the next town to the east, just eight miles away but outside Prozzo's jurisdiction. They wouldn't need him there, and more important, they wouldn't want him.

The transmissions had started with the first officer on the scene, which was in a section of Newport called Kellyville. He had called for detectives. Through the afternoon the summons had gone out for state police detectives, the county medical referee, and a representative from the state attorney general's office.

Prozzo called the Newport station to find out what was going on; at least he could do that much. The dispatcher said that two men had been target shooting, walking in the woods, when they found some bones. They looked like human remains.

The Claremont detective was itching to go have a look, but you had to be careful. Newport was a city but it had less than half the population of Claremont and people were sensitive about being overshadowed by their bigger neighbor. The two towns were only eight miles apart and there was a constant flow back and forth along the conjoined Routes 11 and 103 over the low hills between them; in a way, that only increased the possibilities for tension. There had been bad feelings between the two police departments in the past, Claremont cops taking on borderline cases when they thought Newport didn't have the manpower to get involved, then Newport officers feeling slighted and resentful. At one point the chiefs of the two departments had been barely able to conceal their antagonism toward each other. Things were better now, and Prozzo wanted to keep it that way. Whatever the temptation, he wasn't going to get involved until he was asked. He hung around the station all day, just in case Newport should call him in, but nothing happened.

It was later in the evening, after he had gone home, that the call came. Arthur Bastian, the chief in Newport, invited Prozzo to come to his house in Claremont.

The remains had been found in the woods near the Sugar River, he told Prozzo. The abandoned track bed of the Claremont and Concord Railway, now used as a jogging path, ran along the river. The little heap of bones had been found on a hillside about fifty feet from the path. An ancient hemlock tree lay upended, its huge tangle of roots torn from the ground. They had sawed off a five-foot section of the trunk to get at the remains.

If the driver of a vehicle wanted to get as far into the woods as possible, away from Routes 11 and 103, the spot on the abandoned track bed adjacent to the remains was where he would have to stop. A tributary stream, Sparrow Brook, ran into the river there, cutting across the railroad's right-of-way; the bridge across the brook had decayed, leaving only four heavy beams studded with railroad spikes. It would have been a drive of about a mile. Someone trying to reach the spot on foot directly from the highway would pass the Flexit Shoe Factory out near the road and then make his way through about a half mile of woods and brush.

The remains consisted only of bones; the flesh had long since disintegrated. There was a single sandal. And that was it. There was nothing to help with an identification of the bones. In fact, it never paid to leap to a conclusion; they might not even be human remains. More than once some citizen had reported finding what he feared were human bones in the woods and they turned out to be a deer or cow, or even a dog.

"We don't know exactly what we've got," an assistant attorney general announced.

New Hampshire, famous for its frugality and sparse public services, had no medical examiner. The remains would be sent to the state lab in Concord. The lab would farm parts of the task out to specialists as necessary. It would be some time, a week or more, before they had any answers.

Prozzo had picked out selected materials from the case files on the three missing women to show to the Newport chief. Bastian, a smallish, stocky man with a sober demeanor, fixed his attention on the flier about Ellen Fried.

"Mike," he said, "I'd bet you that's her." He poked a blunt finger at the photo of Ellen Fried.

There hadn't been anything with the skeletal remains that would allow a quick identification. Nobody had known what Ellen Fried was wearing when she disappeared; she had last been seen leaving the hospital and nobody knew if she had changed from her nurse's whites. It had to be a hunch. Maybe it was the sandal, some remote association with Fried's style; people had characterized her life away from work with the word *hippie*.

"I'll bet you a hundred dollars that's her," Bastian said.

It was Ellen Fried.

The news was released twelve days after the discovery of the remains. The announcement had been held up briefly so that Fried's parents, who lived in New York State, could be informed.

The Frieds had remained close to the investigation. A few months before she disappeared, Ellen had taken her parents around Claremont, pointing out favorite sites in her new home, enjoying the chance to display for her parents the dimensions of her independence. After her disappearance, the Frieds had driven to Claremont to tour the city with detectives, trying to identify places Ellen had showed them that might provide leads in the search. They had placed a paid ad in a Claremont weekly paper, asking for word of their daughter. "Help us find her," the ad had concluded. They had kept the ad running for ten months; it had stopped appearing in May, only four months before the remains were discovered in Kellyville.

A dentist in Concord had identified the remains by comparing the teeth with dental records of the three missing women. An autopsy by a forensic pathologist had not been able to determine what caused Fried's death. There were no broken bones that could be attributed to a weapon. The assistant attorney general in charge of the case announced that the investigation would consider all the possibilities: accident, suicide, and homicide.

"There's a lot of unanswered questions," the assistant attorney general told a reporter. "Almost all of the questions are unanswered."

The investigators had little doubt; they were working on a murder case. The attorney general's office might be cagey about it, and there was no specific evidence of homicide, but it was hard to imagine what kind of accident could have left Ellen Fried's body to molder in the woods, she wasn't the type to commit suicide, and there was nothing in the remains to suggest either event.

Officers worked into the night searching the area around the place where the bones had been found. The brilliant glare of the Newport Fire Department's emergency lights looked incongruously harsh against the soft early-fall outlines of the forest. The search went on for several days, but nothing further turned up. Another search, this time with metal detectors, also failed to produce anything useful. Any lead would have to come from some other source.

In the following days, officers in pairs went door-to-door, first along the dirt road on the other side of the Sugar River, then working their way back to Routes 11 and 103. At each house they introduced themselves, mentioned the discovery of the bones, and asked if the residents had noticed anything out of the ordinary, any strangers or unfamiliar vehicles in the area.

The officers, detectives from the Newport and Claremont departments and from the New Hampshire State Police, were working with several handicaps. The biggest was the length of time since Ellen Fried had disappeared. Even if her remains hadn't been in the woods the entire fourteen months, it was clear from the state of the bones that whatever had brought her there had taken place many months before.

Nobody seemed to remember anything specific related to the place where the remains had been found, but slowly, out of the welter of fragmentary memories, a name started to emerge.

A woman standing in her doorway would look away from the officers, avoiding their eyes, and say, "Have you talked to—you know—him?" waving vaguely toward a house off in the distance. A man, sitting in his living room with the two investigators, would offer, almost as an afterthought, "Ya know, there's a guy over here, kinda strange, you know, over by the brook," not wanting to say the name, looking at the detectives to see if they knew the man he was referring to, wanting to let them supply the name.

And suddenly, the police had a suspect in the death of Ellen Fried.

fourteen

The house stood out, even if you didn't know who lived there. It stood close to the road, with cornfields on both sides, nothing to block the view, so that when you came along Routes 11 and 103 from either direction, and especially through the old covered bridge and around the curve from Claremont, it loomed up out of the flat surrounding land, all towers and gables and turrets, a classic, brooding Victorian pile.

Even before the name of Richard Robert Bordeau became common currency, whispered a thousand times a day in the coffee-shop and street-corner conversations of Claremont and Newport, those who lived in the area felt a special chill in passing by, looking up at its dark, gabled front. Many children, even a few adults, referred to it as "the haunted house."

The house's dark, brooding façade seemed to give it a sinister aura, even in bright sunlight. But then, who could tell how much of that was just imagination, a shroud of mystery and menace thrown over an ordinary house by the reputation of the man who lived there?

Richard Bordeau was no stranger to the Claremont police, even before the discovery of Ellen Fried's remains. In late August, Virginia Troy, a waitress at the Mapleview Restaurant in Claremont, had come by the station. The Mapleview was just across the square from the police station in the center of Claremont; a lot of the cops stopped in regularly for coffee, and all of them knew Ginny Troy.

Some of them knew the guy she was talking about, too. A few months earlier he had applied for a job as a cook at the restaurant. Troy happened to be in charge at the time and took the application from him. He had been turned down for the job. Ever since, he had been writing her letters.

At first the letters merely seemed strange, even amusing. They were addressed *Dear Ginny,* and they had a chatty tone, with little nuggets of news about chores he was doing around the house, or how he had spent the previous afternoon. In each letter Bordeau asked her to go out with him. The letters seemed to have been written on a computer and they were signed by hand with a flourish:

Love, "King" Richard Robert Bordeaux

These were letters from one old friend to another. The problem was that except for taking his application and serving him coffee a few times, Virginia Troy had never talked to Richard Bordeau.

Ginny Troy never responded to the letters. She thought he would give up eventually.

It was when he wrote again and suggested that she sleep with him, and then started calling her on the phone, that she got worried, then scared. That was when she came to the police.

The complaint was assigned to Bill Wilmot, the young detective who had worked closely with Mike Prozzo on the disappearances of Bernice Courtemanche and Ellen Fried. Wilmot looked the letter-writer up in the phone book and found a discrepancy in the spelling: in the book he was listed as Bordeau, without an *x* on the end. Over the next few weeks Wilmot tried repeatedly to call him, without success.

Finally, in the middle of September, Wilmot wrote a note: "A matter has come to our attention that suggests I should speak to you personally," he told Bordeau, asking him to call the station.

Two days later, Bordeau phoned. Wilmot told him about Ginny Troy's concerns and asked him to stop writing to her.

Bordeau agreed without protest and Wilmot closed the file.

It was the following day that the two men taking shooting practice in the woods of Newport found the remains of a skeleton, and the entire department was soon immersed in the case of Ellen Fried. The timing was pure coincidence, but soon it became tempting to think it was something else. As the detectives fanned out around the site by the ruined hemlock tree, asking neighbors about anything out of the ordinary, their attention was directed again and again to Richard Robert Bordeau.

Between the site of the remains and the flat expanse of cornfield, the abandoned railroad right-of-way, the Sugar River, and Routes 11 and 103 ran in rough parallel, like three lengths of string stretched out and dropped on the ground. Upstream from the point where Sparrow Brook interrupted the railroad path near the downed hemlock and flowed into the Sugar River, before it drifted under the covered bridge over Routes 11 and 103, the wide stream ran lazily along, through the cornfields, twenty-five yards from the front door of Bordeau's house. Richard Bordeau lived less than a mile from the place where the remains of Ellen Fried had been found.

Richard Pillsbury, Bordeau's neighbor, told police he had seen Bordeau at night, walking up and down the road between their houses.

"He goes over by the brook there," Pillsbury told the officers. "He goes down by the water and talks out loud. You can hear him up on the road. I don't know, he must be talking to the fish or something." On one occasion he had been wearing a tuxedo.

There were times when Bordeau stood for long periods in front of neighbors' houses, staring at their windows, examining their cars. At other times, Pillsbury said, he would open a window and shout some unintelligible message into the night. Pillsbury was worried, for his children, for his wife, for himself. He asked the Newport police to patrol the area regularly.

Mike Prozzo had been one of the detectives asking questions house-to-house along the roads in Kellyville, getting together at the end of the day to pool their information and coordinate assignments for the next day. It was only a couple of days before all the investigators started getting more curious about Richard Bordeau.

Prozzo made a point of taking the big Victorian house for himself and a partner; he wanted to see Bordeau for himself, face-to-face, try to get a feel for what he was like.

Bordeau was sitting in his car in the driveway when the two detectives arrived. They introduced themselves and told him they were looking for information that might help with the case of the woman found in the nearby woods.

"Would you like to go in the house and talk?" Prozzo asked.

"No," he answered, "you do your note taking right here." He spoke in a deep bass voice, but it sounded forced, like a child impersonating an adult.

They asked Bordeau what he knew about Ellen Fried.

"I've seen the posters around town," he told them. "I saw her name. But I didn't know her."

The detectives questioned him about where he had been on the date of Fried's disappearance.

"I don't know," Bordeau replied. "I was probably working. I was working at Wentworth Shoe then. Or maybe I was at home, writing. I really have no idea."

He was familiar with the area where the remains had been found, he said in answer to a question. He went jogging along the old railroad right-of-way in the woods. He had seen the yellow tape the police used to close off the site where the remains had been found. And then he volunteered something that no one had asked.

"I used to run right by there," he said, "right by where she was, in the woods there. I didn't smell anything. There were no foul odors."

He was part of the crime-watch program, Bordeau told them. He called up the police whenever he thought there might be a crime going on.

"One time I heard machine-gun fire and I called the police."

They asked a few more questions but he didn't seem to have much he wanted to say.

"I tend to avoid people," he told them. "I don't like to be around people."

That seemed to be a good cue on which to end the interview.

"If you want to talk anymore, send me a letter," he said.

The visit had been inconclusive; it was hard to tell if Bor-

deau had been hostile or just inept at social interaction. Prozzo
was left with little but a vague impression of the man and a
heightened curiosity.

These were not small places, Newport and Claremont, certainly not by New Hampshire standards. Claremont was a city,
ninth in the state with its population of fifteen thousand, and
Newport the seventeenth-largest town, with a little over six
thousand. And within a week, they were talking about Richard
Bordeau.

Nearly everyone remembered seeing the house at some
time, hovering so dramatically over the road out there between
the two communities. It was easy to imagine that someone who
lived there could be implicated in a violent crime. There were
people who had gone to high school with Richard Bordeau,
who had worked with him at the Wentworth Shoe Company,
who had said hello on the street for years, people who fed
their anecdotes of Bordeau's eerie or eccentric behavior into
the stream of rumor. And now it was common knowledge: he
was a suspect in the killing of Ellen Fried.

As chief of detectives, Mike Prozzo was absorbing all the
reports of Richard Bordeau's strange behavior that were coming to the police. As a lifelong resident of the city, he was
hearing every rumor and casual fourth-hand account of Bordeau's strange and menacing actions that was circulating on
the streets. It was becoming obvious, Prozzo thought, that there
was a slow and powerful tide of fear flowing in the streets,
and it had become focused on Richard Robert Bordeau. No
question the guy was weird, Prozzo thought, but did that mean
he was capable of killing a young woman?

In the last three years Prozzo had talked with other cops in
the Valley about the three women who disappeared without a
trace, about other, similar cases, about Gary Schaefer and the
serial killings in Springfield, just a dozen miles south and
across the river in Vermont. In some of those conversations
there had been mention of a psychologist who helped out on
the Theresa Fenton case.

Prozzo had some things he wanted to talk about.

The theme of violence had flowed through John Philpin's life
like the deep thrumming of the double bass in a symphony,
always in the background, ominous and insistent.

From the arbitrary furies of his father to the reflexive hostility of the convicts he treated for the Vermont prison system, Philpin had been forced to confront the violence of others and the impulse within himself. In his forties he had long since come to terms with all this, but it was taking a toll.

The Springfield Police Department's request that he help out on the Fenton case had come along at just the right time for Philpin. He had been treating men the prison system lumped together as "sex offenders." It was one of those categorical terms that fogged over the thing it described: these were violent men, men who had hunted women and children as prey, who had molested and raped and beaten and sometimes killed their victims, and most of them had done these things once, and again, and again.

Much of the psychological literature said that successfully treating these men, sexual psychopaths, was one of the most difficult of all therapeutic tasks. The rest of the literature said it was impossible. What chance there was depended on keeping them locked up, under the control of prison authorities, obliged to participate in long-term treatment. Certainly there was little possibility of success with convicts who were required only to leave their cells for a therapy session once or twice, at most three times, a week.

John Philpin wasn't quite that pessimistic. Successful treatment, he thought, and with it some professional satisfaction, was difficult to achieve, but not impossible. The problem, Philpin had come to feel, was that he was part of a system in which the therapist had responsibility without control, without resources. Philpin had treated a number of convicts over long periods with what seemed to be success, continuing the therapy after they left prison on parole. But occasionally he had witnessed in one of these paroled men the chilling reemergence of some precursor of the original crime: a convicted rapist drives the highway and picks up a woman hitchhiking, a man who had served time for sexual abuse of children hangs around a schoolyard staring at young boys and girls.

Philpin was left with an impossible choice: cut off the treatment and see the man sent back to prison for violating his parole, or continue treatment and take the risk that the man would repeat his original crime. It was an intolerable choice with no middle ground, no means to temporarily tighten surveillance or increase treatment in times of danger.

More and more often, Philpin found himself in danger of watching a man he had treated go free to brutalize a woman or child, to rape, even to kill. It had never happened yet, but the threat seemed ever present. It was like standing on the edge of a cliff in a strong, gusting wind. Philpin felt he was being forced to gamble with other people's safety, to risk a kind of complicity in some horrifying attack on an innocent person. The burden of that risk had grown intolerable. When Joe Estey called in the fall of 1981 to ask his help in the case of Theresa Fenton, Philpin had begun to withdraw from the work with the prison department.

It wasn't that working with the police on unsolved crimes had removed him from the sphere of violence. In fact it was just the opposite. Early in their work on the Fenton case, Joe Estey had said something one day that made Philpin think he was speaking in code.

"We're gonna pull the jackets on all the types," the Springfield detective had said.

What Estey meant, Philpin found, was standard procedure for a major crime, picking out the police files of men who had committed crimes similar to the one under investigation. In the Fenton case that meant men in southeastern Vermont who had committed sex crimes against children and young women.

Philpin expected to see half a dozen files, maybe a dozen. Even with his work in the prisons, which seemed to hold an endless supply of sex criminals, Philpin was shocked by the results. The row of folders on the floor in Estey's office had reached a foot and a half in length. The psychologist sensed that even Estey was taken aback.

Some of these men would never commit another crime, but Philpin knew firsthand that until American society found a way to stop them, many of them were likely to repeat the coercive or violent attacks against women that had put them in jail. All these dangerous men, Philpin thought, potential threats to women and children, free on the streets, so many, in just this small part of this small and peaceful state.

But at the same time, Philpin's work on the Schaefer cases and then on other crimes was giving him something his earlier work with men convicted of sex crimes had not: working with the police, he now had a way of striking back.

Philpin had never planned to get into forensic psychology, but he found that the opportunity to switch to the offensive, to help the police pursue the criminal, suited him. In 1984 he finished course-work and wrote a dissertation under the direction of a well-known scholar in forensic psychology; by the next year he had earned a doctoral degree from Columbia Pacific University.

What had started as a diversion, with predictions tucked in a desk drawer, had become a solid half of Philpin's professional activity. Some of it was paying work, though never lavish, and much of his time, like the many hours on the Schaefer cases, was given without payment. Philpin still considered himself as much a student in the field as a consultant.

When Mike Prozzo called a few days after the Kellyville remains were identified as Ellen Fried's, the situation wasn't exactly what Philpin would have liked.

In drawing a profile, the last thing Philpin wanted to know about was suspects. That was doing it backward. Philpin wanted to start with the facts and end with the suspect, a profile of the type of person who could have committed the crime.

But Prozzo wanted to talk about a suspect and Philpin was eager to help. He had been following the case of Ellen Fried for a long time. He wasn't about to insist on routine procedure. The next day Prozzo drove to Springfield and introduced the psychologist to Richard Robert Bordeau.

Bordeau had deep roots in the area, stretching back to his grandparents. Both parents had worked in Claremont, his father as a butcher at the A & P, his mother as a nurse and administrator at the hospital. A brother had died young, leaving Richard an only child for most of his boyhood. He had lived all but the first three of his twenty-nine years in the same house, just over the line in Newport, where he had graduated from high school.

The yearbook photo showed a boy with a pleasant, narrow face, but tight-lipped, unsmiling. It was less common in western New Hampshire than in many other places during the late 1960s for young men to defy their parents' standards of grooming, but Richard Bordeau had parted his hair in the middle and combed it in long waves to frame his face; the effect was strangely feminine, incongruous with his neat crew-neck sweater over a shirt and tie.

The information about Bordeau's childhood was sketchy but there were indications that all was not well. He was remembered as a child who acted strangely and sometimes got into minor kinds of trouble, but people had made allowances and he had managed to get through school and graduate on schedule. When he had gotten into trouble, his parents had done their best to back him up. His mother, in particular, had sheltered the boy; working at the hospital, she was able to arrange sophisticated medical and psychiatric treatment. That was how she had known for certain early in his life what his behavior seemed to indicate: there was something functionally wrong with her son. Her reaction had been to treat the information as a secret.

There were reports that his father had been prone to anger and wanted to deal with Richard's problems by demanding more of him, by tightening discipline; his mother, someone said, had protected him against his father's impatience, even to the point of hiding from her husband the results of testing she had arranged: the boy was mentally impaired. She had taken the same approach outside the home as well, acting as Richard's advocate in school, minimizing the little incidents that arose—bizarre behavior, fights—insisting that her son was normal and should be treated like everybody else. She had gotten him some form of medication once, but he had resisted taking it and refused ever to go back to the psychiatrist who prescribed it.

Bordeau had worked from time to time, helping out in the bar at the Holiday Inn on the interstate and working as a stitcher at Wentworth Shoe. He seemed to have trouble holding a job for long, but he didn't need to. His parents continued to support him after high school.

At some point Bordeau had begun weaving fantasies of himself as a powerful figure, occasionally signing himself as *King Richard*, at other times using *King* as a nickname. He had invented a connection between himself and French royalty; that apparently was when he had begun adding the *x* to his name, emulating the spelling of the premier French wine region.

It wasn't clear whether Bordeau had become more eccentric

or just more visible as he had gotten older, but the hastily gathered file contained numerous reports of unusual behavior. For one thing, he seemed to have an invisible friend.

Bordeau had entered a coffee shop in town one day and seated himself at the counter. "Two cups of coffee, please," he said to the waitress. Assuming her customer was expecting the arrival of a companion, the waitress placed one cup in front of Bordeau, the other at the place next to him.

It soon became apparent that no one was going to join him. Bordeau was engaged in animated conversation with a person on the next stool who was visible only to himself. His voice dropped when the companion was talking. They were arguing, it seemed. The companion's name appeared to be Bertram, and he wasn't drinking his coffee.

Richard became increasingly upset with Bertram. Finally, his patience exhausted, he slapped his own face.

That was harmless enough. If all anybody could say about Richard Robert Bordeau had been that he had the kind of imaginary friend that a lot of four-year-olds have enjoyed, nobody would have thought anything more about it. Practically every town in New Hampshire had someone, or more than one, like that, people given to whimsical or bizarre or radically unorthodox public behavior. Often these people seemed to serve a useful function, stimulating wherever they wandered in a community a fellowship of kindness among those who came into contact with them. It was remarkable, often heartening, to observe the tolerance, concern, even material help, the people of a town would offer such local eccentrics. Claremont had several, Newport several of its own. But Richard Bordeau's behavior placed him beyond this category of harmless eccentric. The reports Prozzo had brought to show Philpin included several with a more disturbing dimension.

A Claremont man reported seeing Bordeau dry-firing a rifle in the parking lot behind a store; he seemed to be aiming the unloaded rifle at buildings, perhaps at windows. Several other complaints came from the YMCA, where Bordeau went for karate lessons. He had pestered a number of women strangers with requests for dates. In each case he had refused the woman's repeated requests that he leave her alone. He had tried several times to join an all-female aerobics class; two of the women he had asked for dates were in the class and came to feel that he was pursuing them. When the recreation director refused to let him into the class, he had become angry, raising his voice and clenching his fists. He claimed to hold a black belt in karate and at five feet eleven inches and 180 pounds, he was a menacing figure.

And then there was Virginia Troy's report. Bordeau had sought out other waitresses and asked about Troy, Prozzo told Philpin. "I've been watching her," he told one of Troy's co-workers.

"She's got really nice tits," Bordeau had said, with the neutral expression of a man talking about the weather. He seemed unaware that his words might be offensive or inappropriate.

"You're a victim of love and passion," he had told Troy on the phone, as if he were in the grip of some great force. Sometimes he would lower his voice, so that it was reminiscent of the reports about his conversations with Bertram, his imaginary friend; at other times he would suddenly break into a burbling giggle. Later, one source said, someone had asked Richard where Bertram was.

"I buried him," Bordeau answered.

The story of his observation of Virginia Troy tied in with a complaint from Newport, Prozzo said. A woman who lived near Bordeau's Victorian house had phoned the police with a complaint. A man had called her house, asked for the woman, and said something that made the hair stand up on the back of her neck.

"I've been watching you," he said, "and I like the nightgown you're wearing. It's a nice shade of blue."

The woman looked down reflexively at her blue nightgown, then ran in a panic to pull down every window shade in the house. Later another neighbor reported to her that he had seen Richard Bordeau watching her house through binoculars.

These anecdotes didn't add up to anything conclusive, Philpin thought, but it was at least worth keeping track of Richard Bordeau, even though he had no criminal record. Apart from harassing Virginia Troy, he hadn't come to the attention of the police. But there was a sexualized element to several of these reports, and the spying incidents were disturbing. There were indications in the research literature that some men who committed violent sex crimes had started with less serious offenses and escalated gradually; Peeping Tom violations were a common starting point. It was plausible that such minor offenses could continue concurrently with more serious crimes.

The detective and the psychologist agreed to stay in contact. By the end of 1985 the police had pursued hundreds of leads and checked out a dozen or more suspects in the case of Ellen Fried, but the concern about Richard Bordeau continued to produce a flow of anecdotes and complaints. Among them, two in particular seemed troubling to Mike Prozzo.

A young woman named Carla Rollins had phoned the Newport police at seven-thirty-five on a Tuesday evening. She was nervous about a man who had come in the convenience store where she worked, she said. Could they send someone out? A patrolman arrived at the store a few minutes later.

The officer had known Carla Rollins for several years. As a sixteen-year-old she had run away from her family in New London, twenty miles away, to be with her boyfriend in Newport; the Newport police had been called more than once to find Carla and hold her until the New London authorities could come and take her back. Now she was married to the boyfriend and, at twenty-three, she had two children. The officer remembered her as a good-natured, friendly girl, and she still seemed to fit that description. But she was frightened by what had just happened in the store.

At about five-thirty, she said, a man who looked vaguely familiar had entered the store. He chatted idly for a few minutes with the owner, who soon left. The man had stood by the magazine rack, leafing through a copy of *Playboy,* ostentatiously opening up the centerfold as if to show her what he was looking at.

After a while he had begun talking to her, Rollins said, looking over to where she stood a few feet away behind the counter, asking her questions. At first she had considered it just a friendly conversation.

''Where do you live?'' he asked.

''Newport,'' she answered. ''Where do you live?''

''I live near here,'' he said. ''It's a nice house. Do you want to come over for coffee?''

''No, thanks,'' she said. She felt the need to be polite.

''What's your name?'' she asked him.

''Richard,'' he said. ''I have a computer. I do a lot of writing. I'm writing a book. You could come over and have coffee and see my computer.''

She again politely declined. He turned back to his reading. There were long stretches when he said nothing, looking through the magazine, but he seemed to perk up when some-one came into the store, exchanging a few words with the newcomer, watching the transaction at the counter.

''I think you'd be interested in my book,'' he said when they were alone again. ''We could have coffee.''

She couldn't think what to say to make him stop.

''What's your book about?'' she asked.

''It's about merchandising,'' he said. ''It's so I can pass it all on to my family. I don't have a family yet, but I hope to have one someday. I live all by myself in that big house. You could come and have coffee.''

''No thanks,'' she said.

She knew every corner of the little store, and ordinarily being at work felt almost like puttering around her own living room. Now she was suddenly conscious of the loneliness of the place, of its isolation out in the countryside, the two-lane road outside quiet on a Tuesday evening before Thanksgiving, everybody home with their families having dinner.

''I'd like you to come over,'' he repeated. He was moving closer, edging around the counter so that there was no longer any barrier between them.

''It's not far from here,'' he said. ''The big house by the covered bridge. My family has lived there for generations.''

He took the young woman's hand. She pulled it away. She thought she should do something else, but she couldn't think what.

''I'd like to kiss you,'' he said. ''On the forehead, just on the forehead.''

He pushed his face toward hers.

The big dark house by the bridge, she thought, the haunted house. A conversation from a party a few weeks earlier came back to her. They had just found the bones in Kellyville, not far from the store, the nurse that disappeared. A man at the party, it was Robert Partlow, said to her, ''When they find out who did it, it's gonna be that weird guy in the big house there, the one by the bridge. He had girls coming and going all the time.''

The man's face loomed in her sight.

"Go away," she cried out.

He backed up slightly.

"Well, I've gotta go," he said. "I'm gonna go and work on my computer." She didn't reply.

"How about a kiss goodbye?" he asked. She shook her head emphatically. He seemed to accept the rebuff.

"I'll call you later," he said, as if they were lovers parting after a date. "I'll probably come back." She didn't respond.

"When are you working again?" he wanted to know. She told him the truth, that she was working two jobs every day. She didn't want him to think he could find her there all the time.

At last he left. As soon as his car pulled away she had called the police station. It was about 7:00 P.M. He had hung around the store close to an hour and half.

While she was talking with the officer, the phone rang.

"It's him," she mouthed to the policeman.

"Are you busy?" he asked. She was noncommittal. "I'll be around in about forty-five minutes," he said, as if he felt she were waiting eagerly to see him.

The officer finished taking her statement, then drove off for a few minutes. When he returned to check, Bordeau had not come back. A few minutes after the patrol car pulled away, Bordeau walked through the door.

He walked to the counter and picked out a candy bar. He placed forty pennies on the counter and watched while Rollins counted them. He seemed prepared to hang around. It was a little after eight-thirty.

"Look," she said, "I hate to have to kick you out, but I have to mop the floors. I have to close the store."

Bordeau looked disappointed. "Oh," he said, "okay."

He turned and started to leave, then stopped and looked back at her.

"In case I don't see you, have a nice Thanksgiving," he said, and left.

A few minutes later the officer returned again. The doors were locked. He knocked and shook the door handle.

After a minute Carla Rollins peeked around the display shelf. She told him about Richard Bordeau's return and how

she had gotten rid of him. In a few minutes her husband came
to drive her home.

The incident added to the picture of Bordeau as a man who
routinely disturbed women with his intrusive advances, skirt-
ing the edge of sexual harassment. But there was a boldness
and persistence here that seemed to go beyond the other complaints. Could it be a sign that he was capable of something
still more serious?

The other report that stood out was entirely different from
Carla Rollins's account. It was a phone call, and it was a report
of a rumor, the kind of thing that under normal circumstances
would cause an officer to shake his head and make faces to
the other cops in the room while periodically inserting a "Yes,
ma'am," into the caller's fanciful rambling. But these were
not normal circumstances.

The caller was a woman who said she had heard the story
from a friend. The friend, the caller told the officer, had spent
time in the Claremont hospital a year earlier. The friend didn't
want to talk to the police herself, the woman said; she was
afraid.

The friend knew Richard Bordeau, the caller reported, and
she had seen him in the hospital a lot then. He had been visiting his mother and his grandmother.

"His mother was a nurse there at the hospital, you know,"
the woman said. "But when Richard was there, his mother
was a patient. She was sick. And then his grandmother was
sick, too.

"And that nurse, you know, Helen, the one that died," the
woman said, "she was there, too." It turned out that the
woman was referring to Ellen Fried.

"Well, she just cozied right up to Richard," the woman
went on, "sat out there with him on the sun porch, just went
right out there with him every day. Didn't have time for the
rest of her patients, had to spend all her time out there with
him." The woman sounded aggrieved, probably echoing her
friend's sense that she had been neglected.

There was something else that made this report stand out,
even if it was, at this point, merely a rumor. It was the first
concrete suggestion that Richard Bordeau could somehow be
connected to Ellen Fried. Prozzo set about assembling the
facts.

Bordeau's mother had worked as a nurse at the Valley Regional Hospital, eventually becoming coordinator of discharges. In 1982 she had been voted nurse of the year. The following year she had become sick and died at the age of fifty-seven. Less than three months later, the day before Christmas, Richard's grandmother died. And three weeks later, at the age of fifty-four, his father died. An only child, at twenty-eight he had lost his three closest relatives in less than four months.

It appeared that the big Victorian house had been paid for some years earlier and Richard had received an inheritance from his parents and grandmother—possibly there was some form of disability payment—that allowed him to live on there with nothing more than sporadic earnings of his own.

Richard Bordeau would still have been going through the process of mourning—or whatever his response may have been to the loss of the parents in whose house he was still living at the age of twenty-eight—when Ellen Fried disappeared in July of 1984. And if the woman caller's second-hand story was true, Bordeau knew Ellen, saw her every day for a time, had countless opportunities to collect personal information about her life and routine.

The department was going to have to put some serious working time into Richard Bordeau, Prozzo thought. This collection of reports and incidents and anecdotes was becoming something greater than the sum of its parts.

BOOK IV

Eleven Days

April 1986

Of course it was coincidence, there was no way it could have been anything else, that brought three events together in the tiny space of eleven days, so that there was no time for the people of the Valley to recover from one before the next was upon them.

And if you looked at it with the hard, critical eye of some-one detached, a skeptic, there was no real, concrete proof that the events were even related.

The problem was that at the end of those eleven days, no one in the Valley was in the mood to be detached. There were precious few skeptics left. There was anger, there was fear, in some few places there was an emotion approaching panic. There was very little detachment.

fifteen

Day One: April 15, 1986

There was something about it that bothered him, something beyond the casual irritation you feel when you get to the phone just after it stops ringing and there's nobody on the line. At least that was how he remembered it later, along with a lot of other details that would never stick in your mind under normal circumstances.

Steve Moore had been on the job site with his crew since midmorning. He had built this fireplace and chimney for the Pettersons ten years ago. Back then he had still been mainly just a mason, working nights and weekends by himself or with one helper to get the extra money so they could live better. That was progress, tearing down your own work. This time it was a major remodelling, an extension with its own foundation, and now he had four men working with him.

The Pettersons were staying in the house while the work went on, so Moore had told the men to seal off the kitchen and dining room with thick plastic sheeting to keep the dust out. That meant that if the phone rang when the Pettersons were out someone had to go around the house and in through the kitchen door.

When the ringing penetrated the job noise, Moore called to Roger Curtis, one of the young guys, to get it. Roger was outside loading the dump truck, closest to the phone. It was between twelve-forty-five and one o'clock, they figured later. Roger came back in a minute.

"Couldn't get it," he said. "Stopped ringing."

Moore had given the number to his wife. I wonder if that was Lynda, he thought. She probably wouldn't call, she'd know we'd have a hard time getting to it.

The thought didn't help. There was still something in the situation that was making him uncomfortable. After a minute he walked around to the phone and dialled his home number. The line was busy. The idea of jumping in the truck and driving there crossed his mind; it was only five or six miles. He put the thought aside and went back to work.

He had talked to her less than an hour earlier. He had sent Terry Sanders off to the dump with a load of demolition rubble a little after ten. Terry was to stop by at the house on the way and get a check from Lynda to pay the dumping fee. When they had finished lunch and he still wasn't back, Moore called home to see if Terry had been there. On the third ring Terry drove into the yard. On the fourth ring Lynda picked it up.

"Lynda, I was calling to see if you knew where Terry was," Moore said, "but he just drove in."

"Yeah, okay," she answered. She sounded annoyed. He must have gotten her in from the yard. It had been a typically cool Vermont spring and she had caught a cold. This was one of the first really sunny days with a little warmth to it; she'd take the first chance she could to get some sun on her face. They hung up without talking further.

By the time they had filled the truck again it was a little before three. Terry Sanders lived almost at the Springfield town line, near the dump in Rockingham, and he was due to finish up at three-thirty. If he drove the load down and brought the truck back to the job in the morning, Moore could get in another couple of hours' work with the rest of the crew and he wouldn't have to pay someone to make the round-trip with the refuse.

"Terry," Moore called out, "why don't you take off now with the truck. That'll get you through to three-thirty."

Moore went inside to call Lynda. She could write another check for the dump on the business account and Sanders could stop by and get it on the way. She had been keeping the business books for six months now, along with her part-time job at a clothing store in Bellows Falls; she got bored with nothing to do.

Moore let the phone ring a long time. Obviously she wasn't there. He came out of the house and called over to where Sanders sat in the truck.

"Terry, take off with the truck and head down toward my house. Stop there and I'll be right with you and write you out a check." It was less than ten minutes' drive; he could write the check and get back to finish up with the crew.

Terry had a few minutes' head start on him, but it was an old truck and Moore knew he'd catch up. He always drove fast and he had the speeding tickets to prove it, enough to be in danger of losing his license. Just the other side of Saxtons River, in front of the River's Edge restaurant, Moore swung his El Camino around the lumbering dump truck. They were halfway there, only three miles away, but Steve Moore couldn't stand to go at anything less than full speed.

He slowed for the sharp bend in the road just before the house. Tidd's Corner, it was called, named after a family that had lived there in the eighteenth century. The house wasn't quite that old, but there was a little plaque on the front that said 1829 and he and Lynda had worked hard to get it into good shape. Set in the crook of the curve, which made it visible to cars coming from both directions, the house had become something of a local showplace.

Strange, he thought as he pulled into the driveway, her car's here. She'd had a practically new Saab Turbo, a flashy, expensive car, and just a few months before she'd traded it in on the Volvo. Champagne, they called that color. She'd thought it was classier than the Saab. She liked having the best, whether it was clothes or things for the house or a car.

The dog, a Saint Bernard named Abigail, was lying under a spruce tree in the front yard. She hardly stirred as he drove in.

As he stepped out of the truck he saw the fold-up lawn lounger sitting on the driveway apron by the back door. There was a portable radio next to it and his wife's sandals were placed neatly nearby. Now it was his turn to be irritated.

"Why the hell didn't you answer the phone?" he asked in his mind. Could've saved him the trip. She had to be there anyway, the kids were due off the school bus at three-thirty.

He pulled open the aluminum storm door to the mud room and stepped into the house. He noticed the quiet, a heavy afternoon silence, a deep absence, no washing machine rumble, no dryer or refrigerator hum, no activity.

A few steps along the red carpet into the mud room and he turned left through the doorway into the kitchen.

She lay on her stomach a few feet in front of him, her head propped at an awkward angle against the jamb of the doorway leading from the kitchen into the living room on the left.

"Lynda," he said to her, as if to carry on the conversation he had been having in his mind.

As he stepped toward her his eye caught a flash of red on the baseboard and he thought, "Painting, she must have been painting it red," and then, "She fell, passed out, fell asleep," running through the possibilities.

He reached down and rolled her over and the knowledge that it must be blood caught up with his mind and a great opening appeared in her neck and he saw white—it must be the bone—showing through another slash on her arm.

He looked in her face and his body began to shake. One eye was open partway and the other was closed. One side of her face had turned grayish with pooling blood.

He reached for her wrist to see if there was a pulse. "Dummy, not with the thumb," he thought and switched his grip, but he still couldn't feel anything.

A sudden thought ripped his awareness from the still form of his wife and he started, turning quickly to face the room behind him. There was no one. He stood for a moment, listening. The house was gripped in the same stillness he had felt when he came in the door.

Moore walked across to the kitchen phone. He couldn't think how to find the phone number for the ambulance service. He dialled the operator and she gave him the number. When he had finished making the call he remembered Terry Sanders in the truck and walked back out to the driveway. The truck was parked out by the road.

"Terry," he called, "come in here." Terry was retying the tarp that covered the construction rubble in back.

"Yeah," he called back, "be there in a minute."

"Get the fuck in here," Moore shouted at him. "My wife's been stabbed."

Sanders jumped down from the truck and ran toward the house. They walked inside. Moore was aware of Terry looking down at the body, his mouth agape, the color draining from his face, then turning away. Moore felt a kind of distance from it all, as if he were looking through the wrong end of a telescope.

Moore went to the phone and called a friend, Beryl Wister, at his law office in Brattleboro. He told Wister briefly what had happened. He hung up and called his parents, who lived a few hundred yards up the road. They had come home early from their winter in Florida; Stephen's sister, a pianist, was scheduled to give a recital at the Vermont Academy in a few days. They wanted to be there.

In a few minutes the ambulance arrived. There was a flurry of activity, men running into the house, carrying equipment. The ambulance driver looked quickly at the body lying in the doorway. He stood up and stared at Moore.

"Have you called the police yet?" he asked. Moore shook his head.

The driver glanced at the phone, then at Moore. The phone was red with blood.

"Is there another phone in the house?" he asked.

"Upstairs," Moore told him. He suddenly remembered the nauseated look on Terry Sanders's face. He looked at the ambulance driver.

"Shit," Moore said, "I came here to write him a check for the dump. I'll go up with you, I want to grab a check."

"How can you think about that now?" the driver asked.

While the driver called the police, Moore wrote out a check and tore it from the big company checkbook. Downstairs he handed it to Terry Sanders and sent him on to the dump.

Of course these things never revealed themselves from the start, Mike LeClair knew that, but in the end it was the contrast that was so striking. There was such a stark difference between what he thought at the beginning, when he first walked into the house at Tidd's Corner, and the way things actually turned out.

It was less than fifteen miles from the state police office in

Chester to the Moores' house in Saxtons River. LeClair was the detective on duty when the call came and he arrived just fifty minutes from the moment Steve Moore had walked in the house and found his wife lying on the floor. That alone was a big factor in their favor, the victim and the surroundings almost completely undisturbed. Lieutenant Jim Candon, another state police detective, was in command, and they had the mobile crime lab on the way, all within an hour of the discovery of the body.

The ambulance guy had understood right away that she was dead and hadn't even touched her. And he'd known enough to avoid the kitchen phone and get away from the area where the body was lying.

And then there was the setting, everything about it shouting the word *domestic* at you, giving the word two meanings. One was the house, the home, everything so neat and comfortable, a family with two kids and a dog and a couple of cars and a nice living room and a well-equipped kitchen and there right in the middle of it was the body, a smear of horror across the peaceful domestic scene. And then it was also the police shorthand for anger boiling over between people who knew each other, lived in close quarters, storing up their hurt and resentment and finally taking it out on whoever was near at hand, adding another instance to that huge proportion of all violence that came under the heading of "domestic dispute."

And then there was the husband. Stephen Moore claimed he had found the body and then called the ambulance. He had told the first cops on the scene that the kids were due home in a few minutes and they had put a call out, trying to get a cruiser to intercept the school bus and get the children off. They had stopped several buses, but not the right one. At three-thirty the big yellow bus pulled up in front of the house and the children jumped down, first the boy, who was twelve, then his sister, four years younger, lively with the look of young animals ready to play.

Moore had gone out and met them halfway up the driveway, with the growing collection of detectives and uniformed cops hovering nearby, and the strange mood of the place caught the children before they reached their father, and the eagerness fell from their faces.

Moore had knelt down and put his arms around them.

"I've got to tell you something," he said to them, and as he talked the little girl started crying. The boy looked puzzled.

Moore's father had pulled his car into the driveway and Moore went over and got in with the children. After they had talked for a while, Moore's mother took the children and went back down the road to the grandparents' house. Moore walked up the driveway and went inside to see if the cops wanted to talk to him.

The husband was acting strange right from the start, Mike LeClair thought, what the ambulance driver said about him taking all that trouble with the checkbook and sending the kid off to the dump while his wife is lying there on the floor on a background of her own darkening blood.

And now he's standing there, with blood on his hands, literally, real blood, his wife's blood, and he's talking in this flat voice and he's got this face that hardly moves when he talks and he looks at you as if you just came to the door to try and sell him siding or convert him to your church and he's waiting to see what you have to say.

This did not look like a case that was going to take a long time to solve, LeClair thought.

The detective and the victim's husband sat down to talk.

sixteen

Day Five: April 19, 1986

There was a casual quality in the way the body was found that came to seem shocking in comparison to the terrible meaning it held for so many people in the Valley.

The two men came upon it around noon Saturday, twenty-five yards off a logging track called Cat Hole Road, as they walked up through the woods in the northern part of Kellyville, heading for an afternoon of fishing. There was a small stream running across their path and one of them looked down and there it was. Even the way it rested in the stream, almost as if someone had sat down there to take a bath and never got up, gave it an offhand feeling.

It was in Newport's jurisdiction, a little east of the Claremont line, north of Routes 11 and 103. The first police arrived in a little more than an hour, Newport first, then the New Hampshire State Police, the crime lab, the county attorney's office, the attorney general's representative.

For all that, there wasn't much to work with. There was a skull, and part of the upper torso was still there, encased in the remains of a jacket. Assorted other bones remained, some attached to the torso, a few resting nearby, but much of the skeleton was missing, probably taken off by animals or washed away in the stream. The investigators marked off the site with wide yellow plastic tape and started combing the surrounding area.

The story was on page one of the *Claremont Eagle-Times* the next day, reflecting its potential interest, but it was short, reflecting the lack of information. The remains were being sent to Dr. Henry Ryan, in Augusta, Maine, for analysis, it said. Pieces of jaw and some teeth went to a forensic dentist in Concord, for comparison with dental records of missing persons. New Hampshire still did not have its own medical examiner.

At the same time, twenty-five miles away and just across the river in Vermont, police were investigating several suspects in the killing of Lynda Moore.

The medical examiner had found more than two dozen stab wounds in her body. It was clear that Lynda Moore had been engulfed in a wild explosion of violence, repeated hammering blows of the knife, standing her ground and throwing up her arms to protect herself, only to see the blade drive through her defenses, striking into her center, into her arteries, turning her desperately pumping heart into her assailant's accomplice.

Lieutenant James Candon of the Vermont State Police told a reporter that they had administered polygraph exams to several people. "We've got some prospects in mind and we're in the process of checking them out and checking alibis," Candon reported. Nine state police detectives were working on the case, he said, along with others from the Bellows Falls Police Department and the Windham County office of the state's attorney.

"We are not discouraged," Candon said. "We have a lot of work to do. There's a lot of energy in this investigative team. We're not going to leave a single stone unturned."

Five days into the investigation, Candon didn't sound as if he expected an early conclusion. The investigators needed some sort of break to solve the case, he said.

Day Eight: April 22, 1986

It was Bernice Courtemanche.

The dentist in Concord, the same one who had identified Ellen Fried, had compared fragments from the remains to the missing girl's dental records.

"We're confident that it's a match," an assistant attorney general told the press.

Bernice Courtemanche, who had last been seen in the Beauregard Village section of Claremont setting out to hitchhike to Newport, had been found a year and ten months later. She was five miles from where she had started.

The identity of the remains put things in context. The fates of Bernice Courtemanche and Ellen Fried had moved within a narrow universe of space and time.

The two young women had disappeared fifty-one days apart. The bridge outside Beauregard Village where Bernice had begun her trip was less than a mile from Leo's Market, the last place Ellen Fried had been known to be alive. That was where she had used the pay phone to call her sister in California.

And the stream in Kellyville where Bernice's remains had been found was about three miles north of the downed hemlock near the Sugar River where the two shooters had come upon the skeleton of Ellen Fried.

The chiefs of the Newport and Claremont police departments, Art Bastian and Adam Bauer, announced that they were going to work with the New Hampshire State Police to look into connections between the cases. They would meet regularly to discuss leads and evidence and coordinate the work of their detectives. It was the first public acknowledgment that the investigators shared the concern that had preoccupied people throughout the Valley for months.

Chief Bastian urged members of the public to come forward with tips about Bernice Courtemanche and Ellen Fried, especially people who had provided information anonymously in the past.

The Newport chief also asked that people call in with information about other unsolved cases in the Valley. He mentioned Eva Morse, who had been missing nine months, and three homicides. One of the homicide victims was a young woman named Elizabeth Critchley, whose body had been found in the town of Unity, just south of Newport and Claremont, five years earlier. The other two were a young man, still unidentified, whose body had been found in a rest area earlier in the month, and Sylvia Gray, a seventy-six-year-old woman who had been killed near her home in 1982.

It was just a shopping list. The chief wasn't implying any

connection among the cases, except for the fact that they were all unsolved. Within days, the investigators would be looking at some of the cases in a very different way.

As for Bernice Courtemanche, it would be another day or two before autopsy results would be available from the doctor in Maine, the attorney general's office announced.

Day Nine: April 23, 1986

Henry Ryan looked like a man who could tell you how long it takes for a skeleton to sink into the floor of the forest. Not that there was anything ghoulish about Ryan. His comfortable slope of belly and the pipe that hung from his mouth on its curved stem like a permanent part of his breathing apparatus gave him the solid, thoughtful air of someone who must know a lot about something. It just happened that what Henry Ryan knew a lot about was death.

A medical examiner's interest took up where everyone else's interest left off. While mourners concerned themselves with the soul of the departed, Ryan pored over what was left of the body, searching for clues that would tell the world how it had come to this.

Dr. Ryan had been a coroner in New York State before coming to Maine eight years earlier. The things that Ryan knew were not necessarily the ones that a chief medical examiner in Boston or New York or Los Angeles would find valuable, but they were crucial when you lived among the vast dark woods of a place like Maine. He could estimate how long a body had lain in the woods by the height of the new growth emerging between the bones, and he also knew that the shoots would be well established before the bones sank far into the ground. He knew that any bones dragged off by animals would be no farther than two hundred feet from the skeleton, and he could tell you that if the corpse was found with loose change the newest coin would be dated within a year of the death.

"Try it," Ryan would say, "check your pocket," more matter-of-fact than mischievous.

These insights were especially useful in the early spring or fall, when hunters and fishermen ranged beyond the paths and deep into the forest in search of prey and solitude, and found things that had not been meant to be seen again.

Ryan's rumpled look, a little independent tuft of hair poking above one ear, reflected the detachment of a man grown comfortable with things that most people preferred to ignore. He didn't mind having his picture taken chucking a skeleton under the chin or pointing to the location of a missing bone, and when he turned to examine a little heap of remains, if he needed insulation from the implications of what he was doing it was provided by his religious beliefs.

"I don't feel sorry for the dead," Ryan said. "It bothers me for the living. However the victim died, it was quick, usually. Sure, they suffered for a while, but now they are safe."

And for protection of a more tangible kind in the midst of an autopsy, there were other means.

"I smoke my pipe or a cigar and the smell doesn't really bother me," Ryan said. "When we are busy and have a responsibility, we're not sitting back and thinking how terrible this is. We just go about our business."

Business for the office of the chief medical examiner of Maine involved some twelve hundred cases a year, most of them routine, perhaps a couple of dozen of them murders. So when he had finished his work on cases referred to him by medical and legal authorities throughout Maine, Ryan was willing to look over the remains dug up by a contractor excavating for a house foundation or consult on a case sent over from another state.

"The more bones you deal with," Ryan liked to say, "the better you are at dealing with bones."

There was only one criterion for deciding whether he took on a case from New Hampshire. There had to be a challenge, something to be learned from it.

"It has to be of some interest," he said, "and it has to be somewhat destroyed. Decomposed remains and destroyed remains are the most difficult."

The bones and bits of cloth the New Hampshire attorney general sent over from Kellyville met the criterion. Before Ryan had finished his analysis, the police in New Hampshire had learned from the forensic dentist in Concord that the remains were those of Bernice Courtemanche, but that had no bearing on Ryan's work. He was looking for anything that would throw light on what had happened to the remains before they came to rest in the woods. What he found would have a powerful impact on the investigation of what had happened to the missing women in the Connecticut Valley.

It didn't look like much, just a nick here and there on the bones of the neck, lesions, in the physician's term. No one who hadn't carefully studied a lot of human remains would even have noticed them, much less reached the certainty about what they represented that Henry Ryan did.

"The lesions are rather subtle," Ryan said. "The conservative person is more likely to say, 'That's nothing,' unless he's absolutely sure."

Ryan was absolutely sure.

Bernice Courtemanche had been stabbed to death.

seventeen

It was too much, Mike Prozzo thought, just too damn much. You could forget for a while, throw yourself into the work, but as soon as you left room in your mind, it came back: another murder, another human being killed and left in the woods like so much household trash, another woman murdered.

Except for his time in the service Prozzo had lived in Claremont all his life and he could hardly remember a murder from when he was a kid. Even in his first ten years on the force there had only been two murders in the city. Now he had been chief of detectives for five years and six murder cases had come across his desk. Even though he knew it had nothing to do with him, there were times when Prozzo almost felt responsible for the increase.

Still, if you looked back it seemed more like a series of natural events, like say, the occasional flooding of the Connecticut River, than something anyone could be responsible for. Someone had killed a baby, a woman had killed the husband who abused her, a psychopathic young man and a friend had tortured his sister, a man stabbed another man in a fight; each case was self-contained. It was easy to see these as isolated incidents; if you had to attribute the increase to something, you could say it was a product of all the craziness that was in the air the last ten years or so, families breaking up, new people coming up from the cities, more transients passing through, people losing their connections to each other. Other than that, there was no particular pattern. Until now.

What could you say about Ellen Fried and Bernice Courtemanche? A woman disappears from Claremont, then another woman disappears less than a mile away, and a year later you're out in Kellyville trying to figure out how one of the women ended up there, and seven months later you're back in Kellyville trying to figure out how the other one ended up there.

Detectives in the state police or in large cities could specialize in homicide; in a city the size of Claremont you took whatever came along, and nothing like this had come along before.

Spring had only just started but the day had been warm and Prozzo was feeling grimy and tired when he left the police station. The investigation hadn't turned up anything new in the murder cases and the persistent tension of a hundred unanswered questions lay heavy in the back of Prozzo's mind when the phone rang at his home late in the afternoon.

"Mike? Pete," the voice said. Prozzo hadn't needed the identification. It was Captain Pete Hickey, the man who had been chief of detectives before Prozzo. They had switched jobs, Hickey taking over the uniformed division.

"They just found another body," Hickey said.

"You gotta be shittin' me," Prozzo said, knowing as he said it that it wasn't true. "Where?"

"Out toward Unity, West Unity." It was the town south of Claremont. Unity shares borders with Claremont, Newport, and Charlestown.

Prozzo half-listened, his mind racing through the implications of the news, as Hickey gave him detailed directions to the site.

"What the hell is going on?" Prozzo found himself wondering. He felt as if all the air had been sucked out of his body in a great whooshing rush.

"I'm on my way," he said into the phone.

• • •

The discovery of the bodies of two women and the murder of a third, all in the space of eleven days, had a cumulative effect that descended on the Connecticut Valley like a mudslide, growing broader as it spread.

Dental samples were taken for identification and the rest of the remains were sent to Dr. Ryan in Maine for an autopsy. This time, the identification took only a few hours. The police were fairly certain from the start whose remains they were dealing with; after the discovery of Ellen Fried and Bernice Courtemanche there was only one person still missing from the area. The dental material was sent to a dentist in Charlestown. He quickly recognized work he had done on Eva Morse.

The place where the bones had been found was about four miles southeast of where Eva Morse had been seen for the last time on a July day nine months earlier, hitchhiking outside the veterinary clinic on Routes 11 and 103. The remains had been found by two brothers who made their living at a variety of odd jobs, one of them logging. They offered their services to landowners who wanted a woodlot harvested for firewood or a small load of softwood that could be sold to a paper mill. It turned out that the brothers' discovery of the remains of Eva Morse was a bizarre coincidence with powerful reverberations.

The brothers told police that they had been walking in these same woods with a third man five years earlier when they smelled a powerful odor. They had assumed at first that it was the carcass of an animal, but when they approached they discovered it was the remains of a woman. The spot had been about five hundred feet from where they had now found the skeleton of Eva Morse.

It had taken more than a month, but late in the summer of 1981 the police had finally identified the men's find as Elizabeth Critchley. The twenty-five-year-old Vermont woman had been missing for two weeks. She had last been seen in Massachusetts, starting to hitchhike on the interstate highway, heading for home. Her route would have taken her north on I-91, along the Vermont side of the river, up through the heart of the Connecticut River Valley. There was an exit from I-91 just across the river from Charlestown, New Hampshire; the exit was four miles from where the loggers had found the remains of Elizabeth Critchley, and the same distance from where Eva Morse had last been seen.

The autopsy had not established a clear cause of Elizabeth Critchley's death, but it was classified as a homicide. A lengthy investigation had proved fruitless.

Three years later, after Gary Schaefer was arrested for the killing of Caty Richards and began talking with the police about other crimes he had committed, detectives had questioned him about Elizabeth Critchley. The interstate was part of the route Schaefer cruised, looking for victims, and the exit closest to where Critchley's remains had been found was only three miles from Schaefer's home. Critchley was twenty-five, older than Schaefer's victims in the Springfield cases, but there were at least two reports of Schaefer attacking more mature women. Critchley had disappeared on a Saturday; Schaefer rarely worked on the weekend and had killed twice on a Saturday. But Schaefer had denied any knowledge of Elizabeth Critchley and there had been no solid evidence to connect him to her death. The case had remained on the list of unsolved homicides.

Now the finding of the remains of Eva Morse, with the haunting coincidence of its discovery and the strong circumstantial resemblance to a five-year-old mystery, had revived interest in the death of Elizabeth Critchley.

But that was not all.

It was hard now to recover the feeling of that time when Jo Anne Dunham disappeared. It was the day they buried Bobby Kennedy at Arlington National Cemetery, the same day that General William Westmoreland said goodbye to his troops in Vietnam, trying to put the best possible face on his term of failure as their commander. As he spoke, the Vietcong rained rockets on Saigon, a few miles away. It was June of 1968 and the Valley was a different place then.

For the people of the Valley in that time, killing was something that happened far, far away. Violent death could be shocking, taking away a young politician, a man in whom many in the Valley had placed their hopes. It might even touch the Valley, which had sent dozens of its young men to fight in Vietnam. But in the Connecticut Valley, violence worked at a distance. It seemed there was little to connect that time with the middle years of the 1980s.

Yet the fate of a fifteen-year-old girl formed a link across almost two decades. Jo Anne Dunham, a tall girl with blue eyes and short blond hair, was a sophomore in high school, but people said she looked older than her age. She walked out the door of her home in a trailer park off Route 12 in North Charlestown about seven-twenty on a Tuesday morning in 1968. It was one of the last days of school before the summer vacation. She was carrying a purse in one hand and a single book in the other, heading for the bus stop a few hundred yards away, where she waited alone each school day to be picked up. When the big yellow school bus came at seven-thirty-five, no one was there.

A member of the search party found her body in the woods the next day after his boxer dog led him to the site. A biology report written in Jo Anne Dunham's girlish script lay on the ground nearby. The coroner ruled that she had died of strangulation. The investigation never led to an arrest or an explanation of what had happened.

When the loggers found the remains of Eva Morse eighteen years later, the police chiefs in Charlestown and Claremont, the state police troop commander, the county sheriff, and the county attorney who had come together for the Jo Anne Dunham investigation and had their picture taken together for the front page of the *Claremont Daily Eagle* were long since retired. Several of them had passed away. But Jo Anne Dunham was remembered, and there were those who recalled that the place where she had last been seen was less than a mile from the veterinary clinic where Eva Morse had tried to thumb a ride, and the place where the body of Jo Anne Dunham had been found was an even shorter distance from where the decaying remains of Eva Morse had been discovered. A narrow loop arcing through time to encompass the bodies of Jo Anne Dunham, Elizabeth Critchley, and Eva Morse would enclose a little strip of woods in West Unity a little over a mile long and a few hundred yards wide.

This chain reaction of discoveries and associations between one victim and another acted upon the mind of the Valley community like some cruel form of torture. Each time there seemed to come an end to the stream of shocking news, a chance to understand and assimilate what had happened, another revelation came along to reinforce the appearance of deepening chaos and fearful menace.

The fear was particularly pronounced among women, who identified especially closely with the victims, and for the first time there appeared a substantial organized response. Much of this activity was centered around an organization called Women's Supportive Services and its leader, Deborah Mozden. Mozden had lived in Claremont since the age of nine, working in the family business, Stan's Market, attending parochial school, graduating from Stevens High, going on to earn a degree in sociology at the University of New Hampshire. She had lived through the period of rapid change in the Connecticut River Valley.

Mozden had started in social-service positions while she was in school, continuing after graduation in VISTA, then in the food-stamp and Head Start programs. Around 1980, as feminism and growing activism were expanding women's influence in social services, Mozden helped found Women's Supportive Services. At first the organization worked primarily with the city and other agencies to help displaced homemakers, but gradually their interests expanded to include support for battered women. Mozden and others who had been providing services to women were beginning to realize that whatever other problems their clients brought to them, they were often also victims of sexual violence and incest.

The disappearances of women in the Valley had at first seemed to Mozden like extreme but isolated instances of the problems her agency had been facing in its daily work. Then the bodies of Bernice Courtemanche and Eva Morse had been found in the woods and she began to hear something that was both frightening and disturbing.

Women were calling the agency to talk about the killings, concerned about their safety, wondering if there was anything they ought to be doing to protect themselves. And there was a tendency in many of the calls for women to distance themselves from the danger by distancing themselves from the victims. Bernice Courtemanche was young, they were saying, a bit footloose, it was probably someone she knew, something specific to the way Bernice lived her life. Eva Morse ran with some unsavory people, anything could happen when you hung around with them.

"She was hitchhiking," the callers were saying, and it could apply to either of the women who had died, "and we all know that's not safe," and, "She left herself vulnerable, and that's foolish because you never know who's going to pick you up."

Deborah Mozden found this kind of thinking, which she saw echoed in the columns of the Valley's newspapers, both dangerous and unfair. The danger lay in the complacency this view encouraged toward what seemed to be an emerging threat to all women. The unfairness, Mozden felt, was in shifting the blame for a death to the woman who was killed.

It was necessary to recognize the danger, Mozden told both women and men in talks she gave before organizations in the Valley, but the responsibility for what had happened should rest with only one person.

"We have to know that if we do hitchhike we are leaving ourselves vulnerable," she said. "If we get really drunk and take a ride home with someone we don't know, we are leaving ourselves vulnerable. But we are not responsible for the injury that happens to us from that assault. Had I picked up Bernice Courtemanche, she would have been fine. What happened to her was the sole responsibility of that person who assaulted her."

Beyond that, she found, the thing upsetting both women and men was simple uncertainty. "There were a lot of questions," she recalled later, "and there weren't a lot of answers."

The apprehension took on a particular intimacy in Charlestown and Unity, where women had disappeared and bodies had been found. Doug Rowe, who lived in Unity about a mile from where Eva Morse's body had been found, saw it as the work of an outsider:

"I have to think it's somebody using this area to drop bodies off," he said. "I can't believe somebody from around here did it."

Like some other men, Rowe saw the danger as affecting primarily women.

"It doesn't affect me that much," Rowe said, "being a male. It makes me a little nervous. It's made my friends a lot more nervous than me, actually. I've had a lot of phone calls from friends, asking how close it is."

A Charlestown man told a reporter, "What I'm hearing everybody say is that everyone should be on their guard."

Kim Smith, a young Charlestown woman who worked at a

restaurant in Claremont, said she was worrying more about her safety than in the past.

"I talk to my friends, my mom," she said. "People are confused. You can't even walk out and around anymore. My mom called me up the other day and said, 'Kim, I know this sounds silly, but lock your door.'

"I do think about it," she concluded. "Could there really be someone out there? But I still go about my business. It'd be foolish not to. But I do worry more."

On a brisk spring day in Saxtons River, Vermont, fifteen miles away from Charlestown, a man leaving the funeral of Lynda Moore at Saint Edmund's Church, sounding very much like some of the New Hampshire residents, summed up the feelings of people in the surrounding area: "People are afraid because they don't know what to expect," he said.

Police in the area had been swamped with phone calls from people who needed to ask questions and discuss their fears. Jim Candon, the state police lieutenant who was in command of the investigation into the death of Lynda Moore, offered some advice. "We don't want to alarm people," he said, "but a little extra caution at this time is recommended."

An editorial in the Claremont paper summarized the community's reaction. The editorial listed the unsolved killings and found in them a message that it called "frightening":

Even though we live in New Hampshire and Vermont, the same dangers lurk in our streets and houses as those that lurk in Boston and New York.

Something was happening in the Valley. It had begun with the deaths of three young girls and the unmasking of Gary Schaefer as a killer, a man who took the innocent at random and killed without reason and then went hunting for the opportunity to do it again.

The Valley was losing its innocence.

BOOK V

Counterattack

eighteen

It was time to strike back.

The Connecticut Valley might feel in many ways to the people who lived there like a self-contained enclave, an over-sized village of eighty or ninety thousand people set apart from the rest of New Hampshire and Vermont, distant from the center of things, but it was only fifty-one miles from Claremont to the New Hampshire capital in Concord, and someone had been listening.

What had seemed two years earlier a routine disappearance had become in just eleven days the center of a web of murder. What had been the subject of occasional curiosity among the population of a few towns was now a widespread source of concern and apprehension all up and down the Valley. And now the sound of those anxieties had risen to a level that seemed to demand action.

The second body had been found around midday on Friday and identified as Eva Morse later that afternoon. Saturday morning the attorney general of the state of New Hampshire held a news conference in Concord to announce the formation of a task force to investigate nine unsolved homicides that had taken place in the Claremont area within the last five years. At least one of those killings had happened in Vermont, Attorney General Stephen Merrill said, and he would confer with his counterpart there to arrange cooperation in the investigation.

Merrill acknowledged that there was no definite evidence that any of the killings were related. "But at this point we're not going to rule anything out," Merrill said. "We are certainly troubled by it."

There was a problem, however, one that would bedevil the investigators far into the future. The uncertainty that plagued the people of the Valley had its parallel in the minds of the men and women responsible for solving the series of killings: Which of these cases were related? If there was a serial killer loose in the Valley, which of the unsolved murders should be treated as his doing?

In a way this seemed a simple matter: there is a group of murders for which no one has been prosecuted; go find out who committed them. But from the point of view of the people who would carry out the assignment, it was far more complicated. The attorney general would not have taken action unless a large number of people had grown concerned, including many police and prosecutors; a large number of people would not have grown concerned at a series of killings if they had seemed an ordinary number of isolated incidents. People were worried that a serial killer was at work in their neighborhoods.

But the notion of a serial killer was a tricky one. Until you caught a serial killer, it was impossible to know for sure that he existed. That was especially true when time had erased so much of the information about how the murderer had manipulated and killed his victims. So the attorney general was obliged to take action because of worries about the existence of a serial killer without knowing if he existed, and without knowing which cases might be related. Merrill's response was to list all the area's unsolved murders since 1981, then tack on the 1968 killing of Jo Anne Dunham.

In addition to the deaths of Jo Anne Dunham, Elizabeth Critchley, Eva Morse, Bernice Courtemanche, and Ellen Fried, Merrill said, the investigators would look into the cases of two men, still unidentified, whose bodies had been found in March and April, and Sylvia Gray, the seventy-six-year-old woman who had been stabbed and beaten to death near her Plainfield home in 1982. They would also cooperate with Vermont authorities on the case of Lynda Moore.

A group of police officers and prosecutors would meet Monday in Claremont to set up the task force, Merrill announced. The attorney general didn't say so, but it would be part of the investigators' job to decide which of these murders to focus on. That decision, the thorniest single element of the case, would continue to rest at the center of the Valley mystery, like the monster in the center of the maze, until the day someone was caught and charged with the killings.

Mike Prozzo was fed up with feeling helpless. He had worked more hours on these missing-persons cases that turned into homicides than on anything else that had come along in his five years as chief of detectives in Claremont. And that meant that they had invaded his off-duty life as well. There was a time, not too long before, when Prozzo wouldn't have minded the distraction, would have figured the more the better. He had gone through a divorce several years before and there had been times when it seemed the job was all he had, the only part of his life that was manageable. But now he had been happy in a second marriage for a couple of years and Prozzo felt as if he had restored the balance between work and home, regained the feeling that things were going well and everything was in its proper place. But these unsolved cases, the victims, their families, the sense that it was his own responsibility and his own failure, kept pushing its way into his life. He found himself distracted in the midst of his family or friends, thinking of things he had done or ought to do in the investigation, his mind circling around the details, turning them over and over, worrying at them. Yet no answers had emerged, and in the end Prozzo was left with a feeling that approached a kind of loneliness.

This is what it would feel like, Prozzo thought, if you were stranded alone, your car broken down on the highway at two in the morning in some strange place in the middle of the country far from home, and you look one way and there's no sign of help for miles and you look the other way and there's nothing there, either. You're just helpless, pure and simple, and you think, ''What am I going to do with this lonely feeling?''

Now, at last, there was an answer. It was Monday morning,

less than seventy-two hours since the remains of Eva Morse had been identified, and they were setting up a task force. At last they'd have the means to go on the offensive, instead of just waiting for things to happen and then trying to find the time and people to do a proper investigation.

Prozzo walked from the detectives' office in the Claremont police station to the courthouse next door. There were a few unfamiliar faces, probably from the attorney general's office, some brass from the state police, but Prozzo felt as if he knew almost everybody in the room, several state police detectives from Concord, chiefs and investigators from Claremont, Newport, Charlestown, Unity, and the neighboring town of Acworth. Jim Candon and Mike LeClair, the two state police detectives heading the Lynda Moore investigation, had come over from Vermont with their chief of detectives. The courtroom rumbled with the greetings and gossip of more than two dozen men.

After a period of general discussion the leaders split off to meet in another room. When they returned just before noon an assistant attorney general announced the formation of a five-man task force that would set up an office in Claremont. It would be headed by Sergeant Clay Young, the chief investigator of the New Hampshire State Police. Prozzo was gratified to see that his boss, Chief Bauer, had named him to represent Claremont. The other members were a detective from Newport, Tom Cummings, and two young state police investigators, Barry Hunter and Mike Miles.

They got off to a fast start. The following day the detectives found a vacant space on the ground floor of a state-owned building on Water Street. It had been abandoned by the state liquor authority and the outline of the letters spelling out Liquor Store was still visible above the door. The unemployment office, probation and parole department, and Division of Child and Youth Services occupied the second floor.

The former liquor store was now a single, large, echoing space. It was poorly suited for use as an office, but it was owned by the state, which made it cheap. That was a key consideration. The state of New Hampshire was not about to reverse three centuries of frugality and make the task force comfortable.

The office space, awkward though it might be, had at least

turned up quickly. Furnishing it was another matter. It took weeks to get a phone; nobody wanted to pay for it. Eventually a computer for word processing and managing case data was located in some remote corner of the state system and sent over; unfortunately, none of the detectives knew how to operate it, and there was no money for a secretary or administrative assistant. The city of Newport contributed some desks and chairs, and boxes that could be used to hold files. Later a couple of typewriters appeared.

The balky trickle of support from the state had its parallel in the flow of communication. Now that the state government had turned the bright light of its attention upon the killings in the Valley, the investigation had become tightly entangled in politics. The members of the task force were required to clear all public statements with the attorney general's office. Word of any developments, progress or achievement or simply effort, would come from Concord.

On Saturday, in the first flurry of publicity, an assistant attorney general had announced that the names and even the phone numbers of the task force members would be publicized, to make it simple for citizens to offer tips and comments. Once the five detectives had assembled in the former liquor store, however, the attorney general had imposed a policy of secrecy. Even the names of the five men, though widely known, were not released. That meant all communication would have to pass through several levels in the chain of command, through the state police and the attorney general's office.

Besides the purely political intentions, there were reasonable goals behind the rigid information policy. It was intended to avoid prejudicing any future prosecution, to keep information from potential suspects, and to protect the anonymity of the task force members for purposes of the investigation. But the net effect was to distance the task force from both the public and from state officials in Concord.

At least there was no problem of communication within the task force itself, however. At the beginning the atmosphere felt a little like the fifteen-year reunion of a high school basketball team. Working in small communities in a small state, most of the men had crossed paths frequently. Tom Cummings was married to a woman from Claremont; Mike Prozzo had

gone to school with her brother and knew her father, a fire-
fighter in Claremont. The wives of Barry Hunter and Mike
Prozzo both worked at the hospital; the two couples had seen
each other socially. The three state police detectives, Young,
Hunter, and Miles, had studied and taught in the same training
courses and occasionally worked together on cases. Young,
before his promotion to head the major-case investigations out
of Concord, had been stationed several years earlier in a state
police office near Claremont, where Hunter was now; each of
them had become acquainted with Prozzo and Cummings
while cooperating with the local departments on cases.

Mike Prozzo remembered a night several years earlier when
the police radio had brought a strange call for help from Route
120 in the north of Claremont. The caller was not a police
officer, but he was reporting that a trooper needed help. When
Prozzo and another officer arrived they found Clay Young,
who had been patrolling the road, outnumbered by a burly
father and son who objected to Young's attempt to arrest the
younger man for drunken driving. Young's portable radio
had been knocked loose in the struggle; a helpful bystander had
picked it up and called for help. Prozzo and his partner had
helped wrestle the two men into handcuffs, earning the trooper's appreciation.

Clay Young was a natural choice to lead this group. He had
the closemouthed and deliberate style of a man who likes to
consider at length all the possibilities in a situation. Along with
his military bearing and broad expanse of bald head, this gave
him an air of authority that could seem forbidding, but that
was misleading. In a career of almost two decades that had
made him one of the leading detectives in the state police,
Young had worked at one time or another in almost every
region of New Hampshire. Everywhere he had been, Young
was widely respected by both other officers and members of
the public.

A chief of detectives in the Lakes region remembered Clay
Young as the most systematically tenacious investigator he had
ever known. A woman in southern New Hampshire whose
sister had been killed thought of the detective as almost saintly.
It was several years and the case had never been solved. The
woman's priest never mentioned her loss any more, but Clay
Young continued to call once or twice a year to tell her of

new leads and assure her that the investigation was still active. Whether this was the detective's intention or not, the calls provided what little solace the woman could find in the situation; Young's quiet sympathy and stubborn persistence assured the woman that her sister was not forgotten.

The state police detectives were only called in on cases in small communities where local police departments lacked the expertise to handle major crimes, or on homicides and other serious crimes where larger departments asked for assistance. That meant that Clay Young and the two other state troopers had more experience with murder cases than the two local officers, Prozzo and Cummings, who worked on the whole range of matters that arose in their communities. Young had developed expertise in administering and interpreting polygraph tests; Barry Hunter, whose promotion to detective had been the realization of a boyhood dream, had studied techniques for extracting evidence from crime scenes. Prozzo and Cummings, along with Miles, who had been stationed in the Valley, provided the kind of local knowledge and contacts that often proved more valuable than any technical expertise. The task force seemed a well-constructed team.

The five men quickly fell into a smooth routine. Mike Prozzo, who lived closest to the office, usually arrived first and started the coffee maker. Prozzo enjoyed the quiet time before the others arrived, using it to review reports of the previous day's work. By nine o'clock the rest of the men had arrived and they would sit down to discuss leads and divide up assignments. It was quickly apparent that they would get along well together; the mood was relaxed and egalitarian.

At lunch in Burger King one day, three of the men found some cardboard children's crowns being given away for a promotion. They amused themselves at lunch by assigning each other nicknames and writing them on the crowns. For his sharp face and the aggressive way he swooped upon a lead or a piece of evidence, Prozzo was anointed with the name Hawk. Back in the office, they handed out the crowns to the two who had not been present. Clay Young was ceremoniously crowned with the title Bald Eagle One, in recognition of his shiny head and his leadership role.

Young exercised his leadership with a light hand; assignments and decisions seemed to be made by consensus. Prozzo was voluble and used to command, opposite in temperament to the calm and taciturn state police detective; rather than clashing, their styles seemed to complement each other. The problem, as Prozzo already knew well and Young quickly observed, was that they didn't have much to work with.

It wasn't that the task force lacked information on the cases, far from it. Especially in the Claremont cases, which Prozzo and his colleagues had worked up, everything that could be done had been done thoroughly and well. But homicide investigations typically began from the place where the victim was found and radiated outward. The body and the surrounding area were normally a rich source of information. In the Valley killings, on the other hand, the task force faced an investigation without a center.

Clay Young found himself envying the Vermont detectives working on the case of Lynda Moore. They had arrived at the scene within a few hours after the crime. In the New Hampshire cases, by contrast, it had been months, even years, before investigators got a look at the crime scene. Except in the murder of the elderly Sylvia Gray near her home, no one had even known that a crime had been committed in any of the cases until a body was discovered. By the time the investigators arrived, the forces of nature had erased most of the information that would have gotten the investigation off to a fast start.

Still, the creation of the task force itself was an encouraging move. For the public there was a degree of reassurance in it. The people more directly involved, and especially the task force members, faced the job with optimism. Five experienced detectives working exclusively on the Valley killings would be able to attack the mystery more aggressively than anyone had done to date.

Officially, of course, no one was promising anything.

"We are concerned that a serial killer could be a factor here," an assistant attorney general told reporters, "but we have no concrete evidence on that." The public stance was that the task force was being set up to find out about connections. But behind the public pronouncements there was a general expectation that the task force would produce results. Even the members kept it to themselves, but everybody expected to catch a killer.

The first step was deciding what they were dealing with.

Henry Ryan had reported within a few days on his autopsy of Eva Morse. In a close examination of the bones, Ryan had found telltale evidence: like Bernice Courtemanche, she had been stabbed to death. Like Bernice, she had been stabbed repeatedly, far beyond what was necessary to kill. Like Bernice, she had suffered numerous cuts to the throat; in Eva's case, the cuts had come close to decapitating her. Added to the other similarities—a daytime disappearance, hitchhiking, the locations, the dumping of the bodies—Ryan's conclusions reinforced the correspondence between the cases of Bernice Courtemanche and Eva Morse.

That raised the question of Ellen Fried. An autopsy in New Hampshire soon after the discovery of her remains seven months earlier had failed to reveal the cause of Fried's death. But in several cases since then, Henry Ryan had seen more in a weathered set of bones than other autopsy physicians could. It seemed worth a try. The remains of Ellen Fried were sent off to Maine. This time there was no urgency; it was an old case, as these things went. The task force could afford to wait.

In the meantime, there was still a decision to be made about which cases were the most important. The attorney general's initial list of nine cases was unrealistic as a work assignment. A few of the cases bore only faint similarities to the killings that had provoked anxiety in the Valley. Others, like the killing of Jo Anne Dunham, might be related but seemed too old to make active investigation profitable. The Dunham case, and that of Elizabeth Critchley, seemed to fall into a secondary category; the task force would watch for evidence in other cases that might touch on the fates of the two young women. The Vermont detectives were working on the murder of Lynda Moore; the task force would stay in close touch with Mike LeClair and Jim Candon. That left the deaths of Bernice Courtemanche, Ellen Fried, and Eva Morse at the core of the New Hampshire investigation.

When the attorney general's office made the announcement, there was a fourth case on the list: the unidentified body found in a rest area off Route 12 in North Charlestown, a male in his twenties or thirties, had been added. The body had been discovered only a few weeks earlier; perhaps the publicity would create a break in the case. And the rest area where it had been found was within a mile of where Eva Morse had last been seen. Among people who had been paying close attention to the series of killings, adding the case to the task force workload seemed, as someone said, like "a what-the-hell move."

The odd decision to include the rest-stop corpse did nothing to change the group's working hypothesis, the idea that everyone from Concord, New Hampshire, to the Vermont side of the Connecticut River was waiting for them to prove or disprove: There is a serial killer in the Valley and he has murdered Bernice Courtemanche, Ellen Fried, Eva Morse, Elizabeth Critchley, Jo Anne Dunham, and Lynda Moore.

That was a hypothesis, however, not a belief. Young and the others maintained a public neutrality about the existence of a serial killer. There was no deception in this. It was a political stance, certainly, obedience to the orders of superiors in the attorney general's office and local government. Beside retaining control of the investigation and the credit for any results, politicians wanted to avoid anything, justified or not, that would feed public fear.

But this open-minded stance came in part from the detectives themselves. It was the outlook of the professional investigator, a way of seeing the world. Anyone who might have to take a case into court someday quickly learned to reserve judgment until the evidence singled out a suspect. These were bright, experienced, creative investigators in one degree or another, but they worked within a system that set its own rules.

"You can have all the suspicions and beliefs and intuitions in the world," someone said, "but it's not gonna do squat by the time the judge brings the gavel down."

For a detective, keeping an open mind was a useful work technique. The longer you waited to commit yourself to one theory, one suspect, the longer you put off blindness to other possibilities. It gave you a better chance of seeing other useful things when they came before your eyes. Everyone could describe a dozen leads that had looked like sure things, a dozen suspects who had looked guilty as hell, until other facts had produced the real culprit from somewhere else. It was best to wait until you were sure, and then wait a little longer.

In the case of Eva Morse, there were additional factors that contributed to this skepticism. Those who knew the most about her life—the rough circumstances, her marginal economic existence, her lesbian associations, the disorderly social life of her friends and their brushes with the law—tended to separate the death of Eva Morse from the other cases. And there was one other element to their reservations, mostly unspoken: these were crimes that seemed to depend on the attraction, however deformed, of a man to a series of women. Some of the investigators found it difficult to believe that a man could have chosen this obese, mannish woman as a victim.

John Philpin had no such doubts. The psychologist had been following New Hampshire events in the newspaper when Mike LeClair, the Vermont State Police detective he had worked with on the Gary Schaefer cases, called for assistance a few days after the killing of Lynda Moore. Philpin had helped the detectives discern the shadows of motivation that attached themselves to the physical evidence, shaping an understanding of what had happened when the killer confronted Lynda Moore in the confined space between the kitchen and living room, re-creating the state of mind behind the furious, crushing swiftness of the attack. Starting from the reconstruction, Philpin started working on a profile of the killer for the Vermont detectives to use.

It was a few days after that when Mike Prozzo called from the office of the New Hampshire task force. The detective had talked with Philpin occasionally since the psychologist had helped out with the analysis of Richard Bordeau the previous autumn. More recently, while conferring with the task force, Mike LeClair had mentioned Philpin's work on the Moore case. A quick discussion had produced a decision to ask Philpin to consult with the task force.

The result became an interesting oddity of the investigation into the killings in the Connecticut Valley: John Philpin was to be the only person working directly on murder cases from both sides of the Connecticut River.

Crooks, like traffic and business, moved easily back and forth across the river, and police in Valley towns had long since recognized the need to do the same. Chiefs and detectives, in particular, maintained working relations with their counterparts on the opposite side of the river, and many of them had become friends. But their cooperation always took place in the shadow of political reality: they worked in different states, in different jurisdictions, with different prosecutors, answering ultimately to different political authorities. No detective, however close the cooperation, would ever be allowed the time to make himself an expert in a case from the other side of the river.

In the long run this gap would prove a significant obstacle to the solution of the Valley killings, which showed no respect for the broad expanse of the Connecticut River or the boundary between two states that ran along its western shore. But now, almost by accident, a bearded forty-three-year-old Vermont psychologist who had spent the last five years making himself an expert in criminal investigation was becoming the one man who could span the gap, the boundary that separated a growing list of murder victims.

Beyond the essential question of whether the deaths were the work of a serial killer, the New Hampshire detectives hoped Philpin could help reconstruct the psychological atmosphere of the New Hampshire crimes and devise subjects and techniques of questioning that might separate out the most credible suspects. Eventually, all this material could solidify into a profile, or a conclusion that no single profile could fit a diverse group of crimes.

Philpin wasn't bound by the limitations that reined in the detectives of the task force. The psychologist wasn't about to discuss his conclusions in public; he accepted the ground rules imposed by the political authorities. And intellectually, he resisted any unsubstantiated conclusion as earnestly as the detectives. But as Philpin immersed himself more and more deeply in the case files, he came to feel a presence lurking behind the facts, like some stealthy predator circling in the forest, always just beyond the range of sight.

Somewhere in there, the psychologist sensed, was the outline of a serial killer.

nineteen

All this should have been easier. Certainly the circumstances were more conductive to quick work than a lot of the cases John Philpin worked on, coming to the scene months or years after the crime.

This time the detectives had been on the scene within hours after Lynda Moore was killed, and Philpin had gotten a look within a few days. He had absorbed the dimensions of the small space where Lynda Moore had met her killer and struggled to save herself, then prowled the grounds and stared at the house from all sides, then walked back in, trying to imagine the mood of a killer, the sequence of intention and impulse, that had led him to this savage outburst of fury.

And of course there was the victim, the second party to this intricate choreography of death. Philpin would have liked to immerse himself deeply in the personality of Lynda Moore, using the known as a mirror in which to see the unknown, but there wasn't time. The detectives were eager to move fast. They had been looking closely at the husband as a suspect, though doubts were already emerging. However that turned out, this looked like the kind of case that could be solved quickly. And everybody was aware that any case that wasn't solved in the first few weeks wasn't likely to be solved in the next few months; either you got it fast or you didn't get it for a long time.

There was a problem, though. Often it happened quickly for Philpin, the evidence converging with his imagination to produce a picture of how the crime had happened, then one shape separating itself from the vast army of possibilities, the outline of a killer coming into focus. This time, the focus wouldn't sharpen. It was still early. All the things that might have sharpened the image of the killer were missing so far. Only preliminary autopsy and lab reports were available, and not much was known about the victim. There was nothing to suggest a motive. Philpin was seeing at least two very different pictures of what had happened.

The problem was the confined ferocity of the killing. Looked at from one perspective, it argued first for a spontaneous, unplanned act, an explosive binge of psychotic viciousness, fuelled by rage or panic. It could have been the act of an acquaintance, someone who came to Lynda Moore's house on some pretext, then tapped into a stream of deranged fury. The body had not been manipulated after the killing; there was no sign of any ceremonial or formalistic activity by the killer. The torrent of violence would have been its own reward. Such a man would have derived his pleasure, possibly sexual arousal, from the destruction of his victim, even without any overtly sexual act. It could well have been a singular act, unprecedented, unlikely to be repeated.

The killer's departure from the house, like his arrival, would have been uncalculated, unplanned; he would have been in a state of confusion as he left, incapable of rearranging things, of covering his tracks, of straightening or cleaning his clothes. His escape is a matter of luck; his path may run briefly parallel to the comings and goings of a dozen people or more in the vicinity of the Moore house, but does not directly intersect any.

But what if it were not a spontaneous act, not some kind of confrontation gone wrong? Ordinarily a more deliberate, calculating type of killer would have found his pleasure in the domination and control of his victim. The key to the psychology of such a killer would be his urge to possess his victim. This killer would have taken his time, attempting to stretch out the process, controlling the victim before killing her, or spending time with the corpse afterward, arranging the event and its aftermath to conform with a scenario long cultivated in fantasy. But there were no signs of such drawn-out savoring of the process; on the contrary, the medical examiner's evidence suggested that the stabbing would have lasted a mere thirty to forty-five seconds, the body had been left to lie where it fell, and nothing else had been disturbed.

But as Philpin read and listened to the investigators' preliminary reports about the central position of the Moore house, about all the people who routinely glanced into the yard and spied on the domestic life of the family that lived there, as he walked through the grassy field below the house, noting vantage points near the turnout and along the banks of the river, as Philpin absorbed all these facts and impressions he summoned up the specter of a killer who could have taken possession of his victim without ever touching her. Perhaps this was the answer to the strangely pristine conditions surrounding the corpse of Lynda Moore.

This man is excited by his surreptitious spying; like many repeat killers he is aroused by the risk of getting caught. There is an ecstatic anticipation in his prowling. It is not the first time he has prowled the area around the house, trying to catch a glimpse of Lynda Moore. He has seen her before, savored each brief sighting, drawn her image into his fantasy of anger and vengeance. He has moved easily, quietly, through the field, into the little patch of woods, along the river, making each tree and each shrub and each rise of ground his own, taking possession.

Now he ambles with fake casualness along the river behind the house. At the edge of his consciousness he tracks the traffic passing fifty yards away, coveting the sense that there are others around, enjoying the feeling that he knows where and how to move so that few of them will notice him and none of those will remember. Suddenly he crouches low, like a child playing hide-and-seek, and moves stealthily up the embankment to a point where he can watch his prey without being seen. She is lying in the sun, bundled against the early-spring chill, hungrily consuming the long-awaited early-season sunshine on her face.

He devours the sight, this woman with her big house and nice cars and easy life, he savors her every action. There is a thrill of sexual pleasure in the sight of his victim, vulnerable, open to him. It's almost as if he can see into her mind, and yet her mind holds no idea of his presence. He watches the way she moves her hands, shifts her weight, turns her head to the sun. She thinks she is alone, does what she would do if she were alone. But she is not alone, he is present, and he could reach out and touch her if he wanted to, he could do anything else he wanted to, anything, whatever he wants. She belongs to him.

Perhaps by now it is twelve-forty-five or so, Philpin thought, and Steve Moore calls. His wife hears the phone ringing and rises to go inside, moving quickly to answer before it stops. In her rush she leaves her sandals where she has placed them, resting neatly side by side beneath the lounge chair.

The man watches as she rises suddenly from the lounge and after the door closes behind her he moves to follow, to take possession in the flesh of what he has owned in his mind. He would wait for the phone call to end, or perhaps she was getting something to eat—a package of crackers had been left out—then he would move carefully, feeling his way, making sure she was alone in the house. Did she hear the door close behind him and move to see who had entered?

She challenges him, perhaps even takes the offensive, ordering him out of the house—even a preliminary understanding of her character showed that she was confident, strong-willed, proud and possesive of her house—but he has the knife ready and falls upon her quickly. She puts up a vigorous defense but the confrontation is one-sided and over in minutes.

The killer, still calculating, still in control, does not pause to linger over what he has done. He exists as he has come in, taking his weapon, moving confidently, melting quickly back into the flow of ordinary life, leaving almost no trace.

And yet, Philpin kept returning to the problem of focus, the narrow space, the extreme viciousness compressed into a few short moments. There was an incongruity in the idea of a man savoring his victim beforehand, exulting in his power over her, and then ignoring her afterward, when she is at his mercy, in his complete control. Philpin jotted some notes:

Subject's fantasies and subsequent behavior did not include an extended stay with this woman as his captive. Did not include sexual assault, repeated sexual assault over time, etc. The excitement evident here is with the kill.

And what if the killer had been planning on some further activity when he entered the house and had been panicked into the attack by his victim's aggressive defense, or frightened into flight afterward, before he could carry out his plan?

"It would be my opinion that the area covered in the attack would be much greater," Philpin wrote in his notes.

Philpin looked the notes over, then set them aside. He had already made the point, seesawing back and forth between the two scenarios. There was no getting around it: both stories were plausible, both conformed with what he had seen and felt at the Moores', both fit the evidence that had been found in the house. Less than two weeks after the death of Lynda Moore, Philpin produced two distinct profiles for the investigators.

The man who killed impulsively, without calculation, is a white male between eighteen and twenty-nine years old, Philpin told the investigators. He is of average intelligence or less, and he failed to graduate from high school. He lives alone or with an older female relative, within twenty-five miles of Saxtons River. He works rarely or not at all and spends much of his time roaming, apparently aimlessly, from place to place; consequently he knows the area well.

He is manifestly mentally ill, probably psychotic. He looks sloppy and is careless about personal hygiene; combined with poor nutrition caused by childhood neglect, his carelessness could cause other problems, like rotted teeth. He has no close friend or confidant. He is ill at ease socially, especially around women, and others consider him awkward or strange.

There is a pattern of mental-health problems and trouble with the law dating back to his early teens, including such charges as breaking and entering, morals and sex offenses, and possibly attempted rape. But he probably has not killed before. He killed because circumstance and sudden impulse flowed together; if he had done it before he would probably have been caught by now. He abuses alcohol, but that played no role in the crime; the events leading up to the killing were precipitated by some particularly stressful event in his life, like a fight with someone he knows, the loss of a job, or a defeat in some form of competition with another man.

Knives are important to him, significant in some way. He entertains fantasies of vengeance against those who have wronged him, in which a knife figures prominently. These fantasies are fused with sexual impulses; he may use a knife to mutilate pictures of women while masturbating.

Since the killing, he has felt no guilt and little anxiety about the crime, but he has experienced flashbacks. These episodes were not necessarily disturbing; in fact, he may well have enjoyed reliving his crime. Though in the past he has routinely spent much of his day wandering in the area around Saxtons River and Bellows Falls, his first inclination after the killing was to pull back, even to the point of staying home, hiding out. That phase will not last, though; he will soon resume his meandering, if he hasn't already. He does not worry about getting caught. He has been a visible presence on the street, and he will remain so.

Philpin offered the investigators several pointers for questioning suspects who fit this profile. Oblivious to guilt, he would be likely to talk about what he had done in matter-of-fact terms, or to vaguely acknowledge doing something "bad" without at first recognizing his responsibility.

The two profiles were in striking contrast. The other profile portrayed a man within the same age range but more intelligent, probably a high school graduate, possibly with some education beyond that. He knows the immediate area, too, Philpin wrote, may have lived here at one time, and he moves around freely, but he ranges farther; he lives within fifty miles of Saxtons River. He is unmarried and lives alone or with relatives.

There is nothing special about his appearance, nothing that would attract attention, though he is constantly reassessing himself and changes his appearance regularly.

He has a job but he is not reliable. He has no close friend or confidant, but he is more likely than the first profile suspect to maintain continuing relationships with others, though they remain superficial. In social situations he is like a child mimicking adults; he is good at acting out a variety of social roles, though he does not experience the associated emotions.

His behavior betrays no obvious signs of pathology, and he would deny heatedly any suggestion that there was anything wrong with him, that he was sick. Looking at him, no one would say he was crazy, or even strange, and though he may well have killed before, he has no criminal record.

It was not a distinct event that triggered the sequence leading to the killing, but he may have prepared himself with alcohol, using it to loosen his inhibitions, aware, in a general way if not specifically, of the energies that might be unleashed.

The knife he killed with has no particular significance to this man; he could as well have bludgeoned or strangled his victim. But the act of killing, and its impact on the community, gives him a sense of power. He is following accounts of the crime in newspapers and on television, fascinated by the distant reverberations of his act.

It is not a pure pleasure, however. He is experiencing periods of anxiety. In ordinary times he swings between intense feelings of inferiority and a sense that he is powerful, superior. This pattern persists: since killing Lynda Moore he has see-sawed between a terrible certainty that the investigators are closing in on him and an absolute conviction that he will never be caught.

He tried to cover his tracks after the killing and in his dark moments it is one of the things that worries him. He washed his bloody clothing, or got rid of it where he hoped it could not be traced back to him, and he cleaned himself as soon as he got the chance. He thinks it through, searching for some way the clothes, the blood, could be connected to him. He is worried about the knife: Is there some tiny trace of blood left on it that could become evidence? Could it be traced to him in spite of his best efforts? He may have tried to establish an alibi, dropping in soon after the killing on acquaintances or places where people know him and would remember his visit. Anyone who saw him at the time thought he seemed nervous.

This man will stay as far from Saxtons River as he can for a long time. He will try to match this physical distance from the crime with emotional distance; he will try not to think about what he has done, and try not to feel anything about what he has done. If he is aware of things like guilt and responsibility, it is purely as ideas; he does not feel these things, and flatly denies any possibility that he could have committed such a crime.

It was a little unsettling, Philpin thought, to be suspended between these two portraits of the killer. Surely with more time and more information one of these pictures would fade, the other would take on sharper outlines and more vivid colors, and press itself forward. But there was no time; the investigators needed to move fast, and they wanted him to move fast. And Philpin was already turning his attention to the task force investigation across the river in Claremont. Even the tantalizing question of whether the Moore case might be related to the task force killings would have to be set aside for later. By then Philpin would know more about the New Hampshire killings.

Philpin presented his dual portrait in the Lynda Moore case feeling a little apologetic, but the investigators were glad to have it. Everyone acknowledged that the situation was far from ideal. That was nothing new. There weren't a lot of ideal situations when someone had been murdered.

twenty

For the task force, the daily reality was an endlessly rolling tide of detail. It was easy to forget that the pattern behind all this, what gave it meaning and existence, was the fear of a serial killer.

A man called to say that a woman he knew had told him she had a letter from Bernice Courtemanche with a photo of Bernice and a man. The letter had been mailed after Bernice disappeared, the woman said.

A Connecticut man named George Culbertson called to say he had seen something strange on the day of Eva Morse's disappearance nine months earlier. He owned a summer home in Charlestown that he and his wife used on weekends. They had stayed on after Fourth of July weekend and that Wednesday they had been driving toward Charlestown from Unity when they saw a hitchhiker.

"I remember it clearly because she was wearing clothes that looked like they were twenty years out of style," the man said. "You know, like hippie clothes." He had decided to call when he heard about the task force, Culbertson said.

These tips, like hundreds of others, led nowhere. The woman in the photo was not Bernice Courtemanche, though she looked a little like her, and the hitchhiker's clothes bore no resemblance to Eva Morse's windbreaker and jeans.

There were several factors that kept all this from descending into drudgery. For one thing, each tip, each lead, each interview was a story in itself. The story might turn out to reflect nothing more substantial than the dark apparitions of some twisted soul, but exploring these tales bore its own rewards. Following along the byways of human nature, and talking and speculating about them afterward, provided one of the finge benefits of being a cop. Soon after the task force was set up, one of the detectives received a note from a police officer in Bellows Falls, south of Springfield on the Vermont side of the river.

"I was talking with a subject last night who stated that she was talking with a family friend who just moved to Newport from Claremont. This person lived with a girl by the first name of Claire. Claire's boyfriend's name was Dewey something.

"Dewey's brother is a 'bad character' and is supposedly connected with the Mafia. She stated that the Mafia hired Richard Bordeau to do the killing of Fried and Courtemanche. There is evidence in Richard's house linking the Mafia and Richard to the killing.

"Now Dewey's brother and three or four other Mafia subjects are supposed to kill Richard within the next month. This is supposed to be a brutal type killing, made to look like a revenge for one of the female murders.

"They are going to collect any evidence from the house. I will call you when I get up. I have names and am going to set up an appointment to talk to the girl about this. This may be BS, but we can check it out."

Claire, the officer reported after seeking her out for an interview, was so addled by alcohol and drugs that there were times when she would not have been a reliable witness on the subject of her own date of birth. The Mafia story appeared to be the product of some macabre boasting by her boyfriend, Dewey.

And then there were the calls, like the one from a man in Ludlow, Vermont, that left the detectives bemused. Bernard Greylock phoned a trooper at the Vermont State Police office near his home to describe his wife's recent dream. The dream, he said, concerned the murder of Lynda Moore. His wife had special powers, Greylock said.

"She's psychic, you know," he told the detective, as if he

were describing the color of her eyes. The detective invited Greylock to go on.

"She had a vision of a woman being murdered in a wooded area by a thirty-year-old man," Greylock said. The man drove a greenish blue car with a New Hampshire registration containing the number five.

"There was running water nearby," he continued. "The man stopped the car, got out, and opened the hood. The victim got out, too, approached the hood, and was struck on the head.

"The murderer then removed a hunting knife from the trunk and stabbed the woman twice, once in front and once in back."

The detective dutifully recorded Greylock's account, suppressing the knowledge that this was not the kind of lead that good, professional, investigative technique was based on; not only was this a dream, but it was a dream that came from a woman who claimed to have psychic powers.

"Then he removed her clothes carefully," Greylock continued, "and masturbated on them."

The murderer, he added, lived in a trailer with a pink roof and had a mother who was very fat.

There was no correspondence between the circumstances of the dream—the woods, the car, the nude victim—and the murder of Lynda Moore. Maybe Mrs. Greylock was matching her vision to the wrong murder case. The state police detective thanked Mr. Greylock and told him that the task force would be getting in touch with him later.

Detectives always seemed a little bit defensive when they talked about the psychics who seemed to rush to an important investigation like wintering mice to an old house. Nobody would admit thinking a psychic might come up with anything truly useful. But almost without exception they explained their response to these self-proclaimed clairvoyants with sentences that started, "Of course we never expect to get anything out of it, but if they *did* have it right and we ignored them. . . ." In a time when increasing numbers of Americans thought they could predict their prospects in romance or business by examining the alignment of the stars or consulting a set of dice engraved with unreadable foreign symbols, it seemed prudent to check out the dreams of a middle-aged woman as if it were any other kind of lead. And it always made a good story.

However eccentric or mundane the investigative work might

seem on any given day, there was an element of professional excitement surrounding the task force that made even the smallest job seem significant.

It was not just the visibility of the case and the danger of the prey. For the five detectives of the task force, this assignment was a unique professional event. If there had ever before been a special force set up to bring a handpicked group of detectives from various jurisdictions together for a single investigation, no one could remember it. And it was not the kind of event that only seems significant in retrospect. The intense public interest, the resulting close attention of politicians and police superiors, the carefully selected colleagues, the special office—all these were clear indications to each of the task force members that this was something extraordinary, an assignment that might never be matched in a professional lifetime.

And always, suspended just out of the mind's reach, was the sense that this tip, or maybe the one that followed it, would be the one that brought a successful end to the quest. Each new tip or lead, no matter how many had failed before it, retained the capacity to awaken this eager hope of victory.

It was rare that the cycle of hope and failure and new hope could be repeated so many times in just a few hours, but the experience of one morning in late June was representative. The first call, soon after Clay Young arrived at the office, was about the man's body found in the rest area off Route 12 in North Charlestown. The caller said he thought he knew who the man was. The caller knew a man who had gotten in a dispute with some other men; they had a reputation for violence. He described the conflict in detail. The man, he said, had been reported missing May 7. That was the end of that lead. The unidentified body had been found April 1.

Minutes later, a man walked into the former liquor store. He introduced himself and sat down.

"What can we do for you? Young asked.

"I haven't seen my neighbor in about three months," the man said. The neighbor had been in trouble often; he had done time in the Grafton County Jail.

Young thanked the man and called the jail, where the neighbor's fingerprints were on file. A quick comparison to the corpse eliminated the possibility that it was the neighbor.

Soon a phone call came with information from a medical report on a missing man.

"He's had his appendix removed," the caller said. "How about your guy?" The body from the rest area had no major scars, Young told the man. Three in a row.

And before lunch, one more, a missing person who didn't match. Four leads, each of them heartening for a day or an hour or a few minutes, each fading quickly in the light of fact, each renewing the hope briefly lost in the failure of the one before. By the end of three months, the task force had checked out 115 reports of missing persons from all over the country who were similar to the rest-area corpse; every one had failed to match.

Besides checking out tips, the investigators had to start from scratch with some of the case files, compiling basic information about the final known movements and contacts of the victims, their work and families and friends. Prozzo and his Claremont colleagues had done this work for Bernice Courtemanche and later for Ellen Fried. But Eva Morse had last been seen in Charlestown, in front of the veterinary clinic. Even with the help of the state police, the tiny Charlestown Police Department had neither the manpower nor the expertise to assemble all the necessary information. Nine months later, that job fell to the task force. And along with it, now there was the case of Elizabeth Critchley. For the first time her death would be considered in the light of the other killings of women in the Valley.

As work went ahead on the case files, the detectives began compiling a list of men from the Valley who had been convicted of violent and sexual crimes against women. One by one they were checked out, interviewed, questioned about alibis for the times of the disappearances, asked to come in for polygraph tests.

The parents of Bernice Courtemanche, Albert and Jeanne Laplante, had been impatient with the work of the police since the beginning. They had felt from the start that the investigators had failed to follow up some worthwhile leads. They had wanted a more intense investigation of Bernice's boyfriend; he had some friends who were known around Claremont as troublemakers. Their dissatisfaction hadn't kept them from contacting the police periodically with new tips and ideas for investigation, however. The day it was announced that a second set of remains had been found in Kellyville they went to the Claremont police station and asked for Chief Adam Bauer.

The chief updated the Laplantes on the investigation and the plans of the task force. They were still concerned about Teddy Berry, the Laplantes said. Jeanne Laplante told the chief that her sleep was disturbed almost every night by nightmares about her daughter, terrible dreams in which Teddy Berry and two of his friends hurt Bernice. It had gotten so bad that she had been forced to see a doctor to get help sleeping.

Albert Laplante agreed with his wife's view about Bernice's boyfriend, and he had also been concerned about Richard Bordeau. He worked at Wentworth Shoe, where Bordeau had been employed for a while. A few months before, Laplante told the chief, he had driven past Bordeau's house and seen him burying something in his backyard. Bauer promised to pass their ideas along to the task force and keep them informed of any progress.

Many of the calls to the task force were the product of suspicion, citizens singling out from among their neighbors and acquaintances one they thought might be guilty of murder.

Many of the leads were more concrete. In answer to a query from the task force, a supervisor from the county house of corrections called with the names of three men convicted to sexual assault who had been released within a few months before the disappearances.

Each of these reports was checked out, along with the complaint about a man who had offended his neighbors with long, drunken parties featuring public sex and vomiting, and someone who had been observed loitering near an elementary school, and a man who had been seen following the teenage girls who gathered downtown to play video games and flirt with teenage boys.

Whether it seemed likely that he had anything to do with the Valley killings or not, each of these men had to be checked out, observed from a distance, his neighbors interviewed; perhaps he would be confronted directly and asked a few questions about his regular activities, where he had been at certain times on certain days. There was information to be collected from motor vehicle registrations, work records to be gathered, sometimes criminal records to be researched.

Much of the information from the public looked at first as if it were related to the killings, but probably spoke simply of the endemic plague of harassment of women by men. A typical report came from a North Charlestown woman who regularly walked for exercise up Route 12 toward the southern edge of Claremont. It was a mostly rural area, she said, and she was often approached by men who would slow their cars to offer her a ride, or pass in one direction and then a few minutes later in the other, conspicuously ogling her as they passed, sometimes whistling or calling out a comment.

Intimidated by the attention, the woman said, she had changed her routine. She would drive each day to the Smith Farm, a large, parklike reserve nearby, leave her car, and walk along wooded paths. The area was a short distance from where Eva Morse had last been seen. One day around the time of Morse's disappearance, the woman had noticed what looked like a photograph on the ground in her path. When she picked it up she found that it was a picture of a man, from the neck to the knees; he was nude. She threw the picture down and ran home.

"I think someone knows I walk that same route every day," the woman said, "and put that thing there for me to see." The wife of a friend who walked there had seen the picture, too, she said.

The volume of rumor and suspicion, which had gradually fallen to a low rumble in the seven months since Ellen Fried's remains had been found, erupted again with the news about Lynda Moore and the discovery of the bodies of Bernice Courtemanche and Eva Morse. And, as before, rumor fed suspicion, which fed rumor, and Richard Bordeau became once again the subject of excited speculation.

A man from Wentworth Shoe told one of the detectives about a card of condolence the workers there had made up after Bernice Courtemanche's body had been found. Bernice's father had worked at the shoe factory for many years, and at the time her remains were discovered, Richard Bordeau had been a stitcher there. Every worker in the factory had signed the card, the man told the investigator, except for one. Among the dozens and dozens of names, he said, there was no signature of Richard Bordeau.

Investigation showed that the card contained not signatures but names copied out by a single person. Whoever had done the copying had missed several names; Richard Bordeau, relatively new to Wentworth Shoe, had probably been overlooked.

And someone who had been in Richard Bordeau's house reported that he kept a collection of his father's butcher knives, each one sharpened to a razor edge, displaying them proudly and with gusto to his guest. That report was never discounted, but it was of little use.

Mike Prozzo came back to the office one day to find a piece of paper on his desk. It looked like the draft of a memo by one of the other detectives. There was no name at the top.

"Shortly after the discovery of the body of Ellen Fried," it read, "a suspect was developed by the name of Richard Robert Bordeau. Several reasons for the suspicion have come to the attention of the task force investigators.

"One of the investigators, Lieutenant Prozzo, code name Hawk 1, has had several dreams or visions, none of which have anything to do with the case."

Such moments of comic relief lightened the days of investigative routine, but as the months went by without producing neat answers the pressure seemed to mount a notch with each new week. The *Claremont Eagle-Times* had titled an editorial on the day the task force was established "Fearful Times." Months later a story in the *Rutland Daily Herald* was headlined "Reams of Information, No Solution in Murder." In August the *Boston Herald* ran a story with the headline "Murder Mystery in Forest"; it was typical big-city condescension, seeing New Hampshire as a collection of trees interpersed with unsolved crimes, but it testified to the fact that the detectives working on the case were at the center of something and a lot of people were watching.

The secrecy about the names and phone numbers of the task force members didn't help. Nothing could have made the five men, all of them well known in the Valley towns, seem truly remote. But the decision, imposed from above, to run all publicity through the attorney general's office and keep the members' names out of the papers, did set them off from the community. If there was one way to take advantage of the close-knit nature of the Valley community it would have been to capitalize on the connections of the task force members to the surrounding towns. Instead, members of the public with information to offer were asked to call their local police departments or the New Hampshire State Police's toll-free number.

For the people of the Valley were worried.

Much of the anxiety was general. A clerk at the post office noticed that people who came in to pick up their mail were talking about taking precautions, checking their cars before driving anywhere out of town, making sure to get home before dark. Women in particular were conscious of their routines, making sure to park in heavily trafficked areas in town, taking keys from their purses before reaching their cars. Parents warned their children, especially girls, about hitchhiking, going unaccompanied into the woods, hanging around downtown after dark. At home, people who had routinely left their houses open even when they were away installed new locks and began bolting their doors before leaving. People who had only locked up when they were leaving were now locking their doors even when they were at home, and some who had only locked their houses at night were now locking them in daylight, too.

But there was another kind of fear, as well, the kind that attached itself to particular causes. One was the idea that the killings were connected somehow to nurses or hospitals. It was widely known that Ellen Fried had been a nurse at the Valley Regional Hospital. The news stories had reported after a few days that Bernice Courtemanche worked at the county nursing home. It seemed like a long reach to connect the two, the investigators thought. Still, it was something to think about, and when they did, there was more. Eva Morse, the detectives learned, had worked briefly as a nurse's aide some years before. And Lynda Moore had been active in a hospital auxiliary across the river in Vermont; she had even served as its president.

The Valley Regional Hospital in Claremont, the Mary Hitchcock Hospital in Hanover, and other hospitals on the Vermont side of the Valley alerted their nurses to the danger, handed out lists of safety precautions to female employees, and offered workshops in personal security. The Claremont Rotary Club paid for the purchase of police whistles to be distributed to women in self-defense classes.

The other focus of concentrated fear and speculation was the one man universally believed to be a suspect in the killings, Richard Robert Bordeau.

A woman working in social services overheard two other women talking about the murders:

"His mother was a nurse, and his father was in the hospital," one woman said.

"And he really hated nurses, because they let his father die," the other said, completing the thought.

"Did you hear that from him?" the social-service worker asked, skeptical about what sounded more like fear-spawned myth than information.

"Well, no, but I heard it," the woman replied. Like many other people in the Valley, men and women both, the woman was following the natural urge to make sense of the senseless, whether the facts supported the theory or not.

An executive at the chamber of commerce was worried about his daughter. Not only was she a nurse, but she was in the habit of driving out Routes 11 and 103 to the hospital where she worked in New London, beyond Newport. The route took her past the big Victorian house by the covered bridge. The man told his daughter to change her route. There wasn't anything particularly logical about the idea, he knew, it was just fear, that's all, fear, and a way of trying to put it at a distance.

Mike Prozzo was hearing the rumors on the street, people saying, "Oh, we know who did it."

"I heard you guys arrested him and then let him go," a man said to the chief of detectives one day. He didn't need to say who he was talking about. Prozzo told the man that the police were investigating a lot of people but there were no official suspects.

That was true. There were no official suspects, and never had been. But it was also true that there was no such thing as an official suspect, short of someone who had been the subject of a grand jury investigation or charged with a crime, and even the idea of a suspect was hard to define. By now the task force had interviewed more than a hundred men from the Valley who had been convicted of assault and sex crimes. In a sense each had been a suspect; but there had been no reason to believe any one of them had committed a particular crime. In that sense, none had been a suspect. And in the end, virtually all had passed lie-detector tests or provided alibis; the remaining few had been eliminated from the investigation, as had dozens of other men who had come under scrutiny for one reason or another.

With one exception. The file on Richard Bordeau, with his public anger, his persistent harassment of women, his aggressive eccentricity, and, most of all, his weak alibis, continued to grow.

After several months the work the task force had done on Bordeau looked like the product of a checklist from a textbook on investigation. The detectives had plumbed every source of public information, interviewed every available friend or associate, explored every tip, and tracked down every rumor. It was time, the task force leaders decided, to get a closer look. They would watch him every waking hour for a week, get a sense of his patterns, see how he lived. If he were involved in a serious crime, surely they would turn up some sign. It would be a big investment, but at this point they didn't have much to lose; and at least they would never be left to wonder if maybe, just maybe, they could have broken the case if they had looked at this one suspect a little more closely.

Mike Prozzo persuaded a local car-rental agent to provide late-model cars at a reduced rate. Each morning three or four of the detectives would meet at Prozzo's house to pick up the vehicles for the day. To save money they arranged to get gasoline at the police station, where the town got a special rate. One day the rental cars included a Lincoln Continental; the men spent a few minutes examining the top-of-the-line stereo and the luxurious interior before going off to work. Not the typical patrol unit, they joked, though it should be.

The detectives arranged to wait for Bordeau along the road, a watcher ready to signal the other cars that he had left home. A chaser, waiting farther down the road, would wait for him to pass and then follow to his first destination. After several hours the watching team would call in another pair to take up the pursuit. Every six or eight hours the detectives changed places and exchanged cars. On a day when Bordeau moved around a lot it took three or four cars to camouflage the presence of the detectives.

The surveillance had its moments of slapstick. On the street in Claremont one day, Mike Prozzo was watching Bordeau when his quarry turned suddenly and came walking back toward the detective. Feeling like a character in a bad movie, Prozzo scrambled frantically to unfold the newspaper he was carrying and get it up in front of his face; Bordeau had seen the detective during the house-to-house canvassing and Prozzo was convinced he would be recognized. Afterward he was never sure if he had been successful in his effort at concealment or his quarry had simply disdained to acknowledge his presence.

One goal of the surveillance was to produce photographs of Bordeau for use in the investigation. After several days, the detectives established his schedule. He worked the morning shift at Wentworth Shoe; most days he would go afterward to the YMCA, parking each time in the same spot. The detectives found an empty office in the building across the street and arranged with the building's owner to borrow it for a few hours.

When Prozzo and the others arrived to begin setting up, the owner was waiting for them. He wanted to talk about the investigation and how it was going. Prozzo, appreciative of the man's help, was having a hard time breaking off the conversation to get the cameras set up. Finally, feeling rude, he interrupted the conversation and turned back to his work, just in time for the arrival of Bordeau's car in the lot below.

As Bordeau drove up, one of the detectives, forewarned by the men in a car trailing Bordeau, pulled out of a parking place that was in direct line of the sight of the cameras. The stratagem worked exactly as they had planned; the photographic subject turned into the vacated place. The pictures came out perfectly.

It was one of the few satisfactions of the surveillance. After a week of eighteen-hours days and a good deal of tension, the detectives had little to show for their effort. Richard Bordeau had gone grocery shopping, worked in the yard, tinkered with his car. In short, he had acted for seven days like an unmarried working man living alone and pursuing conventional forms of recreation. Whatever hope the task force members may have held dissolved in a week's worth of unrevealing routine.

As the summer came on and the cramped task force office grew warmer, the early hopes of those first cool spring days wilted under the weight of a thousand hours of unproductive leads.

"It can be real discouraging when you don't turn up anything," Clay Young told an interviewer. "But I believe in time we're going to find the guy who did it."

twenty-one

There was just no way, Mike LeClair thought, no way in hell the husband could have done it.

There were lots of ways to approach someone who was such an obvious suspect. There were detectives who liked to try to scare the person into confessing, or intimidate him, or trick him with faked sympathy, or pretend to think he was innocent to get him relaxed and vulnerable, then use words to hammer a confession out of him.

LeClair wasn't above a little playacting occasionally if there was some prospect of success, but he much preferred a more straightforward approach. That was why the detective had told Steve Moore he was the primary suspect in his wife's death.

It wasn't just that Moore was on the scene when the ambulance arrived, though that was certainly part of it. It wouldn't have been the first time a man killed his wife and then called the ambulance. Moore's eerie calm was another factor. When LeClair arrived, the first detective on the scene, Moore was standing in the driveway, waiting. He said hello to the detective and shook hands with the solemn but unemotional manner of an usher greeting mourners at a funeral.

The body of Lynda Moore and her immediate surroundings looked strangely isolated, LeClair thought, as if they had been sealed off from the rest of the house. An antique chair, a marble-topped table, a wine rack, all within a few feet of where she had fallen, were undisturbed. Even a first look told LeClair of an explosive attack and a vigorous attempt by Lynda Moore to defend herself—the victim's arms and hands were criss-crossed with slashing wounds from blows aimed at her body. So much had happened in such a confined space. How had the killer gotten so close to his victim?

The ambulance driver's account of Steve Moore's behavior, his cool persistence in writing the check and sending the truck off to the dump, reinforced the air of unnatural calm. As more investigators arrived and crime-lab technicians moved around the house, gathering evidence, Moore went about his business, making phone calls to his office, talking with friends who had come to console him. The detectives noticed that one of Moore's first phone calls had been to his lawyer. Was this a defensive move, instinctive or calculated? As Moore moved around the house, passing between the kitchen and the entry hall, he stepped without apparent hesitation over the blood-soaked body of his wife.

Later in the afternoon, LeClair took Moore aside for a private talk.

"Okay, look, Steve," LeClair said, "I want to be up-front with you." Moore was impassive.

"Ninety percent of these"—LeClair gestured vaguely, taking in the house and Moore and the body of his wife—"ninety percent of these involve the husband." The word *involve* was a euphemism, but LeClair could see Moore wasn't having any trouble understanding what he meant.

"You know that you're going to be the number-one suspect in the case," LeClair went on, "and we're going to have to treat you like that for a while until we can either arrest you or clear you."

It was a peculiarly delicate situation, LeClair knew. In a case like this you were looking at either a killer or a horribly grief-stricken victim. It was night and day, and no way of telling which. You had to treat the man as a suspect, but at the same time you had to acknowledge the possibility that he was a victim.

"I know this is your wife that was murdered," the detective told Moore. "You've got your kids here that you've got to worry about now. They're here without a mother and I'm sad for you, I'm concerned." Moore listened without comment.

"And I also want you to know," LeClair continued, "that you're the best witness I have in this case and I need your help." LeClair was aware that a suspect put in this situation had no choice; he had to give at least the appearance of co-operating or he would seem defensive and guilty.

But even as he spoke with Moore, LeClair was entertaining his first doubts that the man could have killed his wife. Moore recounted his movements throughout the day in a flat, emotionless voice that seemed consistent with his behavior; the man was obviously tightly controlled. Would a man kill his wife when he knew his employee would arrive at the house no more than two or three minutes behind him and his children were due home from school in less than half an hour? The rest of the day, Moore had been in view of four or five men at the Petterson house, except for ten minutes when he went to the store to get a sandwich; in his truck Moore found the cash register slip from the store with the time stamped on it. Even the presence of the lawyer looked less suggestive when LeClair learned that the man was Moore's best friend, a natural person to call in the circumstances; in any case, he specialized in commercial law and said he wouldn't know how to handle a criminal case.

The timing of Moore's arrival at home reinforced the idea that he couldn't have been the killer. LeClair had seen a lot of bodies in his five years as a detective and he had an instant reaction as he looked down at the body and felt the skin.

"This lady's been dead a couple of hours, at least," LeClair told himself. The ambulance driver, Jimmy Perrault, agreed. He had made a cursory check of the body and quickly decided even the most remote chance of helping Lynda Moore had long since vanished.

"If she'd only been dead even half an hour," he told LeClair, "I'd have put her in the ambulance."

The victim's arms and legs were cold and her hands were clenched into fists, except for one finger that pointed grotesquely, as if assigning responsibility for her death. The finger was probably due to a cut tendon, LeClair thought; otherwise it would have pulled into a fist with the others. The cooling of the body and the stiffening that follows death were already well advanced. It seemed certain that Lynda Moore had been dead a lot longer than the forty-five minutes or so between the time Stephen Moore said he arrived and the moment when LeClair examined her body.

In the following days, LeClair and the other Vermont detectives interviewed dozens of witnesses about Moore's story and the timing of events around the house throughout the day of the murder. The investigators' view of Moore as a suspect was slowly dissolving, but there were two more critical questions.

LeClair asked Moore to go in for a blood test, coupling the request with expressions of sympathy for the difficulties of adjusting to the family's loss. Moore and the children were living with his parents; he had simply assumed the children didn't want to go home. LeClair made it clear that Moore could take care of the blood test whenever it was convenient.

The day after the funeral, Moore went in for a polygraph exam. The readout showed no sign that he had told anything but the truth. A few days later the blood test results revealed that the only blood on Moore had been his wife's, smeared on his hands when he turned her body over. Witness by witness, Moore's account of his movements was corroborated, the midmorning phone call just as Terry returned to the job site, the quick trip for a sandwich at lunchtime, the fast run past the dump truck just minutes from the house.

"If this guy killed his wife," LeClair said, "he's got to be some kind of Houdini."

In addition to confirming Steve Moore's version of events, the investigation had turned up a multitude of people who had passed the house during the day of the killing. Roadblocks on two different days, interviews with neighbors, and a public request for tips brought in reports of sightings of Lynda Moore and a number of strangers around the house.

The detectives weren't surprised that a lot of people remembered what they had seen at the Moores' house. The curve of the road at Tidd's Corner slowed traffic and showcased the house. It was a handsome, well-kept old structure, with open areas on both sides that provided long, unobstructed views of the house and swimming pool. And there was one other attraction. Lynda Moore had enjoyed sunbathing by the pool in a bikini. Even a couple of the detectives admitted among themselves that they never passed the house without surveying the scene.

The list of sightings of Lynda Moore around the house grew longer by the day. A paving contractor had come a little before 11:00 A.M. to talk about some work that had been done; he had left his card with Lynda Moore. Her husband had called around eleven about the check for the first dump run. A man said he had driven by and seen her sunning herself in the lawn chair at eleven-fifteen. Others claimed to have seen her between then and twelve-thirty. Her husband had called again at twelve-forty to ask about Terry Sanders and the truck; the terse mutual acknowledgment of the inconvenience as Terry returned to the job site was Steve Moore's last conversation with his wife.

From the flood of calls and interviews, the detectives selected out reports of men who had been spotted in and around the house. A passerby had seen a young man standing in the field below the house around 11:00 A.M. A blue van had been seen in the driveway before noon. Someone had noticed a pair of apparently drunken men walking along the road sometime around noon. A salesman who lived in the area spotted a young man with a knapsack on his back walking near the house around twelve-forty. A woman driving by had seen a man leaving his car with the hood up, going down to the Saxtons River behind the house to fill a water can. Another driver had sighted a man who had parked at the turnout just down from the house, apparently going into the woods to urinate.

Nine or ten detectives were working full-time on the investigation. By the end of the first week they had sifted through these reports, trying to identify the individuals involved, refining estimates of times, checking one story against another. By the end of a week's work all the potential witnesses and suspects had been accounted for or eliminated. Except one.

The witness who had reported seeing the young man with the knapsack was a salesman who lived with his wife not far from the Moores' house. He said they had always admired the house at Tidd's Corner, so they looked it over each time they passed, evaluating any improvements, watching to see if the lawn was mowed and the bushes trimmed. He was quite sure of what he had seen. The man walking toward the house had looked to be about five-foot-eight or five feet ten inches tall, of medium build, maybe a little on the stocky side, with a round face. It was a youthful face; he could be in his mid-

Sheri Nastasia was thirteen years old when she disappeared from Springfield, Vermont, in 1979. It seemed an isolated incident at the time, but her abduction turned out to be the first in a series of crimes that would not be solved for almost four years. (*Rutland Herald*)

Sheri Nastasia

In the summer of 1981, twelve-year-old Theresa was kidnapped while bicycling on a road near her home. She was found near death in the woods outside Springfield the following day. Her abduction aroused the first suspicion that there might be a serial killer loose in the Connecticut Valley.

Theresa Fenton

What Joe Estey saw in the woods off Mile Hill Road would stay with him for the rest of his life. The subsequent search for a serial killer brought Estey together with state police detective Mike LeClair and a local psychologist named John Philpin. Six years later, the three men would be reunited in the hunt for another serial killer.
(*Rutland Herald*)

Joe Estey

Vermont State Police Troopers Lead Gary Schaefer into White River Junction District Court in April 1983

The capture of Gary Schaefer put an end to one series of killings but served as a forerunner to a much more intense siege of murder in the Valley. (*Rutland Herald*)

It was on one of the last days of the school year that Jo Anne Dunham, a fifteen-year-old high school sophomore, walked to the school bus one morning in 1968. Her body was found in the woods of Unity, New Hampshire, the next day. The case was never solved. When the body of a murdered woman was found in Unity eighteen years later, detectives were intrigued by the fact that it was only a few hundred yards from where they had found Jo Anne Dunham. (*Keene Sentinel*)

Jo Anne Dunham

The circumstances surrounding the death of Betsy Critchley made it look similar to the murders committed by Gary Schaefer, but investigators could never make the connection. After the body of another murder victim was found only 500 feet from where Critchley's body had turned up, the detectives began to wonder if she should be considered a victim in the Valley's second series of killings. (*Keene Sentinel*)

Mary Elizabeth Critchley

Bernice Courtemanche, seventeen, set out to hitchhike to Newport, New Hampshire, where her boyfriend was waiting for her. It had been raining heavily all month, and when she didn't show up, the investigators feared she had drowned in one of the flooded rivers around Claremont. It would be almost two years before they learned the truth. (*Keene Sentinel*)

Bernice Courtemanche

Lieutenant Mike Prozzo

Mike Prozzo had grown up in the little New Hampshire city of Claremont, and he had always felt closely connected to everything that went on there. When someone started murdering young women, Prozzo was Chief of Detectives in the city's police department and he felt extra pressure to find the person responsible. (*Valley News*, Lebanon, N.H.)

Life had been difficult for Eva Morse, but she was doing her best to turn things around. She bought a special present for her daughter's tenth birthday, and Eva's sister couldn't remember when she had seen her looking so happy. A few days later, she was gone. (Courtesy of Noreen Crocker)

Eva Morse

Ellen Fried

"I need a house, a job, a chance to live and see," Ellen Fried had said, and now she had found all that in the Valley. She enjoyed living simply, leaving the doors unlocked, with the natural world all around. How could there be any danger in such a peaceful place? (*Keene Sentinel*)

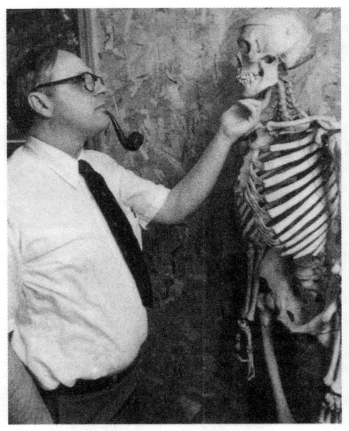

Dr. Henry Ryan

After months of exposure in the woods, the bodies of the Valley victims were badly decayed, leaving little evidence of what had happened to them. Dr. Henry Ryan, the pipe-smoking medical examiner in neighboring Maine, was an expert on the effects of the environment on the human body. He was able to find crucial bits of information that no one else could see. (*Valley News*, Lebanon, N.H.)

The Home of Lynda and Steve Moore at Tidds Corner

It was a handsome house with an attached barn, old and well kept, and its location at a bend in the road gave anyone who passed a glimpse into the lives of the Moore family. Detectives wondered how long the intruder had spied on Lynda Moore before the deadly confrontation in the hallway next to the kitchen. (*Rutland Herald*)

The Moores had worked hard to build a comfortable life. Lynda was proud of their home and kept everything in immaculate condition. Their knowledge of her character, and the likelihood that she would have fought to defend her ground, helped the investigators reconstruct what happened. (Courtesy of Stephen Moore)

Lynda and Steve Moore and Their Children

**Police Search the Banks of the Saxtons River
Behind the Home of Lynda and Steve Moore**

Several men had been spotted on foot near the Moore home the day of the attack, and the woods by the river provided good cover for anyone trying to approach without being seen. The attack on Lynda Moore was the first of three events in just eleven days that sent shock waves throughout the Valley. (*Rutland Herald*)

John Philpin

Since the Theresa Fenton case had introduced him to forensic psychology several years before, John Philpin had studied for a doctorate and become a consultant to police. Almost from the first, he sensed that the murders in the Valley were not isolated incidents. The pursuit of the killer would lead him into his own world of personal danger. (Lee Associates)

Barbara Agnew

Barbara Agnew disappeared the night of the winter's heaviest snow. A few days later, detectives traced her to a car that had been towed from a snow bank in a rest-area parking lot on the interstate highway. One look into the car told them something violent had taken place.

Police Search for Clues in the Disappearance of Barbara Agnew

Digging in deep snow, near the abandoned car just days after the blizzard, police found traces of evidence that helped them visualize what had happened to Barbara Agnew, but where was she now? (*Rutland Herald*)

**A State Police Officer Questions a Motorist
at the Rest Area on Interstate 91**

Police mounted an intensive investigation into Barbara Agnew's disappearance, but they were unable to pick up her trail after the attack in the parking lot. (*Valley News*, Lebanon, N.H.)

Ted LeClair (left) and Mike LeClair

Both the LeClair brothers were troopers in the Vermont State Police, both became detectives, and both were drawn into the investigation of the murders in the Valley. They dreamed of finding the killer, but the investigation turned out to be the most frustrating either of them ever worked on. (*Rutland Herald*)

**Police Block Off the Road Where the Body
of Barbara Agnew Was Found**

The isolation of the spot and the difficult terrain suggested that before going out to look for a victim the killer had carefully planned the details of what he was going to do. (*Valley News*, Lebanon, N.H.)

**Detective Sergeant Ted LeClair Points to the Spot
Where the Body Lay in the Snow**

Cold temperatures had preserved the body during the two and a half months it lay on Advent Hill. For the first time, the investigators were able to gather an array of evidence to help in pursuing the killer. (*Rutland Herald*)

**A New Hampshire Woman Practices Using Her
New Gun in a Firearm Safety Course**

The death of Barbara Agnew set off an unprecedented run on gun shops throughout the Connecticut Valley. Many of the purchasers were women, or men buying weapons for their wives. Some of the new gun owners (like the woman above) signed up for instruction courses, but not all were so prudent. A Vermont woman approached a police officer on the street, opened her purse to show him an automatic pistol, and asked for help learning to use it; the officer was relieved to find that there was no ammunition in the clip. (*Valley News*, Lebanon, N.H.)

**The Supermarket Parking Lot Where
Jane Boroski Was Attacked**

The store seemed so close to the road when you drove into the parking lot, and so far from the passing traffic when you were desperately calling for someone to help save your life. (Lee Associates)

The composite portrait and the physical description of the attacker raised the hopes of police in the Valley that for the first time they were on the trail of the killer.

**Composite Portrait of the Man
Who Attacked Jane Boroski**

**Actors Re-enact the Attack on Jane Boroski for the
Television Program "Unsolved Mysteries"**

Even in a re-enactment, the violence of the attack was shocking to
the people who were looking on. (Lee Associates)

**Jane Boroski (center) and Actors from
"Unsolved Mysteries"**

It took some time, but it seemed that Jane had finally come to terms
with the terrifying events of a hot summer night when she stopped
to get a soda from a machine. (Lee Associates)

twenties or younger. He had short, dark hair that hung low on his forehead, and wore glasses with heavy, black frames. The knapsack had been small and bright blue.

The salesman said he had been driving from one appointment to another; he had been able to narrow the time down by checking his appointment book. His estimate would have placed the man with the knapsack at the door close to the moment when Steve Moore talked to his wife for the last time, possibly a little later.

The police issued a description and asked for anyone who had seen the man to call.

"We checked and double-checked," Jim Candon announced, "and we think that this really may be a significant lead."

Candon didn't say so publicly, but the timing was right. Someone claimed to have seen Lynda Moore in the lawn chair around 3:00 P.M. That report seemed shaky, and if it was eliminated, the man with the knapsack could have been the last person to see her alive.

Your basic garden-variety psychic was usually some amiable citizen, pretty ordinary in fact, except for believing that he could see through walls and trees and time, and most detectives responded to them in the same spirit, listened with a genial forbearance and made a few phone calls afterward to check the psychic's supernatural vision against the facts and confirm what the detective had half—or more, or less—suspected from the beginning: this fantasy has nothing to do with the crime I am getting paid to solve.

This one, Mike LeClair thought, was different. It was early June, a little less than two months since the killing of Lynda Moore. The story sounded like the typical extrasensory adventure: a man claims he saw the murder of Lynda Moore before it happened. But it wasn't the usual pattern. This man didn't come forward with his story. He was telling it around Bellows Falls, and he wasn't the kind of good citizen who volunteered to help the police with his vision. This was a twenty-nine-year-old guy who caught occasional work putting up drywall or cutting firewood or doing odd jobs and spent the rest of his time sitting on a barstool wasting his life until closing time.

The man's name was Franklin Triplet and LeClair thought

he sounded worth talking to. It was surprising how many cases
got solved because a guy bragged in a bar about a crime he
had done and somebody who heard him ended up with a reason to tell the police about what he had heard. Telling people
you had seen a murder before it happened could be just another
way of bragging about something after it happened.

LeClair and Herve Bernard, another state police detective,
found Triplet at the Friendly Inn, a bar in Bellows Falls. It
was daytime, and in this case he wasn't a customer. He was
working, hanging drywall in a renovation. He wasn't shy about
discussing his gift.

"I have this supernatural power," he told the two detectives. "I see things."

In October 1985, Triplet said, six months before the death
of Lynda Moore, he had been walking along Route 121 in
Saxtons River with a friend named Walter Krivas. He had no
car and often hitchhiked or walked around the area. As they
approached Tidd's Corner he looked up at the Moores' house
and experienced a premonition: a woman was going to die in
that house. He told Walter about it and they continued on their
way to Bellows Falls.

A few days after he learned of Lynda Moore's death, Triplet
said, he had experienced another vision. In this one he saw the
murder taking place.

"What did you see?" LeClair asked.

"She was sitting in a lawn chair in the driveway," Triplet
said.

The man is alone, carrying a green knapsack on his back,
walking along Route 121 from Saxtons River to Bellows Falls
when he sees her there. He is familiar with the area but pre-
tends ignorance and walks up the driveway to ask her directions to the nearest southbound exit on the interstate, which is
about five miles away. Mrs. Moore becomes frightened and
tries to run into the house, but the man catches her.

The man is wearing gloves and he carries a hunting knife
in a sheath on his belt; its handle is black. Still holding Lynda
Moore from behind, he stabs her twice in the stomach, but she
breaks loose and runs inside. She is unable to lock the door
and the man follows her.

He catches her just inside the doorway between the kitchen
and living room. Holding the knife against her, cutting her with

it, he tries to question her about some valuable papers, but she refuses to cooperate. Now he stabs her repeatedly in the chest and stomach, then releases her. She falls with her head facing into the living room and her feet pointing out toward the kitchen. She lies facedown, on her right side.

The attacker removes a bandanna from his neck or from a pocket, wipes the blade and handle, and puts the knife back into the sheath at his waist. He uses his T-shirt to wipe blood off himself; later he will dispose of the T-shirt.

The man in the vision had a name, Triplet said, Taylor or Tyler, and it may have a French spelling.

The two detectives experienced a jolt of recognition as Triplet described the vision in his matter-of-fact voice. He had a remarkable cluster of details right, and others that were consistent with the facts the detectives had assembled in the case. He could have learned about the knapsack from the description of the man wanted for questioning, but the placement of the body was right, and so was the weapon: the medical examiner had measured and analyzed the wounds and concluded that they had been made with a seven-inch hunting knife. The gloves would fit with the absence of marks and fingerprints. This was definitely interesting. LeClair asked Triplet if he could describe Lynda Moore's wounds in more detail, beside the two to the stomach she received in the driveway.

Triplet listed the wounds: She was stabbed in the right side of the chest, he said, the left shoulder, and he went on, patiently enumerating the wounds and locations in detail, more than a dozen in all, including several in the abdomen, and ending with a stab "right into the heart.

"She put up one hell of a fight," he said, "but it was over very fast. She died within five minutes.

"He was in and out," Triplet said. The man spent fifteen or twenty minutes in the house, then walked outside. As he left the house, a cream-colored car drove past. He walked to Route 121 and hitched a ride. Triplet described the man who picked up the killer. His name was Bob and he was between thirty-eight and forty-eight years old, with curly hair. He drove the killer to the Westminster exit of the interstate, where he dropped him off.

His vision had told him one other thing about the killer, Triplet said. "He's gonna do it again," he concluded. It would be in Vermont, in Brattleboro, Dummerston, or Putney.

Again, LeClair noted, Triplet's vision was remarkably close to the facts. His description of the number and placement of the wounds was uncanny; almost every wound he listed was an exact match for one on Lynda Moore's body. The nature of the struggle as he described it—the rapid-fire sequence, Lynda Moore's fierce resistance—was exactly the way the investigators had reconstructed it. This whole story was growing more interesting every minute.

There was something else. Beyond the accuracy of the facts, two elements of Triplet's account seemed to bear an eerie significance. The killer Triplet described, walking along Route 121, heading toward Bellows Falls, was doing exactly what Triplet himself had been doing at the time of his first "vision." And Triplet said the killer was going to strike again, with three possible locations that were all within fifteen miles of Lynda Moore's house.

There were two obvious possibilities about Franklin Triplet to be faced right away: either there really was such a thing as clairvoyance, or what this man was describing as something he had seen in a vision was really something he had seen— and something he had done—in life. If you didn't believe in extrasensory perception, Triplet's prediction about the killer striking again could be a warning about what he might do next if he weren't stopped.

This had a familiar ring to it, a strong feeling of plausibility. Law-enforcement lore was full of stories about people who committed crimes and then started to feel strangled by the guilt. Sometimes they would experience an irresistible need to confess, to relieve themselves of the burden. Every cop had seen it: the suspect is being questioned after the arrest and instead of denying everything he seems pathetically eager to admit what he did and describe it in detail. Could Franklin Triplet's story simply be a more creative, and more evasive, way of doing the same thing?

The detectives shifted the conversation to Triplet himself and his activities on April 15, the day of Lynda Moore's death. He seemed to recall that he had been working for a woman named Linda Portman in Brattleboro, Triplet said, cutting firewood.

Triplet said he had not known the Moores, but he admitted

that a few years earlier he had met Steve briefly when he tried to get work on a renovation job Moore was doing in Bellows Falls. Moore hadn't hired him. Another time he had noticed a tree that had fallen on Moore's property, blown down by the wind, he thought, and he had phoned several times to ask if Moore would like him to cut the tree up for firewood. He had never reached Moore, Triplet said; he knew the Moores were seldom home during the day and Steve worked long hours away from the house.

LeClair asked Triplet if he carried a knife himself. Oh, no, he answered, he didn't believe in knives or guns.

Would he be willing to take a polygraph exam to verify his account and clear himself of suspicion as a suspect? the detective asked. No problem, Triplet responded. They made an appointment for the following day.

Later that day LeClair and Bernard went to Triplet's house to talk with his girlfriend. Her name was Jennie Elwell. She had been living with Triplet for about two years, she said. They had a baby nine months old and she was pregnant with their second child; Triplet had told the detectives he planned to marry her someday.

Jennie Elwell said Franklin had told her about his premonition that something was going to happen at the Moores' house; it was definitely before Lynda Moore was killed. She said they hadn't talked about it much after the murder was in the papers. She thought Franklin had been working in Brattleboro the day of the murder.

At eleven o'clock the following day Franklin Triplet arrived at the state police office in Rockingham to take the polygraph exam. LeClair watched and recorded the interview from behind one-way glass. The spiked path of the pens as the paper unrolled beneath them revealed no clear pattern. The results were inconclusive. The polygraph technician said he couldn't conclude that Triplet was lying, but he couldn't conclude that he was telling the truth, either.

The polygraph was no use as evidence, but sometimes it could reinforce or contradict other findings, helping to clarify the investigator's thinking. In this case, it did the opposite. The situation was murkier than it had been. LeClair sat down with Triplet for another interview, hoping to find some explanation. It only made things worse. Triplet continued what was starting to seem like the kind of dramatic performance you'd see in a movie.

Triplet repeated his precise description of where Lynda Moore's body had fallen, adding a few details. He then launched into a remarkable description of the Moores' living room. He had seen it in his vision, Triplet said, a very long room, with a brick fireplace protected by a metal screen. A cluster of furniture was arranged facing the fireplace. There was an antique wingback chair with a rounded back and curved legs, covered in beige fabric. He saw floral-pattern drapes that were bunched and frilly at the top, and half a dozen other features of the room, a lamp with a yellow globe, a rug, a sofa, and more, all in detail. The sofa was an antique with wooden arms partly covered in leather, the rug was an Oriental with a gray fringe that matched the carpet. And all the descriptions, with the single exception of the lamp, were exactly as LeClair had found them on the day of Lynda Moore's death.

The room, Triplet said, was "very, very neat," far beyond the ordinary, and the colors of the drapes and rugs blended well with the furniture. It was like an echo to LeClair; Triplet could have been reading from the interview reports the investigators had gathered after talking to Lynda Moore's friends. They all said she was a meticulous housekeeper, intolerant of even the slightest clutter, and she had taken great pains decorating the house, coordinating furniture and fabrics.

How about the kitchen? the detectives asked, bemused by Triplet's accuracy. He described the round wooden kitchen table and chairs. It came as something of a relief when he faltered on the rest of the kitchen. He said the floor was wood; in fact it was a patterned vinyl. And his description of the layout of the cabinets and counters was wrong.

Still, Triplet's account was impressive. He had a lot of the details right, and an amazing percentage of the rest matched up neatly with the deductions of the investigators. How could he have gotten this information? Could he be the killer? An accomplice or acquaintance?

There were too many questions here, but LeClair couldn't resist asking one more.

"Why did he do it, Franklin?" the detective asked. It was the kind of question that might reveal more about the person answering than he meant to tell. "Did he go in there meaning to kill her, or was he intending just to rob her, or maybe rape her, and killed her unintentionally?''

''He went in to kill her,'' Triplet answered, ''not to rape or rob or anything else. He's programmed.''

The answer, with its certainty about the killer's murderous calculation, was chilling. Once again it raised the obvious question: Could Triplet be talking about himself?

''Where did you say you were on April 15?'' LeClair asked.

Triplet said he was pretty sure he was working in Brattleboro, but he'd check his work records at home to be sure.

When they were finished, LeClair drove Triplet home. After rummaging through a pile of papers for a few minutes, Triplet came up with a receipt for work from April 12 to April 15. It showed that he had worked twenty-eight hours in the four days. He had been wrong about working in Brattleboro; he had worked for a woman in Bellows Falls named Helen Eddo.

The next day LeClair called Helen Eddo. She remembered very clearly that Franklin Triplet had helped her clean the yard and cut and stack wood at a rental property she owned in Bellows Falls. They had started about 8:00 A.M. and had worked together until about four in the afternoon. The only break they took was at noon, she said, and it was a short one.

And that was it. Over the course of two days Triplet's remarkable ''vision'' and the accumulation of facts that seemed to authenticate it had begun to create a mood of anticipation, the germ of a hope that at last the detectives had found a path that might lead to some answers. Mrs. Eddo's confirmation of Triplet's work records crushed the hope.

The question was, How had Franklin Triplet produced his remarkable version of the killing of Lynda Moore? Logic suggested a range of possibilities. First, Triplet could have learned all this firsthand. He could be the man who killed Lynda Moore. But Helen Eddo's evidence ruled out that explanation.

But then, how did he know about the killing, the placement of the body and other details? He could have heard about the killing from the man who did it. In that case, though, it was unlikely he would have heard and remembered so much detail. All you had to do was picture two tough guys, half-loaded, sitting in a bar in Bellows Falls and talking about flowered drapes that were bunched and frilly to grow skeptical about this explanation. But if he wasn't the killer, was it possible that he knew who was?

As long as Triplet stood by his version of events, there would be no final explanation. But then, it wasn't a detective's job to explain things. It was a detective's job to catch a killer.

The following day LeClair searched out Triplet's friend, Walter Krivas, the one he claimed had been walking with him near the Moores' when he saw his first vision. Krivas confirmed Triplet's story.

There were still loose ends to pursue, always loose ends, like Krivas's own alibi for the day of Lynda Moore's death, other friends and acquaintances of the two men who could verify the story about the vision, the unanswered questions about how Triplet had gotten his information. LeClair and Bernard dutifully plowed their way through several days of interviews and phone calls to make sure they hadn't overlooked anything important, but nothing they found contradicted what they had known since the interview with Helen Eddo.

It was a little like panning for gold. You sifted through huge volumes of ordinary stuff, all the people who had seen something, anything, around the Moores' house or in the vicinity of Tidd's Corner on April 15, and in the end you had a few little nuggets left, rough stories that might bear the promise of something more interesting.

There had been a remarkable flow of activity around the house that day. The man getting water for his car, the blue van, the man urinating in the woods. These and a dozen more had been tracked down and eliminated. When it was all done, the man with the blue knapsack remained. And so did the joggers.

Someone had mentioned them during the door-to-door canvassing around Tidd's Corner in the days after the murder. "Did you see anything unusual that day?" they would ask, and one woman said, No, nothing real unusual, but there were two guys jogging.

One of them had a "messed-up face," she said, and the other was wearing a T-shirt with some writing on it. "Messed-up?"

"You know," she said, "kind of bad-looking. Something wrong with it." She couldn't say anything more about it. She hadn't wanted to stare. And she had no idea what it said on the T-shirt. It was sometime between nine and ten in the morning.

It took three weeks, what with all the other leads to check out, but other sightings accumulated. A jogger had been seen by a woman hanging out her wash in Gageville, the village next to Saxtons River, around 11:00 A.M. A man working in his yard nearby had seen someone fitting the same description, but at 4:00 P.M. And there was a piece of luck. He remembered the T-shirt, the man said. He had served in the Philippines during World War II, remembered MacArthur landing in Leyte. That's what was written on the T-shirt, he said. *Mac-Arthur?* No, *USS Leyte Gulf,* he replied. A Navy ship, definitely.

It took several days of chasing down leads, but they finally identified the man in the T-shirt. His uncle, Barney Allen, lived less than a mile from Tidd's Corner. Sure, Allen said, his nephew was in the Navy. He was stationed in the Philippines. Just went out there. Got that T-shirt as soon as they told him his assignment, real proud of it. Do you remember the date? they asked. I can figure it out, he said. He looked at a calendar. Jeffrey—that was his name, Jeffrey Miller—went back on April 18. That was three days after Lynda Moore was killed.

Does he have a friend who has something wrong with his face? the detectives asked.

"Oh, sure, you must mean his brother, Stanley," Allen replied. "He was burned when he was a kid. Chemistry set blew up in his face. Been having operations ever since."

In the next few days the detectives interviewed Allen about the Millers, trying to reconstruct their movements on the day of Lynda Moore's death. It took several days of following one lead on to another before a timetable of Jeffrey Miller's movements on April 15 began to emerge.

Stanley Miller seemed intelligent and well-spoken, but he had a habit of turning his face sideways when he talked, as if he were addressing someone at his shoulder. He seemed to be trying from long habit to spare his listener a direct view of his scarred face, but it made him difficult to understand. Nevertheless, he seemed to want to be helpful.

He and Jeffrey had gone jogging early that day. They had started sometime around eight in the morning, run along Route

121 toward Gageville, and returned home within an hour.

Barney Allen had been driving home around five in the afternoon when he spotted Jeffrey jogging on Route 121 just past Tidd's Corner. He had taken his nephew home and given him dinner. Jeffrey had left about 7:00 P.M.

Did Jeffrey say anything else about where he had been that afternoon? the detective asked. One of those days while he was home, Allen recalled, probably it was that same day, Jeffrey had stopped off to see Alma Hayden. Mrs. Hayden was a former high school teacher of Jeffrey's. She had always been kind to Jeffrey. He didn't have a lot of friends; she was one of the few people he felt he could confide in. She was retired now, lived in a trailer just down from Tidd's Corner, across from the Moores.

Alma Hayden remembered Jeffrey's visit clearly. It had been the day Lynda Moore was killed. Everybody was scared, she said, the neighborhood was in an uproar, police coming and going, people slowing down to gape at the house. And she was worried herself, a woman living alone with some killer on the loose. She had told Jeffrey about Lynda Moore, it had only happened an hour or two before, but it had just gone right over his head. All he had wanted to talk about was his new assignment in the Philippines; he had never been out of the United States. He was wondering how they'd treat Americans; he had heard there were guerrillas who attacked sailors in uniform sometimes. She had been preoccupied with the murder; Jeffrey hadn't showed any interest in the subject. A gap soon opened in the conversation and after a few minutes Jeffrey had left, Mrs. Hayden said.

When they reinterviewed Barney Allen he produced a letter that Jeffrey had written after arriving in the Philippines. There was a line in it that caught the detectives' attention.

"How are things going on the Lynda Moore homicide?" Jeffrey had asked. "That was crazy."

Mike LeClair had assembled the outline of a description and personal history of Jeffrey Miller. He was nineteen years old, just a year out of high school. He was five feet eleven inches tall and weighed about 180 pounds; he was in excellent physical condition from his Navy training.

The Miller boys had grown up amidst constant turmoil in the family. Their mother had been unreliable and emotionally volatile. She had suffered a breakdown and spent time in the state psychiatric hospital. Their father, a bookie and petty con man, had left the family when Jeffrey was eleven years old. Lorraine Miller had seemed to alternate between erratic helplessness and fury. She had disciplined the children severely at times. As the oldest, Jeffrey had been the first target of her anger; at times she had shut him in his room and padlocked the door.

Jeffrey Miller had intended to stay with his mother while he was home on leave, but had changed his plans after a few days when a friend named Todd Banker had invited him to stay at his apartment in Saxtons River. Banker tried to recall his friend's possessions for the detectives: there had been a leather suitcase, he said, a duffel bag, and what he described as a tote bag. It was nylon or canvas, dark, he couldn't remember exactly what color. Banker remembered the T-shirt with the name of the ship on it, and also a windbreaker that said *U.S. Navy*. It was blue.

There were a number of interesting elements buried in this preliminary collection of information. Jeffrey Miller had been seen in the area of Lynda Moore's house twice on the day of the murder, two or three hours before her death and again the same length of time afterward. The man standing in the field near the Moores' house had been wearing a windbreaker, according to a witness; Jeffrey owned a windbreaker. The "tote bag" described by Todd Banker sounded as if it could also be referred to as a knapsack, which might correspond to the description from the passing salesman of the man walking up to the Moores' house on the day of the murder. And there was Jeffrey's odd reaction to the murder, first flatly refusing to acknowledge it or show any interest during his visit with Alma Hayden, then asking for news in his letter two or three weeks later.

Mike LeClair set about verifying the descriptions of the jacket and knapsack and put in a call to the Naval Investigative Service at Subic Bay in the Philippines. An officer at NIS said they were always glad to cooperate with civilian authorities. It was arranged that Navy investigators would interview Jeffrey Miller and collect physical evidence—the T-shirt, windbreaker, and tote bag. They agreed to take a photograph and send it to Vermont.

Several days later the Navy investigator contacted LeClair to say that they had taken possession of the three items and Miller had agreed to submit to a polygraph examination. Questions were sent back to the Philippines for use with the polygraph.

It was the end of June before the transcript of the interview and the polygraph results reached Vermont. The results were striking.

The polygraph operator had first established the context for the questions. He was going to ask about Miller's recent leave in Vermont and events surrounding the death of Lynda Moore.

"Did you attack this woman?" he asked. "Did you injure this woman? Were you in the house of Lynda Moore?" Miller denied any knowledge or contact with Lynda Moore.

Out of ten questions, seven produced explosions of agitation on the polygraph charts.

The operator told Miller that his reactions seemed to indicate that he wasn't telling the truth. Did he have any idea why that could be?

"I can't explain why your machine reacts like that," Miller replied. He seemed deeply indifferent.

In spite of what the charts showed, to all appearances Miller had been exceptionally calm, the operator reported, "cool as a cucumber." Afterward he had talked easily with the investigator. He recounted his activities on the Tuesday of Lynda Moore's death. He claimed he had run twice with his brother; Stanley had turned back the second time, he said.

After lunch, Miller sat down for a second session on the polygraph machine.

"Have you ever lied to anybody in authority?" he was asked. It was a standard question, used to calibrate the test, a basis for comparison to other answers. Almost everybody answers yes. Jeffrey Miller answered no. The needles swung wildly on the moving paper.

He repeated his answers to the other questions: he had never met Lynda Moore, had never been in the house. Again his demeanor betrayed no hint of emotion. Again the polygraph operator concluded that there was some deep source of agitation accompanying his answers, like crackling static coming out of a speaker with the music. There were no absolutes with polygraph testing, but there were strong indications in these charts of something wrong.

"One way to explain it," the operator said, "is that this guy knows something about the murder."

The photograph of Jeffrey Miller arrived. It showed a handsome young man, but there was something disconcerting in his stare; it was a glaring intensity, a slightly bug-eyed look, that seemed too sharp in a young man standing for an informal snapshot. Maybe that was due to the circumstances, naval investigators ordering him to pose for a portrait; that would make anybody tense. But there was something more, a strong facial resemblance to the composite drawing of the man with the knapsack who had been seen walking up the Moores' driveway the day of the murder.

The investigators began sorting through the leads and contradictions in all the evidence surrounding Jeffrey Miller.

The discrepancy between the brothers' stories about jogging together disappeared when Stanley was reinterviewed. The first time the detectives had asked him, Stanley said, he had forgotten starting out again with his brother. It had been a few hours after their first run. He had tired quickly and turned back, he said. Jeffrey had gone on; that corresponded to the sighting of a single jogger around 11:00 A.M. by the woman hanging out her wash.

LeClair went back through all the sightings of men near the Moore house, searching for any that might be connected to Jeffrey Miller. The two most promising possibilities were still the young man with the knapsack and the man standing in the field wearing a windbreaker.

The detectives rechecked the report of the man in the field. The witness who had reported seeing the man confirmed that his jacket had appeared to be light in color. The windbreaker that arrived in the package from the Philippines was dark blue. There was no way to identify Jeffrey Miller with the figure in the field.

The evidence in the other sighting was more confused. In addition to the facial similarity, there was a degree of correspondence between the physical descriptions: the man with the knapsack had been described as between five-foot-eight and five-foot-ten and slightly stocky; Miller was five feet eleven inches and weighed 180. But Miller's tote bag was dark green, a color that the passing salesman would probably not have confused with a bright blue. In addition, it had not been designed for carrying on the back. There was no conventional knapsack among Miller's possessions, and no one remembered him owning or carrying one.

But the glasses were another story. John Philpin had pointed out that the eyeglasses the salesman had described on the man approaching the Moores' house were an inexpensive type that was favored by the welfare department and the military. Jeffrey Miller had been wearing contact lenses in his picture; he said he had worn glasses in the past, but he couldn't remember where he had bought them. The detectives left it to Philpin to check around, and he eventually located an optometrist in Bellows Falls who had made the glasses for Jeffrey Miller. They were similar to the ones worn by the man with the knapsack, and there was something else that drew the detectives' attention: Jeffrey Miller had received them less than a year earlier. It seemed unlikely that he could have forgotten so soon where he had bought them. Could he be lying about the glasses?

The investigators continued sorting and verifying the information on Jeffrey Miller. Stanley Miller and Jeffrey's friend, Todd Banker, both submitted to polygraph exams. Both seemed to be telling the truth. The detectives told Stanley Miller that his brother's polygraph results had seemed to indicate that Jeffrey was lying.

"Really?" he said. He seemed stunned by the news. "That's weird."

They talked about how a polygraph works and what Jeffrey's results might mean.

"That scares the shit out of me," Stanley said. "I know he didn't do it."

The detectives were not so sure. LeClair had passed the information about the Millers on to John Philpin. The psychologist couldn't say much on the basis of an incomplete file, but he was intrigued by the hints of pathology in the family history. Jeffrey's indifference to the news of the murder and his unemotional responses in the interviews with the Navy investigators sounded alarms.

The detectives had reconstructed Jeffrey's movements on the day of Lynda Moore's death. Miller had filled in some of the details himself in a second interview with the Navy investigators. After returning from the first run with his brother, Jeffrey said, he had put on pants over his shorts and started out again to visit his mother in Bellows Falls. He had persuaded his brother to go along, but Stanley soon changed his mind and turned back. Jeffrey had gone on by himself. After a short time at his mother's apartment he had gone over to the high school, where he had graduated a year earlier. He had visited with teachers and some of his friends for a couple of hours, he said, leaving a little after the lunch bell. That would have been about twelve-thirty or so.

And that was where a large, unexplained gap opened up in the record of Jeffrey Miller's movements on the day Lynda Moore was killed. The investigators timed out the segments of the schedule and verified the Millers' stories where possible. The brothers had come back from the first run around nine-thirty. Jeffrey had quickly become restless and the second run had started around ten-thirty. Allowing time for a brief visit with his mother, Jeffrey had arrived at the high school sometime after eleven. If he had left the school when his friends went to lunch, he could have been in Saxtons River by twelve-forty-five.

Steve Moore had talked to his wife on the phone at approximately twelve-forty. The medical examiner had placed the time of death between noon and three. The ambulance driver was sure Lynda Moore had been dead a long time; that would place her death closer to the early limit of the medical examiner's estimate, soon after her brief phone conversation with her husband.

That left the question, Where did Jeffrey Miller go after his visit to the high school?

Miller said he had gone back to Todd Banker's apartment and stayed until three o'clock, when he went for another run. He couldn't remember how he had spent the time in the apartment. Banker was at work, no one else had been there, and Miller couldn't think of anyone who had seen him along the way or at the apartment. That left a crucial three hours unaccounted for.

If he had attacked Lynda Moore, how would he have gone about it? The investigators tried to put together a hypothetical schedule: He arrives at Todd Banker's apartment from the high school. He puts on jeans over his shorts. Placing a knife from his gear with the eyeglasses in the tote bag or some other carrying bag—could he have a knapsack that no one else had noticed?—he walks along Route 121 to the Moores'.

He knows where he is going; he has passed Tidd's Corner at least three times this day. He has seen Lynda Moore moving around the house, sitting in the sun at the top of the driveway, near the back door.

Perhaps he pauses for a moment just before turning up to the house, hiding himself from the road, to put on the glasses, to disguise his appearance with other clothing he has carried in the bag. He turns in at the driveway, going over in his mind some pretext that he has prepared long before, gone over and over in his mind.

He may not intend to kill; he may imagine merely talking with his victim, or stopping after raping her, but something causes him to panic, to lose control—perhaps he is recognized, or challenged, or overcome with an unanticipated rage of lust.

Afterward he creeps back along the riverbank to his uncle's apartment, a distance of less than a mile, completely under cover. He knows this area intimately; he has played for long hours by the river as a child while visiting his uncle. He knows that no one will see him along the way, connect him to the Moore house. He disposes of the bag, bloody clothing, knife, and glasses.

It is a short walk back to Todd Banker's, where he is staying. He visits briefly with Alma Hayden; he is distracted, feigns indifference to the murder that has taken place just across the road. He is spotted at four-thirty as he continues his run, then is picked up by his uncle around five o'clock.

It was plausible, the detectives thought, but not enough by itself. Maybe the clothes would provide some support. Several hairs had been found on the T-shirt the Navy investigators had seized, and there were stains on the running shoes that looked as if they could be blood. Hopes rose for a break in the case.

They were soon crushed. The hairs matched Miller's own, not Lynda Moore's, and the stains were not blood. Certainly Jeffrey Miller could have killed Lynda Moore, but there was no way to place him at the house and no evidence linking him to Lynda Moore.

The detectives continued to pursue leads, collecting odd bits of information on Jeffrey Miller. Friends and family members volunteered for interviews and John Philpin filled out the picture of a deeply injured family, a young man who had been severely abused psychologically, if not physically. It was highly plausible as the kind of environment that could produce a killer. But there was nothing further to know, and no further evidence turned up to make the crucial connections in time and place.

How had Franklin Triplet gotten his information? Had he come in contact with the killer of Lynda Moore? Who was the man with the knapsack? Could it have been Jeffrey Miller? Had Miller lied about the glasses? What caused his wild responses on the polygraph exam? The investigators would always be left to face mysteries within the mystery.

twenty-two

Richard Bordeau simply wouldn't go away.

In the spring he had started writing again to Virginia Troy, the waitress at the Mapleview Restaurant he had been pestering seven months earlier, just before Ellen Fried's remains were discovered. She hadn't worried at first, thinking, hoping, it might be an isolated relapse; after all, the police had ordered him to stop before and he had complied.

Then she got another letter. That was it, she thought, and took it to the Claremont police, who passed it on to the task force. And after that, the letters kept coming, some of them great batches of computer printouts, printed haphazardly, folded across the perforations.

The new letters included long sections Bordeau said come from a book he was writing about business administration. He seemed to have taken bits and pieces from legitimate books on the subject—a word here, a phrase there, a technical term from somewhere else—and stitched them together in a crazy quilt of nonsensical verbiage. Some of them ran to six or eight or a dozen pages of incomprehensible ramblings, interspersed with more personal messages awkwardly sprinkled with formal or technical words.

"How can we make this communication work for your advantage?'' he asked in one letter. "How is the family? When would you like to introduce me to them? How can I better our relationship and work with you? How about a nice big smile? This sentence is written to secure and maximize your joy." It was signed, "Love, Richard Robert Bordeau.''

The letters seemed to be tortured love notes, tokens of a mutual passion that existed only in the mind of one man. Another letter, written by hand, included an invitation to Virginia Troy to visit the Victorian house.

"I am preparing to make the very finest French apple pie of your life!'' he wrote cheerily. "At 11:00 P.M. I will be removing your French apple pie from the oven and want you to come over and enjoy it, if you would like. Yours very truly, Richard Robert Bordeau.''

The letters were strange, the detectives thought, and, to Virginia Troy, sometimes frightening. It was eerie to think that someone you didn't know, had hardly even seen, was sitting there in his house thinking about you, pouring out this stream of weird and incoherent tribute. But at bottom it seemed harmless, and other than asking him to stop, there didn't seem to be much that the police or anybody else could do about it. It was only when the letters were put together with other bits of information that they added up to something more troubling.

There were several complaints from local radio stations that seemed connected to Richard Bordeau. A woman who had worked as a disc jockey at the Claremont station had received several phone calls from a man who described the kinds of sexual activities he wanted to perform with her. When she moved to another station nearby, the calls continued. The caller eventually invited her to come to his home and told her where he lived: his house was the big Victorian near the covered bridge on Routes 11 and 103.

Mike Prozzo discussed the complaints with John Philpin and directed the psychologist's attention to another set of reports. The program director of a radio station nearby in Vermont reported that a man had called repeatedly, obsessively, to request a song called "Bad to the Bone." The song had been used as the theme of the movie made from Stephen King's book, *Christine*. The detectives had become convinced that the caller was Richard Bordeau.

Philpin listened to a recording over and over until he had the song's lyrics copied out.

The singer recalls the day he was born, a child so special that all the nurses gathered around the viewing window in joyous celebration. But one nurse—perhaps she is the head nurse, an authority figure, but she has some special insight, possibly an affinity with this infant—steps forward and warns the others away; she has seen immediately that this child is "bad to the bone."

The rest of the song boasts of the singer's mastery over women, young and old, rich and poor. All fall under his spell, all do his bidding. His control, the singer insinuates, is sexual, psychological, total. Even kings and queens give way when he passes.

The singer is addressing his words to a woman he wishes to possess. His bragging about his special aura, his rare power, is meant to both draw her to him and let her know that he will be in control of whatever happens between them, in control of her.

It was possible, Philpin thought, that the obsession with the song of the man who repeatedly requested it could be taken as a form of identification with the singer. Taken more or less literally, as an obsessed radio listener might hear it, the song indicated an inflated, grandiose kind of thinking that was common in paranoid personality disorders. The theatrical element—seeing himself as dramatically evil, "bad to the bone"—and the boasting about his sexual power over women fit this picture of the caller's personality.

There were odds and ends that reinforced this psychological portrait of Richard Bordeau. The x he had put on the end of his surname when he wrote it out matched the spelling of the famous wine region in southern France. In one of his letters to Virginia Troy he had enclosed a photocopy of a chapter from a book on wine; it discussed the production of wines in Bordeaux. In the letter he implied that his family was descended from the original landowners of the region, and that he had inherited more than simply the name.

The identification with France was carried out in other ways. Bordeau favored the nickname King. He sometimes signed his letters "King Richard," and he had referred to himself as a man with the heart of a lion; it was a reference to the medieval

English king who campaigned in France, Richard the Lion-hearted.

All this further supported the idea of paranoid grandiosity, a distorted and disruptive view of the world. This was not a way of thinking that was necessarily associated with violence. But there was something else in the song that led in another direction, as well, something more concrete, and more disquieting. That was the image of the nurse.

The extraordinary child in the song is surrounded by nurses, receiving their adoration in a scene that echoes the birth of Jesus. And then there is the one nurse who stands apart from the others, in a special relationship to the child. "Leave this one alone," she says to the other nurses, as if to both protect the child and reserve him for herself; she is the one, the only one, who recognizes the extraordinary qualities of this child, who understands him fully. Does the man obsessively requesting the song on the radio respond to some perverse echo in this relationship? Does this special nurse, who both protects the child in the song and sympathizes with his charismatic wickedness, remind the caller of some key figure of his own life?

By now the Valley killings had become associated irreversibly in the public mind with nurses and hospitals. The task force detectives had looked into the idea every way they could think of and all they were left with was skepticism. Ellen Fried was a nurse at the Valley Regional Hospital, that was true, and Bernice Courtemanche had worked in a nursing home. But Bernice had only been employed part-time, and her work had little to do with nursing; she was an aide, helping to bathe patients and change beds. The connections to Eva Morse and Lynda Moore were even more tenuous.

Where was the association between a nurse at the hospital in Claremont, a part-time nurse's aide at the county home in Unity, eight miles away, and a woman who had worked as a nurse's aide ten years earlier, apart from the word *nurse?* And how did any of these connect with a married, middle-class woman working as a volunteer fund-raiser, president of the auxiliary organization, in a hospital twenty miles away?

And yet, and yet, the detectives thought, you just couldn't ignore it. For one thing, it had become an obsession with the public. It was common to hear people on the streets refer to "those nurses that were killed." Hospitals in the Valley had instituted safety classes for nurses and other women workers. And what if there was some remote connection, one place or habit or person connected to the idea of nursing that had touched all these women at some time, that could be followed like a frail but continuous thread to the moment of their deaths. The possibility had to be kept in mind.

With that thought, the detectives had looked more closely at a series of apparently unconnected reports. It began with Richard Bordeau's mother. Richard's young brother had died when Richard was eight. Already protective, she had turned to Richard with an even more intense energy. She appeared to some to be obsessed with protecting and insulating him, not only from the world outside, but also from his father. She had understood that he was different from other children, which seemed to justify even more firmly a passionate defensiveness on his behalf. She had interceded for her son repeatedly. Out of a desire to protect him she had controlled his life, managed his every move.

How had Richard himself perceived all this? Had his mother seemed smothering, overwhelming, seductive? It seemed likely that Richard's relationship with his mother had been, at the very least, intense. And, for what it was worth, she had been a nurse. Could he have responded with some form of vengeance fantasy against nurses?

A dispatcher at the police station had taken a call from a woman who refused to give her name or a phone number where she could be reached. Three years earlier, the caller said, Richard Bordeau had invited her out "to supper." Instead of going to a restaurant, he drove her to Hanover Street in Claremont and parked at the edge of a field behind the Valley Regional Hospital.

When they got out of the car, the woman went on, standing in the tall grass with a direct view of the hospital, Richard Bordeau had taken off his pants and informed the woman that he wanted to have sex with her. After she refused he eventually put his pants back on and drove her home. The date was taking place on a Tuesday and before leaving Bordeau got her to agree to another date for the following Tuesday. The date, again, was to be "for supper."

A week later, she continued, Bordeau had picked her up and

repeated the sequence, driving her to the grassy field behind the hospital, removing his clothes, and telling her that he wanted to have sex with her. Eventually she had talked him out of it, and once again he agreed to take her home, though not without trying to persuade her to let him come in.

In talking about himself, the woman said, Bordeau claimed to work at Hanover Hospital.

"I have a girl for every day of the week, you know," he had told her. The woman wondered why, in that case, he was pursuing her.

"Something happened to my Tuesday girl," he explained.

Of course it could be coincidence. The woman caller refused to elaborate on the story or provide a phone number, so the investigators couldn't call her back to pursue some of the details. On the other hand, one of the detectives said one day when they were talking about the incident involving the woman they referred to as "Miss Tuesday," what if it were not just coincidence?

"What if the guy gets off on putting it all together: mother, nurses, hospitals, sex, maybe some violence?"

Certainly it was somewhat farfetched, but just suppose there was something real there.

Looked at in this context, the words about nurses leapt from the raucous song "Bad to the Bone." The caller to the radio station obsessively requests again and again to hear about the nurses all gathered joyfully, gazing in awe through the nursery window, while another nurse, the boss, the supervisor, holds up this extraordinary child and declares her special bond to him, commanding the others authoritatively, "Leave this one alone," this one is mine, mine alone.

So far, though, there was simply no evidence to lift Richard Bordeau from the category of unofficial suspects. The puzzle remained unfinished.

John Philpin had been doing criminal profiling for five years now and he was used to analyzing people he hadn't met, enjoyed it, in fact, the intellectual challenge, the purity and abstract quality of the enterprise, along with the opportunity to let imagination and intuition run loose among the facts.

Still, he was having trouble reconciling his own emerging view of Richard Bordeau as a confused and impaired character with Mike Prozzo's sense that the man was dangerous, a potential killer. And Philpin had never met the man, never even seen him, though Bordeau lived right there, only twenty miles or so from Philpin's own home. The psychologist had been thinking for a while that it might help if he could observe Richard Bordeau at first hand, but he hadn't found an opportunity to pursue the idea. It was a mundane errand that provided the occasion he had been looking for.

Philpin had dropped off his son's tape deck at Johnson's Audio in Claremont for repair a few weeks before. He figured to combine the trip to pick it up and do a few other errands in Claremont with another look at the places where the three women had last been seen. Perhaps there would be some detail, some arrangement of facts, that he had not seen before, or not noticed in reading the reports.

But when Philpin arrived at the shop in Claremont, it turned out that they had sent the tape deck to their store in Newport, eight miles farther east. Philpin pictured the route leading off toward Newport, past the big Victorian house where Richard Bordeau lived, out near the covered bridge.

Philpin had studied the man intensively and talked about him endlessly, it seemed, with Prozzo and the rest of the task force members. There was even a videotape of Bordeau talking to Bertram, his imaginary companion.

"What the hell," Philpin thought, "I know all this stuff about the guy and I've never seen him or talked with him." It was like going to see the places where key events—Ellen Fried's last phone call, the starting point of Bernice Courtemanche's trip to Newport—had happened. It was the same with people. No matter how much you knew about someone from the printed record, there was a dimension of understanding you could only get face-to-face. And there was an undeniable element of curiosity.

"As long as I'm going over there," he thought, "I might as well see if I can stop and get a look at the guy."

When he had finished his errands in Claremont, Philpin stopped by the task force office to tell them what he was planning to do and get directions.

"You don't want to do that, John," somebody said. "You don't want to mess with the guy."

"Geez, John," someone else joined in, "he's a big guy, a

black belt in karate. You go out there, you might never be seen again.''

The members of the task force didn't know enough about Richard Bordeau to be sure he could do serious violence, but they knew enough to fear he might.

Philpin took their comments in stride and when they saw he was determined to go, someone came up with a plan. There had been a sleek red Camaro with a For Sale sign in the window, sitting on the lawn in front of the gloomy Victorian house. It would make a good excuse for Philpin to stop.

The detectives felt uncomfortable about letting Philpin go by himself.

''We'll keep an eye on you,'' someone said.

As Philpin passed through the old wooden covered bridge and rounded the curve, the house loomed before him. The Camaro was still on the lawn. He drove past the house at full speed, then pretended to notice the car and brought his pickup to a stop at the side of the road. He waited for another car to pass, then backed up and pulled into the driveway. He felt a little silly, like a man dressing up for Halloween to go trick-or-treating.

As he brought the truck to a stop he looked out at the Camaro. The For Sale sign was no longer there.

What the hell do I do now? Philpin wondered. He realized that the trepidation of the cops, joking or not, had gotten to him. He decided to say that he had been by before and seen the For Sale sign. He mentally practiced his line: ''Hi, is the car still for sale?''

Philpin got down from the truck and started to walk toward the car. And now he noticed in the front yard, on the other side of the car, something he hadn't seen before: a sign declared Keep Out, No Trespassing. The sign looked huge, its message uncompromising. And just beyond, a face appeared in the window of the house. It was Richard Robert Bordeau.

Philpin stood rooted to his spot, staring at the Camaro but hardly seeing it, preoccupied with the presence in the house, resisting the temptation to look back to the window. Maybe if he sees me admiring the car he'll come out to talk, Philpin thought. He wondered where his bodyguards were; there had been no sign of them since he had left Claremont. With that big sign there on the lawn he was technically guilty of trespassing. Could a man legally use force to defend his property against trespassers? Philpin wondered. I'm not about to go up to the house, he decided.

Philpin recalled the report that Bordeau had inherited his butcher father's impressive collection of exquisitely sharp knives. And guns, didn't somebody say he had guns, too? Someone saw him dry-firing a rifle in Claremont, that's what it was. It seemed to Philpin he had been standing on the lawn a long time.

There was no sign that Bordeau was going to make an appearance outside. Philpin decided he had stayed long enough to allow for an honorable retreat. He returned to the truck and drove on to Newport to pick up the tape deck. When he passed the big Victorian house on the way back he kept his foot on the gas, resisting the temptation to slow down for another look.

The failed attempt at a face-to-face confrontation made Philpin feel that the extended history of Richard Robert Bordeau as a murder suspect was ending in farce rather than tragedy. It was hard to take the man seriously as a suspect, the psychologist thought. He was crazy, yes, but homicidal? Probably not. He was too scattered, disoriented. The conversations with Bertram, his imaginary friend, didn't seem like an act; it was like so much of his behavior, the bizarre speech patterns and writing, the assumption of intimacy with people he had barely met, the delusions. These were the hallmarks of a personality falling apart, disintegrating. That, Philpin thought, was the opposite of what you'd expect from the kind of killer they seemed to be dealing with.

A killer who hunted his victims, who spent long hours cruising the roads looking for the perfect time and place and person, selecting the scenery and fellow actor for his lethal production—that kind of predator would have to be organized, controlled. All this suggested an integrated personality, psychopathic, to be sure, but displaying a certain kind of control. Richard Bordeau seemed incapable of acting with such systematic authority.

And don't forget, Philpin pointed out one day in a discussion of Bordeau as a suspect, now they were talking about a serial killer. A scattered, disorganized killer might get lucky and escape once, even twice, but he would be almost certain to get caught eventually.

"After all," the psychologist said, "what if Bertram appeared suddenly in the middle of the crime and wanted to talk?" The joke was intended to make a point: the kind of personality that produced an imaginary companion didn't seem consistent with complex and efficient killing expeditions.

And yet, despite Philpin's misgivings, Prozzo thought, there was just something about all this that wouldn't go away. The task force hadn't been able to build a case against Richard Bordeau, but they had never convincingly eliminated him as a suspect, either. He had the flimsiest alibis, and there were so many things that made him look like a plausible suspect. Bordeau even matched the profile that Philpin was starting to put together for the task force in a number of ways—his solitary life, his ineptness with women, his mobility. It was a whole collection of little things that added up to a continuing, low-level suspicion; Prozzo couldn't shake it, but it never became persuasive enough to act on. It was like a little stone in the shoe, big enough to get your attention, but not irritating enough to make you stop and take the trouble to unlace the shoe.

Prozzo would never be fully convinced that Richard Robert Bordeau was not somehow involved in the Valley killings. It might be all he had, this little stone in the shoe, but there was no getting rid of it.

twenty-three

You had to be patient. It didn't do any good to push too hard, move too fast. The image of a killer would follow its own rules, hiding in a thicket of facts, yielding up a glimpse here, an impression there, emerging only when the time was right, when you had seen enough and thought enough and felt enough with your mind and your heart to capture a sense of who he was, how he lived his life, and why part of his life was killing.

That was one of the things that had made the Lynda Moore profile difficult: time, the need to try for quick conclusions. It couldn't be avoided; the investigators needed to move quickly; in order to be useful, John Philpin had tried to match their pace. But it had left him balanced between conflicting views of the killer, lacking the perspective nurtured by time that would have enhanced one of the portraits and caused the other to fade away.

Philpin liked to recall, for himself and for others, a newspaper story he had read about an agent in the FBI's Behavioral Science Unit at Quantico, Virginia, who specialized in criminal profiling. The agent, Philpin said, kept a clipping about a murder case displayed in a prominent position above his desk. The FBI had prepared a profile of the killer before he was caught, but the article was not a memento of a great triumph. Just the opposite, in fact. The agent could go through the characteristics of the convicted killer one by one, showing how not a single point matched the FBI's profile. The agent kept the article to caution himself against excessive pride in his craft. Philpin identified with the agent and shared his humility.

The first question for Philpin was which cases might be related. The similarities among the cases of Bernice Courtemanche, Ellen Fried, and Eva Morse placed them at the center of the investigation. There were reasons to consider Jo Anne Dunham along with the others, but her death was so remote in time—sixteen years before the disappearance of Ellen Fried—that it seemed unlikely a close investigation of her case would shed light on the others. Perhaps it might eventually work the other way: a solution to some of the others might answer the question of who had killed Jo Anne Dunham. For now, her case was set aside.

That left Elizabeth Critchley. She had not been placed on the official list of task force cases, but her death was one of those that bore the greatest similarity to the ones on the list.

The task force investigation had fleshed out the portrait of Elizabeth Critchley. As the investigators came to know more about her they referred to her as Betsy; that was what her friends had called her. She had been thirty-seven years old when she disappeared. It was 1981, close enough to the seventies that her long hair and easy manner had been thought of as hippie style. Her pictures showed a pretty face, but when she smiled it was with her mouth closed. Her bite was deformed in a way that made her self-conscious about her looks. Her condition was unusual; a dentist in Massachusetts had been providing corrective treatment at virtually no cost, in return for the experience.

It was a Saturday in July. After a long session of work on her teeth, the dentist, accompanied by his assistant, drove her to the interstate. She was planning to hitchhike northward on I-91 along the Connecticut River to her home in Vermont. She was never seen again alive.

The body of a young woman was found two weeks later in Unity, New Hampshire. It was clothed in maroon denim jeans and a maroon sweater over a pink sleeveless blouse with a floral print. There were two rings on the right hand, one on the ring finger, one on the little finger. The description was published, but in spite of the details, it was almost two months before it was identified as Elizabeth Critchley.

The task force investigators had found several reasons to suspend judgement about whether Betsy Critchley's death was related to the other cases they were working on. For one thing, although the autopsy had never established a cause of death, it was clear she had not been stabbed. If the Valley killer's routine included a knife, that argued for separating her from the others. So did the fact that her route passed through the heart of the territory where Gary Schaefer had hunted for victims.

In his discussions with the detectives after his arrest in 1983, Schaefer had talked of "driving around" to relieve frustration or anger. That was how he had found Dana Thurston, the woman he had abducted and then released. His other victims had not been so lucky, and Betsy Critchley had disappeared only a month before Schaefer killed Theresa Fenton in 1981.

There was evidence that Schaefer had assaulted several women outside Vermont. The investigators, along with police in other places where Schaefer had lived, suspected that he had killed before, as well, though there was no grounds for prosecution in any of the cases. The murder of Betsy Critchley seemed to fit Schaefer's pattern. She had disappeared on a Saturday; Schaefer rarely worked on weekends and had killed both Theresa Fenton and Caty Richards on Saturdays twenty months apart.

Philpin and Mike LeClair had talked with Schaefer about these suspicions, but he had never admitted to anything and there was no evidence to connect him to Critchley. He met questions about the case with the same blank wall of denial he had thrown up against the out-of-state cases.

Critchley had been heading into the heart of the region where the other victims had been abducted, she was on the road, she was hitchhiking, alone and vulnerable, and her body had been dumped in the town of Unity, within two miles of where Eva Morse and Jo Anne Dunham had been found. The old suspicions about Gary Schaefer undermined Philpin's inclination to connect the Critchley case with the other Valley killings. He added the name of Elizabeth Critchley to his mental list of related murders in the Valley, then his uncertainty marked it off with parentheses.

The psychologist found himself returning repeatedly to the

telephone in front of Leo's Market where Ellen Fried had made the call to her sister. Philpin's wife, Jane, liked to shop at Joe Sclafani's Warehouse, a cut-rate factory outlet store in west Claremont. It was just a quarter mile down the hill from Leo's. Philpin couldn't stand to go into the store, with the crowds of avid shoppers picking over the bargain merchandise, so it worked out fine. He made the twenty-five-minute drive to Claremont with Jane from their home in Vermont, then while she was shopping he would wander over to look at the pay phone and the small parking lot in front of the store.

The psychologist would stand on the sidewalk across from the little market, watching the comings and goings of customers, delivery people, the mailman. He pictured Ellen's ancient Chevelle parked facing the front wall of the store, the young woman standing at the phone a few feet away, talking to her sister, Heidi, then interrupting the conversation, something about a passing car catching her attention—was that surprise in her voice, mild concern? Heidi hadn't been sure:

"That's strange," Ellen had said.

Now she leaves the phone for a moment. When she returns she lets her sister know that she has started the Chevelle's motor, so it will be ready, just in case . . . of what? What did she see in the passing stranger, what was there about him that concerned her, what did she imagine might happen?

Then Philpin's imagination turns to the stranger, watches him pass by, follows along behind him, prowls the edges of his consciousness, probes for the shape and patterns of the life that brought him here, follows him to his confrontation with Ellen Fried and onward to her death, seeking the keys to the mood that carries him along, the urge that drives him to search for a vulnerable woman, to end his search by killing.

The psychologist pondered endlessly over the scene, walked through the surrounding neighborhood looking for anything that might speak to him of two people who had passed there many months before. Then he drove down the hill, past the bargain outlet, to the road where Ellen Fried's car had been found, two miles away from Leo's Market, then back eight miles in the other direction, eastward to the woods in Kelly-ville where her body had been discovered near the downed hemlock by the abandoned railroad right-of-way.

The essence of it was in the arrangements, Philpin reflected, a complex series of moves if you thought about it. The killer must have had his own car, he took a woman from her car, he left her car, clean, innocent of any sign, two miles away with the keys locked neatly inside. He retrieved his own car, transported a woman eight miles and disposed of her in a place where she was not likely to be found soon, was not found, in fact, for fourteen months.

Halfway between Leo's Market and Jarvis Lane, the dirt road where the abandoned Chevelle had attracted the attention of the police, lay Beauregard Village, the section of west Claremont where Bernice Courtemanche had begun her hitch-hiking trip toward Newport to meet her boyfriend. Philpin drove down the hill from Leo's Market toward Beauregard Village, the same route that led to Jarvis Lane, imagining a man who moved along familiar paths like a hunter checking his trapline, alert to the factors of time and place and activity that would shield him from the attention of bystanders, watching for other signals that set off alarms of recognition, of readiness, that said to him, This is my prey.

This was somebody who spent many of his hours in motion, circling like a feeding shark, hunting along the roads and highways of the Valley, Philpin thought. Was he rootless, free, one of those people who float ceaselessly between occasional jobs and loose attachments?

"You've probably seen me on the road," Franklin Triplet had told Mike LeClair. "I hitchhike all around here," Triplet had said, sounding as if he felt his drifting conveyed some form of ownership, like a farmer who has just finished pacing the boundaries of his land.

Or could this flowing stream of movement be related some-how to the killer's job? Philpin went through catalogues of occupations in his mind. He imagined the killer delivering beer or crackers or bread to convenience stores, servicing vending machines or video games, collecting money from pay phones. He considered a dozen, a score, a hundred occupations that would require or allow a man to move unnoticed through the daily life of the community. But the victims had been taken at three different times of day, four if you counted Elizabeth Critchley. And Bernice Courtemanche and Eva Morse had disappeared on Wednesdays, Ellen Fried's last phone conversation had been early in a Friday morning, and Elizabeth

Critchley had last been seen on a Saturday. There was no pattern; it all suggested flexibility.

The Philpins ate occasionally at a Chinese restaurant in Claremont with their nine-year-old son, Steven, who enjoyed playing video games to while away the time until the food was served. The game machines were in the bar, which had become the regular hangout for a crowd of marginal-looking men, so Philpin accompanied his son and sat nearby while he played.

The psychologist found himself observing the men, some loud, some sullen, who populated the bar. He thought of them as floaters, men carried along by the current of daily events, and he tried to imagine what they did in the rest of their lives, when they weren't sitting on a barstool absorbing enough alcohol to maintain some distance from their daily realities. Could this be the type of person he was searching for amidst the facts of the investigation? he wondered. Was one of them the man who had killed, and killed again?

Probably not, he concluded finally. The man who had stalked his victims and captured them and moved them and killed them was no feckless drifter. The killer had managed circumstances, controlled his victims. He was purposeful. He was not a man who would sit idly and let time drift untouched before him. He is a man who works; either the nature of his work or flexible time off allows him the freedom for his hunting.

And what of Eva Morse? Some investigators continued to set her apart from the others. She was oversized, heavy, unkempt, too different, they thought.

But these victims possessed a tragic equality of femaleness, of solitary vulnerability, that attracted their killer. That was the beauty they shared in his eyes; no other mattered.

And with Eva Morse, the autopsy made it clear, there must have been a profusion of blood. Her neck had been brutally slashed, almost severed clean through. Somehow this killer had managed to deal with the blood, cleaned it from himself, from his vehicle, controlled it, Philpin thought. The same would have been true with Bernice Courtemanche; the autopsy showed she had been stabbed. That left Ellen Fried. There were no results yet from the second autopsy, but Henry Ryan had done remarkable things with the other victims, and the pattern of what Philpin had learned led him to expect similar results. If that was true, at least three of the victims had to be considered together.

There was something else: the killer had gotten past the first defenses of his victims. He would have been presentable, plausible. If he picked up a hitchhiker the presumption of trustworthiness would have been in his favor: he was doing a kindness. After that, he would have to be a man who could preserve his victim's trust. Bernice Courtemanche was probably too young, too unsure of herself, but certainly Eva Morse, and probably Ellen Fried, too, would have resisted him if he had revealed himself too soon. Eva was brave, not easily intimidated; she probably would have fought him. He was cool, cagey, controlled.

These crimes were sexual, Philpin thought. That didn't mean that the killer forced physical sexual activity on his victims; because of the deterioration of the bodies it was impossible to be sure, but there was no sign of this type of sexual activity or manipulation. There were other forms of sexual urge could take, however. It could be diverted, redirected, to fuel a rage that was expressed in cruelty or domination. That was what had happened here, Philpin theorized.

Sexual murder typically involved a knife, strangling, or physical beating. This kind of killer often cruised in a car or stalked his victims; typically he was well organized, prepared for what he was going to do. He would not gamble with circumstances. Usually he brought a weapon with him. The entire act, from long anticipation, to preparation, to the hunt and the capture and the killing, was an exercise of his control over people and events, over time itself. He affirms his mastery by preparing himself and his implements, by choosing with care the time and place of the act, by enacting and savoring his domination over the victim, and by the final act, the killing, the ultimate form of dominance.

Philpin reconstructed the crimes: Bernice Courtemanche was knocked unconscious, perhaps killed, then stabbed; the wounds were too confined to have been inflicted on a person capable of fighting back. Ellen Fried was taken in her own car by force or intimidation, made to undress, then killed. Eva Morse must have been forced to walk into the woods and killed there. In each case, the element of control, the need for some extended period of domination, was apparent.

Once in a secluded place, this killer feels safe, confident that he will not be interrupted. He is familiar with this area, knows where to go. He senses the patterns of use and movement of others in these woods, which reinforces his confidence: he can take his time.

The killer's personal characteristics are interwoven with the style of his crimes. He is a rigid man, meticulous. The victims who were found clothed may have been dressed by the killer. In his personal habits he is neat, well groomed. He enjoyed watching his victims undress; he may have kept some of their clothing afterward, taken pleasure in it as a reminder, even if only temporarily.

He is white, between twenty-five and thirty-nine; a younger man would not appear so controlled, experienced, an older one would have been caught, or perhaps shifted to another pattern, even stopped killing. The range was typical for this type of crime. His familiarity with the back roads, the woods, suggests that he lives nearby, say, within twenty-five miles of Claremont. He cruises the roads, and his range may extend farther than that. The sporadic timing of the killings suggests that he may leave the area at times.

If he is employed, which is likely, it could be in sales or service, or in a business that has several branches or offices in the area. He looks normal, not strange or threatening; he is well groomed and dresses neatly. He is strong, in good physical condition. He engages in regular physical activity, but it is something he can practice alone, like jogging, hiking, or weight lifting. He collects something as a hobby, coins or stamps or baseball cards, and he goes to church, though his attendance may be sporadic.

This fairly conventional exterior conceals a deformed spirit. He harbors a grievance over some persecution, real or imagined, at the hands of a female. It could be physical or sexual abuse, failure to protect him as a child from victimization or humiliation by another male, domineering intrusiveness. He is driven to seek revenge for these torments. He manufactures fantasies of revenge in which other women, all women, stand in for the one who abused him. The knife, as is often the case in psychology and literature, plays an essential role in his dream of vengeance. It is a weapon for close quarters, for intimate confrontation with the demon who oppressed him; it is a means to reverse the balance of power, seize dominance for himself.

He views his own experience as merely a sampling of what is universal: Relations between men and women are evil, impure, dirty. Sexuality is merely a means for women to subjugate men with their power of rejection. That is the way the world works, and it is wrong, it is cruel; women exist in fact for the possession and use of men. He feels nothing for those he victimizes; where is the wrong in reversing this cruelty? In fact, his victim has invited what happens to her, by doing things that no intelligent woman should do, placing herself in a situation where her own power is nullified and she is rendered vulnerable: displaying herself in revealing clothes, hitchhiking, driving alone late at night.

The mental mechanisms that separate him from his acts separate him also from all forms of feeling, but he is a practiced imitator. He is expert at simulating the behavior of a complete human being, and his intelligence makes him clever at choosing the correct face for any situation. He is like an actor assuming a role. His tone of voice, his gestures, even the set of his face, all may change at will, seeming to indicate attitude or intention, but there is nothing behind them. He is hollow, without mature emotion.

He may sustain his impersonation of the ordinary and appear immersed in routine for long periods, but eventually the turbulent brew of primitive feeling within him builds to a level of pressure that he cannot ignore. He is feeling restless, uncomfortable, confined. He begins to entertain random fantasies. He seeks the solitude of his car, driving for long hours without apparent purpose or destination. He is entering a cycle of danger. Philpin thought it was like a circle of videotape playing out a series of acts and feelings, then coming to its end and beginning again. He began to call this lethal cycle a "tape loop."

The killer repeats a sequence of thought in which each event must follow in fixed order, and then he must convert it from thought to action: he cruises, selects women and watches or stalks them, imagining that one will become available to him. He savors images of violence against vulnerable women, repeating and adjusting his mental pictures to what she sees in his hours of cruising. He feels a stirring inside; there is a thrilling intensity of anticipation in these moments. He knows what he is preparing to do, knows that he will kill. It is a matter of days, perhaps less, until he converts his fantasy to action. At last he finds the perfect confluence of victim and circumstance. He portions out the gathered excitement in a meticulously managed ritual of vengeance. He kills a woman, kills the power of all women.

Afterward he subsides into a period of lethargy. He lacks energy, feels that his life is empty. Activities that he would ordinarily enjoy seem dull. He may go on like this for weeks or months. During this time he may find the energy for some predatory but milder form of sexual activity, like prowling voyeurism, something he has done frequently over a long period. When he feels the aggressive impulses building, he may attempt to suppress them, engaging in some ritual of purification, a special diet, an exercise regimen, forsaking drink, or masturbation, or the use of pornography. These efforts are typically short-lived.

To others, he seems to be functioning normally. He feels no remorse for what he has done, though he remains concerned about the possibility of being found out. The care he showed in managing his attacks and covering his trail afterward persists in his close attention to newspaper accounts of the crimes and the investigation. He may even have saved clippings from earlier crimes.

When he recovers his energy and confidence, he may swing toward the feeling that he is untouchable, invulnerable. In this mood it is even possible that he might inject himself into the investigation. Part of what thrills him in his attacks on women is the risk, taking it and surviving. Philpin speculated that he might seek out some shadow of that excitement by revisiting the scene of the attack or contacting the investigators with some peripheral observation or information in the crime. If he is questioned, the psychologist said, he may adopt a taunting posture, though without directly exposing his guilt.

Finally, Philpin told the task force, this man is experienced. He has performed other types of illicit sex-related acts, like voyeurism, harassment, or low-level molestation, and these acts may well have brought him to the attention of the police. He has spent endless hours cruising and these outings have led to other attempts at abduction; either he was interrupted or he chose to break off his approach. Or perhaps he has completed assaults, even killings, in some other jurisdiction.

There was a problem with the timing of the killings, Philpin concluded. There had been a hiatus of about a year since the death of Eva Morse. All the killings had taken place in the warmer months. Possibly the killer was excited by the increased exposure of women in summer clothes and bathing suits, by their seemingly increased vulnerability. The interruptions would make sense if the killer were a summer resident or someone who leaves the area seasonally, for school, or periodically, for military service. The break since the death of Eva Morse could be due to the intensified investigation since the discovery of Ellen Fried's body in 1985. But that would not explain the gap between the death of Betsy Critchley and the disappearance of Ellen Fried, three years almost to the day.

"It is my opinion that Ellen Fried and Bernice Courtemanche were killed by the same person," Philpin concluded in his report to the task force. "I consider it highly likely that Eva Morse was killed by the same person." There was a possibility that Betsy Critchley was another victim of the same person, but Philpin now thought it was remote.

There was another obvious question to ask, and that was whether there was any connection between these cases and the murder of Lynda Moore. But the members of the task force were too preoccupied with the New Hampshire cases to give it much thought, and the subject didn't fall within the scope of Philpin's assignment. Still, the psychologist couldn't help reflecting back on the dual portrait he had prepared in the Moore case. As time passed, the more impulsive killer seemed less likely; for one thing, such a man, acting strangely, babbling of his fantasies, blurting out secrets, would probably have been exposed by now in such an intensive investigation.

That left the more controlled killer, the same general type that Philpin was describing in his task force profile. But the speed of the assault and the attacker's apparent lack of interest in his victim before or after the killing seemed to differentiate him from the New Hampshire profile. Philpin thought the differences looked greater than the similarities at this point, but he was keeping an open mind. He set the question aside for a closer look at some later time.

For the task force, Philpin had one final point to make. On the question of whether the killer would strike again, he said, there was good evidence on both sides. In the end, he said, he was persuaded by the power of the compulsion the killer must feel.

Even when the restraints that normally kept him from killing were at their weakest, Philpin wrote, this kind of killer would be capable of logical thinking and deceptive behavior. But his responsiveness to the cues that excite him and begin his deadly cycle "is intense and unrelenting," and he has no inclination to restrain himself.

"My own opinion is that if he is still here he will kill again," Philpin told the task force.

The psychologist took satisfaction from his work with the investigators. It was intellectually challenging, and there was the feeling that he was contributing something useful to the community. He put in long hours preparing a profile and had come to take some pride in his results. The more accurate the profile turned out to be, the more likely it was to aid the investigators.

But this was one case where Philpin would have been satisfied if his prediction had been less accurate.

There was no fanfare, no formal announcement. It had been a little more than four months and the detectives had simply run out of leads and suspects, and even ideas, worth pursuing. With the tight rein on publicity, there hadn't been much in the papers for a while. The task force had been shut down two weeks before the Claremont paper caught up to the story. The *Valley News* took two months.

The assistant attorney general who had overseen the task force told a reporter that the detectives had carried out hundreds of interviews and cleared as many as twenty suspects through alibis. Dozens of others, men with records of violent crimes against women, had also been questioned and ruled out.

"We feel we've covered all the bases and we've done everything we can do," he said. "It's not necessary to keep the office open and dedicate personnel to it full-time." He advised the public not to worry, but to "be cautious." The murders made clear the dangers of hitchhiking, he said, especially for women.

The official view was that the deaths were unrelated, that there was no evidence of a serial killer. "I don't think we're at a point where we can say there is a link," the assistant attorney general said.

Mike Prozzo, returning to full-time work as chief of detectives in Claremont, was no longer inhibited by the task force ground rules. A senior officer in his department, working for the city of Claremont, Prozzo was also outside the chain of command flowing from the attorney general. He enjoyed more freedom to speak his mind than his state police colleagues on the task force. In any case, Prozzo combined the skills of a big-city ethnic politician with the confident, straightforward manner of a man who works among people he's grown up with.

With his characteristic candor, Prozzo spoke to reporters of the Fried, Courtemanche, and Morse murders as a single case, as one investigation that would lead to one killer. There was no conclusive evidence of the connection, he was forced to concede, but after a time an experienced investigator developed a sense about these things.

"I suppose deep down, subconsciously, I believe they must be related," Prozzo told a reporter. Low-key though it was, Prozzo's statement became the first public acknowledgment that a serial killer was loose in the Valley.

The loss would never become anything else, never become a thing softer or easier to bear, but all the people who had seen someone they loved taken by violence in the Valley sensed that a small corner of the pain might be lifted from their lives if the killer were caught. They rarely said it unless they were asked, and when they were asked they said it in different ways: they wanted to see justice done, they wanted to see somebody pay, they wanted some explanation. But in the end they were all speaking variations on a universal human theme: the story of a life must be complete. If we know the beginning of a life, if we know something of its living, we must know how it ended. It was the knowledge that people needed, and it was the knowledge that no one, in spite of the best efforts of the investigators, could yet offer.

Still, from the pain and confusion of their loss, the survivors all seemed to find the patience to accept the situation as it was, to view what had been done in search of answers as the best that could have been done.

"I'm sure they've searched, checked out everything humanly possible," the father of Bernice Courtemanche said. "They searched until they ran out of clues."

Ellen Fried's father, a doctor in New York State, had been closely involved in the investigation, visiting Claremont, placing the newspaper ad after his daughter's disappearance, and he expressed similar feelings: "The police are doing everything in their ability," he said.

And Eva Morse's older half sister, Noreen, who lived with the sadness of so much left undone, so much unsaid, still found in her heart a reservoir of patience for the people involved in the effort to make an ending to the mystery of her loss.

"Some things take time," she said. "Some things are never found out."

She paused to choke back tears.

"It's hard," she said simply.

twenty-four

Winter 1986–87

It was deep winter when Jeffrey Miller came home again on leave, and he was angry. He went to the state police office at Rockingham to pick up his T-shirt and running shoes and windbreaker, and he confronted Mike LeClair. He looked as if he had gained weight since the Navy had taken his picture, and he seemed very nervous, agitated. Maybe it was the anger.

"You made my life miserable," Miller told the detective. He had tried to cooperate, submitted to all those polygraph exams, and still the NIS had called him in again and again to ask him more questions. Obviously the questions had come from Vermont. In a few months it would be a year since the murder and they were still hassling him. The Navy investigators had called him in for another session just a month before he came home on leave.

LeClair tried to mollify him, describing the procedures of an investigation. In fact, there were still a few questions they'd like to talk with him about, things to clear up. Miller wasn't satisfied with the explanation and seemed uninterested in talking about it anymore.

"I'm gonna talk to a lawyer," Miller said. "I'll get back to you."

Activity on the Moore homicide had dwindled with the

passing months, but LeClair had continued to keep an eye on it. Thousands of man-hours of investigation had reduced a long list of suspects to three or four. Jeffrey Miller was one of them.

The naval investigators' last session with Miller had produced some interesting information, which LeClair passed on to John Philpin. Miller had been defensive. Perhaps it was a combination of fatigue with the repeated interrogation sessions and resentment of the investigators' apparent suspicion, but rather than proclaiming his innocence he seemed to take a legalistic stance.

"They don't have enough to detain me right now," he said. "All this is leaving a bad taste in my mouth, 'cause they're grasping for straws and they're not finding any."

There was something eerie about this tone, Philpin thought. It reminded him of Ted Bundy, the notorious serial killer, who had almost taunted detectives at times with his knowledge of his rights and confident assertions that he was beyond their reach. Bundy had displayed an arrogant self-assurance at times, as if it were beneath him to proclaim his innocence; he didn't seem to care whether the detectives thought he was guilty. He had merely defied them to prove it.

"They could detain me," Jeffrey Miller had told his Navy questioners, referring to the Vermont police, "but they would have to have evidence. They don't have enough.

"And they're not gonna find anything else, I'll tell you that right now," he concluded. It was the kind of statement that could be read two ways: Was he saying, "They won't find evidence because I didn't do it so there couldn't possibly be any evidence that I did"? Or could he be saying, without realizing how revealing it sounded, "I'm confident they won't find anything else because I was very careful about disposing of all the evidence."

And that was it. Once more, new answers had led only to new questions that had no answers. It was interesting, Philpin thought, all this psychological information and speculation, but there was no way to go any further with it unless some new lead appeared.

The Moore case rested through the winter in the backs of the investigators' minds like a hibernating bear. And then the investigation took a strange turn.

Mike LeClair had been in line for a promotion; at last it

came through and he was made a lieutenant. He returned to the uniform he had traded for street clothes eight years before, and exchanged his detective slot for command of the regional state police office in Rockingham.

The Moore case was turned over to a new detective named Buddy Walker, and Steve Moore soon became aware that Walker and his partner were taking an intense interest in his activities. There were whisperings that the word had come down through the chain of command, starting with the attorney general's office: Let's go back and take a close look at the husband again.

Wherever the impetus had come from, Moore became increasingly annoyed with the intrusions into a life he had only begun to feel was getting back to normal. Through the winter he heard of friends and acquaintances who had been interviewed intensively in April and May now being visited again by detectives. Eventually Moore himself was summoned to an inquest and asked a series of questions about the day of his wife's death. Moore felt it was a replay of the process he had gone through in the weeks after April 15. It was clear that he was once again the chief suspect in the murder of his wife. Irritated, he cooperated fitfully at first, then angrily tried to take the Fifth Amendment at the inquest, with only partial success.

Mike LeClair viewed this activity with bemusement. He was enjoying his new job, the responsibility of command, the variety of activity. Still, he had been a detective eight years, he had developed a sense of pride in his professional abilities, and he wasn't going to leave it all behind just like that. He had closed half a dozen murder cases after the death of Lynda Moore, and it was the only unsolved homicide he left behind when he returned to uniform and became a shift commander. He respected the professional boundaries that cut him off from direct work on the Moore case, but he found it hard to see how Steve Moore could be taken seriously as a suspect.

"If this guy ever went to trial," LeClair told somebody later, "I'd probably be called as his best witness. I did everything in the world to arrest him. But it's also my obligation not to arrest the wrong man, and I believe in that."

Book VI

Twenty Heartbeats

twenty-five

January 1987

The car was there, jammed backward into the snowbank, when the attendant arrived to unlock the rest-area service building on Sunday morning. The door on the driver's side was open, a pile of snow wedged against the inside panel.

The dense, wet flakes had fallen steadily much of the night, the heaviest storm of the winter so far, and by morning the car wore a thick cap of snow. The rear of the car was resting on the lawn at the back of the building, its front sticking out into the access road.

During the night the two snowplow trucks had come through, one with a right-hand blade, the other with a left-hand blade, one behind the other. They had been forced to swerve around the car in order to open a lane through the inner road of the rest-area loop. They were moving fast, trying to keep up with the snowfall, and when the driver of the second truck saw the car standing awkwardly astride the inner lane he thought maybe his partner had clipped it with his blade. They stopped and walked back to check. The two men looked the car over, but there was no sign that the plows had done any damage.

The drivers returned several times during the day on Sunday to clear out the new snow and open up the parking area, expecting each time to see that the owner of the car had come back with a tow truck and hauled it away. By the end of the day they were getting impatient. People had been making their way around the abandoned vehicle all day. One of the drivers asked the attendant to notify someone. It was too late for that day, so she promised to do it the first thing in the morning. There didn't seem to be anything special about a car stuck in the snow; dozens of drivers had been forced to abandon their vehicles all along the interstate during the last twenty-four hours.

The attendant made the call to the Hartford Police Department at seven o'clock Monday morning. Hartford passed the word on to the Vermont State Police office in Bethel, which notified Ed's Sunoco in White River Junction. It wasn't long before a wrecker backed up to the abandoned car, winched it onto the tilted ramp, and drove back to White River Junction. The car was unloaded and pushed into a parking place behind the Sunoco station. Nobody gave any particular notice to the dark stains on the front seat and the inside of the door.

It was interesting, Jane North thought, how much Barbara had changed since they first met. It hadn't been all that long ago, sometime in 1984. Barbara had joined Parents Without Partners and they had seen each other at the weekly meetings at the Owl's Nest in Lebanon. Jane was well into her second divorce and her kids were in their twenties by then, pretty much on their own, and Barbara thought of Jane as strong and independent.

Barbara hadn't been feeling either strong or independent herself. She had been separated from her husband for a couple of years at the time, the divorce was just going through the final stages, and her son was four years old. She was still getting used to being a single parent, taking back her family name, starting a new life at the age of thirty-six. But she had dealt with the situation in a way that Jane later came to realize was typical of Barbara, energetically going about making it better. She had kept herself busy and joined things and made a point of meeting new people.

The two women hadn't become close at the time, but there had been enough contact at the Parents Without Partners meetings and social events that both had become aware that they liked each other and had a lot in common. So even though they didn't stay in contact after that, when they ran into each other the next winter at the Thetford Clinic, they started talking right away like old friends.

Jane—her friends called her Jage, to rhyme with *cage,* an odd blend of her first name and her family name, Grey—was working at the clinic as a nutritionist when Barbara brought her son, Neil, in to see the doctor. It turned out that Barbara had arranged to rent a place in New Hampshire for a week of skiing with Neil, and there was room for another person. She invited Jage to come over and spend a few days with them. Jage didn't know how to ski, but Barbara's warmth overrode her hesitation and she agreed to go.

It rained most of the four days that Jage was with them, so there wasn't much skiing, but that turned out to be a blessing. They went shopping at the outlet stores in North Conway one day, spent a lot of time sitting by the indoor swimming pool, and through it all they had plenty of time to talk and get to know each other. By the time Jage was ready to leave they felt as if they had known each other all their lives. Jage was seven years older than Barbara, in her early forties, an age and circumstance where close, trusting friendships were increasingly hard to come by. It was a blessing to feel that you had made a friend for life. Neither of the two women could have begun to guess how short a time that would turn out to be.

Barbara had been born in Canada and had three sisters, all of them living in the United States. Her mother had died a few years before, but her father was alive in Canada, though their relations had been strained at times. Barbara had gone to nursing school in New Jersey. That was where she had married Doug Tallon, a dentist, and when he had a chance to set up a practice in New Hampshire, they had moved to Hanover. Barbara worked as a nurse at Mary Hitchcock Memorial Hospital, which was affiliated with Dartmouth College.

Hanover was a quiet place bordering the Connecticut River, in many ways a close match to the stereotype of a traditional college town. It tended to inspire widely divergent attitudes. There were those who thought of Hanover as a neat, peaceful town with good schools and attractive stores a cut above anything in the surrounding area; others thought of it as stuffy, snobbish, and exclusionary, a temporary haven for the spoiled and irresponsible children of the affluent. In fact it was all of these things, and more.

Hanover was also an expensive place to live, and the summer after they reestablished contact, Jage helped Barbara move across the river to Norwich, Vermont. Norwich was home to an institution of higher education, too, Vermont College, but one whose students were more likely to be working adults with children of their own than recent high school graduates. Norwich was more like a typical Valley town, with a wider range of income levels and occupations among its residents.

Barbara and Doug arranged for Neil to live alternate weeks with each of them, and Barbara set about establishing the patterns of her new life. She was taking courses at Vermont College, intent on earning a bachelor's degree in nursing, working part-time in the coronary-care unit at Mary Hitchcock, and travelling periodically throughout the country for a medical equipment company, training nurses and doctors in the use of the firm's products.

In the following months the two women explored their mutual interests, going to dance performances at Dartmouth, enjoying hikes and other outdoor activities as the weather got warmer. Feeling a little restless with the coming of spring, eager to revive her social life, Barbara joined Single Vermonters. It was a matchmaking organization, where each member submitted a short biography and received the biographies of potential dates.

Barbara urged her new friend to get involved, too, but Jage was reluctant at first. Joining a dating club seemed like an act of desperation; the idea was a little tacky, too, and even dangerous. There was no way of knowing what kind of person you were going to meet. But Barbara's enthusiasm was contagious and soon they were reading the statements provided by men in the club, trying to figure out how to describe themselves. Barbara was five feet four inches tall, with blue eyes and brown hair that fell to her waist. She always felt that at 140 pounds, more or less, she was heavier than she ought to be. How much of it should she admit to? What was the right adjective?

And some of the biographies they received in return were

hilarious, men trying to make themselves sound attractive who ended up just seeming foolish. But there were some that sounded interesting, and Barbara sent out three responses to the first batch. All three called her for dates. It turned out to be a mixed experience, justifying both Barbara's cheerful optimism about the singles club and Jage's trepidation.

Barbara went sailing with one of the three men, but nothing much came of it. She seemed to like the second man, though Jage thought it was more a matter of compassion than romantic interest. His name was Barry Washburn; he had been in trouble with the law as a boy, he told Barbara, and now that he was straightened out he wanted to help young people. He was hoping to set up his own counselling practice, specializing with kids who were getting in scrapes at school or minor brushes with the law, to help them avoid further trouble and turn their lives around.

Barbara brought Barry to Jage's one time for a drink. Jage wanted to like him, but she ended up feeling he was strange, possibly a little crazy, with an intensity that seemed unnatural. Meeting him revived all her fears about the singles club. When she thought about him afterward, the word that came to mind was *creepy*. It even occurred to her that he might be dangerous, and she was a little worried for her friend. But Barbara was oblivious to all this; she seemed to share Barry's hopes that he could make a new life for himself and help others do the same. Barbara was like that, always concerned for the underdog, ready to offer sympathy and support to someone in need. They never talked politics, but Jage was sure Barbara must be a liberal Democrat.

Later, after Barbara stopped seeing him, they were talking about men one day and the conversation came around to Barry.

"I did something I don't think you'd approve of," Barbara said.

Jage's curiosity was aroused, but Barbara pulled back from the subject; obviously she didn't want to go into detail. Jage found out later that Barbara had loaned Barry Washburn several thousand dollars. He had told her he needed it to help start up his counselling practice. Apparently he never paid it back.

The third man Barbara met through Single Vermonters was Randy Ogden, and that connection turned out better than the others. He was a Vietnam veteran, divorced a few years, with his own landscaping business. He lived an hour or so from Norwich and Barbara travelled on business in the weeks when Neil was with his father, so a lot of their communication was by letter. They dated during the summer and by fall they were lovers.

Barbara enjoyed their time together, but after a few months it was becoming clear to Barbara that she and Randy felt differently about the relationship. He was much more conservative than she was. There were times when her open, casual ways made him nervous. She never wore a seat belt in the car or locked the doors, and he was constantly reminding her to lock up her apartment when she left. Neil was seven now and they included him in some of their activities, but it didn't turn out well. Randy felt that Barbara wasn't firm enough in her discipline, that she was spoiling Neil.

When school resumed in the fall, Barbara's time was taken up with being a mother in alternate weeks, her own nursing studies, her business travel, and work at the hospital. Combined with the distance between Norwich and Randy's home, Barbara's busy schedule meant that their time together was confined mainly to weekends. They continued to write notes, partly to save on phone bills, and late in the year Barbara wrote to tell Randy that she thought they should taper off their relationship, perhaps continue as friends.

During Christmas vacation Barbara and Jage were planning to go skiing for the day and once again their plans were disrupted by rain. Instead they spent the day at Barbara's apartment, working on a wreath they had planned to make out of hydrangeas. Barbara talked about a minor romantic adventure she had enjoyed during a trip to visit her father in May. She had sat next to an attractive European man on the flight from Boston to Toronto and they had gotten to talking. He was Swiss, she said, but he had a business in Rhode Island that distributed X-ray equipment and he skied frequently with his three daughters at Stratton Mountain in Vermont.

She hadn't thought much about him since then, Barbara said, but the approach of the ski season brought the encounter back to mind. That, and the fact that her relationship with Randy was winding down; it was clear to Jage that her friend was ready to start something new. The man on the plane was an accomplished skier, a member of the ski patrol at Stratton and an occasional instructor. Barbara had talked to him about how much she enjoyed the sport; it was possible that her enthusiasm, stoked by his attractiveness, had left the impression that she was a slightly better skier than was, in fact, the case. His name was Paul Hartmann. They had exchanged business cards, the way people do on planes, Barbara said, but she didn't expect anything to come of it.

"Why don't you go ahead and write him?" Jage suggested.

Barbara was reluctant at first, but Jage thought he sounded attractive and tried to tease her friend into it. "Go for it," she said. "Send him a Christmas card."

And then she said something, so insignificant at the time, that would come back later to dwell on her mind like an apparition of loss.

"What have you got to lose?" she said.

Barbara was persuaded, probably not entirely reluctantly in the end, and she sent off a Christmas card the next day. She added a brief note:

I hope we get to ski together this winter.

Paul Hartmann called just after New Year's. He was going to ski at Stratton the weekend of January 10.

"Why don't you come over for the day?" he suggested.

They arranged to meet for breakfast at Stratton on Saturday and then get in a few runs together before he taught his first classes. They chatted a little about skiing. He had a friend, Hartmann told her, whom he envied. Like Hartmann himself, the man was divorced and an avid skier.

"He fell in love with a woman who skis," Hartmann said, "and now they travel together all over the world and ski."

"No problem," Barbara said, mixing cheerful rejoinder with romantic fantasy. "I'm sure we can work something out."

Jage's daughter and her boyfriend were coming up from New York for a visit that weekend. The boyfriend was allergic to cats, so they couldn't stay at Jage's house; Barbara offered to let them stay at her apartment.

The weather report was predicting snow for the weekend. Friday afternoon Barbara took her car in for routine service at Northeast Foreign Cars in White River Junction. It was a BMW, but far from the classic yuppie chariot. It was twelve years old, with almost a hundred thousand miles on the odometer. Old as it was, Barbara took good care of the car and it was running well. You had to pull up on the driver's side window and crank at the same time to get it closed, but that was no problem, especially in the winter; she just left it closed.

Jage had met a man through Single Vermonters, too, a doctor at Mary Hitchcock. Friday night they went to a dance performance at the Hopkins Center at Dartmouth; afterward they drove to Barbara's apartment, changed their clothes, and went with Jage's daughter and her boyfriend and Barbara to Joseph's Waterworks, a popular Norwich bar with a dance floor. By midnight Jage and her date were preparing to go home, but Barbara was still going strong. She was at the bar talking to a woman friend from New Hampshire. Jage and her date said goodnight. Barbara was looking forward to skiing with Paul Hartmann the next day. Jage figured she would see her Saturday night.

Jage's daughter heard Barbara in the shower early the next morning. It was already snowing hard, and the plows were having trouble keeping the roads clear. The drive to Stratton, about seventy-five miles, took longer than usual and Barbara arrived late, but there was still time for a quick breakfast with Hartmann and a couple of runs before he went off to give his first lesson at nine-forty-five. They arranged to meet for lunch with a couple who were old friends of his. After lunch Paul went off to his afternoon lessons and Barbara skied with the friends.

When the lifts closed for the day they found each other at the base lodge and stood in a crowd for a while listening to an oom-pah band, then went to get her car to return to his condo. She had parked in the large, multilevel garage near the base lodge and now she couldn't remember where the car was. They searched for several minutes on one level, then found the BMW on a different level.

Hartmann's three daughters, young teenagers, were at the condo when they got back, relaxing after a strenuous day in ski-racing training classes. Hartmann assembled a simple dinner for the girls, then he and Barbara headed off down the mountain for dinner at the River Cafe, an informal place in Winhall. He would have been willing to go somewhere a little fancier, but she hadn't brought any extra clothes except a zippered sweatshirt and a second ski sweater. They took Barbara's car because it was better equipped for the snow than Paul's Mercedes. He offered to drive and she agreed. When they left the house she was still wearing her ski overalls.

Paul gave his name to the hostess and they sat in the bar to wait for a table. After what seemed like a long time, he went to find out why they hadn't been seated. The hostess said she had already called their name and they hadn't answered. They would have to wait until their name came around again.

By the time they were summoned to a table they had been chatting amiably for close to an hour. Hartmann thought Barbara seemed reasonably satisfied with her life. She was making a good income from her job training medical personnel and she seemed proud that she had stayed on good terms with her boss for several years; it was a good job, but several people hired before Barbara hadn't been able to stand working with him for more than a few months. She wasn't happy about her divorce, but she felt she had gotten her life back under control, she was enjoying her new apartment with its view of the river, and things were going well with her son, Neil. Even her relations with her father, which had been difficult for many years after her parents were divorced, seemed to be improving.

There was nothing glamorous about her, Hartmann thought, and he got the impression from the conversation that she didn't have much of a social life. When they had met on the plane she had been dressed up, but here she didn't wear makeup and looked as if she didn't spend much time worrying about her figure or her clothes. Her only gestures toward ornamentation were a gold bracelet on one wrist and a pair of earrings. She hadn't brought a purse and she was carrying only forty dollars, of which she spent thirty on her lift ticket. She gave the impression of solid practicality.

"She's a true Vermonter," Hartmann found himself thinking, "a true New Englander."

They left the restaurant a little after ten o'clock. It was

snowing and on the way back they talked about whether she should stay over. The apartment was small, only one bedroom, and crowded already with the three girls there. They really didn't know each other all that well, Hartmann thought, and as far as romance was concerned, he didn't have any designs along those lines. By the time they reached his place they had decided that she would head for home. The snow was falling heavily now, in thick, wet flakes, and Hartmann was a little concerned, but she seemed to feel comfortable with the idea of driving back to Norwich.

"I'm a Vermont girl," she said lightly. "I can take care of myself."

Hartmann started to put her skis in the rack on top of the car with the soles together. Barbara said she preferred them lying flat, so he changed their position, then fastened the poles in next to them.

They kissed each other lightly on the cheek and she was off into the dark, the car quickly disappearing from sight behind a thick curtain of snow.

Sunday morning Paul Hartmann was the first skier on the North American trail down Stratton. It was an exhilarating run, cutting new tracks through pristine, virgin snow under bright sunlight. Barbara had been disappointed that they had only skied two runs together the day before; she would have loved this skiing. Hartmann always enjoyed his time on the slopes, but this was a day that deserved the word *magnificent*.

Jage went to Barbara's place about ten-thirty Sunday morning to pick up her daughter and her boyfriend to go skiing. She was hoping Barbara might join them, but she wasn't there. Jage had been expecting Barbara back Saturday night, but it wasn't too surprising that she hadn't made it. She probably decided to stay over because of the snow, Jage thought, or maybe something developed with the man from the airplane. She'll ski today and come back tonight.

Barbara still wasn't there when they came back from skiing later in the day. Jage kept expecting to see her come sailing in, all ruddy from the skiing and her usual high spirits, lighting up the place with her energy. After her daughter and her boyfriend left for the return drive to New York and Barbara still hadn't arrived, Jage felt a little tremor of concern edging into her thoughts.

"But that's Barbara," she reassured herself, "always spontaneous, the adventurer." She had been so excited about a day on the slopes with this attractive man who was such an excellent skier.

Monday morning Jage called Barbara's house as soon as she arrived at work. The answering machine was still on. She left a message, asking Barbara to call immediately when she got in.

After she hung up, Jage considered the situation. Really, she thought, this was nothing out of the ordinary for Barbara. Neil was with his father this week and Barbara didn't have to work. She didn't have any obligation until her nursing classes started on Thursday; that was something she wouldn't miss. She was probably off on a fling of some kind, Jage told herself. She'd turn up on Wednesday.

"She's a big girl," Jage told herself, searching for some reassurance. "She knows what she's doing." Then the anxiety pushed forward again.

"Jeez, you'd think that she would have called and let me know what was going on," she thought.

At a few minutes before seven on Tuesday morning, a twenty-two-year-old attendant named Toby Ferris was standing at the window of the service building in the rest area off Interstate 91 a mile or two south of White River Junction. The building, which housed rest rooms and a telephone, stood in the island formed by the two parallel access roads on the northbound side of the highway. As Ferris gazed idly out the window, he noticed a man reaching into the rest area's dumpster. When the man drew his hand back he was holding an article of clothing. He stretched the garment out and held it up for examination. Ferris walked out of the building to see what he was doing. As the attendant approached, the stranger dropped the garment back into the dumpster and walked away.

Ferris put his arm down into the garbage container and pulled out the garment the man had been examining. It was a ski jacket. It seemed to be in good condition. Ferris looked over the edge of the dumpster. A turtleneck sweater and a zippered red sweatshirt lay on top of the pile of refuse. Ferris reached in and pulled them out. As he walked back to the building with the clothes he noticed the stranger getting into his car and driving away.

Back inside the building, Ferris looked over the three garments. He couldn't see anything wrong with any of them; they didn't seem like the kind of thing someone would throw away. He rummaged through the pockets of the sweatshirt and ski jacket, not really expecting to find anything. In a front pocket of the jacket his hand touched something leather. It was a small wallet. There was no money, but in a window compartment he found an identification card.

The card had been issued by the Mary Hitchcock Memorial Hospital, across the river in Hanover, New Hampshire. Someone had printed in the name: Barbara Agnew. Underneath there was an address and phone number in Norwich, Vermont. Norwich was just the other side of White River Junction, twelve miles north of the rest area. Ferris dialled the number from the card. After a few rings the phone was picked up. He was getting ready to speak when he realized it was an answering machine. I'll try again later, he thought, when she's home.

Throughout the morning on Tuesday, Toby Ferris tried the number several more times. Each time, he heard the answering machine click onto the line. When his shift ended in the afternoon, he turned the bundle of clothes over to someone in the district office of the highway department in White River Junction.

Tuesday afternoon, the clothes and the wallet ended up on the desk of Helen King, a data entry clerk in the office. Something ought to be done about the clothes, she thought; the owner should get them back. She phoned the number written on the identification card. Her first call reached the answering machine. The card was from the Mary Hitchcock Hospital. She dialled the hospital and reached a receptionist.

"I don't know anything about it," the woman said. King tried to explain the situation, but the receptionist insisted she was too busy to do anything.

When Helen King came in Wednesday morning, the clothes were still there. It bothered her to think of these perfectly good things separated from their owner when there was a lot of good use left in them. She phoned the hospital again. This time a different receptionist answered and she was more interested in trying to help out. Helen King described the clothes. Nobody knew how they had gotten into the dumpster, she said, but they were in good condition and the owner ought to be informed so she could get them back.

It was easy to imagine a lot of places in the world where a rest-area attendant like Toby Ferris wouldn't have bothered with the clothes, or where, if he had bothered, an office worker like Helen King wouldn't have taken the trouble to call, get rebuffed, and call again. But this was the Connecticut River Valley, and more often than not, people acted as if they were connected to other people.

Barbara Agnew's hospital personnel record listed Dr. Douglas Tallon as the person to be notified in case of emergency. There was an office number in Hanover. He returned the hospital's call at nine-fifteen and an administrator told him about the clothes in the dumpster. He told her that he and Agnew were divorced, but he would try to locate her and tell her about the clothes. When he hung up, Tallon called Jage North, his former wife's closest friend. She was at home in Sharon. Tallon told her what he had heard about the clothes.

"Do you know where she is?" he asked.

North told him about Barbara's plans to go skiing. It was a relief finally to tell someone the whole story. Barbara's boyfriend, Randy Ogden, had been calling, obviously worried, but Jage hadn't wanted to tell him that Barbara had gone off skiing with another man. He had kept calling, sounding more upset each time, until finally she had broken down and told him the whole story.

Tallon and Jage talked for a few minutes, trying to decide what to do. Tallon started to recount the sequence that had led from the clothes to the phone call alerting him at his office. When he mentioned the wallet in the pocket of the ski jacket, a chill of fear slithered down Jage North's spine. It was so typical of Barbara, Jage thought: She liked to keep things simple, she hated to carry anything bulky when she went out. She would almost never carry a purse. She would stick a little money in her pocket, or at most slip it into a slim wallet with her driver's license and a minimum amount of identification. The wallet in the pocket of the ski jacket was something she would never have parted with intentionally. Jage North was overtaken by the knowledge that she had been fending off for three days now: something had happened to her friend.

Jage still had the key to Barbara's apartment. She arranged with Tallon to go there and see if they could find any indication of where Barbara might have gone. She drove across the river to Hanover to pick up Tallon, then drove back with him over the bridge to Norwich. Jage opened the door and entered, looking quickly around the familiar rooms. Everything appeared as it had been when she left with her daughter Sunday evening. Just sixty hours. Everything was the same, and everything had changed; Barbara had not been back since Sunday.

She pressed the playback button on the answering machine and they listened to the messages. There was a message from Randy Ogden, asking Barbara if she wanted to go skiing Tuesday or Friday. Then Jage heard her own voice, pleading with Barbara to call immediately when she got home. There was another voice, a woman, asking if Barbara wanted to go skiing sometime.

There was one more message. It started off innocuously, a man talking about a condo in Utah. Then his voice took on a tone of sly innuendo, something about how they might get together, a double entendre implying sexual intimacy. As he went on, Jage's stomach knotted and she was seized again with the fear she had felt on hearing about the wallet in the ski jacket. The thought flashed through her mind that this man, with his sneaky sexual maneuvering, could be connected to her friend's disappearance. And there was something else in it, too, the unaccountable feeling that she was in direct danger from this stranger herself.

Tallon quickly reassured her: Barbara owned a share of a condo at Snowbird. The man was an old friend of his and Barbara's; apparently he was planning to rent the condo from Barbara. But the experience, the memory of her fear, with its personal menace, would linger in the mind of Jage North long after she and everybody else knew what had happened to Barbara Agnew. The predatory note she had sensed in the caller's insinuations would come to seem a foreshadowing of her friend's fate.

But it was clear that there was nothing in the apartment to tell them what they had hoped to learn. It was hard now to say what they might have hoped to find, but it was evident that they weren't going to find Barbara Agnew on their own. Doug Tallon dialed the number of the Norwich Police Department. An officer named James Cushing took the call. Tallon briefly recounted the phone call he had received from the highway department. Cushing told them to stay at the apartment and he would come right over.

Sifting through some papers, Jage came across a business card. She recognized the name. It was the Austrian man Barbara had planned to meet for skiing at Stratton, Paul Hartmann. She called the office number in Rhode Island. Hartmann's secretary said he was out but she would pass on the message.

There was nothing to do but wait. There wasn't much to say. The apartment building was quiet on a Wednesday morning. You could see the Connecticut River from the living room of the apartment. It was bordered by streams of ice coated with snow, and the water flowed sluggishly in the channel. It was as if life itself was coming to a stop.

After a time a police car pulled up in front of the apartment and Officer Cushing appeared at the door. Tallon gave a more detailed account of the call about the clothes at the rest area; Jage North told about spending the evening with Barbara at Joseph's Waterworks Friday night and her friend's plans to go skiing Saturday. The last anyone knew for sure was that somebody—it must have been Barbara, although Jage's daughter hadn't seen her—had taken a shower here in the apartment at five-thirty Saturday morning. North showed the officer around the apartment and handed over Paul Hartmann's business card.

Cushing promised to look into the situation and they left. It was 11:45 A.M. Barbara Agnew was officially a missing person.

Jim Cushing entered Interstate 91 at the Norwich on-ramp and drove south six miles, past the busy interchange with the east-west Interstate 89 at White River Junction, then crossed over to the northbound lane and pulled into the rest area. The trip from Barbara Agnew's apartment had taken about ten minutes.

Cushing walked around for a few minutes, looked into the dumpster, walked back into the service building. There wasn't much to see. He talked to the attendant on duty. The only unusual thing in the last few days, beside the clothes, was a car that had been abandoned. The rest area, like the community of White River Junction, was in the town of Hartford, so that was where they had called to report the car. That was on Monday, the day before yesterday.

Back at his desk, Cushing checked with the Hartford Police Department. Since the rest area was on the interstate, they had passed the call on to the state police in Bethel. Someone at Bethel had run the plates; it was routine with an abandoned car. It was a New Hampshire registration, number 435758. The car was a 1974 BMW, model 2002, green. It was registered to a Barbara Agnew of Hanover.

That was it, the same name that was in the wallet found in the dumpster. This was not going to be the average missing-person case.

Cushing waited anxiously for Chief William Luczynski to come back from lunch. When Cushing had finished laying out what he knew, the chief put in a call to Lieutenant Ed Farmer, the commander of the state police office in Bethel, twenty miles west. Beyond the fact that the interstate highways and the rest areas fell under the jurisdiction of the state police, all but the largest departments routinely called for help from the state police detectives, with their crime lab and specialized training, in a major case. And this was starting to look like a major case.

"There's a possibility of foul play here," Chief Luczynski told Farmer when he returned the call, using the stock phrase for the feeling that something bad had happened. Farmer promised to get someone working on it right away.

Sergeant Ted LeClair was carrying out a routine investigation in White River Junction when the call came from the Bethel office. Lieutenant Farmer told LeClair to drop what he was doing and go over to the Hartford station. Jim Cushing would fill him in about a missing-person case he was working on.

Ted LeClair had been in the Vermont State Police nineteen years, ever since his brother Mike had prodded him into realizing a boyhood ambition, and yet a call like this still had the power to bring a little rush of excited anticipation. There was a combination of urgency and mystery in it, the possibility and challenge spreading out ahead of you. The beginning of a case carried the promise of its end, of a successful solution.

Much later, looking back with the knowledge of how this case would end for Ted LeClair, these expectations at its beginning would take on a deeply melancholy quality, but as Jim Cushing finished briefing LeClair at the Hartford police station, there was no hint of what was to come.

The first step, they decided, was to go get the clothes. A Hartford detective went along with them to the highway department office. From there they went to look at the car at Ed's Sunoco, not far from the police station. Cushing pulled the patrol car around to the side of the station, where several vehicles were parked in uneven rows. The three men got out of the car and walked along the row. They quickly found the green BMW. A thick coating of snow still obscured the top and the hood and trunk lid, but the sides of the car were exposed.

LeClair walked around the BMW, looking it over. A removable ski rack had been fastened to the roof. There was nothing in the rack, but the clips were open. The door on the driver's side of the car was open slightly; the detective pushed on it gently. It wouldn't close. He pulled the door toward him. It moved more easily. He opened it wide enough to lean into the car. He noted a couple of clumps of snow on the floor near the brake pedal.

The detective pulled the door open a little wider and leaned into the car. There were ski boots on the floor, poles resting against the passenger seat, but LeClair barely gave them a cursory glance. His eye was caught by something on the dashboard. Snow covered the windshield and the light was dim inside, but LeClair could see well enough to distinguish a pattern of spots forming a flat arc. In the dim light they seemed to have a dark, brownish color. His eyes followed the pattern upward. More spots speckled the headliner. It was like a spattering of paint from a flicked brush. A word began to take shape in his mind.

LeClair followed the direction of the pattern backward to where it ended in front of the steering wheel. A drizzle of tiny specks dotted the leather cover of the steering wheel. The detective pulled back slightly and looked down at the door. There were more of the small spots on the inside of the door. The same dark color was repeated on the wide inner handle of the door, but here it had a smeared, liquid look. The word in his mind became speech.

"Blood," LeClair said, "that's blood."

twenty-six

It was funny the way things turned out. It was the older brother, Ted, who had wanted to be a state trooper when they were young, who had looked up to the tall men who patrolled the roads, with their gleaming boots and buckles and their military bearing. Mike, the younger brother, had never given much thought to what he wanted to do. But when the time came, Ted had lost sight of his boyhood goal and it was Mike who had decided that he wanted to become a trooper. And then it was only after a long siege of Mike's prodding and teasing that Ted went ahead at last and applied to take the exams.

Ted LeClair was twenty-four by then. His life hadn't felt unstable at the time, he was a young man and he'd always had a job, but looking back it seemed as if he'd been drifting for six years since graduating from high school. Maybe he was just continuing the pattern of the LeClairs' family life. In retrospect it felt as if they had lived in half the towns in central Vermont, not to mention a sojourn of seven years out of state. Their father had worked for many years in the great marble quarries of Vermont, until the stonecutters went on what turned out to be a long, bitter strike. When he found a job at Pratt and Whitney, the manufacturer of aircraft engines, the family moved to Connecticut. But they had left behind a large, close family, and with his wife increasingly eager to go home, the boys' father found a job as a route salesman back in Vermont with the Grand Union Tea Company, the grocery chain.

Eventually there were six children, five of them boys, with a fifteen-year span between Ted and the youngest child, Doug. Ted and Mike were the two oldest and they had always been close, but it was just an accident of the military job-selection process, not his brother's boyhood ambition, that got Mike assigned to the military police when he joined the air force after high school. By the time Mike was thinking about what he was going to do after the military, Ted had worked in construction, delivered bread for Nissen, done factory work for International Silver back in Connecticut, worked on the line in a plastics factory, and spent time as a mechanic in a motorcycle shop.

In the meantime, Mike had decided on a career. Talking with Ted about his police work in the air force and his decision to apply for the state police when he got out, Mike sensed that his brother was in a rut. All Ted's jobs had seemed interesting or challenging at the beginning, but none of them had stayed that way. Mike's own enthusiasm about his future was contagious. Go ahead, he urged his older brother, give it a shot. Less than a year later, Ted passed the exams and became a member of the Vermont State Police. Six months after that, Mike was accepted. Their careers had run in rough parallel ever since.

Ted was the smaller of the two brothers, a couple of inches short of six feet, and thinner than Mike as well. He wore a standard-issue police officer's moustache that turned down around his mouth and combined with his long, narrow face to make him seem mournful. That impression was misleading, for he was a cheerful and good-natured man with an easy sense of humor, but as he got older and by degrees settled down there emerged in him a purposeful, focused quality. Many of his state police colleagues, perhaps because of the physical and predominantly male environment they worked in, seemed to retain a youthful lightness of personality, but there wasn't much of that in Ted LeClair. It might have been the inheritance of a first child in a large family, born of an early awareness of responsibility: the word *serious* came to mind.

In contrast with neighboring New Hampshire, Vermont politics was given to a kind of eccentric liberalism, which occasionally elected a socialist mayor or an antiwar senator. But beneath that level the two states shared a personal conservatism, born mainly of small-town life. That made Ted LeClair's independence and nonconformity somewhat surprising.

Ted LeClair joined the Vermont State Police in 1968, grateful for his acceptance and for what promised to be a secure job. By the end of the year he was helping to lead an insurrection. LeClair was never quite sure what the cause was, but apparently he had offended someone in the state police command. One week he was stationed in Bellows Falls on the Connecticut River, near his family and the central part of the state where he had grown up, and the next week he had been transferred to Hardwick, a tiny town in the remote section of Vermont near the Canadian border called the Northeast Kingdom. It wasn't so much working up north that bothered him; all troopers, and especially rookies, were moved around from time to time. It was the arbitrary way decisions were managed that seemed unfair to Ted LeClair. He could have resigned from the state police, run away, but even after just a few months he knew that this was a job, with its physical activity, its constant challenge to learn new skills, and most of all its daily newness, that he wanted to keep for a long time. He wasn't about to let anybody make him quit.

Like most things in business and government in those days, the Vermont State Police was run in a personal way left over from a simpler past. The people in command positions had a way of cramming things down the troopers' throats, often without system or explanation; regulations and procedures weren't enough to restrain personal malice or quirk. In addition, the troopers felt themselves underpaid and poorly equipped.

Ted LeClair wasn't the only one who saw injustice in the situation. By the end of the year he had joined with a few other officers, including his brother Mike, to revive the long-dormant Troopers Association; the man elected first president of the association in its new era was Ted LeClair.

His own role in all this came as something of a surprise to LeClair. The nation was consumed with political ferment and hippie dissent. Ted LeClair was used to thinking of people like that, people who organized and resisted authority, as rabble-rousers; he was bemused to think that now he had become one of them. Still, to anyone who knew his independent nature and his resentment of injustice, it seemed entirely in character.

The association and its leaders faced rough going in the early years, but slowly they gained respect. They fought for and won procedures that protected troopers from arbitrary action, along with improvements in pay and working conditions. Even so, it was more than a decade before superior officers began giving Ted LeClair and the other activists professional evaluations that were free from bias, and promotions that came when they were earned. By then, a less tangible benefit had come to Ted LeClair that he was too modest to talk about, maybe even too modest to acknowledge. His work for the association had made him one of the most widely known and respected officers in the Vermont State Police.

During that first decade as a trooper the tension and disruption in Ted LeClair's professional affairs found its echo in his private life. He had married a woman with two children and later adopted them. The couple had a son of their own, but the marriage broke up after nine years. LeClair stayed involved with the children, but it was a difficult time.

Through it all, there were a few constants: his work as a trooper, the large, extended LeClair family, and always, and especially, his cherished pastime, hunting. He had begun as a boy and now his time in the woods with Mike and other companions had come to seem essential for his well-being. It was almost as if the rest of the year revolved around the hunting season. The off-season provided time for anticipation, for the care and preparation of the weapons and equipment, for loading ammunition. He kept busy and sharpened his eye with skeet- and trap-shooting, practicing regularly and competing in tournaments. When the time came he spent every hour he could spare from work and family ranging through the Vermont woods, hunting wild turkey, game birds, deer, each in its season.

The year LeClair took his oldest son, Shawn, hunting for the first time, something happened that changed forever the way he looked at his pastime. It was time, LeClair thought, with Shawn turning eleven, to introduce him to the mysteries and satisfactions of the woods. They were hunting turkey, dressed in the camouflage outfits necessary to elude the notice of the notoriously wary birds. Father and son had been crouching for some time in front of a white birch tree at the edge of a clearing, partly concealed by a low wall of brush, waiting for full daylight. A friend of LeClair's who had come with them was hunting some distance away. Shawn cradled his 20-gauge shotgun, proud to be in the woods on the business of grown-ups, proud to be among men.

LeClair laid his head back and closed his eyes momentarily. They had risen early to seek out the turkeys in their active time. Suddenly Shawn sensed movement on the other side of the clearing. He had begun rising, his arm moving upward before his face, when a booming explosion tore the morning quiet. The boy fell back toward the tree, struck by a burst of shotgun pellets. In that moment Ted LeClair gave a shout, a wordless bellow of surprise and shock. He began rising to his feet, turning toward his son. A slash of bright red stained the white bark of the birch tree behind Shawn. A first attempt to understand what had happened raced across LeClair's mind:

"Shawn shot himself," he thought.

Instantly there came the roar of another shot and LeClair was rocked sideways by a blow to the hip and back that knocked him to the ground. It was several moments before he could recover his equilibrium and move to his son's side. He quickly checked the boy's wounds. Shawn had seen a hunter preparing to fire and had instinctively thrown his arm up in front of his face. The main force of the buckshot had struck him on the wrist and forearm, but some of the pellets had hit him in the face. There was a lot of blood, but these were not wounds that would threaten his life.

LeClair turned in the direction from which the shots had come. A hunter stood at the other side of the clearing, fifty yards away, still not sure what had happened. LeClair was possessed by a cold fury.

"Get your ass down here," he shouted at the man. "Get down here and give us a hand."

When the man approached, LeClair identified himself as a state trooper and ordered him to help them get out of the woods. The man and his partner carried the guns while LeClair, his own wounds relatively minor, braced his son and half-carried, half-walked him from the woods.

The hunter claimed he had spotted a turkey in the clearing between himself and the LeClairs, but it was a transparent invention, the product of the guilt he was already feeling for an act of blatant carelessness. There had followed a long cycle of legal activity between insurance companies that confirmed the shooter's responsibility. It had required an even longer course of physical therapy for Shawn to recover from his wounds and regain full use of his arm and wrist; he would carry a few of the pellets in his face and arm for the rest of his life. Ted LeClair would never again go into the woods without bright orange safety clothing, and he would never again go turkey hunting.

Something more profound had happened, as well.

It was not that the incident had undermined LeClair's love for hunting. "I live for it," he could say some years later. The experience of the outdoors, the solitude, the excitement of the pursuit, the clarity and simplicity of the outcome, his respect for the prey and the primal satisfaction of eating what he killed, all this was a part of Ted LeClair's passion for hunting.

But now it had become in some way a different experience, more dangerous, more complicated. That shocking smear of brilliant red against the white bark of the birch clung to his memory. There had once been an element of innocence in the hunt, in the pursuit, even in the killing. Now, that innocence had been compromised by an awareness of something harsher that inhabited the woods. If he had tried harder to identify it, if he had been less a man of action and more a man of words, LeClair might have said that he had discovered the possibility of tragedy at the core of his beloved pastime.

In most ways, though, LeClair's life moved in a calm and steady progress. In later years he wore horn-rimmed half glasses for reading, which seemed incongruous for a cop and gave him a thoughtful, studious look. Except for his jaunty, bandy-legged stride and disproportionately large, powerful-looking forearms, he could have been the vice president of a small-town Vermont bank.

He remarried, to a woman with a degree in criminal justice who had worked for a number of police departments. They enjoyed bicycle trips in the summer, skiing in the winter; when time and money were available, they went on vacations to Hawaii and the Caribbean. Pauline couldn't share in the hunting trips, but her police training had made her comfortable with guns and Ted taught her to shoot skeet and traps. She became good at it and they enjoyed practicing and going to tournaments together.

Once the tensions of the association's early years subsided, LeClair was promoted to corporal, then to sergeant. He became a detective and found first pleasure in the work, later confidence in a growing proficiency. As a younger man, like other troopers, he had faced physical danger from time to time, a disturbed man with a gun, an angry one with a knife. Now those confrontations seemed remote from his experience; he had the skill to manage events away from risk if necessary, but he also had reason to avoid risk, more to lose if something went wrong. And he no longer had any need to prove himself.

He was assigned to the Bethel office, with investigative responsibility for a sizeable segment of southeastern Vermont, not far from where he had grown up. And his brother Mike, now also a sergeant and a detective, held the same responsibility in an adjacent state police district to the south. The brothers, who had always been close, now had professional reasons to talk on the phone at least once or twice a week, and more, as much as two or three times a day, when one of them needed a professional confidant, or when a case straddled the district line between them. The murder of Lynda Moore in her house in Saxtons River, which took place in Mike's territory and produced a wealth of suspects and connections on Ted's turf, had been one of those. Now the case of Barbara Agnew, and the question of whether it could be related to the death of Lynda Moore, would become another.

twenty-seven

The work was almost like doing archeology, but if anything, it was even more delicate, digging in the snow for any trace of matter that might help explain what had happened to Barbara Agnew.

Late Wednesday afternoon they had connected the green BMW found in the rest area to the missing woman, Barbara Agnew, and Ted LeClair had found the blood in the car a few hours later. The troopers had worked late into the evening organizing a search of the rest area for the following day.

Thursday morning, state police officers from all over Vermont, even the specially trained mountain rescue team kept on standby to search for lost hikers and skiers, assembled at the rest-area service building. They were joined by off-duty police officers and firefighters from the town of Hartford. Two men set up stanchions and stretched strips of wide plastic ribbon to block traffic from entering the access road at the back of the service building. The search area around where the car had been found was divided into rough sections.

The weak sunshine of the last few days had brought some thawing; the cold nights had refrozen the softened snow and there had been some additional snowfall on top of the resulting thin crust. Each officer was assigned a few square feet and by nine o'clock they had begun, brushing carefully at the surface of the snow, pushing each paper-thin layer off to the side, sifting through the moist clumps, then scraping at the frozen crust, watching intently for anything that might be a trace of human presence.

The searchers had been working for more than an hour, dark shapes scattered over the bright, white surface, when an officer on his knees near the border between the blacktop and the grassy center island called out for a commander. He had found a hair; it looked as if it had come from a human head. Five minutes later a state police sergeant searching nearby uncovered some dark spots frozen into the snow; they bore the shape and congealed look of spattered blood. Other finds followed in the next hour: more blood and some bits of fiber, a piece of chewing gum, a strand of hair nearby, then a longer, thicker hair at the other side of the search area.

At noon the mobile crime lab arrived and the technicians took over, establishing a perimeter and laying out string in taut perpendicular lines to form a grid. The search quickly resumed and more blood, hair, and fiber was uncovered. The finds seemed to trace a line between where the car had been and a spot diagonally across the parking area.

By four o'clock the searchers had examined the upper layers of the snow. There had already been substantial snowfall before the car was abandoned; it was unlikely that any more small bits of evidence would be found at lower levels. The officers moved off and a backhoe was brought in to push the remaining snow into piles. Officers watched the snow accumulate in front of the steel bucket and pawed through the mounds in search of larger items; nothing turned up.

It was dark by the time the technicians had packed up their bits of evidence, each in its own clear plastic bag, each a potential answer to a part of the larger question. The lab van pulled slowly out of the parking lot, heading back to headquarters in Montpelier. The searchers scattered to their homes. Their day's work had produced only a first, dim outline of what happened in the rest area four days earlier, but it was a start.

Whatever had happened to Barbara Agnew, hers was not an isolated fate. Even without knowing whether she was alive or dead, it was hard to avoid the thought that she could be the latest in a series of victims.

Ted LeClair was too much a professional to come right out and say what he was thinking, but he was a man with the habit of truthfulness. His comments to the press made clear what was on his mind. There had been several murders of women in New Hampshire and Vermont during the last two and a half years, he pointed out, all within thirty miles or so of the place where Barbara Agnew's car had been found. These events gave a special impetus to the investigation of Agnew's disappearance.

"In light of all the problems we've had in the past year," he told the reporters, "and the disappearances of some of these ladies, we're jumping into it with both feet. We're going to try to get a head start on it."

LeClair had finished going over Barbara Agnew's BMW with the lab technicians. The lab people had found several fingerprints, though they couldn't say how many of them might be Barbara Agnew's. They had taken the blood spots, some fibers, and other bits of material for analysis. There had been toiletries and a hairbrush on the seat, along with ski gloves and a wool hat.

In the glove compartment LeClair found a work order for service on the car. It had been in the shop in White River Junction on the previous Friday, the day before Barbara Agnew went skiing at Stratton. That was a lucky break; it might help them trace her movements Saturday.

There had not been anything remarkable about the ski boots and poles on the passenger side of the car, but their presence had raised a question: Where were the skis?

Another state police detective, Ron DeVincenzi, had contacted Paul Hartmann, the man she had skied with at Stratton Mountain. Hartmann was in Europe on business and DeVincenzi had finally reached him in Vienna. Hartmann had described his day with Barbara Agnew on Saturday, the dinner afterward, her departure for home. His daughters had been watching television, the detective show "Hunter." It must have been about ten-thirty.

Hartmann remembered putting the skis into the rack on top of the car because Barbara had asked him to change their position. They were Olins, Mark IV, red or orange, with M-40 bindings. They were a little longer than average for her height, about 180 centimeters, because she was a strong woman.

After they had talked for close to an hour, Hartmann became aware that something in the detective's persistent questioning had been making him uncomfortable. He blurted out his concern. "It sounds like I'm a suspect," Hartmann said.

"No, no, not at all," DeVincenzi told him, rushing to allay his anxiety. He had been a great help in reconstructing both the personality of the missing woman and the events of the day, the detective told Hartmann.

He had received a call from his secretary, Hartmann said, telling him that someone in Vermont wanted to talk to him about "someone by the name of Barbara." The news that she was missing had come as a shock.

"I've been, you know, rather thoughtful ever since," Hartmann said. The detective told him more details about the discovery of the car. The implications of the evidence were not lost on Hartmann.

"This is absolutely horrible," he told the detective.

"Yeah," DeVincenzi told him, "we're suspecting the worst."

It was impossible to do anything but think about Barbara. Jage North had tried to concentrate on other things, to take her mind off it. It didn't work. She was Barbara's best friend, she was the one who had been in the middle of things from the start. The police were calling to check the facts, the newspapers and television reporters were calling to fill in their stories. Barbara's parents, her sisters, her friends were calling to get the latest news, and each call was disturbing, filled with the sense that so much was left unfinished, unresolved. And everything was made more difficult by the lack of knowledge, the uncertainty about what had happened and where Barbara might be now.

Randy Ogden was distraught. He had been Barbara's lover, as close as anyone, and it was almost as if he felt he was at fault somehow, as if there had been something he could have done to prevent Barbara from coming to harm and he had failed to do it. He had been interviewed by the police and he had told them everything about Barbara and himself, about their relationship and their ups and downs and their disagree-

ments over her disciplining of Neil. They had asked him in
detail about what he had been doing Saturday night. When
they checked with his landlady she told the detective that she
hadn't seen Ogden come home Saturday night at the time he
had told the police. They seemed suspicious, Ogden thought,
as if his differences with Barbara could have been reason for
him to harm her.

All of this, everybody's worries, everybody's fears, seemed
to drain into her life, Jage North thought, gathering to form a
great knot in the pit of her stomach. She tried to keep up with
work, tried to keep all her appointments, until finally it got to
be too much. She got out her appointment book and opened
it to the current week and scrawled in large letters across the
top of the page, NO MORE. She turned to the next page and
wrote it again, and then she found herself obsessively turning
the pages and writing, until page after page, week after week,
far into the future, the words NO MORE stared out at her in
heavy, somber black letters.

Slowly the pieces came together, forming themselves into a
picture of Barbara Agnew's movements from the time she left
Stratton Mountain Saturday night. It seemed clear that she had
been attacked at the rest area, but where had her attacker come
from? Could she have gone somewhere else first, somewhere
there might be a clue to how and when she had met the man—
the assumption that it had been a man, at least one, was automatic—responsible for the blood in her car?

The work order from Northeast Foreign Cars showed that
she had taken the BMW for service on Friday. The service
department had recorded a mileage reading of 99,318 miles
when she brought the car in Friday morning. Someone at the
dealership confirmed that Agnew had picked it up at 5:00 P.M.
Friday afternoon.

When Ted LeClair looked into the BMW a few days later
at Ed's Sunoco, the heater, fan, and defroster switches were
all in the on position and the odometer showed 99,466 miles.
The car had travelled 148 miles between Friday evening and
the time it reached the rest area. A detective was assigned to
drive from Stratton Mountain back to the rest area, using the
route that Barbara Agnew was most likely to have taken, to
measure the mileage.

The snowplow drivers helped place the time they had first seen the car in the parking area Saturday night between 11:00 P.M. and a little after 1:00 A.M., when they had headed back to the highway department garage for a break and a short nap.

When the two drivers had returned later in the morning to plow the access road, one of them had also noticed footprints in the snow on the passenger side of the car leading off toward the parking area. In addition, the snow on the car roof above the passenger door had been disturbed.

The drivers' information suggested that the skis had been taken from the rack on the passenger side of the roof sometime after the car had been abandoned. That information didn't say much about the fate of Barbara Agnew, but it combined with the observations of Toby Ferris, the attendant, to create a disturbing picture of the rest area. In a follow-up interview, Ferris told the detectives he had seen some clothes on the seat of the abandoned car Sunday or Monday. Looking back, he thought they must have been the same ones he rescued from the dumpster. The man Ferris had seen at the dumpster must have been either disposing of the clothes after taking them from the car, or scavenging among items previously removed from the car by someone else and then abandoned. Somebody had stolen the clothes from the front seat of the car; someone else, it appeared, had stolen the skis from the rack on the roof.

The police had appealed for help from the public and reports were coming in that reinforced the idea of the rest area as an unpleasant and often unsafe place. A man called to say that his married daughter had gone to use the rest room and come upon a man masturbating; she had called her husband and the man had run away. A member of the cleaning crew reported that homosexuals used the rest area as a meeting place. They parked their cars in the lot and followed each other into the bathrooms for sex. Loiterers and men in pairs, usually one older and one younger man, could be found there at all hours, but especially late at night. The employee said he had gone into the rest room to clean up one night and had found two men, naked, in the bathroom. He had thrown them out. Later, after he had threatened to take license-plate numbers and report some of the men he recognized as regulars, he had come out one night to find that his tires had been slashed.

And a Hanover woman called to report something she had

heard from several sources. A local resident named Libby Bannerman had been attacked at the rest area, the caller said. A detective called Ms. Bannerman to ask about the details. The report was correct, she said. She had come out of the rest room and a shabby man wearing sneakers—she had noticed that he had terrible body odor, she said—had made a sexual comment about her appearance. As she passed, trying to avoid the man, he grabbed her arm. She swung her purse and hit him in the groin. He let go and she ran to her car. He chased her, got into his own car, and followed her. She drove to the police station in Weathersfield and reported the incident. When had this happened? the officer asked. Six months earlier, she said, in the summer of 1986.

These reports and others like them, though they made the rest area sound like the rural counterpart of a big-city bus terminal, appeared to have no bearing on the investigation of Barbara Agnew's disappearance. Other callers reported seeing the green BMW stuck in the snowbank during the day Sunday, but their observations failed to add to what was known already. A man called to say that his girlfriend and her mother had seen two men apparently forcing a woman into a van on the interstate highway near the rest area. It had happened Saturday afternoon, too early to have any bearing on the Agnew case. And so the calls came in, two dozen or more every day, interesting, disturbing, and, as the days went by, increasingly repetitious, but none reporting an observation of Barbara Agnew after ten-thirty Saturday night.

The men who were closest to Barbara Agnew had to be treated as suspects. Paul Hartmann was eliminated by the testimony of his daughters and others, and Randy Ogden agreed to take a polygraph examination, which indicated that he had been candid with the investigators and knew nothing further about his friend's disappearance. There were several calls about men in the community who had behaved in suspicious or menacing ways toward women. One caller reported on her neighbor, a man named Barney Stillman. He had been bothering the woman and her seventeen-year-old daughter since Thanksgiving, she told the detective who took her call. Stillman was in his forties, she said, tall, thin, and balding, with long, stringy, unwashed hair. He had a "pointed" face she said, and was missing a front tooth.

"He's very ugly," she said, somewhat redundantly.

The detective thought the name sounded familiar. He checked on Stillman's record and found a long history of assault charges, some involving use of a weapon, some just with fists. He had served time in jail for assault. Stillman went onto the growing list of potential suspects for further investigation.

The trooper assigned to check the mileage had driven down the access road at Stratton Mountain and made his way through Londonderry, Chester, and Springfield before driving north on I-91 along the Connecticut River to the rest area. Conditions were similar during the test to those the night of Barbara Agnew's trip. It was snowing heavily again and there were about four inches of snow on the road. The trip took one hour and fifty-one minutes. The distance was 65.8 miles.

The detectives added up the mileage for Agnew's known travel; there was the short drive Friday evening, maybe four miles, from Northeast Foreign Cars to her home, a short round-trip in Norwich that night from her home to Joseph's Waterworks and back, then six miles to account for the distance from her home as far as the rest area Saturday morning, plus the distance to Stratton measured by the detective, the short trip down the hill with Hartmann to the restaurant in Winhall and back, then the mileage back as far as the rest area. The total would come very close to the 148 miles that had registered on the odometer of the BMW between the time Agnew picked up the car after it was serviced and the time the car was found at the rest area. That appeared to rule out any side trip or unknown destination. It appeared that she had driven straight to the rest area after leaving Stratton.

And that raised another crucial question: Why had she pulled into the rest area, when another ten minutes or so of driving would have brought her safely home? It was plausible to think that she had needed to go to the bathroom; she had drunk a large amount of liquid during the long wait in the bar at the restaurant and then more with dinner, and the dinner had ended a relatively short time before she started the drive home. In addition, because of the snow the trip would have taken longer than usual, perhaps much longer than she anticipated. Even with a visit to the bathroom at Hartmann's condo before she left Stratton, she could have been looking forward to another opportunity. But would a mere ten minutes have made a difference? It seemed unlikely.

Then what about the effect of the heavy, wet snow on the driving visibility? Could she have stopped to clean off a buildup of snow on her windshield? That was at least possible, but it didn't explain why she had pulled into the relatively dark area behind the service building when she could have used the shorter route through the brightly lighted front access lane. And another possibility: She could have stopped to use the phone in the service building. She was an energetic, social person; could she have been planning to call someone, even at this late hour, to see if she could get together with friends? But she had gotten up early, spent a busy, active day, and endured a long, tense drive home. It seemed unlikely that she would still be looking for entertainment around midnight after a day like that.

Concern about Agnew's disappearance had produced an unprecedented flood of phone calls from people who wanted to help. A newspaper had quoted Ted LeClair as saying that one of the questions the investigators were working on was the motivation for Agnew's stop at the rest area, and soon after, a Hanover woman called to suggest an answer. She said she had been travelling north on I-91, heading toward home, the Saturday Agnew disappeared. It had been snowing, the woman said, and she was feeling tired and a little tense about the driving conditions, when she saw a sign leaning against a pole by the side of the road just south of the rest area. When she drew close enough to read the hand-lettered words, Coffee Break, the woman recalled that civic organizations sometimes provided coffee and snacks during a storm or on weekend nights as a public service and a fund-raising device.

She decided to take advantage of the opportunity, the caller said, but as she pulled into the rest area she was taken with the feeling that there was something strange about the situation. It came to her that when she had stopped for coffee in the past there had been lots of cars and visible signs of activity. This time the rest area seemed deserted. The scene had made her uncomfortable, the woman said, and she had driven on through the rest area without stopping. But perhaps her experience could explain why Barbara Agnew had stopped.

In the following weeks the investigators tried to verify the existence of the sign or of anyone serving coffee at the rest area, but no further evidence turned up. The report would remain one of the puzzling loose ends in the investigation.

There was at least one other possible explanation of how Barbara Agnew got into trouble. Many of her friends had remarked on her kindness and empathy for others; Jage North had summarized it in political terms with her guess that her friend was a liberal Democrat. Could she have picked up a hitchhiker or someone with car problems? Randy Ogden, for one, didn't think it was consistent with her personality; she certainly wouldn't pick up a hitchhiker, he said. But others judged that in addition to feeling sympathy for anyone in need, she was inclined to think the best of people. And beyond that, she had the Vermonter's commitment to self-reliance, which made her confident of her ability to handle whatever might come up.

To the people who knew Barbara Agnew best, these thoughts only added a dimension of cruelty to the advancing sense of loss. For they knew her as someone singular, one who combined qualities that were not often found together, independence with generosity, strength with openness, great bursts of activity with quiet attentiveness to other people. Barbara Agnew was too vital, too much a presence, to disappear so suddenly, without explanation, amid intimations of horror. She had too much force of will for that.

Of all people, her friends were thinking, Barbara Agnew was someone to whom such a thing could not happen. Of all people, they thought, she was someone to whom such a thing should not happen.

And yet, as day followed day without news of her, the certainty grew among them that she was now the latest in a series of women to whom it *had* happened.

At some point in the first week someone had asked Jage North if she was scared. It had seemed an odd question at the time and she had just said no and dismissed the idea. She had been scared at first, before they knew Barbara was missing, when she had heard about the wallet, and again when she had gone to her friend's apartment and heard the message on the answering machine with the ominous sexual overtones. In those moments she had been afraid for her friend. But now those brief passages of fear had yielded to something that stayed with her, that wouldn't go away, like a sharp pain giving way to a ceaseless, throbbing ache. It was the growing certainty of loss, of a great emptiness in her life where there had been brightness.

And then, about two weeks after Barbara disappeared, the phone rang a little after four o'clock one morning.

There was the automatic shiver of fear that comes with a phone call in the hours of deepest sleep. The only news that comes in those hours is news of death or its approach. She picked up the phone.

"Hello," she said. There was no sound. "Hello." No response. "Hello, who is it?" There was only silence. After several moments she heard a click and the tone that indicated the line was dead.

It was unsettling, but she put it out of her mind.

A few nights later she was staying with a friend in White River Junction. They were asleep when the phone rang. He picked up the phone. His greeting was answered by silence. He tried again, listened for a moment, and again. When there was still no response, he hung up. North looked at the clock. The hands were within a few degrees of the position she had seen when the call had come a few nights earlier.

Her name had been in the paper. Could the caller have located her at home, then followed her by phone here to White River Junction? How much must he know about her to find her here? If he knew this much, how much more, how much of what she held in her most private thoughts, must he also know? Could he be outside? Nearby? Watching, waiting? Now she was scared, truly scared.

The next day she called a friend, a man who worked as a dispatcher at a local police department. He minimized the danger at first, but soon he yielded to her perception of danger.

"I'm not supposed to do this," he told her, "but if you come on over here, I'll give you something."

At the station he took her outside and handed her a small canister of Mace. He took a few minutes to show her how to use it.

Afterward she felt a little better, but it didn't last. After eleven years of living in a small town without a thought of danger, for the first time she had begun locking her doors. And now those moments of unexpected sound that used to pass almost without notice—a rattling window, a noise in the yard, something on the roof—now those things were enough to bring back that chill of fear she had felt the night the phone rang and nobody spoke.

As the days passed and the detectives gathered ideas from interviews and observation, from lab analysis and phone tips and deduction and intuition and experience, they came to feel they had enough information to reconstruct the path of Agnew's car in the rest area. From that they would attempt an educated guess at what had happened to her.

The tow-truck crew had found the car's front wheels turned hard to the left. Along with the position of the car and the tracks noticed by the snowplow drivers, this suggested that the vehicle had moved in a curving path to the point where it ended up. Following that path backward from the snowbank, the detectives reasoned that Agnew had pulled in on the right-hand side of the service lane, across from where the car ended up and several yards farther ahead. That would have placed her under one of the light stanchions spaced out along the snow-covered ground at the side of the lane. It would also have located her across from the dumpster, which raised another possibility, though a somewhat remote one, about the purpose of her stop: perhaps she had containers or remains of coffee or food to dispose of, possibly in combination with some other purpose.

In any case, the car offered further clues to what had happened next. The difficulty of closing the door on the driver's side turned out to be due to damage on the leading edge; it was the kind of crushing that would have been caused by force on the inside of the door pressing it beyond the limit of its opening swing. Along with the clumps of snow inside the car and its position in the snow bank, this made it seem likely that the car had rammed backward into the snow with the door open.

The lab results were not conclusive about most of the troopers' finds from the parking lot, and some of the hairs turned out to be from dogs. But there were tentative matches with Barbara Agnew's hair and blood, and with fibers from the sweater Paul Hartmann had described her as wearing. Like algebra students laying out a curve with only a few coordinates, the investigators plotted the points where the items had been found on the forensic specialists' grid, each corresponding to a location in the parking area. Then they filled in the gaps and connected the points with a curving line that swept across the traffic lane, tracing the movement of the car and the path of Agnew's struggle with the man who attacked her. The track corresponded neatly to the movement of the car suggested by the other evidence and deduction.

Ted LeClair had found tiny blood spatters on the ski clothes from the dumpster. And the smear on the inner handle of the driver's side door suggested an attempt to pull the door closed with a bloodied hand. The fan had been running, driving the heater and the defroster, when the ignition was turned off. Now it was possible to lay out a hypothetical sequence that tied all these facts together:

Barbara Agnew pulls to a stop and starts to get out of the car, to clean the windshield, dispose of some refuse, or carry out some other task. She leaves the car running to keep it warm and to continue the flow of warm air to the windshield. She has left the car, or she is starting to get out, when she is approached by a stranger. Perhaps he uses some pretext, an offer of help or a request for help or information. The stranger quickly converts the approach into a confrontation; he shows her his knife, his power, and orders Agnew to go with him to his vehicle. But Barbara Agnew is not one to be easily intimidated; she resists. She would have used words at first, speaking in the controlled, firm tone of a woman used to dealing with tense situations, crises where a patient's fragile heart, where life itself, depends on a nurse's ability to remain calm and choose instantly the correct response to an emergency.

But the stranger is beyond the reach of words, implacable, unrelenting. If he attempted first to take control of her physically without using the knife and she resisted, he displayed no slow patience, no willingness to cajole or argue or persuade her into compliance.

He strikes out with the knife, and at least some of his blows strike home. She is wounded and blood quickly appears.

The wounds could well include cuts on the hands or arms sustained when Agnew tries to defend herself against the knife. Either she eludes the attacker and flees to the car, or she is still partly inside. She attempts to pull the door shut, but the stranger catches her, holding the door and stabbing her again. The poor footing and the awkward position, perhaps with the car door interfering, limits the effectiveness of this attack. The wounds are relatively minor, but Agnew's frantic attempts to escape, to close the door and shift the gears into reverse and turn the wheel, fling tiny droplets of blood around the interior of the car, spattering the dashboard and the headliner and the ski clothes sitting on the seat beside her.

She has seen blood before, in her work, and she is not intimidated. She struggles to free herself. She shifts the car into reverse—is she blocked in front by the attacker's vehicle, or is this merely the best she can do?—and she steps hard on the gas. Perhaps he attempts to grab the steering wheel, reaching through the partly closed door, pulling it downward, counterclockwise, or perhaps Agnew is attempting to back away from the curb and overcorrects, but the position of the steering wheel controls the outcome of the confrontation.

The shallow arc of the bits of blood and hair and fiber traces the tragic path of her attempt to flee. Instead of surging away from her attacker into the open traffic lane ahead or swinging at a flat angle into the clear space behind, the car lurches backward, the rear end swinging sharply to the left, across the lane, pushing a growing pile of heavy, wet snow beneath it, and slams into the snowbank created by an earlier pass of the plows.

She tries desperately to pull the door closed, but it has acted like a plow, swinging open and scraping snow from the pile at the side of the traffic lane until it has opened to the limit of its hinges and jams in the open position. The attacker—could he have slipped, fallen to the ground, or been knocked down by the open door?—now catches up to her. Standing by the open door of the car, he threatens her with the knife. Tired, bloody, defeated, she has exhausted her ability to resist. He reasserts control, drives and drags her across the parking lot. Within moments they are in his vehicle, pulling out of the rest area onto the interstate, heading north.

And there Barbara Agnew disappears from the mind's view, lost now in that place out beyond the reach of even the sparse mix of fact and deduction that has allowed Ted LeClair and his colleagues to follow her to this point.

In the end, for the detectives, as for all the people along the

Connecticut Valley who had been touched and frightened by the steadily expanding reach of murder, who had recognized in this latest event something familiar from the past, action and emotion alike were undercut by the one looming question for which even speculation could not provide a useful answer:

Where was Barbara Agnew now?

twenty-eight

March 1987

This wasn't the best possible time to show off the Vermont countryside to friends from the city, even if there was still a foot of snow on the ground. The little towns and wooded hills still had the picturesque quality that flatlanders expected to see when they went north in the winter, but only if you didn't look too closely. When you walked up the back roads and the mud stuck to your shoes and you saw the dark clots of half-thawed leaves and felt the deep chill of the frozen woods under the shade of the dripping trees, romantic thoughts of gossamer snowflakes vanished, at least for the season, perhaps forever.

Still, many New Englanders found visitors tolerable at this time of year, when one could be tempted to almost anything for a distraction. February, when the flow of blood in the veins seemed permanently slowed and the imagination could not reach beyond the idea of eternal, immutable winter, and March, when the sloppy chill of mud season at certain moments evoked nostalgia for February, were times when one accepted, even welcomed, the fruits of half-forgotten invitations. On certain days one would embrace even distant, vaguely familiar relatives, old college acquaintances, friends of a friend, querulous parents, adult children with their unsuitable lovers, brothers and sisters with their alien spouses and clamorous children.

And so it was that a woman in Hartland, Vermont, took her visitors, a couple from Boston and a man from New York, for a walk on a Saturday afternoon near the end of March and discovered a horror that had lurked in her imagination for two and a half months.

A week or two earlier it had been difficult to see over the high banks, a whole winter's accumulation of snow plowed into piles at the edge of the road, but now they were beginning to yield to the warming air. It was the other woman who spotted it first, a dark shape on the snow off to the right of the road.

The two men walked through the slushy snow to the small clearing where the body lay facedown near an apple tree. One of them bent over to touch it briefly, just to be sure, but their host knew immediately, even from a distance, that there was no life in that still form, and she also knew, felt with a certainty, whose body they had found. Even from the road she could see the ski clothes, the blue nylon bib overalls and the purple sweater. It had been two and a half months, but the image of a woman driving alone through the night and the storm was still very much on the minds of many people in the Valley, especially the minds of women, who could imagine themselves stopping at a rest area in a snowstorm, who could feel a woman's vulnerability before a man's brutal force.

"I had been thinking a lot about her," the woman said, "and about when they were going to find her. I thought instantly that that was who it was."

A large stain radiated outward around the head and neck, an ugly dark red against the snow. The two men hurriedly retraced their steps through the snow to join the women. Together they all headed back to the house to call the police.

It was a remote area of Hartland and the dispatcher who took the call at the state police office in Bethel tried to get detailed directions to the site, but it was difficult. The woman sounded shaken. Thinking about a missing woman, imagining what might have happened to her at the rest area and where she might have ended up, even anticipating that she would be found, was no preparation for coming upon that dark form just half a mile from your own house, lying in the melting snow surrounded by a billowing stain of her own blood. It took several minutes for the dispatcher to piece together the route to Advent Hill Road. The paved road ended two miles north of Hartland, a town of twenty-four hundred. From there it was close to four miles more, over rutted dirt and spotty patches of mud. A small brook ran perpendicular to Advent Hill Road and passed near an apple tree where the body was lying.

Houses were few up here and far apart, and except for the home of the woman with the visitors, all were owned by city people and occupied only in the summer. Almost all the land-owners along the road, present or not, had posted signs warning passersby against trespassing and hunting, trying to protect themselves and their property against outsiders.

Sergeant Ron DeVincenzi, who was working on the case with Ted LeClair, walked gingerly down toward the little copse of trees, stepping daintily in the footprints made by the two men before him, trying to avoid further damage to any evidence. The body, a dark foreign presence amid the snow, would have been clearly visible to anyone moving along the road, but the mud and slush would keep most people away at this time of year.

The body lay facedown on a slight slope in about a foot of snow, the head higher than the feet. It had settled down through the snow to rest on the ground. The ski clothes had been slashed and internal organs were protruding slightly through the resulting wound in the abdomen. Amid the blood stains, DeVincenzi could see a pale, brownish filigree of mold, an indication that the body had lain in this spot for a long time.

There were a gold ring with an amethyst on the left hand, a silver ring with an oval green stone on the right, a gold bracelet, and earrings. DeVincenzi made a record of the jewelry to help with identification. The facial features were visible but there had been some deterioration and it was hard to match them to a photograph. Still, the detective had little doubt about the identity of the body. A ski pass hung from a stiff wire loop fastened to the front of the bib overalls. It said Stratton Mountain.

The disappearance of Barbara Agnew in January had drawn the Upper Valley area surrounding the New Hampshire towns of Hanover and Lebanon, and their Vermont counterparts of Norwich and White River Junction, into the same circle of intense concern that the earlier disappearances and deaths had produced around Claremont and Charlestown and Springfield, twenty miles to the south. The discovery of the car and the bloodstains on the snow at the rest area had revived the fears provoked by the previous incidents, but the lack of certainty about what had happened to Barbara Agnew had created in many a kind of suspended emotional state.

Now the doubt was gone. The surge of anxiety radiated outward from the hospital, where Barbara Agnew was known as a warm friend and a responsible worker, and from her wide circle of friends and social acquaintances, who knew her as an energetic, cheerful companion. The community's reaction to the death of Barbara Agnew, powerful in itself, also reawakened and intensified the emotions aroused by the earlier kidnappings and killings.

Gun shops throughout the Valley experienced an unprecedented run on their stock. In ordinary times, early spring was a slow time of year for gun sales, but now handguns in particular were selling as fast as the shops could restock them, and many of the customers were women.

"They have been doing a lot of thinking," the owner of a gun shop in West Lebanon, New Hampshire, said of his women customers. His sales to women had increased at least 50 percent, he reported.

"Some are scared, and tired of being scared," he went on. "If you're in trouble, you're probably not going to have time to call the cops, and you probably can't wait until they come."

A salesman at a gun shop in White River Junction said he tried to talk most women, who were unfamiliar with guns, into buying Mace instead. He was usually successful, the salesman said, but some women persisted, and men were buying guns for their wives. Ordinarily, he said, the shop sold two or three handguns in three weeks; since the discovery of Barbara Agnew's body, he had sold between thirty-five and forty in the same time. Typical sales of Mace were forty cans in a year; now he had sold sixty-five in less than a month.

In Woodstock, Vermont, a woman approached a police officer on the street and opened her purse to show him something inside. She wanted help learning how to use it, the woman said. Lying on top of her wallet, car keys, lipstick, and other ordinary items of everyday life, the officer saw an automatic pistol with an ammunition clip inserted. The weapon was cocked. He snatched the weapon from the purse and was relieved to find that the clip was empty. He advised the woman to get rid of the gun.

A Hartland woman was frightened one night by a knocking on the door. When the knocking persisted she became terrified. She called the police, then cowered in the bedroom. It turned out to be her son-in-law.

The gun salesman who spent a lot of time trying to talk people out of buying pistols and revolvers was concerned that some of the reactions he was seeing were far out of proportion to the danger. "There may be a nut out on the street somewhere," he said, "but there also may be someone who really needs help. For all the murders, no one has ever broken into a home to kill. It snowballs into paranoid fear."

A martial-arts school placed a newspaper advertisement that said, "Protect yourself! Don't be the next victim of a violent crime," and enrollment in a self-defense course offered by a women's organization increased by a third. An advertising agency prepared public-service ads offering safety tips, and radio stations throughout the Valley donated time to broadcast them. Newspapers ran similar ads, and a printing company made up brochures for free distribution.

Joe Estey, who had been the chief investigator in Springfield during the investigation of the Gary Schaefer killings in the early eighties, was now chief of police in Hartford, the municipality that contained the rest area where Barbara Agnew's car had been found. He felt the same concern the salesman had voiced.

"Panic is the key word here," Estey told a reporter. "It's a concern." But Estey also acknowledged that there were grounds for reasonable caution.

There had been persistent rumors, the chief said, of drivers, especially women, being pulled over by men using flashing blue lights on their cars to masquerade as police officers. There had been speculation that such a ruse could provide the answer to one of the puzzling questions of the Agnew case: What had caused her to pull into a deserted rest area when she was so close to home? But no police officer had heard a first-hand account of such an incident, Estey said. He urged anyone who had been stopped in this way to call the police. Since Barbara Agnew had disappeared there had been incidents in which drivers refused to pull over for legitimate police officers, apparently out of fear.

Among those who had been closest to Barbara Agnew, the discovery of her body, which confirmed the tragedy they had feared at the same time it put an end to uncertainty, brought a confusing mixture of feelings. Agnew's former husband expressed the common response: "We're saddened, but relieved to know what's going on," he said. "Our minds were starting to play tricks with us."

The sadness, the sense of loss, had been there for a long time; almost no one had still held out hope that Agnew might be alive. But the details of what had happened to her brought a fresh intensity of emotion for some who had known her. A woman friend of Agnew's, Jan Carter, couldn't stop thinking about the manner of her death.

"The hard part about it for me," Carter said, "is knowing she suffered a great deal. There was always a small, small glimmer of hope that maybe she had an easier death. It's real hard to know that she suffered some really brutal violence, and knowing that she was brutally killed is a hard one that will take me some time to deal with."

At the Mary Hitchcock Memorial Hospital, where Barbara Agnew had worked in the coronary-care unit, her disappearance in January had touched many people personally. Now those feelings were reinforced by the news of her death. She had worked at the hospital a long time; many of the people there had known and worked with her, liked her and had become her friends, but that was not the only reason for the intensity of the reaction. Like nurses and other hospital personnel all over the Connecticut Valley, virtually everyone at Mary Hitchcock knew that some of the women who had disappeared over the last three years—Was it all of them? How many was it, three, four, five? More?—had been nurses. Or had they? No one was sure of all the facts, but everyone knew enough to be worried. Was there someone out there—a former patient, a disgruntled orderly, a psychotic physician?—with a macabre fixation on nurses? Could there be someone prowling the hospital corridors, hanging around the hospital parking lot, even now lurking in the dark, waiting for the next shift to get off work, hungering for his next victim?

The police discounted the idea, and logic contradicted it. Except for Ellen Fried, the earlier victims' only connections to hospitals and nursing had been tenuous or nonexistent. Besides, Barbara Agnew had been attacked after a day's skiing and a two-hour drive through heavy snow. How could her attacker have identified her as a nurse, much less followed her to the rest area?

These arguments, to the extent that they were heard, did little to reassure worried nurses. Yes, but . . . , they might say, there was Ellen Fried, who was a real nurse, full-time, and the others did have nursing or hospital connections, however tenuous, and Barbara did have a hospital ID, and she must have had a Mary Hitchcock parking sticker on her car, didn't she?

The hospital leadership announced formation of a reward fund and contributed $5,000 to get it started. A nurse at Mary Hitchcock named Pamela Rowe thought more should be done.

"I was amazed at how sluggish the reaction was when Barbara disappeared," Rowe said later. She took her concerns to the hospital's education department, which responded by producing a film called *Increase Your Personal Safety, Decrease Your Vulnerability*. The film offered tips on avoiding trouble at home and on the road. It was shown first to eight hundred members of the hospital's staff. In the following months public presentations would reach another two thousand people throughout the Valley.

In January, a little more than a week after Barbara Agnew disappeared, a number of her friends sought comfort in a Sunday morning service at a church in Norwich. The minister, Mark Pickett, took note of their presence and spoke of the missing woman and the effect of her abduction on the community.

Everyone had heard the reports of the earlier abductions and murders, Pickett said, and had responded with sadness and anger. But this was different, he said, "because Barbara Agnew was a resident of our small, intimate community." Her disappearance raised a frightening question in an intensely personal way: "If Barbara Agnew can be abducted on a major highway just a few short miles from where we gather here today, then who among us is truly safe?"

The minister went on to argue against the surrender to despair that might be tempting in the face of such terror, and he expressed the conviction that God had been present with the victim in the face of her attacker, that God was with her still, wherever she might be. And Pickett urged his listeners to stand against the fear that would destroy the fabric of their community.

"If you and I look into the faces of those we encounter at the post office, Dan and Whit's, the Nugget Theater," he warned them, listing popular local gathering places, "and see only the eyes of potential assailants, then evil has triumphed and hope is dead. But if instead we are able to look into those same faces and see people who are as vulnerable as you or I, and no less fearful, then perhaps in our unity we can find strength and healing."

Later, after the body had been found, Jan Carter, the friend who had been so powerfully affected by the violence of Barbara Agnew's death, echoed the thoughts of Agnew's former husband and many others in the Valley. She identified one other element that would be essential for the healing the minister had talked about.

"I want whoever did this caught," Carter said. "I want them apprehended and I want justice done. It will make me feel like people in the Upper Valley will be able to start gaining a sense of community trust again."

It was too easy, distracted by the public impact of events, by the shock and pain a whole community felt at the latest in a series of terrible crimes, to lose touch with the fact that at bottom these were private events. Each of the victims had been torn from the web of connection, ranging from love to mere acquaintance, that grows around each person in a community. Each was an individual taken from the lives of other individuals.

Jage North recalled how Barbara had been going through a difficult period when they met, working through her divorce, adjusting to the rhythm of alternate-week parenthood, easing her way back into a social life. Barbara had seen Jage as a veteran, someone who had been through it all and knew how to handle things. Eventually Jage had admitted to Barbara that she didn't feel as firmly in charge of things as she had seemed.

It wasn't that long since Jage herself had gone through her second divorce, her second time watching friends feel forced to choose between her and a husband, and it wasn't any easier to rebuild a life just because you had done it before.

She had been grateful for Barbara, who had been the solid center of that rebuilding process. Too many of Jage's friends had turned out to be takers, people who accepted help and moral support when they needed it and then just disappeared when you needed something from them. After a while you just came to take it for granted that you had to make it on your own, that whatever you were going to give to other people, you weren't ever going to get much back. And then you met someone like Barbara, and having her as a friend made Jage realize how rare it was in life, what a true blessing, to find this kind of balance in a friendship, both people giving as well as taking. Barbara was one of a kind.

And now she was gone.

twenty-nine

It was strange about the idea of death, the way you could live in the world four decades and see it all the time, even do a kind of work where death in its starkest, most brutal form was shoved in your face at least a half a dozen times a year, and yet it never quite touched you in a personal way. And then you're doing something so ordinary, like going for a hamburger with your wife and son at the fast-food drive-through—drive-thru, they probably spelled it—and something happens, and in a few hours you're on intimate terms with the idea of mortality, and afterward for a good long while you can hardly think about anything else.

The Philpins had been up to Hanover, shopping in the Dartmouth Book Store, enjoying the chance to pore over the rich variety of books and records it stocked to serve the academic community. When they finished, Steven was hungry, so they decided to get him something in West Lebanon. It was on the New Hampshire side of the river, only a couple of miles off their route home along the interstate heading south. It hadn't been so long ago that this was a quiet New Hampshire country road serving dairy farms and an occasional house set far back in the trees. Now it was a strip of gas stations and little business plazas and fast-food restaurants that looked as if it could have been assembled out of cookie-cutter pieces taken from some developer's impoverished imagination.

Philpin had just handed the money through the window in the Burger King driveway when a pain ripped through his gut with such force that it almost made him let go of the steering wheel. He pulled over to the side of the parking lot and got down from the truck, hoping the change of position might ease the pain. He could barely straighten up. Jane wanted him to go straight back to the Mary Hitchcock Memorial Hospital at Dartmouth, but Philpin wanted to continue on home.

"It's got to be gas, constipation," he said, hoping it was true, wondering whether something so mundane could produce a pain so fierce.

As Philpin drove toward home he broke out in a sweat and the pain came on with full force. At home he tried lying down, moving around, just waiting it out, but nothing seemed to make much difference. By late afternoon it was becoming obvious that this wasn't just another stomachache.

"This isn't going away," he said to Jane. "You'd better take me to the hospital."

They operated at midnight. An infection had punched a hole in his intestine, allowing the contents to leak into the abdominal cavity, carrying the poison into his system. The doctors stopped it in time, but afterward Philpin had to confront the knowledge that it had come close to killing him. He also had to face the fact that it was going to be with him, a chronic problem, all his life. He could control it with careful attention to his diet and other habits, but the danger, the possibility of another attack, would always be there, a permanent form of vulnerability.

The constant round of tests didn't help his peace of mind, the X rays and blood tests and ultrasound, the poking and prodding, until it felt as if they had invaded every orifice and every square inch of his body. After a few days, when the reality of it struck him, the lifelong, inescapable menace of this intestinal condition, it came with a chilling thought:

"It's like walking around with a time bomb in your stomach," Philpin thought. The phrase stuck in his mind, irresistible, obsessional.

The next day the doctor came to see him. Before Philpin could talk about his concern, the doctor spoke. "Now, I don't want you to feel as if you're walking around with a time bomb in your stomach,'' the doctor said, all sympathy and practical solicitude.

''Oh, thanks a lot,'' Philpin said to himself. The doctor's choice of the same frightening metaphor had the perverse effect of cancelling out his attempt at reassurance.

Philpin had plenty of time to think about it, eight days in the hospital, then home to rest. He had been home a week when the body of Barbara Agnew was found. The next day Ted LeClair called.

Mike LeClair had introduced the psychologist to his brother at a meeting, and after that Ted had called Philpin every once in a while to get his thoughts about something the detective was working on. Usually it was the kind of case that seemed to have some peculiar psychological element. The detective would lay out the facts for Philpin, maybe send him some information, and then they would talk on the phone about the possibilities, what kind of person might make a plausible suspect, how to approach someone brought in for questioning, where the sensitive areas might be.

Philpin had come a long way since those late summer days of 1981 when he worked with Mike LeClair and Joe Estey in Springfield on the case of Theresa Fenton. All he had set out to do was respond to a request for advice, to help the local cops confront something terrible that seemed to be attacking the community he lived and worked in. Now, six years later, it had become what amounted to a second profession.

In hindsight, there was almost an inevitability about it, as if Philpin had been unconsciously preparing himself all his life to take on this new speciality. Almost everything he had done seemed to have contributed to his preparation: his work in the prison system, the private counselling of prisoners and men on parole, his teaching. Even his childhood, a boy's life in a home that seemed always on the brink of eruption, had played its role. Long before he ever sat down for the first time with a convicted child-abuser whose rage pulsated like a latent infection just beneath his skin, Philpin had lived with violence, with its threat in others, its potential in himself. The doctoral degree in forensic psychology he had earned just a few years earlier seemed like little more than icing on a cake.

For several years now, Philpin had been receiving a steady stream of requests for help from detectives in Vermont, in both the state police and local departments, who had passed his name from hand to hand. More often than not there was no money to pay for his services, but Philpin didn't mind. He almost always came to respect the cops who called for advice, and he valued the feeling that he was making a contribution to the welfare of the community. Most of all, he enjoyed the work, the chance to look for a solution to a particularly complex kind of puzzle, one that involved the mysteries of human behavior at the extremes. Increasingly the calls came from outside Vermont, as well, and offered consulting fees. With the accumulating experience and constant study he had felt a growing sense of mastery.

The psychologist had helped out on several cases since preparing the profile of Lynda Moore's killer a year earlier, and even in that time he had refined his approach. Philpin had first learned to approach a case by carrying out a prescribed series of steps in gathering and analyzing information. Now, that mechanical process had become second nature, and Philpin felt liberated, free to open his mind to impressions, to allow his intuition to build on a foundation of fact. It was a way of illuminating the evidence with a whole additional category of information, the subtle understanding of other people's thoughts and feelings that came to Philpin from a place beneath consciousness.

That process of letting his mind make associations—Philpin sometimes used the psychologist's term, idiosyncratic thinking—had sharpened his ability to see beyond the physical evidence to the person who had committed the crime. In one case, a few months after the death of Lynda Moore, Philpin's methods had produced a remarkable result.

The psychologist had been called in to work with detectives as they reconstructed the murder of a young woman. Then he had gone beyond the theory. The woman had been killed by strangulation, and as Philpin walked through the killer's reconstructed movements, trying to match his own imagination to what must have been in the killer's mind, he felt something odd. At first he couldn't pin it down, and later he had trouble reconstructing exactly where it had come from. Philpin sensed a peculiar stealthiness in the way the killer had operated, an indirectness in his movements, and a kind of furtiveness in what he had done to his victim's body. Philpin could feel the killer hiding himself, but it was not just the concealment of a man who is ready to kill. There was something more. It formed itself in Philpin's mind into a vision of somebody who saw himself as disfigured.

In addition to painting a detailed psychological and social portrait of the suspect, suggesting to the detectives that they look for someone who had seen the victim before, who lived and worked in the area, who had a criminal record for sex offenses, Philpin described a man bedeviled by an extreme self-consciousness. In particular, he said, look for someone who is embarrassed by a physical problem, a limp, say, that he has had since childhood, or especially something to do with his face, like crossed eyes, for example, or scarring from a bad burn.

Philpin had followed his policy of cutting himself off from knowledge about suspects while preparing a profile, but early in the investigation the detectives had identified five men with at least a theoretical possibility of having killed the woman. With the profile in hand they checked each of the men against a dozen or more elements of physical evidence. Only one of the men matched virtually every point. In addition, he fit Philpin's profile, right down to a record of sexual assault against women. A detective who went to question the man in more detail found him to be extremely self-conscious, averting his eyes while answering questions, moving his hands over his face as if to hide from his questioner's gaze. His face had been badly scarred by acne. Relatives said he was convinced that people on the street stared at his face and made fun of his appearance; he considered himself an outsider. From a mixture of fact and feeling, John Philpin had virtually conjured up the face and, even more importantly, the mind of a man he had never seen.

The suspect had become alarmed by the detectives' interest and fled to another state. Unable to locate him at first, the detectives learned of his whereabouts when he was convicted of attempted kidnapping and sexual assault and sentenced to a long prison term. He was never brought to justice in the case Philpin had worked on—the detectives were prepared to bring him back for trial if he should ever be released from jail—but the experience reinforced Philpin's sense that with each new case he was refining his skill in this mysterious new art of imagining a killer.

When Ted LeClair phoned the day after Barbara Agnew's body was found, Philpin was ready to be distracted. He had talked at length with Ted about the case around the time of Agnew's disappearance, and after that he had followed developments closely in the newspaper, but in the days since the operation he had been preoccupied with the state of his health and the slow progress of his recovery. The timing of LeClair's call was perfect: it was something to grasp Philpin's attention and turn it in another direction. There was a problem, though: Philpin hadn't resumed driving and was still moving only with difficulty. In that case, LeClair said, the detectives would come to him.

The following day Philpin, wearing a robe over his pajamas, greeted the LeClair brothers and another detective at his front door. The day was a gift from nature, sunny and mild, something more precious because it could not be anticipated with any confidence in the first precarious fortnight of a New England spring. It was the kind of day that had drawn Lynda Moore outside slightly less than a year earlier to sit for a few moments with her face to the sun. The four men sat on the screen porch at the side of the house and the detectives sketched out for Philpin what they had found so far.

Ted LeClair outlined the reconstruction of Barbara Agnew's movements; much of this was familiar to Philpin from his conversations with LeClair, but there were a number of details that he hadn't heard before. They ran through the list of suspects. There were a few who had attracted particular attention, and one of them, a man named Henry Barker, had been mentioned by several callers.

The discussion moved on quickly to the unanswered questions about Barbara Agnew's actions the night she was killed: Why had she decided to stop so close to home, and why had she pulled in at the back of the rest area, instead of taking the shorter, better-lit route through the front?

Was the death of Barbara Agnew connected with the other killings of women in the Valley? The question had been pushed to the back of everybody's mind by the urgency of getting the Agnew investigation started, but there was no danger that anyone would forget about it. Part of Philpin's assignment would be to help with the answer.

Investigators from all over the Valley were meeting the following day at the state police office in Chester, Ted LeClair said. Philpin would have to get someone to drive him, but he was determined to be there. It was time to start moving back into the part of the world where people did useful things.

More than a dozen detectives, along with state and county prosecutors and medical examiners' representatives, gathered the following day in Chester. They listened to Ted LeClair's description of the theories about what had happened to Barbara Agnew and then the discussion turned to suspects. LeClair parcelled out assignments, asking the investigators to gather information about potential suspects who lived in their communities, check on where they had been in January, try to establish where they might have been on the night of the second Saturday of the year. Once again they would be at a disadvantage, looking back across the gap between the victim's disappearance and the discovery of the body. But this time there were two factors that made the job easier. The interval, just two and a half months, was not nearly as long as it had been with the other victims, and the snowstorm, the heaviest of the winter, made it a memorable night. People should find it easier to recall where they had been that night, what they had seen and heard.

Among the suspects, LeClair paid special attention to Henry Barker. Many of the detectives knew him, or had heard the name. Barker had lived in Vermont as a boy, but several years ago he had moved a few miles across the river to New Hampshire. He had been in trouble often, first as a juvenile, later on adult charges. Ted LeClair asked detectives on both sides of the river to gather information about Barker. Another meeting was set for a week and a half later.

The Agnew investigation was starting to look like a reunion of the people who had come together to work on the Schaefer murders six years earlier. Joe Estey, who had been responsible for bringing John Philpin into the investigation of the Theresa Fenton killing, had offered the facilities of the Hartford Police Department, where he was now chief, as headquarters for the Agnew investigation. Mike LeClair, who had cooperated with the Springfield police on the Schaefer murders, was now involved in the Agnew case as a member of the select standby squad of state police detectives pulled together for major investigations. And John Halpin, the Hartford detective who had investigated what turned out to be Schaefer's abduction of Dana Thurston, had picked up the Agnew case at the rest area on the interstate in his town's jurisdiction and was now working on it full-time.

In retrospect, the murder of Theresa Fenton, then the murder of another young girl, Caty Richards, and finally the capture of Gary Schaefer and the link backward in time to 1979 and yet another victim, Sheri Nastasia, had introduced the Valley to a new kind of horror.

Eight years was a long time in the police business, long enough for a detective to see a lot of people he'd arrested serve their sentences and come back out again, long enough to see some of them begin to lead lives within the law, and long enough to arrest others again and send them back for another jail term. The investigation in Springfield, a mere twenty-five miles south of where Barbara Agnew had been found, now seemed long ago and far away. Gary Schaefer had been in jail three years. And yet in some ways there was a straight line through time from the death of Sheri Nastasia to the gruesome discovery made by four strollers off Advent Hill Road.

The Schaefer investigation had also introduced the police, LeClair and Estey and Halpin and their colleagues, to a new and terrible kind of responsibility in their profession. And in the end it had prepared them for what they were facing now, a case that brought even the most conservative among the detectives a step closer to the conclusion that once again there was a serial killer on the hunt in the Connecticut River Valley.

People were calling in with tips, bits of information, suspicions, fears. The detectives patiently wrote them down, typed up the reports, passed them around, followed up with phone calls to a detective in another town who might be able to add information, to help weigh the usefulness of the report. Sometimes a detective went to see the caller in person, not only to augment the information, but also to weigh the source, get a sense of how seriously the story should be taken.

A woman in Lebanon, New Hampshire, told a story. She and her husband were teachers, living in an old house on a dirt road near the top of a hill, somewhat isolated. She was a serious gardener, comfortable with her hands in the soil, the kind of person who seemed to know exactly what each variety of vegetable and flower needed at exactly the right moment. Each summer she sold vegetables to a local farm stand, as much for the satisfaction of knowing her work was productive as for the money.

The only thing she didn't do herself was till the garden. For that she hired a local man named Donald Barker. Each year in late spring he would drive up the hill in a battered truck, unload a gasoline-powered tiller, and open the earth to the new growing season. He was a small man, getting on in years, but wiry and strong. Sometimes he helped out with other jobs in the yard and barn.

Each year Donald Barker spoke of his health, heart problems, and though he always showed up on schedule and did whatever work needed doing without faltering, his complaints seemed to become more dire with each passing year.

"This will probably be the last time you'll see me," he would say, and then he would show up the next year, looking much the same, his pleasant, modest manner intact, his health complaints another notch more ominous than the year before, but otherwise seeming the same, so that it came to seem that he would go on forever in this way.

Then one year Donald Barker's prediction came true. When the woman called to ask him to drive up the hill, a man answered the phone.

"He died," the man said. After the woman had expressed her regrets and talked about Mr. Barker for a few minutes, she asked for a recommendation of someone to help out with the garden.

"I can do that," the man said. He was Donald's son Henry, and the woman arranged a date for him to come till the garden.

When Henry Barker showed up on the day they had arranged, the woman was uncomfortable from the first moment she saw him. He was not tall, but he seemed unnaturally broad, and he was so muscular that he seemed to intend his body to make a statement, like the men in bodybuilding contests.

As the woman talked with him, outlining the areas for tilling, pointing out the obstacles, the man's presence first became disturbing, then almost unbearable. It was the way he stood, a little too close, perhaps, and the way he looked at her, with a steady, cold stare. And his talk, his words, had an insinuating quality, something hinted at that was unnerving, aggressive, ultimately sexual. In those first moments she was sure, knew with a certainty as clear as if he had spoken it out loud, that this man was capable of harming her.

It was all the woman could do to let him go ahead and till the garden, to allow him to stay that long, a foreign, contaminating presence, in the place where she had spent so many hours in peaceful, satisfying contemplation. She paid him quickly when he was finished and knew that she would till the entire expanse of her garden with a hand rake before she would ask this man back onto her property.

Two months before, Philpin had wandered over the rest area, looking at the place where Barbara Agnew had been taken from her car, thinking about the distances and the relationships of things. Now he needed to do the same thing with the place where her body had been found. Joe Estey volunteered to drive him up to Advent Hill.

It was about five miles in a straight line from the rest area to the place where the body had been found, maybe twice that by car over the zigzag route required by the hilly terrain and the layout of the country roads, but it seemed much farther when you passed from the man-made order of a rest area on the interstate highway to the lonely clump of trees and brush standing amidst melting snow off a dirt road high on a hill. It was like taking a trip backward in time from the Valley's future into its past, and Philpin was struck by the loneliness, the deepening isolation of the place as they moved up the hill toward their destination.

Once again, as he had with Bernice Courtemanche and Ellen Fried and Eva Morse, Philpin formed a mental picture of a man moving purposefully over terrain he knew well, no stranger from a distant place feeling his way in alien territory.

As Estey guided the car over the ruts and mudholes of the dirt road, Philpin imagined the killer, his prey thoroughly under control now, intent on carrying out a plan he had prepared long before. He peers intently through the windshield, trying to penetrate the thick curtain of snow, but he is not deterred. He is determined to follow his plan through to its conclusion, to take from his mind the details he had imagined so often, had enjoyed so intensely in his long, solitary reveries, and make them into reality.

They pulled in at the side of Advent Hill Road and Philpin surveyed the scene. The distance from the road to the tree was about thirty yards; the killer had negotiated that distance through heavy snow, in low visibility, with his victim in tow. It all suggested that the place was not casually chosen, and that the killer must have been both strong and determined. There was material here for the beginning of a portrait.

Philpin looked over the site. It was probably the last, vestigial remains of a once-thriving orchard, with the apple tree at the center of the composition, a couple of other, smaller trees standing nearby like attendants, a clump of brush filling in the blanks.

Perhaps it was just the knowledge of what had happened there, the red stains still visible in places on the melting snow. Maybe, too, it was the bleak, unkempt desolation of winter's dregs, but there was a sadness hanging in the air about the little clearing.

It was enough for a first look. Philpin knew he would come back when he could linger alone and let his mind see beyond what his eyes could take in.

Now the investigation was under way and it was almost visible in the atmosphere as the detectives gathered again a week later at the Rockingham office. This time everybody was bringing something to the meeting, the results of a week's work on the Agnew case, information and speculation, answers to questions, and more questions that had grown out of the first answers. It was as if the emanations from all this work filled the room.

One by one Ted LeClair called on the detectives to summarize what they had learned. When they had finished there was a break as they prepared to hear a report from the state medical examiner, Eleanor McQuillen, on the autopsy results. John Philpin drifted into conversation with Ron DeVincenzi, the state police detective working out of the Bethel office with Ted LeClair.

This time Philpin had driven his own truck to the meeting. It was the first time he had been behind the wheel since the

She didn't have to finish the thought: just like Bernice Courtemanche, Ellen Fried, Eva Morse, Barbara Agnew, and maybe another two or three or more women whose bodies turned up in weather-ravaged bits strewn about the woods of Vermont and New Hampshire.

If that were true, Philpin thought, it highlighted the similarity of the Moore killing to all the other murders. Now there was a whole new range of possibilities to consider. In his mind, Philpin took the Moore case file, which had been sitting off by itself, and moved it over next to the pile of Valley cases. Not right on the pile, but close enough so that now, for the first time, one sweep of the mind's eye took it in along with the others.

The caller said he had been driving on Advent Hill Road, heading across from the Quechee Road to Route 12, when he passed a man on foot.

"I thought at the time it was a little strange, someone walking up there," he told the officer who took his call at the investigation headquarters in the Hartford police station. "But I didn't think anything more about it. Then they found the body up there three days later. So I thought I ought to call and tell someone."

The caller lived in White River Junction, seven or eight miles from Advent Hill, and he said he thought he had recognized the man.

"I think he lives in White River," the caller said. "His name's Eddie something. He's kind of strange."

A detective who lived in White River Junction knew immediately whom the caller was talking about. "That's Crazy Eddie," he said.

It took a few minutes more to find someone who knew the man's full name, Edward Strugnell. He was kind of quiet, someone said, kept to himself, worked at construction jobs sometimes. Nobody knew why he was called Crazy Eddie. A few phone calls turned up Strugnell's home address, and two detectives went to interview him. They found him at home. He seemed to have no hesitation about talking with the two visitors.

Oh yes, Strugnell said, he knew Advent Hill Road, drove past there sometimes on the way to work in Windsor. He installed windows over there for a man who built houses. Strugnell said he was surprised that someone said they had seen him walking on Advent Hill Road.

"I never walk," Strugnell said. "I always take the car."

The man must have seen someone else, Strugnell said. He was sure he had never gone walking up there. He wouldn't have any reason to do that. Sometimes he would drive around on the back roads, he admitted, "maybe have some brews," but always alone. He drove a ten-year-old Ford Fairlane.

He was thirty-seven years old, Strugnell said, and he lived alone. He didn't go out much or date very often. It wasn't that he had any problems with women, just that he didn't care to go out a lot.

While one of the detectives was talking to Strugnell, his partner made a discreet inspection of the small apartment. The place was sparsely furnished but neat. On a shelf next to the dining table the detective's eyes came to rest on a long-bladed carving knife with a wood handle. He sidled over to get a closer look. There was no sign of a stain, nothing that could be blood.

"How'd you get the nickname?" one of the detectives asked. "You know, Crazy Eddie."

"Oh," Strugnell answered, "I shot the TV."

He was fifteen years old, he explained, trying to fix the television set, and it gave him a shock. He got angry and blasted it with a shotgun.

"I have a short temper with things," he said, "but not with people." He didn't own any guns now.

The detectives asked if he would be willing to take a polygraph exam, and he agreed. As they left the house, the detectives followed a roundabout path back to their car that took them past Strugnell's old Ford; it was like his house, neat and free of litter, and there were no visible stains.

Eddie Strugnell came in a few days later for the polygraph and the results were negative. Crazy Eddie might be a menace to television sets, but he seemed to be telling the truth about Advent Hill Road.

The tip about Eddie Strugnell was no more than a drop in a flood that washed over the investigators' headquarters at the Hartford police station, streams of fact and speculation, from which Ted LeClair tried to extract any ideas that might lead the investigators to something useful.

The intense public interest also meant that LeClair and the other detectives were called on to deal with the press. It was no simple job. All the detectives had faced the curiosity of reporters before, but this was something different. There was an intensity of interest on the part of the New Hampshire and Vermont media that no one had seen before, and now the story had also spread far beyond the two states. Reporters were calling from newspapers all over the country, some of them coming to take a firsthand look at the places where victims had last been seen and walk through the woods where the bodies had turned up. The detectives were forced to perform a balancing act, trying to encourage public caution while discouraging panic, communicating a sense that the investigators were doing everything they could, without stimulating false hopes for an early solution.

Responding to the worries of the public, the local reporters repeatedly raised two sensitive issues. The possibility of a serial killer roaming the Valley, which had seemed remote at first, had gathered plausibility with each successive death, until now, with the death of Barbara Agnew, many people in the Valley were treating it as an absolute certainty. Ted LeClair decided the most effective approach was to be candid about the detectives' thinking.

"It's premature to decide that they're linked," he told reporters, "but sure, there are similarities between Barbara Agnew and some of the others." In particular, he pointed out, there was the use of a knife, the multiple wounds, and the stabbing to the neck. He didn't go into the other similarities, the common patterns of abduction and handling of the victims. There was no need to get graphic about it, he felt. Beside contributing to the fear, too much detail could alert the killer to weak spots in his concealment. It could also provide material for the kind of screwball who worked out his personal fantasies by confessing in a highly visible case like this.

The public's other obvious preoccupation was what some people were calling "the nurse connection." On that question, LeClair didn't hesitate. There was nothing to it, he said, other than minor coincidence.

The police switchboard had been flooded with calls, LeClair said, and they were glad to have them. Many of the calls were silly or useless, but that was another point LeClair kept to himself. You never wanted to say anything that might discourage someone from offering information; there was no way of telling which call might turn out to provide the one crucial bit of information.

So the flood continued. Three different psychics had called in the weeks before the discovery on Advent Hill, claiming that they had seen the body of Barbara Agnew in visions. One had seen her lifeless form by the railroad tracks in Norwich, another had pictured her lying along the banks of the Connecticut River. They had missed by thirteen and six miles, respectively. The third psychic had benefitted from making a more general prediction: Barbara Agnew would be found by a body of water. If a turgid brook could be considered a body of water, that psychic had come closer than the others. Still, it was not surprising that the dreams of a psychic, or anyone else living in the Connecticut Valley, might be furnished with the trickling, bubbling, gleaming presence of water in all its natural forms. The Connecticut River and the variegated network of rivulets and creeks and brooks and streams and rivers that fed it inhabited virtually every corner of the Valley. Now the fears of people who claimed to be psychics, much like the fears of anyone else, were placing the body of a murdered woman in the places they passed amidst the routine of an ordinary day.

One tip brought an answer to the question of what had happened to Barbara Agnew's skis. A man arrested in Brattleboro for trying to sell several pairs of stolen skis told the police that he had bought them from a man who snatched equipment off cars in parking lots. The seller had bragged of stealing the skis "off that woman that was killed in the rest area."

The investigation of the death of Barbara Agnew was more than two months old, but the discovery of the body had made it seem as if it were new. The detectives were awash in possibilities.

thirty

The first trip to Advent Hill had been helpful, a good start, especially with the company of Joe Estey, who looked at the scene through the eyes of long experience as an investigator. Now John Philpin wanted to go again. He had agreed with Ted LeClair on a short deadline for the Agnew profile. Before he tried to fill in the outlines of his portrait of the killer, he needed to see more. This time he would drive himself up the hill, move more slowly, try to see more deeply into the place.

There was a lot more background information now, too, and one crucial piece of evidence had emerged. A driver for the town of Hartland named Warren Bernearth had been plowing the area around Advent Hill early in the morning of the January storm. He had followed his usual route, plowing the Quechee Road first, then crossing over to Route 12. The drivers always left Advent Hill Road for the end because almost no one was living there. That was why Bernearth had noticed the tracks.

There were eight inches of snow on the ground and it was still falling heavily. Even in the cab of the plow, Bernearth said, with its high vantage point and powerful headlights, the visibility was poor. You'd have to be crazy to come out here if you didn't have to, and yet someone had driven up Advent Hill before him. The tracks had gone up the hill to the Samowicz house, where they turned in to the driveway. Rather

than ending there, though, the tracks continued up the hill to
a house owned by a family named Darnell, where they again
turned in to the driveway; it looked as if the driver had turned
around there and headed back down the hill. Both the Samow-
iczes and the Darnells were summer people, so the tracks
couldn't have had anything to do with them. Bernearth was
struck by the signs of some other human presence on such a
night, but at the time there hadn't seemed to be any reason to
look further. He had come to regret that.

"I wish I had looked for footprints," he said, "but there
was so much snow I could hardly see as it was. I was con-
centrating on plowing. As a matter of fact, I had a hard enough
time getting up there myself."

It would have been helpful to know what time Bernearth
had seen the tracks, but there was a problem. He first estimated
the time as between 2:00 and 3:00 A.M. The next day he told
detectives that it probably had been later than that, between 4:
00 and 4:30 A.M. It had been two and a half months ago, and
now there was no way to decide which estimate was more
reliable.

In any case, Bernearth had said the tracks seemed "pretty
fresh." Even under a continuing, heavy snowfall, tire tracks
left in seven or eight inches of wet snow might look distinct
for an hour or more. And the Darnell house, where the tracks
seemed to end, was less than a quarter of a mile from the
apple tree where the body of Barbara Agnew had been found.
The driveway was the closest place to turn a car around, and
it was just across from where a person might enter the field to
walk down to the apple tree. It seemed likely that Warren
Bernearth had seen the traces of the man who killed Barbara
Agnew.

There were two routes the killer could have taken to approach Advent Hill. Philpin followed one first, then the other,
trying to see what the killer might have seen as he drove
through the storm. He counted the places where the killer
might have turned off the road with his captive, places where
he could have found some sanctuary, the space and privacy to
act out his murderous fantasy. Philpin passed one likely spot
after another, simple rest areas and turnarounds and small
parking lots along Route 4, clearings and a trailhead and little
dead-end paths off the Quechee Road. On each route he

stopped counting after a dozen. No matter which way the killer had gone, he had repeatedly passed up convenient places where he could have been alone with his victim. Philpin thought of Gary Schaefer, who seemed to have preselected places adjacent to roadside pullouts for later use with his victims; and Ted Bundy, the notorious serial killer, had taken his victims to remote places he had found earlier while hiking.

Even on Advent Hill Road, if the plow driver's report was reliable, the killer had pulled into one driveway, then backed out and gone on to another. Why would a man moving inexorably toward the destruction of his victim behave this way? Why would he resist the desire to yield to the storm, to reduce the risk of getting stuck or having an accident, unless he had already chosen the place where his drama would end? Philpin saw him finding his way through the storm, driven on by the need to see in life what he has played out so many times in his mind, thinking he has reached his destination and turning in, then discovering his mistake and forging onward up the hill.

Philpin parked his pickup and walked down toward the apple tree, pressing on with his re-creation of the killer's odyssey. The killer picked this lonesome spot in advance, Philpin thought, planned out what he was going to do, prepared himself, prepared his vehicle, must have been confident in it. Even the man on the street had decided by now that it must have been someone from around here, someone who knew the roads, and it must have been a four-wheel-drive vehicle, a Jeep or a Blazer or a pickup with a lot of weight in the back.

This was the place. All thought and desire had driven the killer onward to this spot, to the consummation of his waking dream. Ninety feet through heavy snow, his victim struggling, terrified, to the apple tree, "don't sit under the apple tree with anyone else but me," the song Philpin's older sister sang when she was baby-sitting for him, warm memories, the brook nearby, cheerful, a pretty view, a nice place for a picnic, being with women, mother, sister, being special, then killing, ripping open the body, the abdomen, like a twisted version of a birth, a surgical birth, something that harmed the mother, turned her against the child, made her want to hurt him, taught him anger and the lust for violence.

Later, when he had studied therapeutic hypnosis and used

it with some of his patients, Philpin realized that what he had been doing in his forensic work was a form of self-hypnosis. As far back as the Theresa Fenton case, when he had knelt over a little heap of forest debris and sensed the religious element in Gary Schaefer's manipulation of his victim's body, Philpin had listened to the part of his mind that would not settle for facts and logic alone. With time it had become an indispensable part of the way he worked. And now he was ready to start on a portrait of the man who killed Barbara Agnew.

Slightly more than two weeks after the body had been discovered, Philpin gave Ted LeClair the finished profile. To anyone who was familiar with the earlier killings in the Valley, the report could seem vaguely familiar, like a story read in childhood and all but forgotten. With each successive killing, the picture of what had happened became a little fuller. In part that was because the cases had come to seem slightly varying examples of the same thing, an attack and killing of one woman after another by the same man. But it was also because with each case there seemed to be a little more evidence left behind. There was a body reduced almost completely to skeletal remains, then another that was somewhat better preserved, then a body with some clothing. There was a car in one case, and the evidence of a final phone call. And there was Lynda Moore, a victim discovered while she still held some remnant of the heat of life.

Even if the Moore case was left out, the evidence of what had happened to Barbara Agnew now added another layer of richness and detail to the detectives' picture of a killing. The body had been found closer to the time of death than the earlier victims and the cold weather had preserved much of the details in tissues and clothing. And there was the car, and the evidence of what had happened at the rest area. This was the best collection of evidence Philpin had started with in all the cases he had worked on to date.

"I didn't really feel I knew this guy until the Agnew case," Philpin said later. "I couldn't get into his head the way I wanted to until then. We had so much more to work with. We had fragments before that, and I had a sense of him, but there was a lot missing. The Agnew case brought everything all together."

Philpin built on the detectives' picture of the attack, the man waiting for her to leave her car or luring her out on some pretext, then showing her the knife. The mystery of her reason for stopping remained, but the stranger's vehicle had probably been parked in front of hers, forcing her to back up in her attempt to escape.

The wounds that showed Barbara Agnew had fought against her attacker, and the autopsy finding that she had died where her body was found, indicated that this was not an all-out attack. It was a deliberate attempt to bring her under control, subdue her just enough so he could take her away still alive. But his obsessive, waking dream of what would happen had not allowed for the humanity of his victim, the brave spirit of this woman. She resisted him, ruined the perfect flow of his fantasy almost before it had started. Her refusal to be intimidated breached the smooth illusion of absolute control that fuelled his dreams. She may even have come close to escaping, and he may have feared for a few terrible moments that he would lose her, lose everything. He exploded in an angry burst of force that reasserted his mastery of his victim, of the movement of events and time.

If it is true that he has already chosen the place where he will take his victim, and if that place is some distance from the rest area, his plan, his fantasy, must have filled in the time between the first act, the capture, and the final act, on Advent Hill. His vehicle becomes a place for this middle passage, a place to take possession of his captive through terror, to show her that her soul is no longer her own. And he needs time, time to dramatize his power over her, and through the fear reflected in her eyes, to see this power for himself. It is a way to vent an enduring rage at this woman and, through her, at all women, and on through the psychological generations, at some very specific woman in his own life, in his past, probably in his childhood.

This is a man who is prepared in his mind for this moment, and he has prepared the conditions to bring it to reality. In addition to choosing the site, perhaps renewing his familiarity with it in recent days, even earlier that same day, he has made sure that his vehicle can handle whatever conditions he might encounter, and he has probably filled the tank with gas recently, perhaps changed the oil, checked the tires, or carried out other servicing. There are avenues here for investigation.

He is a powerful man, bigger and stronger than average, and sure of his strength. Barbara Agnew is not passive nor easily intimidated; she fights him in the rest area, she resists him on the drive to Advent Hill. Yet he is able to subdue her, force her into his vehicle, control her as he drives—if they went directly, the trip must have taken half an hour at least, and more if he took a longer route. And then, once they have arrived at Advent Hill—has his overwhelming force brought her to complete surrender, so that she walks before him, or does he render her helpless and carry her?—he is able to move her from the vehicle to the clearing.

If Barbara Agnew has surrendered, it is only temporarily. Her determination, her courage, is recorded in the traces of what happened on Advent Hill. There is a furious struggle. He stabs her in the neck, once, and again, and again. These wounds seem to have been inflicted from behind, but their position suggests that the victim was below her attacker. Philpin sees her forced to her knees, the killer standing behind her, insisting that she beg, or pray, replicating some brutal apparition of his experience, some horrifying moment of pain and shame in his own life.

Barbara Agnew has only moments to live. It was these first wounds that killed her, and it was possible to estimate the amount of blood that drained from them with each contraction of her heart. It was also possible to estimate the amount of blood loss that would render a woman her size unconscious. From the first brutal thrust into an artery until the moment she was released from awareness of what was happening to her, Barbara Agnew had lived for twenty heartbeats. In another minute or two, she would be dead.

But her killer was not finished with her. As she lies unconscious, he kneels over her. The snow swirls around him, muffling all sound, casting a delicate veil of serenity over the scene that forms a terrible contrast with what he is doing to this woman, this stranger. He raises the knife and drives it down into her body, and he does not stop. These blows bear no relation to his need for domination, for control of his victim. She is inert, absent. He has moved on to something else. He continues until he has opened her body, as if she were an element in some ritual, a sacrifice. She is dead, and still he does not stop, until at last he has acted out the final scene of his ruinous fantasy.

He rises from the body and looks around. His heart is beating fast from the exertion, but he quickly regains awareness of where he is and what he must do. He is already turning his attention to the knife, to disposing of the woman's car keys, cleaning the blood from his vehicle, restoring his clothing and appearance to normal.

The killer returns to his vehicle and drives off down the hill. Hidden by the snow from the notice of others, he is quickly returning to the secure anonymity of his daily life. He does not have far to go, and even in the difficult conditions he is at home within an hour or less. As he goes, the snow slowly fills in the tire tracks behind him, erases his footsteps on the hill, covers over the signs of what he has done. The scene on Advent Hill is once again enveloped in stillness, but now it is a false tranquillity. Beneath the surface of this calm he has left a specter of horror for the people of the Valley.

Philpin pulled himself back from contemplation of this wrenching scene and completed his portrait of the killer. There was something perversely impressive in the man's character. He displayed rigidity—he had set his plan in advance and adhered to it in the face of the unexpected. But he had also showed flexibility—he had adapted his script, reacted effectively, when circumstances required it. This was a key to the man, Philpin felt, and today it had brought him closer than ever before. It made him seem an even more formidable threat than they had feared.

The clues to the man behind the threat are in the details of what he has done, and in the growing literature about the relationship between those details and the fine points of personality and experience that mark a man who preys upon women. And always, too, there is the viewer's own humanity, the insight it offers him into the soul of another. Philpin sees a man in his late twenties or early thirties, incapable of intimacy, suffering from sexual dysfunction, a man of rigid control that is interrupted occasionally by outbursts of fury. His work involves a degree of organization and attention to detail, possibly some form of record keeping. He enjoys set routines and he collects something; these activities give him the illusion of structure and control. He is probably not married, and even if he lives with a woman she is probably older and their relationship is not much closer than that of two boarders who occasionally find themselves in the same room at the same time.

The most significant relationship in his life has always been that with his mother; his father was aloof, abusive, or absent a great deal. The treatment he received as a child, along with certain traumatic events, left him feeling powerless and eventually rendered him insecure about his masculinity. His treatment of his victim suggested that he might be replicating some early experience, Philpin thought.

"For example," he wrote, "it is possible that as a child this subject was immobilized by fear, required by the threat of violence to act in certain ways, witnessed or experienced the use of knives in the context of violence, and/or developed an idiosyncratic association to the cutting of the abdomen, e.g., legitimate surgery, the birth of a sibling by caesarean section, etc."

The killer was likely to have a history, perhaps a police record, of voyeurism or child molesting, Philpin said, but there would be no trace of him in the thick stack of files of habitual sex offenders the detectives had pulled out for close scrutiny. He was too calculating for that, too good at concealing the truth of his interior life and the predatory activity that grew from it. Philpin described the killer's return to ordinary behavior after the crime, his lack of guilt and his apprehension about being caught.

The automobile was essential here, Philpin said, the killer's reliance on his vehicle and the likelihood that he spent long hours on the road. The driving could induce a form of self-hypnosis, not unlike that which Philpin used in his investigation, but for the killer it would be a time of controlled reverie. The cruising would also have its practical side: he would be searching out places to take his captives. And then, when he was ready, when the cycle had reached its critical point, the hours of cruising would become a time of hunting, searching for the one perfect victim and the one perfect moment. Here was another area where Gary Schaefer, who had mentioned in passing the many hours he spent driving without apparent purpose, had introduced Philpin to something about the ways of a certain type of killer. The pattern had been identified since then in research about serial killers and rapists.

"I expect that he is a rather constant cruiser/watcher," Philpin wrote, "and that he drives many miles while cruising. Prior to cruising I expect he is nervous or restless."

This man is subject to rapid changes of mood, but he is at least average in intelligence, perhaps above average, and along with his rigid control of his behavior when he is not moving into the critical part of the killing cycle, this helps him to conceal his activities and his emotions from others.

"Only someone fairly close to this man on a regular basis could be expected to note the mood swings and the changes in manner," Philpin wrote, "but subject's control may be so thorough that all the public would see would be a quiet, calm, private individual."

And finally, there were the two inevitable questions, and Philpin went on record. The killer had used Barbara Agnew to end the cycle, what Philpin had likened to a loop of tape, that unreeled in his mind. He got what he needed, what he desperately wanted, from this woman, the outlet for his rage, the domination, the possession, the ritualistic manipulation that used her as a stand-in for the demons of rage and humiliation that inhabited his soul. But this would not be enough.

"I consider the relief he achieved here to be transient," Philpin wrote. "He experiences periodic outbursts, and I would expect him to kill again (and he may well have killed before)."

There it was, on paper, once again, the idea that would force those few dozen people in all who would read Philpin's report—Ted LeClair and the other detectives working with him, some police commanders and a few prosecutors and other public officials—to confront the notion that a rampant murderous force was loose in the Valley.

And Philpin had tacked on, as if incidentally, the idea that linked this man, this hypothetical figure who seemed to be taking on ever more concrete reality each time a woman died, to the fears of every woman and every man who had been watching events of the last several years: "he may well have killed before."

He made it explicit for the detectives. They would have to decide whether to pass on this opinion—and that was all it could be, an opinion—to the public. Philpin knew that they would keep it to themselves, and he understood their reasons for doing so. That was their responsibility as they saw it, and he had never hesitated to cooperate with them. But his responsibility was to tell them what was true as he saw it.

Philpin ran off a copy of the profile he had written for the New Hampshire task force just a year earlier and slipped it into a manila envelope. He reminded the detectives that at the time he had thought it "highly likely" that at least three of the New Hampshire murders had been committed by the same person. And Dr. Henry Ryan, the forensic wizard in Maine, had finally reported, long after the task force had disbanded, on his follow-up autopsy of Ellen Fried's remains. Ryan had found among the bone fragments subtle indications that Ellen Fried had been killed with a knife, like the others. She had been stabbed repeatedly, he said.

And Philpin mentioned his recent conversation with the medical examiner, Eleanor McQuillen, and the way it had caused him to reconsider the possibility that the killing of Lynda Moore was yet another in the same pattern.

And now, Philpin said, there was the killing of Barbara Agnew. His language made him seem uncertain, or perhaps it was the enormity of what he was saying, but Philpin told the investigators that there was a high probability that the thing they most feared was true.

"The similarities that I documented in the New Hampshire cases seem relevant," he concluded, "especially in the context of the Agnew homicide."

He inserted the new profile into the envelope with the copy of the New Hampshire profile and sent it off to Ted LeClair.

Even Philpin, a man of almost religious candor and directness, seemed reluctant to speak of this evil without softening his words, but there was no mistaking what he was saying: Now there were five killings in the Valley, and maybe more, that looked like the work of one person.

thirty-one

The detectives had been interested in Henry Barker almost from the moment in January when it became clear that something terrible had happened to Barbara Agnew. There had been calls: someone had seen him on the road the night of the storm, someone else just thought he was eccentric, possibly dangerous. Several of the detectives knew him, remembered tales of a strange, powerful figure and his encounters with the law. But as long as there was no proof that a crime had been committed, as long as the abduction and death of Barbara Agnew were no more than a suspicion, there was a limit on what the detectives could do. Then, ten weeks later, the body was found, and they set about assembling a detailed picture of Henry Barker.

There were a lot of people in the Valley like Henry Barker, men and women who had grown up in rural areas and in the smallest towns during the sixties and seventies, and then suddenly emerged into young adulthood and found that the life they had prepared to lead didn't exist anymore. The hill farms and orchards and dairy producers were surrendering one by one to waves of economic and social change, falling before an army of developers and their clients, people who could afford the time and money to flee the city for a second home, vacationers who took their interlude of peace in smaller doses, Valley town-dwellers longing for their own few acres of land in the countryside.

As the domain of rural and agricultural life shrank, many of the Valley's displaced young people adjusted to the new way of things. They finished high school, acquired new skills, went on for more study, learned to live in other places and other ways of life. But others seemed to lose their grip on things and slip away from the broad, smooth current of life. They existed on the fringes of the towns, lived in rundown houses with rusting refrigerators in the yards, worked occasionally at odd jobs, brought forth children they never quite felt capable of managing, and struggled with poverty and a sense of dislocation, the feeling that there was something important about the world around them that they just couldn't quite understand. Henry Barker was one of these.

It was misleading to say that Donald and Louise Barker had raised their six children. It was more accurate to say that they had given them life and then tried to coexist with them on their barren farm south of Woodstock. By the time Henry, their last child, was born, it was rare that both of them were living at home at the same time. Donald left for long periods looking for work, and Louise would disappear to one of the Valley towns for weeks at a time, fleeing the hardship and strain. Henry had little contact with his parents, much less warmth or support from them. What meager attention he received came from his older brothers and sisters, and that was not always benign.

Eventually Louise Barker left home altogether, going to live across the river in New Hampshire, collecting welfare payments, supplementing them with irregular work cleaning houses. Henry moved to New Hampshire to live with his mother, but as he got older Louise's grip loosened and he fled at every opportunity. Several times, following a fight with his mother or trouble in school, he moved back to the farm in Vermont for long periods. He spent many school days hanging around a rundown gym in White River Junction, exchanging janitorial work for time in the weight-lifting room. The resulting exaggerated muscular development combined with his habitual scowl to give him a menacing look. It wasn't entirely misleading, for he was known to be aggressive and hostile at times, but there was another element to his character. Some of Barker's friends called him Abner, after the comic-strip country boy, L'il Abner, who was known as much for his amiable innocence as for his muscles.

Barker liked the nickname, seemed to feel it expressed the respect of his schoolmates, but there wasn't much else that could draw him into the classroom, or make him use the time to any purpose when he was there. School officials eventually lost track of him, and by the time he was old enough to legally quit going to classes there was no school official in either state who noticed. Henry Barker was almost out of his teens and functionally illiterate.

He had already been in trouble with the law. At first there were tickets for speeding and reckless driving, then a conviction for disorderly conduct after he got into a drunken fight with a man on the street, followed him home, and broke several windows trying to persuade the man to continue the fight. The fight was a violation of one of the conditions of an earlier sentence of probation. After several more arrests involving cars and drinking, during one of which he fired a gun into the air, he was put on probation again and prohibited from driving. When he was stopped yet again for speeding, he was in violation of his probation.

The cumulative seriousness of these violations, even with time in jail, never seemed to make an impression on Henry Barker. He always pleaded no contest, the equivalent of guilty, and seemed to float through the legal proceedings without accepting responsibility for anything that had happened.

None of this was what brought Henry Barker to the attention of Ted LeClair and the other detectives working on the killing of Barbara Agnew, however. After the body was discovered, several callers responded to the request for help by suggesting the detectives check up on Barker. There was a woman who said Barker had picked her up after her car broke down and then tried to force her to have sex with him. A detective phoned from New Hampshire to alert the investigators to several cases involving Henry Barker in attacks on women. And the detectives quickly learned that he had been seen drifting through the night of the big snowstorm, offering to help stranded drivers on the interstate highway.

As the detectives brought back each new fragment of information about Henry Barker, a quiet excitement built slowly in the investigation headquarters. Barker had been charged in several cases with picking up women on the road and attempting to have sex with them. The first time had been eight years before, when he was in his early twenties. He had been working in a filling station, pumping gas and assisting the mechanics, when a young woman accused him of trying to rape her. She had hitched a ride in southern Vermont with a man who dropped her off at the gas station. She had gone inside to get a Coke from the machine and afterward walked back out to the road to try for another ride northward. Henry Barker had apparently spotted her in the station; he left work, picked her up, and after driving aimlessly for a while, asked her to have sex with him. When she refused, he drove to a remote place and tried to take her clothes off. She had fought him and eventually he had pulled back. He drove her to a main road and threatened to come find her if she ever told anyone what had happened. She had ignored the threat and in the end he had pleaded no contest to a relatively minor charge.

That had been the first of several similar incidents over the next few years. Eventually he had been convicted of rape. The courts had twice referred him for psychological evaluation, most recently five years earlier, and twice he had been committed to the state mental hospital. The psychiatrists had concluded that Henry Barker was legally sane and capable of standing trial, but that he fit the standard definition of a psychopathic personality. Psychopaths like Henry Barker tend to appear presentable at first, even charming, but harbor a great emptiness underneath.

The psychopathic personality is vastly egocentric. Whatever exists outside him, other people's rules, thoughts, concerns, or pain, disappears in the face of his internal preoccupations. He is incapable of empathy, or of much feeling at all; he is a stranger to love or remorse, lies without hesitation or regret, and instinctively takes advantage of the need or weakness of others.

There was a fascinating consistency to the cases involving Henry Barker. Each time he was picked up for an offense involving a woman he denied responsibility. The pattern of his defense was similar in each case: the woman was eager to have sex, he would say, he never used force, she led him on. There was no sense that anything the woman said, her fear or pleading, had any impact on him.

And there were several factors in all this that fascinated LeClair and the others. In at least one of the cases, Barker had ostentatiously toed a knife out from under his seat and drawn his victim's attention to it, in an attempt to intimidate her. On another occasion he had told an investigating officer that he spent many hours "just cruising," driving without purpose up and down the Valley. And in the several incidents involving women, some resulting in charges, others set aside for one reason or another, Barker had been driving a car or truck. It appeared that Henry Barker saw the highway as a place to go hunting.

And there was more. He was apparently in the habit of stopping to help drivers stranded on the highway. He had picked up some knowledge of cars, enough at least to make himself plausible as a rescuer to someone in need. He carried mechanic's tools, jumper cables, spark plugs, a can of gas, and a few miscellaneous spare parts in his truck, and he had installed a citizens-band radio so he could listen for calls for assistance from police officers and truckers who had located a breakdown. Sometimes he succeeded in helping to restart the car; other times he called a towing service, or drove the motorist to town. It was a way to make a little money. Could he also be hunting for something more sinister?

There were two reports from the night of the snowstorm in January that seemed as if they might be related to Henry Barker. In both instances a man in a pickup truck had stopped to offer help to motorists, one on I-91, the other on a local road in Vermont. Both locations were within ten miles of the rest area where Barbara Agnew's car had been abandoned sometime around midnight.

And there were the stories, odd bits of informal observation about Henry Barker. Like a lot of men in the Valley who knew their way around the woods, Barker tried to make a little money from time to time by cutting and selling firewood. One of the investigators, Phil Arthur, had arranged to buy some wood from Barker. Several days later Arthur had been in his yard splitting wood, setting each length upright on a stump, lifting the splitting maul overhead with both hands, and swinging it down through the wood.

Suddenly, Barker appeared in the yard, his truck at the curb loaded with cordwood. The detective had put down the maul, a heavy tool that combines an ax head with a sledge hammer, and walked over to show Barker where he wanted the wood stacked.

Arthur had made the instructions quite explicit, warning Barker against damaging flower beds and a walkway. As he moved back toward his chopping block and stopped, he felt Barker moving closer to him, not speaking, and he turned to find the visitor staring at him with an intense, unblinking gaze. It occurred to him that Barker might have taken offense at his instructions about the delivery, resented his assumption of authority over the man delivering his wood. And Barker knew he was a cop. He was not the type of habitual offender who acknowledged that cops were just doing their job when they ran him in. Perhaps that added fuel to his resentment.

There was a fierce, hooded look to Barker's eyes as he moved closer, uncomfortably close, the cop thought. Suddenly Barker bent over and with one hand picked up the splitting maul from where it lay. He handled the heavy tool as if it were a willow stick. His fierce stare hardly wavered from the cop's eyes as he placed one booted foot on a thick, twenty-inch length of ash and swung the maul backhand, upward, away from his body. Arthur wondered if the other man could feel the uneasiness he was inspiring, and then he knew that that was the purpose, the only purpose, of this little demonstration.

The maul descended in a short ferocious arc and smashed into the end of the log, splitting it neatly in two. Barker looked over at the splitting stump and then back at Arthur. The detective was sure Barker was telling him that he knew, had observed before he was noticed in the yard, what a laborious process this could be for an ordinary man like Arthur. With his expression of disdain, Barker had reasserted the dominance he thought had been taken from him. This was clearly not a man to be taken lightly.

In all this mass of fact the detectives found several intriguing points of correspondence to John Philpin's profile. There were the external facts, the man's strength, his record, the sexual character of his crimes, the fact that he had been on the road the night of the storm, even the use of a knife in one incident to intimidate his victim.

Philpin had uncovered some of these facts, but that was not why LeClair had come to appreciate the psychologist's help so much. It was Philpin's ability to tie all the physical details together, and then to connect them to an intimate psychological portrait of the killer, that made his profile a valuable asset to the detectives.

Beyond the physical facts, there were the more subtle elements in the profile that made Henry Barker look like a plausible suspect, the apparent parallels in his psychological history, the hints of neglect by his parents, the possibility of abuse. In addition to the record of sex-related incidents and arrests, there was the association of cars with sex. He was a man at ease in the woods, familiar with the back roads, and he was given to cruising for long hours, searching for something elusive.

And Philpin had described the killer's probable state of mind, suggested ways to approach the type of person who would have killed Barbara Agnew. After the killing, he will ordinarily seem to be under control; only those fairly close to him on a regular basis will notice changes in his behavior, but beneath the surface he will be anxious about the possibility of being discovered. Most of the time he keeps this anxiety out of sight, and he will handle himself well in a routine interview with police. But he will be more vulnerable to a steady build-up of pressure in an investigation, with surveillance, interviews of his co-workers, questioning of his relatives. If such a process culminated with a longer interview by the police, particularly if it disrupts one of his regular routines, he would find the stress less tolerable.

The killer is following the progress of the investigation through the newspapers or television. If the police take a continuing positive approach in their public statements, making it seem as if they are moving inexorably closer to the killer, he will feel the pressure. It will become more difficult for him to distance himself from what he has done and to wall off his anxiety. The tension might stretch him thin, make him transparent, unable to conceal what he had done from himself, maybe from others.

LeClair laid out the task for the detectives: They would have to look into every report that might place Barker on the road the night of Barbara Agnew's disappearance, talk to every witness who would have seen him if he had been at the rest area anytime that night, check with all the towing services and patrol officers who might have come into contact with him. They needed to track his movements, whatever he was doing, right down to the minute, or as close as they could get. And LeClair was going straight to the source; he wanted to talk to Henry Barker himself.

Barker was standing in the yard of the old farmhouse when LeClair arrived with another detective. His truck, a big pickup, stood in the dirt-track driveway. Several other vehicles were scattered around, some so rusted that they almost seemed organic, like tree stumps ready to crumble back into the forest floor. The ground was littered with car parts, some in small heaps, others looking as if they had fallen from the sky.

There was nothing hospitable in Barker's greeting, but he agreed to talk. It quickly became clear that he was not going to invite his guests to go inside, or even to sit down in the yard. Even to the two detectives, whose work required strength and physical self-confidence, he projected an almost overwhelming presence. It was easy to see how Phil Arthur had found him intimidating. He seemed wider than any ordinary person should be, and muscular in a way that made you think of materials like steel or marble rather than flesh. As they talked, Barker would look away, then suddenly turn to the detectives and stare, as if he were trying to see through their heads.

He had been out in the truck the night of the storm, Barker conceded, looking for people who needed help. The detectives tried to get details, specific things they could check on. He had caught a few calls on the CB, Barker said, he'd come upon a few others along the road; he didn't write them down, couldn't remember the details. Helped a few people, he said. Didn't get any names.

It was like pulling old nails out of a fence post. Barker was giving the minimum amount of information, forcing the detectives to ask for every bit of detail. He had called for a tow truck several times, Barker said. He supplied the names of the wreckers; there weren't that many to choose from in the area, and the lack of cooperation would be too blatant if he refused to name them. The necessity of giving up the information seemed to sharpen his growing irritation.

"Why you bothering me?" Barker said. "Why don't you go bother somebody else?" His voice was a growl.

"We're talking to a lot of people," LeClair told him. "You're just one of them. You were out there that night."

That didn't seem to soften Barker's mood. They asked several more questions, trying to bring out more useable information, but Barker's answers seemed to get shorter and shorter, until he was down to a combination of yes, no, and a variety of guttural grunts. There was no point trying to go any further. They might as well try one more thing, LeClair thought.

"We'd like to take a look at your truck," the detective said.

Barker's suppressed anger boiled into fury.

"Get the hell out of here," he shouted. "Get off my property."

Bits of spittle flew from his lips. He bent and picked up a rusted wheel rim that lay on the ground near his feet. He handled it easily, like a large yo-yo. What does that thing weigh, LeClair wondered, fifteen, twenty pounds? Without hesitating Barker turned slightly and skimmed the wheel rim through the air, like a man throwing a Frisbee in the park. It sailed twenty feet across the yard and crashed through the front window of a dilapidated van.

"I ain't the one," Barker shouted. "Get the fuck out of here. Go piss all over somebody else. Go on, get out."

The detectives moved backward toward their car. Barker followed, shouting at them, making shooing motions with his hands, but keeping the distance constant between himself and the two detectives. They reached the car, trying not to appear to be hurrying.

"That's a wild man," LeClair said. The understatement relieved the tension. They both laughed.

You wouldn't call that the most successful interview of all time, LeClair thought, but they had learned a couple of things. For one, they had quickly observed that Barker's truck was big and heavy, and they had gotten close enough to see that it had four-wheel drive. With snow tires or chains, whatever preparation Barker had made for going out on the interstate and the main roads on the night of the winter's heaviest storm, he would have been able to move confidently over the dirt roads as well, even up a grade at a place like Advent Hill. That would be especially true if he were carrying something heavy in the back of the truck, like an engine block and a couple of salvaged truck axles, or a half cord of firewood.

The other thing they had seen was the capacity for fury that Barker hid just beneath the surface of his stolid demeanor. It was one thing to hear about it from cops trading street gossip; it took on a whole new level of seriousness when you saw the man scale a hunk of steel across his yard and you knew that if he had turned 180 degrees he could have taken your head off with it. And he had done it as if it were just part of the conversation, just another way of expressing himself. It had become much easier to imagine how a man like Barker could control and then destroy a tough, brave woman like Barbara Agnew.

February 1988

It had taken months to work out Henry Barker's movements on the night of Barbara Agnew's abduction. Several weeks into the investigation the number working on the case was doubled to a dozen and Ted LeClair announced to the press that the informal headquarters at the Hartford police station was now a "command post," with more space and an air of permanence. The politicians were taking the investigation seriously enough to put in more money, and there was a feeling of optimism in the air: with enough resources and hard work, this case could be broken. And with it, they would break several others.

When the results of the fingerprint analysis from the green BMW came back, there was one print that didn't match Barbara Agnew or any of her friends. The investigators announced the results to the newspapers; the print could be used to check out any new suspect, Ron DeVincenzi said. And if John Philpin was right, the news would keep the pressure on the killer.

Then finally, one day, LeClair realized there were enough fragments to mark out virtually every minute of Henry Barker's activities the night of January 10, 1987.

Some of the times were exact because police logs showed calls from police cars asking for wreckers or other assistance in cases where Barker had been involved; the calls from the tow-truck drivers and police officers announcing their locations at the end of a job were also recorded, and some of those could be matched to Barker's presence. He had actually been seen at the rest area earlier in the evening.

The detectives had tracked down other people who had encountered Barker on the road that night, and still others who could help pin down the times of those sightings. They had driven the routes from Barker's various locations to the rest area, from the rest area to Advent Hill, adding in estimated times for the various parts of Philpin's scenario for the abduction and killing. The result brought the detectives agonizingly close to the conclusion that they had found the killer; it brought them just as close to the conclusion that one more possible killer, the man most of the detectives considered the most likely of them all, had to be eliminated from the ring of suspicion.

There just didn't seem to be enough time for Henry Barker to have killed Barbara Agnew. Depending on how much time they allowed for various segments of Barker's activity that night, there were between three and seven minutes unaccounted for. Even with seven minutes, even if he could have killed Barbara Agnew in thirty seconds, there was just no way he could have travelled to the rest area from the place nearby where they had the last verified sighting, carried through what they knew was a precarious abduction of his victim, fitted in the round-trip to where he was sighted later, and still carried out the minimum activity indicated by the killer's movements on Advent Hill.

It was no exact science, and some of the times could be off, and some of their assumptions could turn out to be mistaken, but taken all together, the results of the months of investigation seemed to eliminate the possibility that Henry Barker had killed Barbara Agnew.

The other work had continued, other suspects had come and gone, until after eight months there were 170 files that had been compiled, each representing a suspect or a solid lead to the identity of the killer. Each had been examined from top to bottom, each had ultimately been set aside, eliminated from consideration.

The tips and suggestions had kept coming at a fairly high rate for a while, but inevitably the numbers dropped month by month. Summer came and went, the leaves fell and the cold deepened, and the investigation went on without any new, dramatic development to encourage the people of the Valley.

The investigation of the murder of Barbara Agnew was long past the time of peak excitement. The command post arrangement at the Hartford police station had been dissolved and the investigators had returned to their regular posts. But most of them were still keeping the Agnew case at the top of their priority lists, and most of them were still spending a majority of their time tracking down one piece of the case or another.

And then, in February, Ted LeClair got a phone call that pumped new life into the investigation. It was a break in the case, and though it wasn't the one the detectives had been searching for, it brought them another step closer to the man they had been hunting. And in one stroke it raised the stakes in the investigation of the Valley killings.

The caller reached LeClair at the state police office in Bethel. She had identified with Barbara Agnew, the woman said, because she was a nurse, too, and she had been following the investigation, reading the papers, hearing about it from someone she worked with whose husband was a cop. There was something that she thought LeClair ought to know about. It was an incident that happened at the hospital in New London, New Hampshire, when she was working there back in 1978. She had forgotten all about it, and then recently somebody said something and it all came back to her.

"This man came in," the woman said, "and he had cuts all over his hands and arms. He was very weird."

LeClair asked her what she meant be weird.

"He was behaving strangely," she said, "crying, talking about hurting somebody, saying, 'Help me, help me,' over and over again."

LeClair encouraged the woman to continue.

"Well," she said, "I thought it might have had something to do with the woman who was stabbed to death in New London that year."

LeClair was startled. He interrupted her.

"What woman?" he asked. It didn't sound like any case that he had ever heard of.

"I don't remember her name," the caller responded, "but she was bird-watching, out in the little park there, and she was stabbed."

LeClair asked if she remembered anything else about the

case. She thought for a moment.

"It was very vicious," the woman said. "She was stabbed a lot, stabbed in the throat."

Those were key words to someone working on the Agnew case. The detective admitted to the caller that he wasn't familiar with the case. He thanked her for the tip and assured her that he would definitely look into it.

It was kind of a shock, LeClair thought. The investigators had put a lot of effort into matching the Agnew killing to similar cases all over the United States. They had sent data in to the National Crime Information Center, and then they had checked out any bulletin from anywhere in the country that came back looking even slightly similar. They had tried matching the Agnew information to lists of unsolved cases in all the New England states. They had been in close contact with detectives on the New Hampshire side of the Valley, and they knew everything about the task force cases. And here was a case right under their noses, a few miles away, just across the Connecticut River, and they had never caught a whiff of it.

A few days later, LeClair and his brother Mike drove to New London with John Philpin. Clay Young, the New Hampshire State Police detective who had led the task force in Claremont looking into the New Hampshire killings, met them at the New London police station.

The victim was a twenty-six-year-old woman named Cathy Millican. The New London chief summarized the case for the four visitors. A thick stack of file folders rested on the table at his side.

Cathy Millican was an enthusiastic bird-watcher. Someone had told her that some rarely seen ducks had been sighted in the Chandler Brook Wetland Preserve off Route 11 in New London. On a Tuesday afternoon in October of 1978 she had left her car in the small parking area just off the road and walked into the preserve. The time was between 5:30 and 6:00 P.M. About a half hour later, a New London police officer on patrol made a routine check of the parking lot. He noted two cars, nothing amiss, and drove on.

When Cathy Millican was reported missing the following day, the officer remembered that one of the cars he had seen in the parking lot fit the description of her Volkswagen Rabbit. It didn't take long for the searchers to find the body of Cathy

Millican. She lay in the woods, between the highway and one loop of the path through the wetland. Her skirt had been pulled down and more of her clothing was bunched under her body. She had been partly covered with brush.

The victim's car keys, the binoculars she had used for spotting birds, and other possessions were found at various places along the park paths. Using the locations of these items, strands of hair, and marks on the paths and in the brush, the investigators had reconstructed the attack. The killer had trapped Cathy Millican, waited patiently, then attacked her. He had carried and dragged her along the paths, stabbed her to death, then moved her again and left her in the brush. The detectives had calculated that at the moment when the officer had driven by, the killer was standing a few feet away, screened from view by trees and bushes. He had been waiting just inside the entrance to the park, knowing that whatever path she took, his prey would have to pass this point to return to her car.

The chief handed around diagrams and other materials from the files to illustrate points he was making. An envelope of autopsy materials made its way to John Philpin's place. As he listened to the chief's account, Philpin idly opened the envelope and slipped out a batch of photographs. The top picture on the pile was a postmortem view of Cathy Millican. What Philpin saw jolted him to attention. He pushed the photograph in front of Ted LeClair and pointed to the wounds on the dead woman's neck.

"Look at that," he whispered, "just like Agnew. Just like Agnew."

If he hadn't known where the photo came from, Philpin thought, he would have believed it was right out of the command post files. The pattern of the neck wounds looked identical to the three deep wounds that had killed Barbara Agnew.

They passed the photographs around. The similarity didn't stop with the neck wounds. There was a cluster of wounds on the lower abdomen. The concentration and a distinctive pattern matched up neatly with the wounds that Barbara Agnew had suffered as she lay on the ground. And they matched the wounds on Lynda Moore's lower body, as well.

The analysis of the sequence of the wounds revealed additional similarities. It appeared that Cathy Millican's neck wounds had been administered from behind, and the abdominal wounds while she was lying on the ground. There was a lot here to think about.

In the following days Philpin and the LeClair brothers mulled over what they had learned, talking on the phone, trading insights and speculation. There were problems with adding the case to the list of Valley murders. For one, the most obvious, New London wasn't in the Connecticut Valley. All the other killings had taken place in a corridor covering both sides of the river that was no more than ten miles wide. The Chandler Brook Wetland was almost due east of Claremont, but it was a drive of about twenty-two miles. It was certainly not out of the question that a cruising killer could venture that far from his habitual routes; here again, Gary Schaefer provided a grim example. But more than a dozen sites, the places where victims had last been seen and where bodies had been found, had conditioned the investigators to thinking in terms of a narrow north-south strip no more than thirty-five miles long. The Millican case pushed beyond the edges of their expectation.

The other problem was the time. Cathy Millican had been killed ten years after Jo Anne Dunham, the North Charlestown schoolgirl with the slenderest grounds for inclusion. There followed a gap of two years and ten months until the killing of Betsy Critchley. Almost exactly the same amount of time— four days less—elapsed until the killing of Bernice Courtemanche in 1984. The rest of the deaths—of Ellen Fried, Eva Morse, Lynda Moore, and Barbara Agnew—had come in the following two years and eight months. Setting aside the case of Jo Anne Dunham, there were still two gaps of almost three years each to account for.

Philpin brooded on the Millican case, the killer spotting his victim's car, perhaps seeing the victim herself, knowing she had to come back the same way, straight into his grasp, and then settling himself to wait. The crime had a particularly sadistic quality to it, the way the killer had toyed with his victim. Cathy Millican probably had not known what he was doing as she wandered through the park, watching the waterfowl over the marsh, but the killer must have been taking pleasure from his anticipation of what he was going to do, the knowledge that he had trapped his victim. She was at his mercy, his to possess as he wished. Philpin felt some of the same colors in the killer's cast of mind that he had reconstructed in the other Valley killings.

But there was one significant difference, too, Philpin thought. This was the most sexual of the killings he had seen. There was no evidence of rape, but it was there in the positioning of the body on the ground, the skirt pulled down, the underwear in disarray. Some of the clothing had been ripped from the body and flung aside. Philpin groped for some sense of what had happened: it was as if a sexual attack had been interrupted. But there was no evidence of anything external breaking in upon the attack. It was more as if the killer himself had cut short the sexual aspect of the attack. Could he have started out intending to rape his victim, then changed his mind?

Philpin went over the file, rebuilding the sequence from the point of view of a man who has committed predatory sex crimes. Perhaps he has killed before, but he is relatively new to this kind of hunting, and he sets out thinking that the climax of his search will come in the sexual element of his domination. He captures his victim, tears at her clothing, propels himself onward toward the sexual assault he has imagined, then finds that his murderous rage drains into the physical dominance, into the stabbing, into the fusion of complete physical mastery with the explosive discharge of tension in the killing. The sexual element of the assault has slipped away, and he does not miss it. His satisfaction has come in terrorizing, dominating, destroying.

And he has learned something else. There are cars here, people passing nearby, the threat of interruption. It is too dangerous. He needs time, time to live out his fantasy of control, to live his dream with real flesh and blood, with his woman. He must extend this time outside the limits of ordinary life, stretch it out, control it, fill it with his own version of life as it should be.

The persona of a killer has hardened in its final, purest form.

Later he will accumulate experience, work out a routine, choose places to find his victims and to leave them when he has finished with them. This is an experience that has given shape to his future.

This man in his imagination was close kin to the man who

had killed again and again in the Valley, Philpin thought. He was just emerging from the earliest stage of his murderous career, discovering the destiny that he would pursue over the next few years. It was like plotting points on a graph; the killing of Cathy Millican fit neatly onto the curve that rose later to the New Hampshire killings and culminated in the death of Barbara Agnew.

But why does it take him three years to move on to the next step, the killing of Betsy Critchley? Does it take him that long to sort through what has happened, discover a killer's vocation? Does he resist accepting what he must do? Is he diverted by a daily, continuing relationship with a woman, overloaded by the attempt to constrain his worst impulses? All of these theories seemed plausible, Philpin thought, none of them really satisfying.

Still, on balance, Philpin came to believe that they had discovered another terrible chapter in the brutal record of the Valley killer.

Ted LeClair had reached the same conclusion. Ted and his brother Mike, talking about the Valley cases, had developed what they called "the apple-tree scenario." A hunter who was familiar with a certain patch of woods learned to identify locations within it where deer were likely to congregate, a watering place, or a particularly good source of food. Whenever he returned to that area, the hunter made sure to check these places, approaching them stealthily, watching for prey; sometimes he would hide himself there and wait.

The Valley cases displayed this kind of pattern; almost every victim had been taken in a place where a killer might expect to find prey, near a telephone, at an interchange on the highway, in a rest area. The brothers imagined the killer checking these places, like a deer hunter watching near a familiar cluster of apple trees, waiting for his quarry. Like the man standing near the exit of the Chandler Brook Wetland Preserve, waiting for Cathy Millican to come back to her car.

It all looked very familiar. And LeClair and Philpin, along with all the other detectives who had come in contact with the unsolved murders in the Valley, were forced to the frustrating admission that there wasn't a single useful thing they could do about it.

BOOK VII

Survivors

thirty-two

August 1988

Still upset from her fight with Dennis in the morning, Jane Boroski headed south out of Keene toward home.

It seemed like they had been arguing ever since she gave him the news in March. He had been working part-time days down at the hydro dam on Main Street in the center of Hinsdale. She had driven straight there from Planned Parenthood after they told her the results of the test. Dennis had known where she was going when she left that morning and he was watching for her. When she pulled into the lot by the dam he came out and stood by the car window.

"They say it's positive," she told him. "I'm pregnant." They talked half-heartedly, filling in the details. There was no joy in it.

"Do you want to get an abortion?" he asked her. It was obvious that he wanted her to. They were both twenty-two, too young for a baby, really. She felt the same way. She didn't want to be pregnant. Afterward she cried and cried about it. But she didn't want an abortion, either, didn't believe in it.

Dennis had a good job driving a forklift at Cersosimo Lumber. He was a hard worker, but he wanted his freedom, and he liked to party. That was how they'd met. Jane had been nineteen then, living alone down in Massachusetts after her mother moved to Texas for a better job, and one weekend she came up to a party in New Hampshire and stayed with a girl-friend.

There was a hard-partying group from around Hinsdale that got together every weekend. She met Dennis at the party and she didn't like him at first because he was drunk and obnox-ious. She didn't drink or use drugs herself. But the next day he came by the girlfriend's house in Hinsdale and he was a lot different, quiet and pleasant. The next weekend she came back and stayed over with Dennis at his parents' house, where he was living. A few months later they moved in together.

Things were fine after that, for close to two years. Until she got pregnant. It had been three months they'd been apart now but they still stayed in touch. Dennis's parents always bought tickets early for the Cheshire County Fair in Keene, and the last two years they had gotten two extra for Dennis and Jane. Jane went over to see Dennis in the morning at his parents' house, where he was still living, hoping he'd ask her to go to the fair with him. He did ask, and she said yes, but then they got into a huge shouting match. Afterward she had no idea what it was about. It wasn't about anything, really, and it was about everything. She left in tears.

She went back to the trailer park, where she was living with Cathy and Chris. They were old friends of Dennis's who had become Jane's friends, too. They accepted Jane's decision about having the baby and they were willing to help out. After she got over the worst of the crying, Jane still wanted to go to the fair, but Cathy and Chris had already left; the man Chris worked for had entered a team in the horse-pulling contest and Chris had to be there early.

After a while, though, she saw Dennis's GMC truck parked out by the first trailer. He must be visiting there, maybe even looking for a way to bump into her, making it look like an accident, and fix the damage from their argument. Weather-bee's was a small place, only five trailers, and nothing much happened without everybody knowing about it. Jane just waited, figuring he'd come by eventually and ask her to go to the fair. She even toyed with the idea of turning him down, just for revenge, but she knew she wouldn't do it.

The next thing she knew, he was gone. She was mad at first, but then she was just hurt and sad. A little later Dennis's par-

ents came by. They weren't taking sides in the fighting between Dennis and Jane, and they were feeling sorry for Jane
after the morning's argument. They asked if she wanted to go
to the fair with them.

"No, I'm just going to stay here," she told them. She was
too upset to go.

She spent most of the afternoon crying and thinking about
the past years, going to the fair with Dennis. They would walk
up and down the grounds, stopping to chat with people they
knew, eating fried dough and Jane's favorite, the sausage, pep-
per, and onion grinders. They would throw darts to win pictures of animals and rock groups, and then go watch the
pulling contest between the huge, souped-up tractors.

By seven o'clock she had recovered enough to start feeling
lonely. She wished she had gone with Dennis's parents. Saturday evening was the biggest time at the fair and the trailer
park was empty, so she decided to head over on her own. She
put on jeans and a pair of leather tennis shoes. She had just
bought them a few days before and they still looked new. That
gave her a little lift. Printed across the front of her blouse was
the word baby in big letters and an arrow pointing to her belly.
As if anybody needed to be told, almost seven months gone.

She went out and got into the Firebird, which made her
think of Dennis again. Last year they had only had one car
between them, Dennis's truck, and usually Jane took it to work
at the plastics factory. She was on her way home from the
early shift one day in December when she saw Dennis hitchhiking to the late shift on his job. She picked him up, figuring
to drive him to work.

"Let's go get your Christmas present," he said.

"What do you mean?" she answered, thinking it was just
some game.

He made her drive across the river to Vermont, and all
through the fifteen-minute drive he refused to tell her where
they were going. In Brattleboro he directed her to the Auto
Mall, snaking in among the rows of used cars, until they pulled
up in front of a beautiful two-year-old white Pontiac Firebird.

"That's your Christmas present," he said, gesturing at the
car.

"Don't joke with me like that," she replied. "That's not a
very nice joke."

But it wasn't a joke. He had already bought the car for her. And she had been driving it ever since. And now she was going to the fair in it, without him.

At the fair it was mud-bog night, when local guys could take their cars in and slosh around and crash into each other in a big sloppy mess. She recognized some of the guys from Winchester who were driving. After a while she ran into Chris and Cathy, and then Dennis's folks turned up. Dennis's mother, Ginny, looking to cheer Jane up, strolled with her along the midway. Eventually, she and Ginny settled down in front of a twenty-five-cent game machine.

There was no skill to the game, but they started to win tokens and they got caught up in it. There were rows of prizes the tokens could be exchanged for, including a large selection of stuffed animals. They decided to get as many of the colorful animals as possible, to put aside for the baby. When they finally quit it was past eleven o'clock and they had seven stuffed animals. Jane had won four of them, all in bright colors, including a white teddy bear and a green rabbit and her favorite, a foot-tall elephant wearing a green hat.

As she got her car out of the big parking lot, Jane was still upset by the day's events, but she was comforted by the thought of the cheerful animals on the seat behind her.

A little south of Keene on Route 10 she suddenly felt thirsty. "It's always something when you're pregnant," she thought, "having to drink or eat or pee."

She could get a Pepsi at Gomarlo's, a country store that sold groceries, just ahead on Route 10. The dark of the two-lane country highway was deepened by the overhanging trees, only occasionally broken by the lights of a passing car.

In a few minutes more she saw the orange glow from the tower lighting the gas station next to the store. She turned right into the parking lot, passed between the light stanchion and the store, and glided across sixty feet of concrete, past the darkened front door of Gomarlo's, before swinging the Firebird sharply left into a parking place perpendicular to the building. There was a pay phone on the wall directly in front of the car and a soft-drink machine a few feet to the right.

She had set the handbrake before she realized that the bulky shape backed up against the wall beneath the overhang of the roof, casting its bright red glow into the night, was a Coke machine. She would have to walk down to the left and around the corner, past the front door of Gomarlo's, to get her Pepsi.

She shut off the engine and left the keys hanging in the ignition. Reaching down into her pocketbook next to the seat, she fumbled for her wallet and picked out sixty cents in change from the coin pocket. It was only a few steps forward into the darkness beneath the overhang, several more to the left toward the corner door of the store. Around the corner the bright colors of the Pepsi machine's lighted panel seemed subdued by the shadow of the roof.

She inserted the three coins one after the other and pressed the panel with the Pepsi sign. Nothing happened. She pressed a bit harder. Still no response. She punched the panel more roughly, several times, starting to feel annoyed. This machine wasn't going to deliver a Pepsi. She pulled down on the coin-return lever, expecting to hear the clinking sound of her money falling into the slot. That didn't happen, either. She tried again, then again and again. Nothing.

Irritated now by her thirst and the machine's dumb stubbornness, she walked back to the car for more change. Her wallet produced only a quarter and a few nickels. She reached into the console between the seats and fumbled among the bits of paper and odd junk. Finally she came up with a couple of dimes and walked around the front of the car to the Coke machine. This time she was successful.

As she strolled back to the car, the cold can of Classic Coke soothing against the sweaty heat of her hand, a pair of headlights swept into the parking lot and then narrowed as they slowly approached her car. It was a tall, boxy vehicle, a wagon of some kind, like a Jeep Wagoneer. She saw the driver briefly from the side. It was a man. As she laboriously maneuvered her bulk in behind the steering wheel, he pulled into the parking place on the passenger side of her car. He turned off the engine, then the headlights.

Jane relaxed behind the wheel, opening the can of Coke, savoring its cool sweetness, then resting it on the console. As she prepared to start the car, she became conscious of the man getting down from behind the wheel and walking back between the two cars. The thought made no impression on her, but in another moment he appeared at the window of her car.

"Is the phone working tonight?" he asked in a soft voice,

gesturing toward the wall booth in front of her car. He was a neat, slim man, smallish, dressed in a short-sleeved cotton shirt and pleated slacks. He glanced quickly to both sides as she looked up.

"I don't know," she started to reply. Her mouth was still open when the car door suddenly disappeared from her side. Before she could register the idea of space where there had been solidity, his right hand shot out, closing like an iron vise around her left wrist.

"Come with me," he said. His voice was flat, expressionless; he could have been asking directions to Keene. Dread, a pure, crystalline terror, suffused her body from head to toe, coming on like a sudden flush over the skin.

"What do you want?" she shouted. "Who are you?" Her body responded before her mind could frame an understanding of what was happening. She jerked backward, straining toward the passenger side of the front seat, her hands on the steering wheel, arms pushing for leverage. His grip remained irresistibly tight, implacable.

In a rush of thought she became aware that she was protecting first of all not her self but the life within her. Surely he would respect that feeling.

"Please don't hurt me," she cried out. "I'm pregnant."

There was no response at all. His hand was like some nightmare monster with its teeth clamped to her wrist.

He didn't care, it meant nothing at all to him.

And, as she realized this, her words, her desperate attempt to make sense of the mind-blasting terror that had leapt out of the soft night, dissolved now in a shrieking scream.

She jackknifed her legs up between them and kicked out frantically. Leaning into the car, his knee on the seat, he tried to pull her toward him. Her right foot struck near the steering column and the left drove between his arms. It seemed to slow him for an instant. A moment later she heard the crashing sound of something shattering. Her right foot had punched through the windshield, spraying a shower of glass fragments over the dashboard and out onto the hood.

Suddenly there was a stillness, as if they were squabbling children commanded to silence by a teacher. The man seemed stunned by the crash and the spray of glass. He held his grip on her wrist but he seemed to pull back. The hope leapt within her: was he going to release her?

"All right, if you're going to be like that . . ." he said. There was a threat in the unfinished sentence, and something about the calmness in his voice made it more frightening than if he had been shouting. His left hand reached around behind his back, and when it reappeared she knew he was not finished with her. He was holding a knife.

The gleaming blade moved slightly from side to side. It seemed to beckon gently, but there was nothing soft in his tone.

"Get out of the car, or I'll cut you," he said. She felt suddenly deflated, as if the blade had already punctured her and the strength had leaked from her body.

Hand still clamped to her wrist, he backed out of the car. She emerged and felt the door close behind her as he pressed her backward. His free hand waved angrily in the air. The knife! He wasn't holding the knife. Had she imagined it?

Run! The thought was like a bright light. She could run. She edged along the side of the car toward the front fender. But before the thought turned to action he was on her. She was aware of the front tire filling her field of vision and realized he had somehow knocked her to the ground. His hands, both hands, were locked on her throat, choking her, cutting off the air.

Now there was room for only one thought, a horror flooding her mind, washing out all else: I'm dying. I'm going to die.

She struck out wildly with her knee, feeling it strike home on his body, flailing with arms and hands. And then, as suddenly as they had clamped onto her throat, the hands were gone. She was free.

The man's slight form was rising slowly above her. He looked down and spoke as if chastising a child.

"Wait till I get that knife," he said.

He turned, took a step, and bent over near the car door. When he turned back, the knife was in his right hand. He had dropped it as they left the car.

Jane was on her feet again, struggling to catch her breath, but before she could move, he had closed the small distance between them and reached out with his free hand to grip her right wrist. He pulled her toward him, sliding her along the side of the car, past the door. Now she was pinned against the car and the knife was at her throat.

It was like a dream, where the dreamer sees that nothing quite makes sense but still feels trapped in the magical flow of events. She had to know what was happening.

"What do you want from me?" she asked, with little hope of ever understanding what these events might mean.

"You beat up my girlfriend," he said, his voice still calm, as if they were discussing some minor business transaction.

The change in mood, the shift from unrelenting violence to this conversational tone, was so sudden that at first she didn't understand what he was saying, as if he were speaking some foreign language. He repeated himself.

"You beat up my girlfriend."

"No," she mumbled. "No. I didn't."

He seemed puzzled. "Isn't this a Massachusetts car?"

"Massachusetts?" she said, trying desperately to find some logic in what was happening. He was still pressing her tightly against the car.

"This is a New Hampshire car," she said. And what could that have to do with anything? she wondered.

The knife fell away from her neck. Jane had never been able to look a person in the face when she was angry. It was a bad habit, this shying away from direct confrontation. She had tried to break it, but with no success. She found now that all this time she had been looking away from her attacker. She forced herself to turn, stealing a brief look at his face. He seemed confused.

Once again he moved away from her. It was puzzling, she thought. She felt her fear beginning to subside. He must have the wrong person. I know I haven't hurt anybody, certainly not enough to make someone this mad.

He walked the few steps to the rear of the car. He was going to look at the license plate, checking whether she was telling the truth.

This is all a mistake, she thought. She experienced a sudden surge of relief. He would see that she was telling the truth. It was a matter of mistaken identity. He was leaving.

Now, seeing the situation nearing a resolution, she felt her relief quickly giving way to a wave of resentment. He had put her through all this for nothing, no reason. And suddenly her mind leapt back from this incredible situation, back across the chasm to her ordinary life, ordinary concerns: what would Dennis think when he saw the car, her Christmas present?

"Hey," she cried out at the man, "what about my windshield?" All her anger and indignation at what he had done flowed through her voice.

He stopped and turned. She was not aware of him covering the ground between them but in an instant he was upon her again, pressing the knife against her throat.

"Come on," he said, "you're going with me." He began to pull on her arm.

Furious again, she avoided his eye, looking straight ahead, across the parking lot to Route 10. Headlights approached from the direction of Keene and passed out of view to the right. People! There were people out there who could help her. Another car threw its shaft of light across her field of vision, then another.

She bolted, feeling the side of the car briefly against her, pushing off, then running, two, five, ten steps, fear gathering in the small of her back, as if the knife was stabbing at her from behind, timed to each pace, each running step a leap away from its lethal arc.

And behind her, almost instantly, the brutal, angry steps, his harsh breathing. Ahead she saw cars again, a small cluster of traffic going both ways, three or four cars now. A scream formed in her mind but no sound emerged. She waved her arms wildly above her head as she ran. The odd thought struck her: these motions were like the jumping jacks she used to do in gym class. But it was like being trapped inside an invisible bubble; nothing seemed to be getting out. The cars were close enough for their drivers to see her, but they kept moving, passing on. Nobody was stopping, there was no sign that anybody had even noticed her.

In a few more steps he was on her. The hands came down hard on her shoulders and she toppled backward to the ground. Now he was kneeling at her side, far above her it seemed, and he straightened fully and his arm rose in a wide arc. She was conscious of a sudden whirling flash as his arm fell upon her body. The knife! The knife was in his hand, he was stabbing her.

And in that instant the thought followed: the baby, he's stabbing my baby, protect the baby. Her eyes went to the rounded front of her body. She thrust her hands upward to ward off the blows. She pulled a knee up as a shield. It made no difference. Again and again the arm swung high above her and drove downward, countless hammering blows blasting past her raised hands.

Suddenly she felt strangely serene, as if she were surrounded by the unnatural stillness that follows a sudden summer thunderstorm. He was gone.

Her hands moved as if by themselves to the front of her blouse. It felt wet. She pulled a hand away to look. Blood! She was bleeding.

She rolled over and laboriously forced herself up to hands and knees. She was having trouble breathing. She would have to gather herself before she could do anything.

A sound, the hiss of wheels on a sandy surface, moved through her consciousness. As she struggled to raise her head, a car—*his* car—moved across her line of sight.

She looked up and now she saw his features, clearly, for the first time. The eyes looked unnaturally close together in his thin face, almost blending into one as he gazed down at her, and above them the high, pale forehead seemed stretched to meet his hairline. The dark blond hair was combed straight back. His lips, pressed tightly together, formed a straight, harsh line. He had the neutral expression of a man looking down at an insect squashed on the sidewalk.

They stared at each other for only a moment before he turned away and his car pulled off, moving parallel to the road and heading for the far exit from the parking lot. He seemed in no particular hurry.

Get up, she thought, have to get up, get help. Surprising how easy it was to get to her feet and move toward the car. She was conscious of a slight chill across the front of her body. Glancing down she saw her blouse clinging to her breasts, a dark wetness of blood seeping downward over her stretched belly. The baby. The thought moved dully in her mind. She pushed the idea aside and shuffled toward her car.

She got the door open and flopped into the seat. The Coke can was on the floor, its contents wetting the mat. The key still hung in the ignition where she had left it. As she reached to turn on the engine she couldn't feel the key. Her hand wouldn't do what she wanted it to do. The thumb didn't seem to be working right. She examined her hand with curiosity, as if it belonged to someone else. There was a deep open cut in the joint of the thumb. She had the feeling that it might fall off if she put too much pressure on it. But she didn't have any choice.

Somehow she gripped the key and turned it. The engine caught and she shifted the manual transmission into reverse, backing up enough to get clear of the building, then pushed the lever forward into first gear. She turned for the same exit he had used, heading south. She had to find someone, somewhere, who could help her.

She made the shallow turn onto the road and laboriously shifted through the gears into high. There was nothing on either side of the road except a broken wall of pine and hemlock trees looming in their dark indifference on the left.

"I'm dying," she whimpered. Each time she moved, she felt the blood oozing from her wounds.

"I'm going to die," she said aloud, repeating the words over and over like a prayer. There was blood everywhere. She had never seen so much blood. "I'm going to die."

It was a sensation of drifting, drifting in her car past a low building set back on the right, a place that housed a cluster of antique shops, dark and empty. On the other side a few modest houses squatted snug and secure for the night behind their small lawns. Gotta find a light on, she thought, someone awake, someone to help.

Into the haze of her thoughts there swam a light, dimly at first, then brighter. It was several lights, she could see now, growing in the darkness ahead. On the road. They were taillights. It was a car and she was closing on it.

Catching up steadily, now just a couple of car-lengths behind, and she was seized with a chilling certainty: It was him! It was the man who attacked her! She could see the distinctive, boxy shape of the wagon, the yellowish paint color, the silhouette of the driver. She noticed that there was a thick coating of dust on the rear.

Before she could decide what to do the sound of the wagon's engine grew louder and it started to pull away, widening the distance between them. He had seen her, he knew she was the one behind him. She couldn't see his face, but she was sure. He knew!

The gap between them grew for a moment, then narrowed again and steadied with the wagon still well in view, close enough to chill her with his presence. Would he stop, try to run her off the road, come to finish the job? But her fear of him remained at a distance, as if she were viewing it through a haze. It was the apparition of death, a mist of her own blood and her failing strength, that dimmed the fear of this man who wanted to kill her. It was death, the visible draining of life from her body, that she feared most, even more than this man who had attacked her for no reason. She drove on.

His taillights were the only illumination in view. More dark, slumbering building shapes flowed into view on both sides, but no sign of life. The road passed through a tunnel of trees and she remembered that the pizza place and the miniature golf course would be down there. And then it came to her. Up ahead, just ahead, she knew someone, the house was just up the hill on the right. Robert Grover lived there.

Grover was a friend of Chris and Cathy's, the people she lived with. It was late, too late to bother someone, wake them up. But she needed help, and Robert Grover was a close friend of Chris's. He had been Chris's best man at their wedding, surely it would be all right for her to stop there and ask him for help, ask him to save her, save her life.

Passing Route 10 Pizza and moving slowly up the hill. The Wagoneer was still just ahead, and then she was slowing down, searching for the driveway on the right, passing alongside a neat low fence, looking for the end of the fence, then turning in to the right and pulling hard on the wheel to bring the car back around into the sharply angled driveway.

She turned off the ignition and pulled up on the brake lever, then pressed hard on the horn. Her headlights were shining on one end of the small prefabricated one-story house. There was no response. She honked again, holding the horn down until she started to feel uncomfortable. The sound seemed very loud, almost shocking in the quiet darkness. Still there was no sign of life in the house.

She was going to have to get out of the car. With great effort she swung her legs out and then she was walking, moving across the short distance to the concrete stoop. As she reached the step the door opened and Robert Grover, tall and dark, appeared behind the screen. He looked puzzled.

"Robert," she said, "call the ambulance, some guy just stabbed the shit out of me."

As he opened the door she sat down on the stoop. It took Grover a moment to recognize the woman who had staggered out of the midnight darkness to beg for his help. As he stood above her trying to make sense of the situation, they heard a car braking near the end of the driveway. It was coming from the south, opposite the direction Jane had been travelling. It looked like a Jeep Wagoneer, Grover told her.

He's coming back to finish me off, she thought. But the car soon moved away and she slowly let herself down onto her back on the stoop. The Grovers didn't have a phone, but Robert's sister and her husband lived next door and they did. After offering Jane a few words of comfort Grover ran the twenty-five yards across the lawn to the identical prefab house next door and phoned the Winchester Police Department.

He was back in a few minutes. "They're on their way," he told her.

"I'm bleeding," she said. "I'm going to die. I'm going to die." She couldn't stop thinking it, couldn't stop saying it.

"No you're not," Grover reassured her. "You're going to be all right."

thirty-three

People were bustling around the emergency room, nurses and doctors and others she couldn't identify, getting her ready to go up for the operation, and there was only one thing on her mind.

"I want to see Dennis," Jane Boroski said. "Where is Dennis? I want to see him."

She had lain there on Robert Grover's front stoop for what seemed like a long time, Grover and his brother trying to comfort her and slow the bleeding, until at last she heard the car pull into the driveway. It's the Winchester police cruiser, somebody said, and then suddenly there was a face looking down at her. It was a familiar face.

"Who did this to you?" he asked.

"I don't know," she answered.

"You're Dennis Parker's girlfriend, aren't you?" he asked her.

It took her a minute to place him. It was Petey Farnham; he had worked with Dennis at the lumber company in Winchester. Petey also worked part-time for the Winchester Police Department. He examined her wounds; Jane thought he looked nervous and upset. He ran back to the cruiser to put in a call for the ambulance. Obviously he had decided that she was too badly injured for him to move her in the cruiser. Soon he was back.

"They're on the way," he said. Jane felt a little easier in her mind.

Farnham told Grover to get a pillow for her head, and they applied more first-aid measures. What seemed like another long period passed and Jane felt herself getting anxious again. They had to come, had to save her, save the baby.

"When are they gonna be here?" she asked. The men reassured her, but nothing happened. After a while, she asked again. It seemed like she had been lying there forever.

At last the ambulance had arrived, and in a few minutes they had covered the four miles back north to Keene. Now, as she lay on the gurney in the emergency room, her fear of dying had been pushed aside, and only one thing in the world seemed important. Petey Farnham had agreed to call Dennis, tell him what had happened. He had come back to say Dennis was on his way to the hospital. The fight with Dennis was forgotten, and the time they had been apart, and everything that had come between them.

"I want to see Dennis," she cried out. They had found another wound hidden by her clothes and somebody was putting a temporary bandage or something on it, and there were tubes and bottles of liquid hanging all over the place. Then they were ready to move her up to the operating room and suddenly she heard somebody at the door.

"Dennis Parker is here and he wants to see her," the voice said.

"No," someone in the room answered. "There isn't time. She's going to surgery."

Ignoring the apparatus and all the people around her, Jane raised her head and tried to sit up. Someone at her side reached out to restrain her.

"I want to see him," she shouted, "let me see him," and in a moment Dennis was at the door and then he was bending over her. Petey Farnham was standing at his side, holding him. Dennis looked hysterical, his face bright red, tears running down his cheeks. She had never seen him like this before.

"I love you, Dennis," she said.

"I love you, too," he said.

And as they were wheeling her away, Jane Boroski just had time to say one more thing to Dennis: "Dennis, find the bastard that did this to me," she cried.

• • •

The only sound was the gentle sighing whisper of the respirator. It was hard to imagine that there could be any threat in an intensive-care unit besides the one that came quietly in the night to end a life from within, but nobody was going to take any chances with the man who had attacked Jane Boroski.

Mike Leclaire, a New Hampshire state trooper (and no relation to the Vermont LeClairs), had been on call at home when the first word of the attack on Jane Boroski came in the early hours of Sunday morning. He had dispatched troopers to the scene and Monday morning he had taken charge of the case. It had been practically nonstop for forty-eight hours since. They had posted a guard at the door of Boroski's room as soon as she came out of surgery on Sunday morning, keeping a log of every person who came and went. During the day the guards took standard eight-hour shifts, but during the night they sat half-shifts. Leclaire had drawn the duty starting at 4:00 A.M. Wednesday. The state troopers were sharing the work with the police in Swanzey, where the attack had taken place.

When they had interviewed her the day before, she was barely able to whisper, but she was a tough young woman and she wanted to do everything she could to see the attacker caught. She had been worried at first, but the doctors had been optimistic and Leclaire had tried to add his reassurance. It looked like she was going to be all right, and the baby seemed to be in good shape, too. It was incredible after the way the guy had stabbed her. The operation had taken something like three or four hours, sewing up wounds to her neck where he had cut her jugular vein, and her abdomen, where they had removed a piece of her liver. Both her lungs had been collapsed and she was still on a respirator to help with the breathing. They had operated on her kneecap, and on the wounds she caught on her hands from trying to protect herself, including the severed tendon that worked her right thumb. It was amazing that she had even gotten the car started with that hand, much less driven it almost two miles to get help. She had been stabbed nineteen times in all.

She had come out of the anesthetic on Sunday afternoon and her boyfriend, Dennis, was there. They had moved a reclining chair in and turned on the television set and he had been sitting with her most of the time since then. It was still hard for her to talk, with the wounds to her throat and the breathing apparatus obstructing her mouth, so they had put a pad of paper and a pencil on the bedside table. One of the first things she wrote was a question:

Where are my stuffed animals?

Dennis had no idea what she was talking about, but eventually she made them understand that she had won the animals as prizes at the Cheshire County Fair. The police had found them in the car, still propped up in a row on the back seat where she had put them. She seemed greatly reassured by that.

On Tuesday she had recovered enough for Leclaire and Kim Bossey, a woman trooper, to interview her. All the cops were holding their breath. Everybody was rooting for her to survive, and as the word spread about what had happened, there was also the growing hope that the case might give them a lead to the whole series of unsolved murders in the Valley. Gomarlo's, the country grocery store where Jane Boroski had been attacked, was in Swanzey, a little town four miles south of Keene. That was just a little more than ten miles east of the Connecticut River and thirty-five miles south of Claremont, the center of activity in the three best-known New Hampshire cases, the murders of Bernice Courtemanche, Ellen Fried, and Eva Morse. The rest area on I-91 in Vermont where Barbara Agnew had been attacked was just a little farther north. Swanzey was even closer to Saxtons River, just across the river in Vermont, where Lynda Moore had been killed in her home. Moreover, Gomarlo's was on Route 10, a two-lane north-south road running parallel to the river that would fit neatly into the cruising pattern of a predatory killer.

And this time, lying in the hospital here in Keene, encased in a healing cocoon of doctors and nurses and equipment and medical routine, guarded twenty-four hours a day by police officers, at long last they had a witness, the victim herself.

When the two troopers sat down to interview Jane Boroski and make a composite picture of her attacker, it had been only forty-eight hours since she awoke from the operation. Leclaire had apologized for bothering her so soon and explained the importance of getting the information quickly so they could go after the attacker. She was pale from the loss of blood, and she appeared exhausted, but she dismissed Leclaire's hesitation; she was just as eager to get the search going as they were. She was only able to speak a few words at a time; she filled in the rest by responding to questions from Bossey and Leclaire with a nod or a shake of her head. Her voice was scratchy and it was obvious that she was in pain, but she insisted on completing her account of what had happened.

Leclaire stopped the questioning several times to let her clear her throat or gather her strength. Beyond the pain and fatigue, it was obviously nerve-wracking for Jane, reliving the terror. She stopped at one point to ask a question: "What if he knows I'm still alive?" she rasped out.

The fear behind the question was unspoken but obvious; he knows that I can identify him and he might come back and finish me off. Leclaire reassured her. The guard would be maintained as long as she was in the hospital. After that they would do whatever was necessary to make sure she was safe.

When Jane had finished describing the attack, they took a break to let her rest. When she was ready to go on, Leclaire got out the Identi-kit and explained how it was used to make a composite portrait. The kit provided several different versions of each facial feature on clear plastic overlays. Leclaire held up the choices, starting with the jawline, which gives definition to the face, and one by one, Jane picked out the cheekbones, eyes, hairline, and other features of the man who had attacked her.

Leclaire placed the overlays she selected onto a matrix one at a time, until, step by step, through trial and error, the image emerged. There was the narrow face and the pinched lips, the thinning hair combed straight back, the cold eyes and penetrating stare.

And the car, that was crucial, the troopers told her. Could she remember anything about the car? It looked like a Jeep wagon, Jane told them, like a Wagoneer, and the color was somewhere in the range between brown and gold. It was dirty, she recalled; when she had driven up behind him the car had looked dusty. And how about the license plate? The troopers held their collective breath. She had a general idea that the background was white, but that was all. Could she remember any numbers? No numbers.

Leclaire and Bossey took down the details. The registration

number, or even a few digits, would have been a big help, but even without it Jane had given them plenty to get started with. The two troopers had thanked her and left, with a promise to go right to work on the search.

Leclaire had already held preliminary talks with two Vermont State Police detectives who were working on unsolved homicides in the Valley that looked similar to the attack on Jane Boroski. One was Mike LeClair, who had the Lynda Moore case. The coincidence of the two Mikes' names had brought them into contact in the past—they would get each other's mail or phone calls once in a while—and each was forced occasionally to tell people that he was no relation to the detective just across the river with the same name. The New Hampshire detective had also talked to his Vermont counterpart's brother Ted, who had worked on the Barbara Agnew case. The two Vermont detectives were eagerly awaiting more information about the attacker and the details of the assault. It looked like there would be plenty of chances on this case for confusion of names; the three of them were going to be cooperating closely for a while.

There was another element to the similarity, because the New Hampshire Mike Leclaire had been born in Vermont and grown up there. But the correspondences didn't extend much beyond that. In contrast to his dark-haired counterpart, the New Hampshire trooper's hair and prominent eyebrows were blond and his complexion was fair, and, unlike the Vermont detective, he had inherited his interest in police work. His uncle Marcel had been chief of police in Brattleboro, and his father, Leo, was due to retire in a few days as deputy chief. Leclaire had wanted to join the Brattleboro department, but someone had figured that two was enough from one family in one department, so he had started his career across the river, with the tiny police department in Hinsdale, New Hampshire. He and his wife had moved to New Hampshire after a few years and he had joined the state police.

Leclaire had been stationed in Keene since 1981, building a close knowledge of the surrounding area and a reputation as a first-rate detective. The case that had just fallen to him was about to draw on every bit of knowledge and skill he had acquired in those seven years.

Kim Bossey had written up Jane's account of the attack,

and Leclaire had put the finishing touches on the composite drawing. Now it was early the next morning, Wednesday, and both documents rested in a folder beside Leclaire as he sat in the guard's chair outside Jane's room in the intensive-care unit. He rose periodically to stretch and look in on Jane. Around 5:00 A.M. he found her stirring and soon she was awake. He needed one more session with her before they went to work.

"Could I speak with you a little more?" he asked.

Jane nodded stiffly. She was still having trouble talking. Leclaire told her he wanted to check over the statement and the composite picture with her to make sure they had gotten it right. She nodded again in agreement.

"I'll read it to you and you can just nod yes or no," Leclaire suggested.

He went through Bossey's report of Jane's account of the attack. Jane was able to add a few details as they went along. Then Leclaire showed her the finished composite and checked over her description of the attacker. She had estimated his height at just a few inches more than her own, five-foot-seven or five-foot-eight. His build was average, she thought; he might weigh around 150 or 160 pounds. He was between thirty and forty years old, with sandy blond hair that was thinning on top. He had been wearing a casual, short-sleeved shirt and dark pants, maybe blue, but not jeans.

And that was it. Nothing exact, maybe, not a perfect likeness or an absolutely precise description, but pretty damn close. And now, Mike Leclaire held in his hand something that was absolutely unprecedented. In all the years that investigators had been working on the murders of women in the Valley—it was hard to accept that it had been so long, four years since the killing of Bernice Courtemanche, seven since Betsy Critchley—they had never once found a direct lead to the man responsible for the attacks. They had always been forced to work from the outside in, sorting through a huge collection of possible suspects and laboriously investigating each of them, one by one, trying to work their way toward the one man who stood at the center of a great labyrinth of evidence.

If the attack on Jane Boroski was related—and you always had to keep in mind the possibility, however unlikely, that the similarities in any of the Valley cases could be coincidence—

now, for the first time, they would be working from the inside out, beginning from information that identified the man they were looking for.

Maybe, just maybe, Jane Boroski had given them the means to bring this tragic mystery to an end.

Mike Leclaire headed for the office to set the investigation in motion.

thirty-four

There was a trace of desperation about the idea, but at least it was worth a try. Six months of investigation by state and local police all over Vermont and New Hampshire hadn't come up with anything more in the attack on Jane Boroski. Under the circumstances, hypnosis might be the best shot they had left.

The search for the attacker was badly in need of stimulation. What had looked in August like a tremendous opportunity soon exposed problems that had been lurking at the edges of the Valley investigations all along.

The Valley was a small, confined area, with a population well under a hundred thousand people, but it comprised more than two dozen separate towns and cities, five countries, and, most importantly, two states. Each constituted a separate jurisdiction, with its own political, prosecution, and police machinery. Only the two state police organizations had the scope and expertise to carry out a major investigation, and in this case they were divided by the Connecticut River boundary between New Hampshire and Vermont. Under normal circumstances, friendly relationships, frequent contact, and informal cooperation across the river were adequate to handle any criminal matters that transcended state boundaries. But these were not normal circumstances.

In New Hampshire a computer run had produced hundreds of Wagoneer registrations that matched Jane Boroski's rough description, and a list from neighboring Massachusetts pushed the total into the thousands. Vermont had turned up over four hundred more in the two southeastern counties alone.

The work of checking that many cars, interviewing the owners and finding anyone else who might have been driving them on August 5, would require untold man-hours. And, ideally, a large force of investigators would start immediately with the best prospects and move fast, before memories dimmed, before the Jeep was modified or disposed of, and before the passage of time created other obstacles to success.

That kind of effort would have required a unified decision by political leaders in both states that the search for the Wagoneer presented a once-in-a-lifetime opportunity, a chance to lift a shadow that had hung over the Valley now for years. The unity did not exist; the decision never came.

The New Hampshire authorities never acknowledged a connection between the Boroski case and the murders. Clay Young, the New Hampshire State Police detective who had led the 1986 Valley task force investigation in Claremont, coordinated the search from Concord. And Mike Leclaire organized a survey of New Hampshire and Massachusetts Wagoneer registrations out of the state police barracks in Keene. But only Leclaire's own dedication, along with sporadic help from other troopers and local detectives, distinguished the investment of resources from what might be expected in an ordinary case of attempted murder. After a few months the investigation was competing for the officers' attention with a homicide case, then another, and another, all crimes that placed heavy demands on the time of detectives throughout southwestern New Hampshire.

Leclaire pressed on, checking each Wagoneer, collecting background information on possible suspects, following up tips from people who thought they recognized the man in the composite picture, getting help where possible from other detectives. He stayed in touch with Jane Boroski, calling to check on a detail, asking her to come in to look at a photo lineup of possible suspects, or just bringing her up to date on the investigation and reassuring her about the effort that was going into the search.

The horror of the attack had swept aside the problems that had come between Jane and Dennis. After two weeks in the hospital, Jane had moved back in with Dennis. One day in the second week of October, she woke up early in the morning with pains that she soon decided were the contractions that signalled the beginning of labor. At 7:00 A.M. Dennis took her to the hospital, and two and a half hours later her baby was delivered by caesarean section. It was a girl. She weighed eight pounds eight ounces. There were some complications in the delivery and the baby required special care at first, but eight days later Jane and Dennis took a healthy, active baby home from the hospital. They named her Jessica Lyn. It was just over two months since the night a man with a knife had left a pregnant woman for dead in the parking lot of a country store.

Jane Boroski thought about the attack almost every day and dreamed about it many nights. Most of these thoughts and dreams were dominated by fear, but she also spent time trying to remember new details that might help in the investigation. On the phone one day in December, four months after the attack, Mike Leclaire mentioned that the police had occasionally used hypnosis to help people recall evidence in criminal cases.

"Do you think it might help me remember more if I was hypnotized?" Jane asked. Leclaire told her he would look into it and let her know.

Leclaire had met John Philpin through the Vermont detectives Ted and Mike LeClair, soon after the attack on Jane in August. Philpin had been consulting with the brothers, comparing the Boroski attack to the profiles he had written on the other Valley cases. Philpin's first quick look in August had supported the brothers' feeling that there might be some relationship. The psychologist was especially impressed by the similarities to the attack on Barbara Agnew eighteen months before.

In Vermont, Mike LeClair had organized an exhaustive search for the attacker's Wagoneer. They were working their way through the hundreds of vehicles in eastern Vermont that approximated Jane Boroski's description of the vehicle and its color. With the support of the state police command, LeClair had brought together representatives from departments all over the state. He had given each a pack of printed forms, one for each car on the list in his jurisdiction. The local departments and state police offices were asked to check on the owner and any male who might have been driving the car on the August night when Jane Boroski was attacked, then visit any who came close to the physical description of the attacker.

Anyone who met these criteria was checked for a criminal record. Out of a hundred or so of these "possibles" in Mike LeClair's southern Vermont area alone, the search turned up a dozen with serious criminal records, men who seemed capable of a vicious assault. The detectives were asked to photograph any owner or driver of a Wagoneer who seemed a possible match, and to put polite pressure on anyone who tried to evade scrutiny. The descriptions and photographs were sent to Mike Leclaire in New Hampshire, and a number of them were inserted in photo lineups for Jane Boroski to look at, to see if she could pick out her attacker. Leclaire mixed the mug shots of the suspicious Wagoneer owners with similar photos of police officers and friends. Jane had come in for several tense sessions of scrutinizing the batches of photos with Leclaire; none of the suspects were the man who had stabbed her.

The New Hampshire detective had asked Philpin in the fall to prepare a profile of the assailant and they had stayed in touch since then. In an unrelated incident, Philpin had recently been asked by police nearby in New Hampshire to hypnotize a woman who had witnessed a hit-and-run accident, in the hope that she might recall more information about the vehicle involved. When Jane Boroski expressed interest in hypnosis, Leclaire called Philpin to ask whether he thought it would help.

"Bring her on up here and we'll see what happens," Philpin told the detective. Philpin had been working on the Boroski profile for several months now. It had been seven years since his introduction to this kind of work in the Theresa Fenton case. He had become adept at immersing himself in the evidence and slipping into the mind of a predator. With each case they had come closer to the idea of a single killer roaming the Valley, closer to a picture of the man himself, coming upon fresher, richer evidence of his movements and his mind. But always the image of the killer had died in the eyes of his victim. Now they had taken another extraordinary step closer: A woman had seen the man, even touched the man, who believed he was killing her, killing her knowledge of him. And she had lived.

Philpin had made several trips to Gomarlo's to look over the place where the attacker had carried out his assault on Jane Boroski. As he drove south along Route 10 toward the grocery store on his second visit, retracing the predator's approach to the moment of his vicious assault, Philpin once again played his double game of identity. He matched his consciousness to what he knew of the man from Jane Boroski's description and what he could read from the facts of the assault, reserving just enough of himself to observe the movements of the predator's mind.

It was a little before midnight, the same hour when the man with the thin lips and the dirty-blond hair swept back from his pale forehead had drifted through the night just a few weeks earlier. Up ahead Philpin saw the orange glow from the light tower. He steered the pickup into the parking lot, past the door of Gomarlo's, along the side of the building. He was looking for prey, a woman by herself, unprotected, soft, available. He swung sharply to the left into a parking space facing the walkway along the side of the building. A pay phone hung from the wall in front of his truck, a Coke machine stood a little to the right.

Philpin was sitting rigidly behind the wheel, preparing himself for what the attacker was about to do, when a car pulled into the parking place next to him. He kept his gaze forward as the door opened on the other side of the car and a woman got out.

"Fool," the killer would have thought, "opening yourself up to me like this, late at night, in this dark, solitary place, alone, defenseless, vulnerable."

The woman had a young child with her, maybe four or five years old. She closed the car door and moved toward the walkway, toward the telephone. Philpin turned, the predator turned, to stare down from the height of the pickup truck, the Jeep Wagoneer, and looked at her. As she came around the front of her car she glanced up at Philpin and something in her face froze.

In a moment the woman looked away again, but the expression Philpin had seen in that instant was unmistakable. She had looked in his eyes and she had been afraid.

As he drove away from Gomarlo's, Philpin went back over what had happened, what he had seen and what he had felt. He thought of the woman, and of the look in her eyes, and he felt a little guilty, for he knew that in that briefest of moments he had caused her to feel fear. But she had also been like a mirror to him, for he had seen in her fear the reflection of his own gaze, and he knew that he had looked down upon her with a killer's glare of pure, predatory malevolence. The identification with the murderous attacker that Philpin had been constructing as a tool for creating the profile had reached its peak in the parking lot where Jane Boroski had been stabbed to the edge of death.

His work on the Boroski case had quickly led Philpin back to the other Valley murders. The link to the murder of Barbara Agnew had seemed obvious from the first; that had suggested a connection to the 1978 killing of Cathy Millican in the New London wetland preserve. When Mike Leclaire called to ask him about hypnotizing Jane Boroski, Philpin was nearing the end of a full-scale review of all the cases. He agreed to put off completion of the profile until after he had met with Boroski. So far, Philpin's information about the attack on Jane Boroski had come from written reports and his discussions with the investigators who had talked with her. In addition to seeing if he could help Boroski recall anything useful, Philpin thought, it would be a good chance to get a firsthand feeling for the attacker.

There was nothing in Leclaire's request for help, nor in the simple professional commitment about seeing Jane Boroski, to warn Philpin that he was about to drop off the edge of events into a whirlpool of overwhelming emotion.

thirty-five

In the dream she was alone again, driving her white car, and then she was pulling into the parking lot. It had the strange, disconnected quality of all dreams, so that one minute she was in the car and the next she was standing beside it, by the door on the driver's side. And then suddenly he was there.

She didn't see his features, but she knew who it was, the man who had attacked her, and she turned and started running from him. She ran across the parking lot and she was sure he was right behind her, stabbing at her with the knife, and then she was running into the field next to the parking lot, running, running, running through the field, and then she didn't feel his presence at her back any longer. She turned to look back, to see if he was there behind her, and he was gone.

She felt safe for a moment, she had escaped, and then she turned back around again, and he was there in front of her. He was holding the knife, ready to plunge it into her body. He was faceless, just a looming, horrifying presence in front of her, and she was terrified. The fear woke her up. Her heart was pounding, she was shaky and sweating.

Philpin was assuming that Jane Boroski had gotten some counselling after the attack. Mike Leclaire had told him there was a service at the hospital that would provide her with support. When Boroski and Philpin sat down in his office to get acquainted before starting the hypnosis session, he asked her how she was doing. The stabbing was on her mind all the time, she told him. Had the hospital program been any help? Philpin asked. She hadn't gotten any help, she said.

It had been six months and the dream was still coming every few nights, the killer pursuing her across the parking lot. He was there in the daylight hours, too, haunting her life, shadowing her every move. At odd times the image of his face, his dead eyes looking down at her as he drove from the parking lot, popped into her mind. She worried that he might still find out that she had lived through the attack. Or maybe he knew and he was just waiting until things settled down a little more. Or maybe he was lurking nearby, secretly observing her, stalking her, patiently watching for the perfect moment to finish what he had begun in the parking lot, eliminate the only living person who could tell what he had done.

There was no one to talk to about all this. She had told the police all about it at the beginning, and once in a while she might mention something to Dennis or his parents or a friend, but you couldn't keep bothering people with your problems, Jane said.

It was like a reflex with Philpin, the desire to help anyone who needed it. His work in the prison had contributed to his reputation for dealing with difficult cases. Sometimes the request for help would come as a referral from the police or from another psychologist who didn't want to deal with a particularly troublesome client. Or it might come directly. Someone would leave a beseeching message on the machine at the office while he was in a session, or they would call his home late at night, waking him up, or they would just turn up, desperate for themselves or for someone they cared about.

Even when he knew he should pull back, when he was overloaded with work, worn out and pushing toward the border of mental and physical exhaustion, he always tried to help the people who came to him, either adding them to his own full schedule or spending the time, often great amounts of time, arranging for someone else to help. He knew it was only partly altruism and compassion, that there was something of compulsion in it, too.

Whatever the reasons, there wasn't any question about what to do with Jane Boroski. Philpin asked her if she'd like to talk about the attack and she said she would. The hypnosis would just have to wait, Philpin thought.

They began by chatting about routine things, her life and work and the baby. It was more like an ordinary conversation than a therapy session. Philpin found that he liked the young woman. She was a little nervous at first, but she had an easy warmth and an open, unaffected manner. Philpin slipped easily into the flow of discussion.

She talked about the nightmares and her worries about the attacker coming back, and about how they had leaked over into more ordinary things, how it had become hard for her to trust anyone she didn't know, to feel at ease in public places. Philpin listened, tried to reassure her.

Jane was making a point, gesturing with her hands. Engrossed in the conversation, Philpin noticed in an offhand way that she had scars on both palms. His attention moved upward and he saw a scar on her neck.

"Where did this woman get these scars?" Philpin thought idly to himself, and in an instant the realization jerked him back to reality. Of course they were the result of the attack. This engaging young woman sitting before him had been stabbed nineteen times for no reason at all by a man she had never seen before.

Philpin was shaken by the moment of revelation. It had seemed like an ordinary encounter with a client in his office, but they were talking about events that passed far beyond the ordinary. The image of Jane Boroski's scars juxtaposed against her easy, likeable manner, had caught him off guard, had smashed through his professional composure, shattered the customary barrier between therapist and client. He had experienced a surge of emotion, of empathy and identification.

It wasn't that Philpin had never experienced this kind of psychological connection before. A form of empathy was standard technique in therapy, and it had also become an integral part of his method in preparing criminal profiles. He worked hard to insert himself into the experience of a killer, in order to imagine what kind of person the police might search for. Even in Jane's own case, he had entered the persona of her attacker; in that moment at Gomarlo's when he had glared down at the woman walking toward the telephone, he had felt himself moving within the mind of the predator.

Nor was it the first time Philpin had experienced this empathy with the victim. Ever since his first case, the murder of Theresa Fenton, he had tried in his criminal work to make this same connection with the mind and feelings of a victim, to help in re-creating the action and the thought of her attacker.

What was new here was the *living* victim. Philpin had read about the other women, talked to those who had known them, examined their possessions and the places they had seen, but he had never before sat in the same room with a woman who had experienced the brutal stabbing assault of a man bent on destroying her. He had never talked face-to-face with a woman who had come within a few moments, a few drops of blood, of losing her life. This time, his identification was with a living person, and the reality of her experience had drawn him across a boundary that he had never crossed before.

But for now the swell of emotion passed and its significance was lost on Philpin, as they moved onward in the easy conversation of one who had stored up many matters that needed discussion and one who knew well how to listen and respond. Beyond the worry, Jane had felt physically tight, and Philpin passed on some techniques for relaxation, ways of draining the tension out of the fears and memories. She was also concerned about her ability to remember details, and she had even come to worry that the image of the attacker would fade, that she might be unable to recognize his picture if it were put in front of her. They had been talking for some time at that point, and the psychologist reassured her; from what he had heard and seen, her recall seemed solid.

By the time the conversation came to a natural ending they had been talking more than four hours. Jane agreed to come back the following week. This time they would make a concerted effort to bring back memories of the attack, and then they would try hypnosis as an aid in the process.

Mike Leclaire drove Jane up from New Hampshire for the second meeting. After they had set up a video camera to record the session, Leclaire left and Boroski and Philpin settled down in his office. He asked how she was doing in general. She was still feeling physically edgy, Jane said, tense in the neck and shoulders, as if the worry had settled into that part of her body. Philpin said he would reinforce the relaxation techniques during the hypnosis.

Philpin began by asking if she had any questions left over from the previous session. Jane said the dream had come again, the previous Friday night, plaguing her sleep. Philpin asked her to recount it in detail and she described it again, the man's footsteps behind her, disappearing when she turned around, then his presence, suddenly, overwhelmingly, appearing before her when she turned back. She seemed calmer now about the dream, perhaps from having talked about it, and it had come only once in the week.

They moved on, Philpin leading her slowly through the attack, talking slowly, softly, eliciting details—the music on the radio as she drove south along Route 10, her mood following the fight with Dennis, and her time at the fair—to reconstruct cues and a setting for her memories of what had happened afterward. She recounted the man's approach, the question about the phone, the confrontation, her sense that the attack was over until she challenged him about the destruction of her windshield.

She described the stabbing calmly. She had never realized, Jane said, that he cut her throat from behind as she was running away. It was only in the hospital, when she asked why she had so much pain there, that she had learned about the wound. It must have happened when he grabbed her; then he had pushed her to the ground.

"Then the next thing I knew he was stabbing me," she said.

Philpin probed gently for the details, where the attacker had positioned himself, how he was holding her as he stabbed, his pace and manner as he left her to walk back to the Wagoneer. He asked her about the image that had returned periodically to trouble her, the man driving past where she lay on the ground, looking down at her. It was the only clear picture she had of the man's face. Philpin reminded her that when she had previously described the man's face as he drove off, she had left out his eyes.

"It's hard to describe his eyes," Jane said, "I don't know the color. I don't see any wrinkles, didn't really notice anything specific about his eyes."

She had told Philpin about her inability to confront someone directly, to look them in the face, when she was angry. Yet she had seen his face as he looked down at her, and she was clear about most of the details. It appeared that her mind had protected her against his image by rejecting any memory of his eyes.

When they had finished, Jane again expressed reservations about her memory, whether it would prove reliable if she viewed a photo of the man. Philpin reassured her again.

"From the two conversations," he said, "last week and today, I could probably tell you this until I was blue in the face and you might not believe it: I certainly would trust your ability in that regard." Philpin had been impressed by her memory for visual detail; he thought her lack of confidence was unjustified.

"I think if you do have the opportunity to see a photograph or to observe a lineup or something like that," he told her, "I would have every confidence in your ability to pick out the right person."

It was time to try to go deeper. Philpin asked if she still felt comfortable with the idea of being hypnotized and she told him she did. He began by reminding her of how she had relaxed in their previous session. He talked to her quietly, slowly, evening out her breathing, moving down through increasingly intense states of concentration. Philpin's method required him to enter a mild trance along with the person he was hypnotizing, to share the experience she was undergoing at the same time he was acting as her guide.

Two other therapists, Philpin's partners, had offices in the building, and the coffee room was across the corridor from his office. The sound of women's voices drifted into Philpin's office. Jane told him she heard the voices, but they made no impression on her state of concentration. She wore jeans and a V-neck sweater over an open-collar shirt, the sleeves pushed back from her wrists. Her forearms rested on the wide arms of the chair and her hands hung limply over her thighs. Except for a slight movement beneath her chin when she swallowed, she was possessed of an absolute stillness, as if every bit of her energy was focused on reading what was stored in her memory.

Philpin's voice sounded deeper than usual. He spoke softly, with long pauses while he wrote notes on a yellow legal pad. The breaks also allowed Jane to search her memory for more detail. They had agreed with Leclaire to concentrate on two things, the physical description of the man and more information about the vehicle, especially the license plate.

Once again, Philpin led her back through time to the day of the fair, briefly re-creating the drive to Gomarlo's and then the arrival of the Wagoneer. His questions were like those of a blind man asking a companion to describe a movie he is watching.

Jane was matching Philpin's pauses with her own, as if to let his questions sink to the deepest places in her memory and draw forth their answers. Her body and head were still and she barely moved her lips when she spoke. It conveyed the uncanny sense of some kind of automatic process, each clipped sentence producing a discrete bit of information.

Philpin asked her to describe the Wagoneer. She saw its headlights pulling into the parking lot. She repeated her description of the vehicle, its color and the thick coating of dust on the sides. Then she went on. There was a rack on the roof, she said, and wood-grain panels on the sides. As he sat there behind the steering wheel, the driver turned on the dome-light and looked downward at something in his lap. These were all things she had not remembered before.

Philpin led her on through the events of that night, the man's puzzlement: "Isn't this a Massachusetts car?" She paused.

"What's happening now, Jane?" Philpin asked gently.

"Running," she said. Then, "He won't stop." There was a hint of a whimper in her voice. Philpin responded to it quickly, reassuring her.

"You're safe, Jane," he said, "my voice is with you."

"He won't stop," she said again.

"Where are you now, Jane?" he asked.

"I'm on the ground."

"Where is he?"

"Walkin' away." She paused. "I'm bleedin'." The moment of anxiety seemed to have passed. She was calmly describing the scene again, both actor and audience, distanced, objective.

"You notice that you're bleeding," Philpin said. "What are you doing?"

"Trying to get up," she said.

"What's happening now?"

"Getting up. He looked at me."

That was what Philpin wanted, the image of the attacker's face.

"Freeze that picture," he told her, "hold on to that picture." He paused to let her concentrate on the image of the man's face. "You're getting up and he's looking down at you. What does that picture look like?"

"Lookin' at me," she answered. "Looks angry. Looks worried."

Philpin told her once again to fix the image in her mind, to hold it for later, so that afterward she could come back and examine it again.

Now Philpin moved on to do the same thing with the Wagoneer. Jane narrated her return to her own car, backing out of the parking place, turning onto the road. Her thumb was bothering her. "It's broke," she told Philpin. A moment later it distracted her again. "Trying to shift." There was a long silence.

"What's happening now?" Philpin asked softly. Even with the flattened range of her voice in the trance, the shock was audible in what she said.

"There he is," she said, "right in front of me." She had caught up to him on the road. She saw the red lights on the back of the car. "It's dirty," she said. "It's right there."

Once again, Philpin told her to set the image in her mind, like a photograph, and he began asking her questions about what she was seeing. She described a dirty window, a handle, the bumper, a white license plate with green numbers. There were five or six numbers she said, and the letter N. Philpin asked if she could see the numbers.

She paused, probing, it seemed, for the numbers. She spoke. There was a six, and a two. Then there was a long pause. Philpin held his breath, waited for more numbers. At last, she spoke again.

"Can't see it," she said. "Blurry."

Philpin asked her to focus on the area of the bumper and license plate, letting the plate fill her vision. "What do you see?" he asked again.

Again she was struck by the layer of dust. "It's dirty," she said. "The plate is dirty."

"What else do you see on that plate, Jane?"

"A red sticker." Philpin asked again and she confirmed it.

That was new, a bit of information that should help pin down the state that issued the license plate. Too bad they only had two digits, but Philpin would ask her to hold the image as a posthypnotic suggestion and come back to it later.

"Will you hold this image of the plate, this dirty plate?" he asked her. There was a short pause. Perhaps she was looking at the picture in her mind. Then suddenly she spoke.

"Six, six, two."

"There's a six, then a six, then a two?" Philpin asked, taken off guard.

"Yup," Jane replied. "One, or, no, five."

Philpin took her through it again. She repeated the first three digits. Then there was a seven, she said. That was all she could recall. Philpin asked her what state the license plate came from. There was no doubt in her mind.

"New Hampshire," she said quickly. He tried one more time for information on the registration number.

"Any more letters?" he asked. This time there was no hesitation, and only the briefest of pauses between letters.

"J-E-E-P," Jane said.

Philpin sensed that Jane had done everything she could. He asked her to write down the numbers she remembered on a pad of paper at her side, then brought her out of the trance. She seemed relaxed and comfortable; she lit a cigarette. Philpin reminded her of the two pictures he had asked her to preserve. He questioned her about the two images.

She was sure of the first three digits of the license plate. After that she saw either a one or a seven, followed by a five. She thought there was a letter N at the end, possibly one other letter before that. The red sticker was the type used for annual registration renewals in New Hampshire. She thought it said 88, possibly 87.

Philpin asked about the other image, of the attacker's face. She described it as before. Had she seen the composite lately? he asked. Yes, Jane answered, anticipating the next question. Now she would make it narrower, deepen the wrinkles—she traced a flat arc from the edge of her nostril to the corner of her mouth.

Before they invited Mike LeClaire in to go over the new information, Philpin had one more thing to say. He had spoken with his two colleagues, he told Jane, and both women had agreed: anytime Jane wanted to come for counselling, or just to talk, she should feel free to call. She thanked him for the offer and Philpin went to get Leclaire in the waiting room.

The detective was excited about the new information, especially the registration numbers. Jane had narrowed it down by identifying it as a New Hampshire plate. If the tag was red, Jane's memory of the renewal year as 1988 was wrong; the red tag meant it expired in 1989. And the key was the three digits she was confident about, the 662.

"I can do a lot with the 662," Leclaire told them. "I can do a large number of things with the 662, no question about it." New Hampshire plates had a maximum of six digits. If Jane's memory of the first three numbers was correct, there would be a maximum of a thousand possibilities to check out, 000 to 999 for the last three digits. That would be easy to do through the state computer. He was going right to work on it, Leclaire told them.

Philpin asked Jane once more how she was feeling. She reached up with her left hand and touched the back of her head, then eased her neck muscles. She had a shy look, as if she wasn't much used to being asked how she felt. A broad smile creased her face.

"That tension behind my head went away," she said.

thirty-six

After the two sessions with Jane Boroski, the profile came together quickly for Philpin. All the other information was standard stuff—the police reports, medical information, his own survey of the scene, the latest articles on psychopathic killers—but the hours of talking with Jane had provided Philpin with subtle details for the profile that had never been available to him before.

Once again there was the sense that the scene of the attack was one of many that this man was in the habit of surveying, part of what Philpin now thought of as a "trapline." Like a hunter inspecting his traps, this man spent long hours cruising, checking a set of selected places where he might find his prey waiting, ready to be taken. The summer had been dry, yet the thick layer of dirt on his vehicle had probably come from mud spatter. That reinforced the idea that he drove regularly on rural, dirt roads, the kinds of places back in the shade of the woods that tended to hold moisture; he could have picked up the dirt on the Wagoneer driving to and from his home or exploring killing sites, possibly both.

His manner in dealing with Jane Boroski told as much about him as his actions. He showed no feeling of any kind during the attack; even Jane's plea that he respect her pregnant state evoked not a flicker of response. Her description of his eyes, the terrifying, flat emptiness, was especially revealing. And the fact that she caught up with him on the road suggested that even in fleeing the scene he was driving within the speed limit, moving with caution, under control.

All this evidence of his calm, deliberate manner indicated that he stood apart from the fury that drove him; in the psychologist's term, his rage was dissociated. That meant, Philpin wrote, that he separated his feelings from his behavior. Often a child, faced with violence or other turmoil in his family, learns to separate himself psychologically and emotionally from the unbearably painful events that he is unable to flee physically. It is a child's way of protecting himself. The separation, the sense of detachment it offers, allows him to survive in a world he cannot trust, a world he sees as hostile and threatening.

But this separation, a deep coldness of the spirit, was not easily reversed; as the child grew older the experience of dissociation would have become tied to certain activities, listening to music, for example, or using a certain drug, or daydreaming. Or, Philpin noted, another likely catalyst for this dissociation, this state of mental detachment, could be long hours of driving, cruising the roads. In the midst of these activities, the shame and rage the child learned to push away from his consciousness burns beneath the surface of the adult's mind, animating fantasies of revenge against those who have harmed him. In the long hours of reverie he refines and polishes the script for the drama in which he will use the power and guile of an adult to exact vengeance for the child.

For this man harbors a deep, chronic anger against his family, Philpin theorized. At the least they failed to care for him; more likely they harmed him. The father or some other male either abused him or neglected him entirely; his mother would have ignored him early, rejected or indulged him as he grew older. The result is some mixture of confusion and anger against the mother or another female; either she has abused him physically or sexually, or he believes that she has betrayed him by allowing his father to do so, by failing to protect him from the pain and humiliation. Some in this situation turn their anger against the man who has abused them. With others, the particular combination of fear and resentment feeds a furious rage against the mother, and therefore against all women; that is the case with this man, Philpin believed.

The killer nurtures a fantasy in which sexual and aggressive impulses are fused. The expression of sexual urges has never evolved into ordinary, healthy forms; for him, these urges blend with physical violence and domination, which largely displace conventional forms of sexual activity. At first he may be confused by this, believing he is seeking sexual release, or that his violent domination must take on sexual disguise in the rape of his victims. Philpin had seen this type of confusion in the killing of Cathy Millican, the victim stalked in a long, seductive ritual, some of her clothes removed, but no evidence of sexual manipulation or penetration. It was the uncertain spoor of a predator newly come to the hunt. That was what had made the placement of the crime in time, almost three years before the next killing, seem plausible; the pattern of the crime suggested a killer still finding his murderous vocation.

The fantasy that shapes his attack incorporates elements from his experience, Philpin thought. He reenacts incidents, imagines the characters, from his childhood; he requires some fit between his victim and the image of his mother or other female against whom he craves revenge; he must find a victim with some characteristic—the shape of the face, perhaps, a certain color of hair or habit of movement—that stands as a symbol for this woman who is the object of his vengeance. But now, the version he lives through of what happened to him is his own; in his fantasy he is rewriting these unbearable events. The outcomes of the incidents, the roles of the characters, all are reversed. Instead of enduring humiliation, he humiliates another; instead of suffering pain, he inflicts it; instead of undergoing the death of his emotional being, he kills. In the reversal of the outcome, he finds at last his escape from brutality and humiliation.

But he sees his victim as responsible for her own fate. It's your fault, not mine, he is thinking; if you had not put yourself in danger by going out late at night, entering this secluded place, getting out of your car so you could be seen, returning to sit in the car with the window open, making yourself vulnerable, if you had not done all of these stupid, careless things, if you had not invited me to act, even lured me onward, none of this would have happened. And if you had not fought against me, forced me to escalate my aggression, I would not have needed to harm you.

In Jane Boroski's account, he only produced the knife when she resisted: "All right, if you're going to be like that . . ." he said. The rest of the thought was, ". . . then you will force me to take more severe measures against you." He had even seemed ready to suspend the attack, until Jane had threatened him about the windshield.

There may even be a twisted psychological truth in his version of events: He may require his victim's resistance in order to achieve satisfaction from the attack. Perhaps he needs to feel he is on the edge of losing control, of being overwhelmed, that he is in danger of experiencing again the feelings of helplessness from his childhood, to release his fury. He needs the danger to justify his brutal attack.

There was so much here that seemed to correspond to the seven attacks in the Valley that resulted in murder, Philpin thought. Of course, the victims were all women, all but one on the road, all alone and vulnerable. Six of the seven had been stabbed; the exception was Betsy Critchley, for whom the cause of death was not known.

And one aspect of the stabbings had caught the investigators' attention. The stabbing of Jane Boroski had placed a spotlight on something that they had first noticed in the Agnew case. The wounds to Barbara Agnew's abdomen had been placed in a flattened V pattern. It looked similar to the configuration of some of Lynda Moore's wounds. The match wasn't exact, couldn't be exact where there were so many other variables, like the shape of the victim's body and the circumstances of the killing, but it was close enough to be intriguing.

Then Philpin and Ted LeClair had gone over to look at the file on Cathy Millican, and as soon as Philpin had opened the envelope full of autopsy photographs, the same pattern had leaped out at him. "Look at that," he had whispered to LeClair, "just like Agnew."

And now, there were the wounds to Jane Boroski. The blows of the knife had missed her fetus, which was an interesting fact in itself, and they had fallen into the same flat V-shaped pattern. There was always the possibility of coincidence, but with each additional instance, that became less likely. It wasn't the first time that Philpin had wished the four other victims had been found before all but the barest trace of the killer's actions was gone.

The logistic similarities were also persuasive, Philpin thought. All had been found on the surface of the ground in remote wooded areas, except Lynda Moore, and Eleanor McQuillen's remark had offered a plausible basis for seeing a resemblance there. "Come with me," the attacker had said to Jane Boroski. He was planning to take her away with him to a safe place, a place where he could play out the script he had prepared and polished in his daydreams. All the victims had been transported in this way, again with the exception of Lynda Moore. In the cases where it could be determined, there was no sign of sexual assault.

Then there was the road, the car, the trapline pattern, what Ted and Mike LeClair called the apple-tree theory. The telephone, often in an isolated spot, a place where women were likely to appear alone at odd hours, exposed and vulnerable, was a perfect checkpoint for a killer's trapline; Ellen Fried, who had been talking to her sister, and Barbara Agnew, and perhaps Eva Morse, had all stopped at or near telephones. And there was a telephone just a few feet from the Coke machine in front of Jane Boroski's car.

And where there was enough information on which to base an opinion, Philpin sensed a certain common pattern of restraint in the attacker's use of the knife. Clearly the knife was a key to the killer's way of thinking; it was his ultimate assurance of power over his victim, it was a symbol of vengeance in psychology and myth, it was the instrument of death. But Philpin's intuition told him that the attacker preferred to control his victim first, to track her, to quickly seduce and then dominate her, all without the knife. There was this quality in the stalking of Cathy Millican through the wildlife preserve, the struggle with Barbara Agnew in the rest area before the knife entered the equation, the attempt to take Jane Boroski from the car without showing her the weapon. It felt like the same man in all these cases, Philpin concluded.

The Moore case was still a problem, Philpin admitted, even with the medical examiner's observation that the attacker's intention to take his victim to a remote place and kill her there might have been thwarted by Lynda Moore's fierce resistance. There was another difference: The attacker had prior knowledge of his victim. When he invaded Lynda Moore's house, the killer was attacking that particular woman, not a target of convenience like the others.

Yet there were also points of similarity between the Moore case and the others, Philpin felt. He imagined the attacker's thinking about his victims: This man viewed women in general, his victims especially, as arrogant, haughty; he imagined their disdain for others, especially for men, for men like himself. They felt they could live their lives, make their plans, go where they wanted whenever they felt like it, without even thinking about other people. These bitches just assumed they could get away with doing these dangerous things, the attacker would think, hitchhiking and going out at night alone.

The killer's view of these women had nothing to do with their actual characteristics. It merely fulfilled his need to deflect onto his victims the responsibility for what happened to them. They had been stupid, they had been careless, and they had also been provocative. He saw them as putting on airs, adopting a superior attitude. He saw this assumption of superiority as an act of dominance, and he had learned to make a perverse association between dominance and sex; he saw in their arrogance an act of seduction. Their haughty airs were an enticement, an invitation to a man like him. And that was how the case of Lynda Moore slipped easily into place on the list of killings in the Valley.

Attractive, given to sunbathing in her yard, visible to the whole world in her prominently located home, surrounded by the trappings of wealth and position, Lynda Moore fit the pattern. Her active, visible presence in the community could have offered her up to the killer's attention in the same way that other women's vulnerability on the road or at a phone booth had exposed them. The Moore case had to remain in the same mental file with the others.

There was one more issue Philpin felt obliged to deal with. If some or all of these killings were related, what accounted for the gaps between some of them, especially the lapses of thirty-four months between the killings of Cathy Millican, Elizabeth Critchley, and Bernice Courtemanche? Could the interruptions be explained, at least in part, by the uncertainty of a beginner, the confusion Philpin had found in the killer's handling of Cathy Millican? Or was there more to it?

If there was an answer, Philpin thought, it lay in the killer's style of thinking. The attack on Jane Boroski, with its clear absence of emotion, provided a clue. He does not kill because he is seeking relief from some demon that plagues him, that invades his days and tortures his sleep. There are serial killers like that, men who hear voices or see signs urging them to kill, who are driven to frenzy by the clothes or the skin or the tears of their victims, but the Valley killer is not one of these.

"This subject's actions are less a matter of compulsion," Philpin said, "and more a matter of deliberation, patience, and convenience."

This man calculates every move, chooses each element with care, the place, the hour, the killing ground and the route he will take to get there, and finally his victim. In the attack on Jane Boroski, he had seized his prey in a flurry of movement, he had come in direct, sensual contact with a helpless woman, he had lost control of his victim for a moment, stabbed her repeatedly, satisfied his compulsion to possess a captive female. Nothing, not one moment of this experience, had disrupted his calm demeanor. "He is in control of his plan," Philpin wrote. "It doesn't grab him and take him along; he sets it in motion." And he follows it through calmly, even adjusting it as circumstances change.

A man with this kind of mental process is capable of passing up opportunities when even one element is not perfect, Philpin thought. He is exceedingly wary of being caught, and capable of doing what is necessary to avoid it. He could have suspended his attacks, Philpin thought, even moved somewhere else, in response to publicity about the killings or investigation, increased tension and wariness in the community, or the approach of investigators to his own life or the affairs of relatives or friends.

By the time he handed his ten-page profile to Mike Leclaire, Philpin had lived with the case of Jane Boroski on and off for seven months. In New Hampshire, Leclaire and Clay Young were working on the new leads flowing from the information Jane had recalled in the hypnosis session. Leclaire came over periodically to meet with the Vermont detectives, and Philpin joined them a few times to help sort through suspects and apply the profile to new evidence, but the Boroski case had moved far from the center of his attention. That was why the nightmare came as such a surprise.

It came in the late spring, and Philpin was the central character, but he knew immediately that it was Jane Boroski's nightmare. Philpin was in the parking lot, running, running across the pavement, and then he reached the edge of the parking lot and he ran on, into the field. He ran through the field and then he turned around to look. The man was there, coming on, getting closer, and he held the knife in his hand, ready to stab, ready to kill. Philpin woke up, tense, frightened.

It was upsetting, but as he lay in bed trying to assimilate what had happened, Philpin thought it shouldn't have been such a big surprise. He had spent a lot of time and energy on the case over a long period. He had absorbed so much of the fact and atmosphere of the case, it was natural that some of it should bubble up in his dreams. "No big deal," Philpin thought, and dismissed the matter.

A few days later, it came again. The dream was almost exactly the same, and again Philpin woke up sweating and scared. The fear passed almost immediately, as it does with dreams, but this time it was a little more difficult to dismiss what was happening.

It was less than a week before the dream came again, and after that it became a regular occurrence, once or twice a week. There were small variations: One time the killer came silently, the next there was the sound of his footsteps, and another night the rhythm of his quick, shallow breathing filled the dream. In one version, when Philpin turned, the pursuer was fifteen or twenty feet behind him, in another he was right there, within arm's length, about to bring the knife down, when the vision jolted Philpin awake. But the outline of the nightmare was always the same, with the awareness of the danger, the flight, the confrontation with the killer.

Philpin thought he knew what was happening. His approach to therapy depended on opening himself to the client's words and feelings, drawing close enough to understand and even to feel in himself what the client was feeling. He had used elements of that same method in his criminal profiling, building out of fact and intuition a passage into the mind of a woman who had been murdered, and from there into the consciousness of the unknown individual who had taken her life.

The ability to cross time and space into the mind of a person you had never seen was like any other skill. It could be en-

hanced and sharpened through practice and use. Over the
years, Philpin had cultivated this skill to a high level, and then
he had applied it in the case of Jane Boroski. He had inserted
himself into the identity of the killer, as he had done in many
cases before, and then he had done the same with the victim.

But now there was a difference. The victim, a vital, likeable
Jane Boroski, had sat in his office. He had shaken her hand,
listened to her voice, heard her story from her own lips. He
had made the leap of empathy into her feelings, and now he
was paying for it.

"I should have known," Philpin thought, remembering the
moment when the vision of Jane's scars had hammered the reality of her terrifying ordeal through his defenses, past the wall
of professional detachment that stood between his own emotions and whatever feelings and experience he absorbed from
his client.

Philpin had used several methods for managing his own
emotional experience, the ordinary stress of his own life and
the strains that he took on from his clients. Writing in a journal
both served this function and offered pleasure in itself, but it
had been many months since he had found the time to do any
writing. He had also used self-hypnosis, going into a mild
trance and exploring what was going on in his mind. Now he
tried it on the experience with the Boroski case, his work on
the profile, and the dream. It led him to an understanding of
what was going on.

"I've been a hundred killers," Philpin told himself, "and
I've been a hundred victims, but I've never been a killer and
his victim at the same time."

He had created a split in himself: He had identified with the
man who had set out to kill Jane Boroski, with the experience
and feeling that had brought the man to the parking lot in
search of a victim, with the fury that had driven the knife into
the body of a defenseless woman. And then, Philpin had identified with the defenseless woman, terrified for her life and the
life within her, helpless before the furious onslaught of the
man with the knife. Philpin had felt the limitless rage of the
attacker, and it was enough to magnify almost beyond endur-
ance his experience of the terror Jane Boroski had felt in the
face of that same rage.

He could see all this, but it didn't stop the nightmares, or the toll they were taking on his mental and physical health.

A few times a week now, Philpin would wake up in a sweat. After the first few nights he had found he was unable to go back to sleep. He would get out of bed, wander around the house, try to read, and eventually give up and go back to bed. He would lie awake or sleep fitfully until it was time to get up. The loss of sleep and the worry about whether the dream would come again were starting to wear him out.

One morning when he came back to bed just before it was time to get up, his wife, Jane, stirred beside him.

"Were you up during the night?"

"Yeah, I was just kind of restless," he said, "so I got up and read for a while."

Eventually he told Jane he was having a nightmare, and that it was related to a case, but he kept most of the details to himself. Jane didn't like his criminal work, felt the people and the work were dangerous. He minimized the impact the nightmare was having on him.

He went to a friend, another therapist.

"I'm really rattled," Philpin said.

He described his criminal work, the process of identifying with the killer and the victim.

"You think you're Superman," Philpin said, "you do all this stuff, and you do it time after time, and you get sloppy. You start to think you have a degree of invulnerability, that you can put your head in anybody else's mind and you can think these horrible thoughts, and then you can walk away from it unscathed. You can't do it. Nobody can."

But he hadn't realized that until his life told him it was so. "The experience with Jane Boroski was like a punch in the face," he said.

It helped Philpin to speak about the problem, and the friend was sympathetic, but he had no answers, and the dream continued, haunting his sleep, disrupting his waking hours.

By July it had been coming again and again for more than three months. Instead of losing some of its power over time, the nightmare was setting off reverberations in every part of Philpin's existence. He felt his life was reaching a climax of some kind. His habitual overwork was deepening the exhaustion from the emotional strain and the loss of sleep caused by the dream. It struck him that it had been years since he had taken any time off.

And there was something else going on, he realized. It had been two years since the pain had ripped through his gut in the drive-through lane at the Burger King. The attack had brought with it the chill of mortality, and at first he had been careful about his diet, about getting enough rest and protecting his health. But then a year had passed and he had started to feel safe again. The habits and demands of ordinary life had reasserted themselves and other matters—family, work, community activities—had taken back the high ground of his consciousness.

And then he had slipped off the solid surface of routine into the vortex of fear and emotion that swirled around Jane Boroski. He had lived in the mind of the man who attacked her, and then he had lived in her own mind, and a man with a knife had brought Philpin in his imagination face-to-face with death.

Philpin knew his own experience was nothing compared to the real terror that Jane Boroski had suffered, but in sharing her vision he had felt the nearness of death, and it had brought back to him the moments in which he had felt that same awareness for himself. The feeling of vulnerability, an awareness of the transience of things, had come back.

It wasn't that he was afraid to die, Philpin thought. He was afraid of some things, but that wasn't one of them, and Jane and their son, Steven, would be all right if it happened. But thinking about it in that way made his time seem precious. If he knew he were to die in five years, say, would he want to spend the next five years, his last, doing what he was doing, living the way he was living?

The idea formed in his mind that he needed to get away, to think it through. He needed some time when he didn't have to be who he was, didn't have to be "John Philpin, the local psychologist," or "the guy who does the work with criminals."

He talked with Jane about it, and she was understanding. Maybe she thought of it as a garden-variety midlife crisis. Maybe she was partly right.

"I'm really drained," he told her. "I'm really tired."

In late July, Philpin flew to Florida. He and Jane had gone there together in the past, bird-watching and just getting away, and he knew it was a place where he could relax, be anonymous, think things out. For a week he walked on the beach, something he had loved to do in Massachusetts as a boy. He went fishing, took a bird-watching trip in the Everglades, and enjoyed the great luxury of going to a movie in the middle of the afternoon. He saw *Dead Poets Society,* and he loved the spontaneity of the main character, a teacher. The movie reminded him of a time when Steven, a little boy then, had been worried about something. Philpin had climbed up on a hassock, and when the boy asked what he was doing, Philpin had said, ''I'm trying to get a different point of view.'' After that he had climbed up on the dishwasher or some other piece of furniture from time to time as a reminder to Steven, and perhaps to himself, that it helped to look at things from a different point of view.

It reminded Philpin that he had once been spontaneous himself, and it reminded him that somewhere along the way he had lost his own perspective. He needed to restore the balance in his life. He had worked too hard, given up too much. And the criminal cases, especially the profiling work in murder cases, had drawn him too close, too often, to the worst in human nature.

It was not what he had set out to do. The Valley had seemed a small and peaceful place, and he had started out in social-service work, helping troubled children, offering a hand to people who needed it. But the Valley had changed, and with the murder of Theresa Fenton, his life had begun to change, too. Many new things had come to the Valley, and, certainly, some were good. But one of them was a new kind of death. It was murder, a pure, destructive, totally pointless and cruel kind of murder. Philpin had been drawn into the struggle against this new force. Now, with the perspective of distance, he could see that it had cost him too much.

By the end of the week, Philpin knew he would not let his life return to the state it had been in when he left home. He would say a polite no sometimes, limit his commitments in work, save the time for Jane and Steven, for his journal and other satisfactions. There were courses he wanted to take at the university, and perhaps he could move toward some other kind of work, something to do with writing, maybe, as a serious hobby, possibly even a career someday.

And he would have to do something about the criminal work. It had become too much, the personal cost was too great. The experience with the Boroski case had made that clear. He would drop the profiling work, Philpin decided, simply treat it as a phase of his life that had passed. He reflected on the decision and decided it was a wise move. And it felt good, he thought. It felt good to be free of the strain, free of the responsibility for taking on other people's pain, living through other people's horror.

It had been a truly refreshing time, Philpin thought as he prepared to go back home to Vermont. He was grateful that he had been given the chance to get away, to work things out, and now he was eager to get home to Jane and Steven, to start the rest of his life.

epilogue

The license-plate numbers from Jane Boroski revived the search for the attacker's Wagoneer, and in the following months the detectives pored over lists and checked out owners of countless vehicles. This time they used the three digits to get printouts of all the Wagoneers from all the New England states and New York. Several times the lists produced what looked like strong leads to the man with the knife, and once, Mike Leclaire, the New Hampshire detective, spent several days in upstate New York after receiving a report that a man who fit the description and owned a Wagoneer had been stabbed to death. But the periodic flurries of excitement passed without producing a break in the case.

As time went by, the detectives who had worked on the various Valley killings moved on to other things. Mike LeClair in Vermont and Mike Leclaire in New Hampshire continued in parallel. Each was promoted a rank, exchanged the detective's street clothes for a return to working in state police uniform, and took up duties as a commander of other troopers. The cases of Lynda Moore in Vermont and Jane Boroski in New Hampshire were picked up by their successors. The new men brought new perspectives and fresh energies to the cases; in each state detectives began complete reviews of the thick case files.

Mike Prozzo, the detective who as a boy had blown his

police whistle at passing speeders on Washington Street in Claremont, continued the upward arc of his career with his appointment as the city's chief of police. Command seemed to fit Prozzo comfortably, and he looked as if he had been born to the crisp, tailored white dress shirt and the badges of rank that he wore for ceremonial occasions. He tightened the department's organization and standardized the officers' uniforms, but his heart remained with investigative work and he thought often about the Valley killings he had worked on with the task force. He had passed the cases on to Bill Wilmot, the young detective who had helped on the Claremont investigations, but Prozzo maintained an abiding interest in the cases.

"There's still a feeling in the community that there's somebody out there that committed these murders," Prozzo would say, and you could see the determination that had fuelled his career when he talked about how he was still committed to seeing the Valley cases closed. He knew there were some people who would keep after it for the glory that would come with catching the killer, Prozzo said, but that was no factor with him.

"I could care less if the Royal Canadian Mounted Police cleared these cases," he said. "I'd be happy. The end result is what's important. I don't care whether the Vermont State Police, or the New Hampshire State Police, or Claremont or Newport or Charlestown does it, it'd be nice to clear the cases and get them off the books."

Prozzo felt satisfied that his department and the task force had done everything they could, but there was one suspect he still couldn't get out of his mind: Richard Robert Bordeau. At its most basic, an investigation was a process of elimination: it started with suspects and searched for information to show they couldn't have done it.

In Prozzo's mind, every suspect had been eliminated except for Bordeau, the karate expert who ordered coffee for his imaginary friend, Bertram, and tried to force his way into the women's aerobics class at the YMCA. He had cast a pall of fear over Claremont with his combination of eccentricity and menace, and Prozzo had never abandoned the possibility that someday they would find evidence to link him to the killings.

"But I could be all wet," Prozzo said.

Ted and Mike LeClair, who were both brothers and colleagues, gave an interview to a Vermont newspaper expressing their determination to solve the Valley cases. By now they were thinking in the long term.

"It's probably the toughest case I've ever worked on," Ted LeClair told the reporter, "but I'm certainly not giving up. I still have a lot of faith that we will find out who did this. I'm not going to give up on it unless I retire."

Mike LeClair said something similar. He had eight years before retirement; Ted, who had followed his younger brother into the state police, had slightly longer.

In the fall of 1989, Ted LeClair went for his annual state police fitness exam. With all the hunting, as well as skiing and biking and other activities with his wife, Pauline, Ted stayed in good shape. He passed the tests with high marks. He took off with Mike and several other friends for his annual month-long hunting vacation in New Hampshire and Maine. Shortly after he got home, he felt a strange numbness in his back. At first he thought it must be something related to the weeks of strenuous physical activity and living in rough conditions. He tried home remedies, without effect, then went to the doctor for testing. Nothing turned up, so he was sent for another batch of more extensive tests, including a day with radioactive injections and X rays.

LeClair liked to describe the sequence of what happened next. The day after the X rays, he got a call asking him to come in for an appointment. They had found a tumor on his kidney. He had perhaps six months to live. The following day he received a letter from the governor of Vermont. "Congratulations on your performance on the recent state police exams and your excellent state of physical fitness," the letter said.

LeClair maintained his sense of humor and his characteristic determination in the following months, changing to a macrobiotic diet and enduring a series of difficult treatments. He walked in the woods and accompanied Pauline to trap-shooting tournaments. Eventually, Pauline quit her data-processing job to be with Ted. No one could see anything in her manner but a remarkably straightforward and undramatic good cheer, except, perhaps, for an occasional wistfulness. She was more than a dozen years younger than Ted, and she wondered out loud one day what it might have been like if they had met sooner.

"I wish I'd known you when we were younger," she told Ted.

"If I'd known you when you were younger," he answered, "I'd have been in jail."

LeClair thought from time to time about the case of Barbara Agnew, on which he had been the lead investigator. Some of the detectives were still maintaining their skepticism, at least in public, about whether a single man was responsible for the cluster of murders in the Valley, but Ted LeClair was not one of them. There were a lot of reasons to believe in a single killer, he said, including the wound patterns in several of the murders and a number of more subtle indications, but in the end, he thought, it came down to a matter of simple statistical probability.

"It just seems unreal that there would be more than one knife killer in an area this small," he said. "It just doesn't happen."

Like Mike Prozzo, LeClair saw one suspect as rising above all the others, infusing his thinking about the murders with a continuing uneasiness. For LeClair, it was Henry Barker, the powerful auto mechanic who had been prowling the interstate the night of Barbara Agnew's disappearance. But unless a way could be found to alter the timetable of his activities that evening, he would remain just out of reach.

Several hundred people showed up at a banquet hall some months later for a testimonial to Ted LeClair. The ceremonies were full of the rough humor that cops use to disguise their affection, but the large turnout and the words of appreciation were evidence of the impact that LeClair, his work in the Troopers Association, his humor and generosity of spirit, had had on everybody who knew him.

Ted LeClair died a few months after that. It was more that eighteen months since he had been told he had half a year to live. He was forty-seven years old.

At one time, John Philpin also had considered Henry Barker a good suspect, and one day he drove to White River Junction to pick up Jane and Steven, who were coming back on the train from a trip to Washington. It was late, so they went to a restaurant nearby. Philpin was listening to the story of the trip when he looked up and saw Henry Barker walking through the restaurant. No words passed between Philpin and Barker, but the psychologist was struck by what he saw. He thought of Barker's nickname, an indication that some people had once seen a gentle innocence along with his frightening physical presence.

"There's no more Li'l Abner there," Philpin thought, and he was reminded of the man's physical menace and his record of violence. The deep suspicion among investigators about Barker's role in the Valley cases had not died with Ted LeClair.

Philpin had come back refreshed from his trip to Florida. He had made the changes in his life that he had resolved on, easing his schedule, reserving time for his private life, pursuing his writing as a hobby. He was not as successful with his resolution to give up criminal profiling work. He kept to it for four months, until a particularly interesting case came up, the murder of an elderly couple in their home. Within days, Philpin was roaming through an old clapboard house in a Vermont village, trying to imagine the man who had slipped through the screen door and taken two lives.

The profiling work was too interesting to give up, but Philpin found he had learned something important from his experience with the Boroski case. Philpin had long ago accepted that any profile he might prepare would have its limits, that the killer might all but elude his imagination. It had taken him longer to see that it could also be precarious work. To know the killer, you had to find the elements of his humanity, however deformed, in what he left behind. That required entering his mind, matching something in him to parts of what you knew of others, and to what you knew of yourself. You had to capture the killer's soul, and to do it you had to use your own soul as bait. In that act, Philpin knew now, lay the risk that you might lose it.

From now on, Philpin decided, he would hold back something of himself, and be prepared to pull away when he felt drawn too deeply into dangerous places. Over time he found he could maintain this new wariness without compromising his intuitive reach and his capacity for empathy. His reputation for criminal profiling continued to spread beyond New England, and eventually he was asked to consult on a notorious murder case in Florida.

Philpin stayed in touch with Jane Boroski, who continued

to be troubled by the vision of the man who had attacked her. "I think about it every day of my life," she said. "I think of him watching me all the time. I often wonder who he is, why he did it."

The summer after the attack, Jane and Dennis went camping for a weekend on the New Hampshire seacoast to celebrate Dennis's birthday. Among the T-shirt vendors and fried dough stands along the strip at Hampton Beach, Jane spotted a sign for a fortune-teller and decided to give it a try.

The fortune-teller was a woman who looked to be in her early fifties. She said her name was Linda. She invited Jane through a curtain into a dimly lighted room. She had blond hair that Jane thought was probably dyed, and she spoke with an accent of some kind. She took out a deck of Tarot cards and asked Jane to cut them, then spread them in a row across the table. She invited Jane to make two wishes and tell her one of them. Jane wished that she and Dennis would continue to be happy together and someday they would get married. That was the wish she kept to herself. She told the second one to the fortune-teller: she wished that the man who had attacked her would be caught.

Afterward, Jane wasn't sure exactly what she had told the fortune-teller about the attack, but it wasn't much. And yet, the woman seemed to know a lot about what had happened, she thought.

Moving her hands above the cards, occasionally touching down to turn one over, the woman talked about the attack. Jane had been attacked while she was pregnant, brutally stabbed, the fortune-teller said, and it had been a very difficult time for Jane, hard to accept that she had been attacked.

"Did he ever do it before?" Jane wanted to know.

The attacker had beaten up women before, the fortune-teller told her, but had not done anything as serious as his attack on Jane. He had done it, she said, because he was angry that Jane wouldn't go with him. Jane was impressed. She hadn't told the fortune-teller anything about the man's insistence that she come with him.

The man had wanted her to go with him, the fortune-teller explained, because he was planning to rape and then kill her. He was on drugs; she wasn't sure what kind.

"If you had gone with him," the woman said, "you would be dead right now."

"Is he going to do it again?" Jane asked.

He will attempt it, the woman replied, and he will be caught.

Finally, Jane asked about the thing that had troubled her most, the whole reason she had wanted to talk with the fortune-teller in the first place: where does he live, does he know I didn't die, will he come back to finish me off?

The fortune-teller was reassuring. The attacker is not from anywhere nearby, he is from another state. He doesn't even know you're alive, she said, he thinks you're dead and he's not going to come back.

Afterward, Jane felt a lot better. She had no idea how the fortune-teller had known so much about her, things Jane hadn't told her, like about her relationship with Dennis, but it gave her the feeling that she could rely on what the woman had told her. The session had lasted forty-five minutes. It had cost fifty dollars. It was worth it, Jane thought.

Noreen Campbell's sleep was troubled, too. After her half sister, Eva Morse, disappeared, she had been obsessed with finding Eva, or finding her body if she was dead. One day when Noreen and her husband were driving north on Route 12, she asked him to turn off, along a dirt road that led away from the place where Eva had last been seen, outside the veterinary clinic.

"You're not looking up there for anything," her husband told her. "You let the police do their job, and you stay out of it."

But Noreen felt she must at least try to reach out to her young half sister, and sometime later she got her next-door neighbor, a woman named Marian, to ride up Route 12 with her. As they got closer to the place, Marian became more and more upset, asking Noreen to change her mind. She was afraid not of failure, but of success, that they might actually find Eva's body. Noreen could not be dissuaded. She drove along the dirt road, stopping at the turnouts and walking over to look down the bank to the river. She didn't find anything, but she had felt compelled to make the effort. There was the sense of something unfinished between her and Eva.

Noreen kept thinking of Eva going through her pregnancy alone, tortured by the fact that she might have to give up the baby, and never feeling she could turn to any of her family. Eva had been in a minor auto accident a few days before Jenny was born, and Noreen had been called to the scene. Eva had cried and cried, far more than the accident seemed to justify, and Noreen had comforted her half sister. Yet even then she had not felt free to confide in Noreen.

Now Noreen lived with the grief and the anger, and wondered if she would live long enough to find out who had killed her half sister, and why. That was the hardest question: Why would somebody do something like that to another human being? she asked herself. What is so wrong that you have to resort to that kind of violence, to let somebody suffer that kind of pain or fear?

And that was the hardest part to accept, what Eva must have felt at the end. She had begun to take some pride in herself, and she was so close to her daughter, you could see it in that last picture, Eva and Jenny together at the birthday party just a few weeks before Eva disappeared. And then she was forced to endure the terror of the attack.

"Her fear for herself," Noreen Campbell said, "her fear for her little girl, that drives me crazy sometimes, and there's nothing you can do. Nothing you can change. You go on, you try not to think about it and you try to keep it so it's not on the top of your mind all the time. It's hard."

Jenny had gone through a difficult period at first. She had been ten when her mother disappeared and she hardly knew her father. Noreen had thought of adopting her, but her husband thought it didn't make sense, with their children all grown and twenty-eight grandchildren.

One day Noreen Campbell was at lunch with a local woman, a real-estate agent, and Noreen was upset that Jenny might have to go to a foster home. The woman knew Jenny and liked her; she suggested that Jenny come to live with her. Jenny agreed, and after some time together they decided that the woman would legally adopt Jenny. She was doing well in school, became a member of the color guard. Noreen told herself that the world is not perfect, that many people suffer violence and loss in their lives, and survive, somehow.

Steve Moore, who had always been unsentimental about life and displayed little emotion with people, found that the effect of his wife's death showed up, often very subtly. Except for a few tears at Lynda's funeral, he had never cried; it just wasn't his way. But he found that he was nervous in small ways that he never had been before. If he was on a construction job and somebody out of sight hammered a nail or dropped a load of lumber, he would start violently.

The year after the murder, the old Saint Bernard, Abigail, the one that had apparently lain quietly in the yard the day of Lynda Moore's death, died of cancer. The children, who were thirteen and ten by then, asked for a dog to replace her, and eventually they went out and got a puppy. The children fell in love with the new dog, and their father was pleased to see it. It was something of a new start for all of them. One day Steve left the house and drove to Bellows Falls. When he came back a little later, there was a group of people in the driveway. Someone was holding the limp body of the puppy. It had gone to sleep under the car and Steve had backed over it on his way out. He began crying, and then he couldn't stop; it was the first time he had cried in many years. Later he realized that finally, after two years, he had begun to mourn for his wife, to grieve for his children's loss, and for his own.

Moore had talked to Mike LeClair one time about this crime, wondering how someone could do something that only took a minute or two of viciousness but left profound effects on the lives of so many people for as long as they lived. It was so brutally unfair to the children, especially. LeClair had pointed out that this kind of thought, a concern for consequences and feelings, would never cross the mind of the kind of person who would kill that way. Moore knew that was true, and he thought there was no punishment great enough for a person like that, for one who could do what his wife's killer had done to their children.

Moore thought the killer deserved to die for what he had done to a family, to the children. Like a lot of people, Moore had expressed anger in the past at people who did such terrible crimes, never imagining that it might happen in his own home, and he had thought that he would take pleasure in throwing the switch to execute someone for a crime like this. But something had happened to Steve Moore. When he imagined the situation now, he couldn't picture himself as the executioner anymore. Not even for the man who had killed his wife. He still had the desire for justice, even for vengeance, but he knew too much about death now. He could not do it himself.

After his wife was killed, Moore had renovated part of the house and added a recreation room for the children. He had put in a pool table and a Foosball game, a microwave oven and a refrigerator to hold the soft drinks. He said he had built it as a refuge for the two children, something special. He hoped they would bring their friends in and hang around. There was something wistful in his voice. He glanced around the room.

"It's kind of rough," he said. "It still needs a woman's touch, curtains and things like that."

Fear of the killer lived on in the Valley. Periodically the media reported on a promising new lead or the murder of a woman, or an anniversary of one of the murders arrived and a reporter reviewed the mystery, and then the anxiety and speculation were revived. From the beginning the story of the murders and their impact on this small, rural place had received wide publicity throughout the country. One day in the early summer of 1991, a crew from the television program "Unsolved Mysteries" arrived in Keene, New Hampshire. They talked to the Vermont detectives and Mike Leclaire, and they videotaped interviews with Jane Boroski and John Philpin and Clay Young, the state police detective in Concord with overall responsibility for the New Hampshire investigations. Everyone involved in the murder cases was glad to see them; a segment on the program was certain to stimulate new interest in the cases and inspire a flood of new leads. Maybe one of these would bring an answer.

On the last of their four days in the area, the television crew began assembling late in the afternoon at Gomarlo's to shoot a reenactment of the attack on Jane Boroski. Residents of the area had been informed of the crew's plans by a brief notice in the afternoon's *Keene Sentinel,* and as darkness fell, cars slipped into the parking lot one by one. They lined up at the edge of the parking lot and settled down to watch.

Opposite where they sat, a Jeep Wagoneer and a white car representing Jane Boroski's Firebird were parked facing the phone and the Coke machine beneath the overhang at the side of Gomarlo's. The brief intervals of action—the arrival of trucks, walk-throughs, rehearsals—were separated by long stretches with no visible activity, while cast and crew set up equipment, consulted, repaired to their rented Winnebago to use the toilet or get makeup, waited for something or someone. Still the several dozen people sat in their cars, through intervals of rain, as the chill descended and the late-spring night got colder and colder. Some had brought folding aluminum chairs and sat wrapped in blankets next to their cars.

John Philpin, who had been videotaped in his office talking about the killings and walking in the woods pretending to re-create the killer's actions, arrived with his son, Steven, and looked over the scene. Philpin was probably the only person who noticed that the license plate on the back of the Jeep Wagoneer bore the three digits Jane Boroski had recalled in the hypnosis session several months after the attack. On closer examination the plate turned out to be a cardboard replica pre-pared by the production company.

In the evening Jane Boroski arrived with Dennis, whom she introduced as "my boyfriend." She showed pictures of her daughter, Jessica, now nearing three years old, a stubby, cheer-ful-looking child in a red corduroy jumper. The actress who was to play the part of Jane in the reenactment came over to talk, looked at the picture, gushed over the baby, and shared some laughs.

As it grew darker a bright light on a derrick came on high above the parking lot, casting enough light for taping yet still leaving the impression of darkness. Jane showed no hesitation about watching the recreation of the attack and professed no discomfort at what she was about to see.

The crowd came to attention as the actors rehearsed the scene of Jane running across the parking lot, the attacker pur-suing and tackling her. The actress tumbled to the mat that had been placed on the concrete to break her fall, and as the pursuer fell on top of her she was unable to suppress a laugh at this child's game they were playing as part of their work. Those who were concerned about how Jane would react to this reenactment of a horrifying moment in her own life were re-lieved to see that, along with the rest of the onlookers, director and crew and visitors, Jane Boroski joined the two actors as they laughed.

To those who had only pictured or read about the attack, the rehearsals came as a revelation. Even in mere rehearsal, when the attacker tore open the car door and the actress play-ing Jane scrambled backward across the front seat to escape his vicious, implacable attack, the violence of the scene was shocking even to onlookers who knew it was merely a reenactment, and not even for taping. The panic on the actress's face seemed remarkably powerful and real. Jane Boroski, however, watched impassively. She seemed to have made her peace with this terrible moment.

On a cool evening in early summer, with families wrapped in blankets sitting in lawn chairs at the edge of the pavement, children nodding off as darkness fell, it was hard to accept that something so terrible could have happened here, in the parking lot of this small country grocery store, on the edge of this quiet village, in the middle of this peaceful, rural area in the valley of the Connecticut River. In a small section of the attached one-story building there was a tiny post office, with a bulletin board displaying hand-printed notices that advertised fish taxidermy and riding lessons and a 1979 Chevy wagon for sale. A three-by-five card offered a reward for the return of a springer spaniel answering to the name PJ.

But the surfaces of things here could be deceptive. In fact, this building, with its gray-painted fake barn-board siding, and the modern gas station next door, and the paved parking lot itself, had only been here a short time. As much as anything, they were symbols of the changes that had taken place in the Valley in the decade since Gary Schaefer began the career of murder that introduced to this peaceful place the idea of a serial killer.

There had been a great surge of population in the Valley, an increase of close to 20 percent in twenty years, and of course the new people had brought their cars, and they had needed new houses, and new roads to get to the houses, and minimarts and country grocery stores with fake barn-boards to serve their needs. The houses and roads of the newcomers had covered over many of the orchards and much of the rich bottomland along the Connecticut River, and their cars were parked now where dairy herds had once moved lazily in their pastures.

The newcomers had brought many things with them to the Valley, things both good and bad, and certainly among those things, in a way no one could explain but everyone believed, was a type of crime that had never existed in the Valley before, the repeated, motiveless, random killing of strangers.

It is still possible to feel in the Valley what the early settlers must have felt more than two centuries earlier, the overwhelming presence of the natural world. On a country road just a few miles from the Connecticut River, in the evening of a late-spring day, the sun flares out in a brilliant pinkish glow. The warm, green walls of dense pines and heavily leafed oak trees make the two-lane road feel like a narrow cart track, embracing the traveller as he moves along, and a small stream dances in parallel by the roadside like a faithful companion. The memory of an austere church, reigning in its perfect composure over the center of the last town, bears witness to a human presence and lights the way.

And then, suddenly, the stream turns away, as if abandoning the traveller, the pink glow fades from the sky, and the heavy blackness closes in. Now the trees seem threatening, hovering darkly over the road as if waiting for some mishap that will leave the outsider helpless, vulnerable.

Then it is easier to understand that there is menace here, that the shadow of something never seen in the long history of this place, something mysterious and frightening, hangs over the Valley now, and always will.

index